Eventually Julie

Anthea Syrokou

Eventually Julie (Julie & Friends, Book 1)

Cover Design by BespokeBookCovers.com

Anthea Syrokou
Eventually Julie
ISBN-13: 978-1545341001
ISBN-10: 1545341001

antheasyrokou.com

For Bill

CHAPTER ONE

"We'll definitely need to make some cutbacks." Julie froze as she heard the words. Her chest tightened and a sinking feeling took over. Cutbacks? What did they mean? Were they talking redundancies? Who were they talking about — *her*?

The male voice continued. "Of course, we have many experts on many levels. The more one knows, the more valuable they are to the whole company. Still ... it needs to be done."

Julie tried to move closer to hear what was being said. Feeling slightly guilty, she managed to move a few steps forward without making any noise. Her eyes were fixated on the senior manager of the Superannuation and Investments division, Justin Jones, who was listening intently to the voice on the other side of the telephone line, fixed to his chair, his shoulders tense. His back was turned towards the door and he faced a view of high-rise buildings through large windows.

"It's a shame. You're right though: experience is an invaluable commodity. When will I find out more?" Justin asked, momentarily turning his head to the side as he searched for something on his sunlit desk.

Julie flinched, fearing that he would turn around and see that the door was ajar, and that she was there, listening in on what was obviously a private conversation. Her busy, gold and ruby-red beaded bracelet made a jingling sound as she moved unsteadily away from the door. *Of all the times to wear a noisy bracelet*, she thought. Julie had decided that the edgy piece of jewellery worked well with the black A-line skirt and cream-coloured silk shirt that she had thrown on in a rush that morning.

She had arrived at work early in order to complete an urgent General Ledger report, needed later that morning for a meeting between Justin and her manager, Colin Ferguson, the head of the Superannuation Claims division of which she was an employee. They would discuss the results in their team meeting. The printer near her had jammed, so she decided to use the one on the other side of the floor from her desk to print the first part of the report. As she hurried along the corridor, she had been surprised that Justin was already in his office. She had instinctively begun to greet him but immediately refrained when she realised he was talking to someone. The rest of the floor had been quiet besides the faint sound of typing coming from Accounts.

Slowly, Julie straightened up, and walked quietly and steadily down the carpeted corridor, safely making her way towards her desk. She would sort out the printer jam and print the report back by her desk. She couldn't risk Justin seeing her. He wouldn't expect anyone to be in *that* early, not from her team anyway.

"How's that report coming along, Julie?" Sarah asked from the partition behind her. "If you need any help, just let me know. There's only five minutes until the meeting. Colin is already waiting outside the meeting room."

Five minutes? she thought anxiously. What was she doing? She had to print the rest of the report.

Sarah made her way to the meeting room. Julie was preoccupied; plagued with worry. Somehow, she managed to enter the figures from the General Ledger team and the rest of the report was finally complete. Her mind returned to Justin's conversation that morning. *Who were they talking about? Will any of us from the Superannuation Claims division be affected?*

The smell of fresh coffee made her stomach turn. Sarah had made it as soon as she walked in, her jaw dropping in surprise at seeing Julie already working at her desk. Sarah always made sure she arrived at work at the same time as her, or even earlier. No matter how early it was, she always managed to have her mousy brown hair tied back in a neat ponytail, and her crisp, corporate shirts never had a crease on them. Julie often thought she must have had a steam iron hidden under her neat desk.

Why am I so worried? There's no reason for them to fire me, Julie reassured herself. She had proven her competency to her manager and the rest of the team on numerous occasions. Feeling more confident, she sat up straight in her chair and began to print the completed document, only to suddenly stop and look with consternation at the computer screen. She looked at the date on the document upon it, and then at the date on the sheet that had been handed to her. In a flash she realised the date on the sheet was not for the relevant month. She grabbed the sheet that her colleague from the General Ledger team had handed her and took a closer look. Her suspicions were confirmed. To her dismay, she realised that the debit and credit amounts that she had entered on the screen were the figures for the month prior to the last. Colin needed a breakdown of *last* month's reconciliations. Julie hadn't questioned the figures that were handed to her. She had begun entering the amounts without once looking to see if it was the correct date. She was positive, however, that she had specifically asked for *last* month's reconciliations. As much as she felt like cursing at her colleague, she knew that she was partly to blame. She should have ensured they were the correct figures, but the conversation she had overheard had rattled her.

What would she do now? The timing was unbelievable! She heard Justin's words in her mind: "Experience is an invaluable commodity". A rush of panic took over and her face flushed with heat. Feeling light-headed, she looked at the rows of numbers, but they appeared out of focus and blurry. Her mind raced. They were talking about cutbacks, and she had ruined a crucial part of an important report that Justin *and* Colin needed for the meeting.

"So, is everyone ready?" Colin called. "Julie, you've got that report for me, right? We'd better get to it. There's a lot to get through."

"Um … sure, I'll be there soon," she stammered, feeling the heat in her face intensifying.

Her mind worked over-time. Her heart beat uncontrollably. How would she get herself out of this one? She knew that her so-called colleagues couldn't wait for her to fail, eager to prove that their manager had made an unwise decision in choosing her to be part of the General Ledger reconciliation team. The more they competed with her, the more Julie felt that she had to prove herself. After what she had just heard, if her team was affected … She had to calm down. Taking deep, long breaths, she steadied her heart rate. *Take it easy,* she told herself. *It's not the end of the world.* It was strange that she cared about her job so obsessively when she hated it so much. What else was out there for her, though? She couldn't fail at the only thing she had. Besides, as her family kept telling her, "It's a good, secure job".

With slightly trembling fingers, Julie combed a long, loose golden brown curl away from her face. She took another deep breath as she opened the door of the small meeting room. She prepared for her usual act again, although this time, she would have to ensure it was her strongest performance. *Just be confident. You can get through this. It's only one mistake,* she reassured herself again.

"Julie, there you are. So you've got the report?" Colin asked, gazing at his brand new, very expensive Swiss-made watch.

"Nice watch, Colin. I'd always be looking at the time if I had a watch like that," George, one of the members of the team, chimed in.

Colin continued looking at his watch proudly. "Yes it is nice, isn't it? Um …" Colin cleared his throat. "Anyway, back to the report."

His serious business tone returned. Julie began to relax slightly as she noticed that his demeanour didn't seem to be any different to any other day. He was possibly unaware of anything regarding what she had heard. Maybe it wouldn't affect their team at all. He also seemed completely unaware that George was stirring him. The watch was definitely stylish, but Colin couldn't help himself when it came to flaunting his expensive taste. *Better him than me,* Julie thought as she sat next to Sarah. She would need all her strength to deal with George's smugness once he found out about her mistake.

Julie looked at George, who was smiling wickedly. He looked so confident in himself. She didn't want to meet his gaze, to have his intimidating blue eyes see through her. George Giveski, with his pearly white teeth and smug smile, was always ready to humiliate her. It would be easy for him this time. She would do it for him.

"So, Julie, you're up. What do you have for us?" Colin looked at Julie intently, as did everyone else in the meeting room.

"Well … the reconciliations are all complete. In fact, they have been for a few days." She cleared her throat before she continued. "However, the report may need a bit more work so it can be just right. I don't want any discrepancies before it's shown to senior management, so …"

"What do you mean? What exactly are you telling me?" Colin glared at her. "You know I have a meeting to discuss the results!"

"Yes, I just need to add a few more things …"

"I can't believe this," George interjected. "You mean the report isn't ready? Wow! That's really amazing!" It was as though all his Christmases had come at once.

Julie felt her face flush as everyone stared at her. She once again combed her hair away from her forehead with an uneasy hand. Her bracelet instantly attracted attention with its jingling sound. She caught George noticing it.

5

"Julie, if it's too much work, like I said on numerous occasions, I'll be glad to help. I mean, just by taking a look at your desk, I can tell you're swamped," Sarah offered.

"I'm fine." Julie turned to face Sarah. "I just need another hour or so to complete the report. I can manage."

Julie's anger gave her strength, instantly aiding her in steadying her breathing. How dare they try to undermine her like that? Sarah was always highlighting how much work Julie had on her desk, as though she was crumbling under the pressure — the pressure that she had created for herself, as she always agreed to complete any outstanding claims, or any work that had been tossed in the "too hard" pile.

"That goes for me too, Julie. I'll be glad to help, we are a team, after all!" George interjected once again.

"Like I said, I can manage on my own. Thanks for your offer though, and for being such a *team player* and all." She forced a smile.

George looked at her without responding.

Julie looked at her notes, conscious of his stare and struggling to keep up her façade of confidence. From the moment she had first seen George, striding down the corridor as though he were on a catwalk, all his female colleagues staring at him in curiosity, she immediately decided that he was arrogant and she wouldn't fall under his spell. She knew his type too well.

"Julie, George is right. Leave some of the fun for us!" Stacey joined in as she looked up from her phone, tossing a lustrous strand of blonde hair to the side as she spoke. *She looks even more glamorous than usual,* Julie thought.

Colin chipped in. "Ah! Stacey, how lovely. We finally have your undivided attention. Do I need to remind you about the meeting rules?"

"Sorry, Colin, but I need to organise a birthday. It's for Jasmine. You know her, she works in Redemptions. She's turning thirty. There are *so* many birthdays this month. It's not easy being the President of the Social Club."

Julie sighed. She remembered meeting Jasmine when she just started working at the company five years ago. It had been Jasmine's birthday when she had been introduced to her. "Are you coming to my birthday lunch?" she had asked her. "Everyone on this floor will be there."

"Sure," Julie had responded, surprised that the whole floor would attend a birthday lunch at the same time. *What a fun place to gain some office experience,* she had thought, way back when she was a twenty-two-year-old fresh out of university.

Colin interrupted her thoughts. "Julie? I need to know when you can have it ready so we can move on with other items. I still have that meeting."

"Um … I should be able to have it ready after lunch or maybe in the afternoon sometime …"

"This isn't like you, Julie! I think you've taken on too much."

George interjected. "Julie, don't you also have to complete that urgent claim by this afternoon? You did mention that the client insisted on collecting the cheque personally. If that's the case then it makes more sense that someone else completes the report. Don't worry about it, I'll take care of it. I'm good with numbers anyway. I should be able to speed things up so you can focus on your other work."

Julie couldn't believe George. Could he not take a hint? Was he so into himself that he couldn't understand that she didn't need his help? "George, once again thanks for the offer but I *will* have the report completed by this afternoon. I know you're good with numbers, but I have managed on my own for the last two months and all the transactions have balanced and have been accounted for, so I think I might be okay with the maths part of it," she responded, a bit too loudly.

She would not allow him to make her look incompetent. More importantly, she didn't want George to think she had lost her nerve.

George looked at Julie from across the table. "Please, Julie — I come in peace. I'm just trying to be a team player. In fact, I was really surprised that you finally *didn't* complete a task on time. It's a miracle! I don't think that has happened before. Forgive my astonishment."

Julie was used to his theatrics. George was definitely one of a kind. He always spoke in a formal way as though he was reciting lines from a literary classic. Sometimes it was difficult to distinguish whether he was teasing or if he was being genuine. Julie always assumed the former. When she *did* notice him striding down the corridor on that first day, she had already been working at the company for a year. Stacey had introduced her to him. He had smiled at her, flashing his perfect white teeth. "Hi George," she had responded with a tight-lipped, rigid smile. "Nice to meet you," she had continued, looking at him with non-committal eyes before continuing her work, refraining from giving him the attention that he would be used to receiving from most women. From then on it was all business between them. But he always tried to outsmart her after their initial encounter.

"Well, it makes no sense to accept more work if there's a tonne still to do," he had challenged in one of their meetings, after she had avoided him the first few weeks. Colin had just made her the Complaints Officer for that month, after both Sarah and he had also volunteered to take on the role. She could feel the weight of his stare when she intentionally ignored him as she walked out of the meeting room that day. She was positive she heard him utter the words, "I just don't get it," as she passed him. She refused to let him, or his type, humiliate her. She had to focus on her work and look out for herself.

Well, she wouldn't allow him to make her look like a fool again! Just as she was about to blurt out that the report wasn't complete due to circumstances that weren't completely under her control, George continued. "You know, many of the great minds of our times ask for help when they need it. Many seek guidance from mentors. They're open to new possibilities and ideas. The outcomes are usually more positive than if they work alone." He was still eyeing her from across the table with a steady, serious look.

"Well, like I said, I'll be sure to ask for help *if* I need it. As for a mentor, I'd gladly be open to suggestions — from someone who has the required credentials, of course." Julie forced another smile as she spoke. "However, for the moment, I'm fine on my own."

George looked at her intently. Surprisingly, he didn't respond, instead opting to look down at his notes.

"George, your team spirit is commendable," Colin said. "Very wise words. Sarah, you'll complete the report and George can help the General Ledger team with next month's reconciliations. Julie needs to focus on the outstanding claims. She already has a lot on her plate and we are the Superannuation Claims Division after all."

"Colin, I can do—" Julie stuttered.

"My decision has been made."

"I just think it would be counter-productive to get someone else to complete it so late in the game. I mean, I've been in the General Ledger team for months—"

"Julie, it has already been decided — end of discussion! Now, we'll have to cut this meeting short. Justin is already outside waiting for me. Meeting adjourned!"

Julie watched as Sarah gathered her notes. She couldn't bring herself to look at George. Not only did she now appear disorganised and overwhelmed by the amount of work she had to complete, she also appeared to be inflexible, and not a team player. It wasn't enough that her maths skills were being questioned. Anyway, how could she keep up her confident façade when she knew that she hadn't been honest about the report being *almost* complete. Now she would have to redo some of it before allowing Sarah to actually complete it — *if* she still had a job. She looked at Justin who was waiting outside the meeting room. An uneasy feeling dug at her heart.

The wilted plant in the corner of the room caught her attention. It looked as though it had had enough of the stuffy environment. Just as the plant needed nourishment, so did she. She had to get out of the small, cramped meeting room. Feeling that the walls were closing in on her, she packed up her things, stood up and attempted to storm out of the meeting room. Her attempt was hindered by Colin and Justin in conversation in the doorway.

"Hey Justin, did you watch the game last night? I can't wait to hear the highlights. I missed the first half. I know it's early but how about some lunch? How does Thai sound?" Colin asked, looking at his watch, and making sure Justin looked at it as well.

Justin was not in a jovial mood. He acknowledged Colin with an artificial smile. Great! Now he would find out that she had made a huge blunder; a blunder that could overshadow all her hard work over the years! She might as well wear a sign saying: "If you want to cut costs, pick me." She tried to pass without him noticing her; however, her eagerness to escape had once again come to a halt as she bumped into George, of all people. She was standing so close to him that she could smell his cologne. They looked at each other. Julie noticed the stubble on his tanned face. She broke the stare, and hurried down the corridor. Stepping into the filing room, she pressed her back against the wall and took a deep, heavy breath, suppressing the bout of anxiety that was threatening to spill out, knowing once she allowed it to come to the surface she would not be able to hide her despair any longer.

CHAPTER TWO

That afternoon, Julie's great escape from the office was preceded by an e-mail notifying all staff of an urgent meeting.

Feeling her heart sink further, she tried to repress what she had read. As much as she detested her job, it was a constant in her life: her safety net.

Why can't they leave me in peace to enjoy the weekend? Julie fumed as she pushed her way through the crowds headed for the pubs and nightclubs on the north side of the bridge.

Remembering that she had to cancel her plans to visit her parents that evening, she took out her mobile from her bag, wanting to get the phone call out of the way. She already had too much on her mind.

"Hi Mum, it's Julie, how are you?"

"Julie, I'm so glad to hear from you. Are you okay?"

"Sure, why wouldn't I be?"

"You don't usually call this time in the afternoon, and you're coming over for dinner later. Is anything wrong? I've been worried about you lately."

"I'm fine, Mum! I'm just calling to tell you that I can't make it tonight. I forgot that I made plans. I'll come over sometime next week."

"Oh, that's okay. So you have plans? It's good to see that you're going out. You know, I've been worried about you!"

That's the second time she said that, Julie thought as she continued walking through the Market Street crowds. She wasn't in the mood for another one of her mother's lectures. The way she had been feeling lately, she knew her mother would pick up on her negative state of mind. She usually smiled and never complained to her family. There was no point. They would never understand where she was

11

coming from. Lately however, it was getting harder to keep up the charade.

"Mum, of course I go out. Why would you think I don't? And why are you so worried about me? I'm fine!"

"I know you go out, Julie. I just feel that lately you aren't yourself. I thought having some fun would be good for you."

"You don't need to worry. I'm just a bit stressed about work."

Julie found a quiet place to talk, in case anyone from work was nearby. For a moment, she felt that perhaps her mother would be able to offer her some support. "I just feel really unmotivated at work at the moment. I feel so uninspired and today I heard something—"

"Why don't you talk to Christina about it? She's usually good with those things. I'm sure she can give you some good advice. I've been out of the workforce for a while. It seems like it was all *so* long ago. Anyway, the way things are going these days, you should be happy that you even have a job. I guess with every job you have good days and bad days. We just have to learn to deal with both and appreciate what we have. God knows I always imagined doing something different when your father and I had the business, but sometimes we need to be realistic."

Julie's jaw dropped. *So much for her not having any advice to offer her on the subject*, she thought with pursed lips. She had become used to that, though. What she couldn't believe was that she was telling her to ask her sister for advice *yet* again. Did she have any faith in her at all?

"Anyway, a good night out may change your outlook. I'm curious, do you have a date?"

"No, I'm going out with friends!"

"Well, you never know, you could meet someone. Do you know that one of my neighbour's daughters met a wonderful boy at one of those church over-thirties parties? That's why it's good to get out there. Work will always be there, but if you don't get out much … well, it's difficult these days to meet the right person."

"Leave the girl alone. She knows what she's doing." Julie heard her father's voice in the background. Her father always defended her. Julie sometimes felt that he was the only one in her family who had faith in her.

"Mum, don't worry about what I said. I'm fine! I just had a bad day. No need to worry," Julie quickly responded, eager to change the subject. "I'll be okay. I'll be my positive self again in no time."

"I just want you to meet someone special. It can't be easy being all alone. Anyway, I know you always see the bright side of things. Your sister, on the other hand …"

"Mum! I really have to go now! Bye." Julie hung up feeling drained. She threw her phone in her bag and continued walking.

As she waited for the pedestrian light to turn green, she stared at the Sydney Tower, and replayed the email in her mind:

To: Insurance.group
From: Colin Ferguson

Dear team,
Please be advised that Monday morning's meeting will be held in meeting room two at 8:30am as there is a pressing issue that needs to be addressed immediately. There will be no need for anyone to take the minutes. It is essential that everyone is punctual as time is of the essence, and we don't want to fall behind with proceedings. Enjoy the weekend and I'll see everyone at 8.30am sharp.
Regards,
Colin

There was no need for anyone to take the minutes! The words plagued Julie's mind. She would not let him, *or* the company ruin her weekend, Julie tried to convince herself, as she buttoned her black woollen coat against a sudden chill. It may not involve her anyway. She was being paranoid.

As the wind picked up, her hair slapped her in the face. *Boy from a church group!* Julie shook her head, remembering her mother's words. *A relationship is the last thing on my mind,* she thought as she hurried across the road, nearly knocking over a young couple wearing matching knitted beanies. Julie felt a twinge of envy wash over her as she gazed at their every loving, affectionate move as they hugged each other tightly, sneaking a kiss while they crossed the road. She glanced back at them as they strolled hand-in-hand, completely oblivious to the fact that she had nearly thrown them both to the ground.

Her mother's words must be getting to her, she realised, taken aback by her reaction. Her mother and her sister were always relentless when it came to her love life. Her twenty-seventh birthday was a perfect example. Most of the evening had been spent with both of them wondering if every single, available man they knew would be someone worth considering for "poor" Julie.

"You should really try to get back in the game, Julie," were her mother's words. "It's just a shame that someone as pretty and intelligent as you is still single," she had continued, with obvious pity in her eyes.

"That's how she'll remain, unfortunately, if she doesn't agree to see anyone. You shouldn't just focus on work. Mum's right; you need to focus on your personal life as well," were her sister's words.

They both took turns telling her what she ought to be doing in regards to meeting "the one".

"You already have a great job. 'Mr Right' isn't just going to appear on your doorstep, you know," her sister had continued.

Julie had spent that night in the upmarket restaurant squirming in her seat, glancing over to her father for support. He had sat in his seat rolling his eyes, trying in vain to steer the conversation in another direction. She herself had given up on responding. The "wise female elders" had already decided what she needed to do to prevent a life of spinsterhood.

Julie rolled her eyes at the thought. The truth was that she was never the type of girl that would dwell on thoughts of marriage and the "perfect" wedding. She had never even imagined herself in a wedding dress as many of her friends had. In fact, she never even thought about marriage. All she really wanted was a connection with someone who understood her, someone who was madly and passionately in love with her, and she with him.

A sudden drop of rain welcomed Julie back to the present and she swiftly took out her umbrella, making her way past frantic commuters searching for shelter. With a triumphant smile directed at the loved-up, umbrella-less couple, Julie rushed downstairs into the train station and onto the platform.

"You seem pleased with yourself." A familiar voice appeared beside her as she boarded the train.

George Giveski.

"Oh ... hi George," she managed, eyeing him suspiciously.

"So, what has you smiling so smugly? Surely, it can't be the e-mail we just received from our beloved leader?"

"Yes, that's it, George. I was just thinking that I can't wait to see what exciting news we'll hear 8.30am sharp on Monday morning," Julie responded with an exaggerated smile, matching his sarcasm. She flicked a slightly wet strand of hair away from her face as he studied her with his deep blue eyes.

"That's strange! Judging by the look on your face this afternoon, you looked like you wanted to be anywhere but at work," he said.

Still trying to hold the exaggerated smile, and trying not to look surprised that he had been observing her that afternoon as she had tackled the backlog, all she could manage was a defensive, "I love my job, that's ridiculous."

"I never said anything about your job satisfaction. I just mean that you looked like you had other things on your mind. We all know how much you love your job. I mean, not wanting to let go of that report this morning …"

"What's that supposed to mean? We know? Who's 'we'?" Julie snapped. "And what does the report have to do with it? It only made sense that I should complete it since I started it." She gazed up at him, unflinching. George's eyes studied her so closely it was as if they were taking notes.

"All I'm trying to say is that everyone knows how focused and committed you are to your work. You always concentrate so much and volunteer to do extra work for Colin. At times, you look like you're uncovering some secret formula that could save humankind from an epidemic," he said with a teasing smile.

Julie could not believe her ears. Is that what everyone thought of her? *They* were the ones always trying to undermine her ability when she volunteered to do something. She could never let her guard down with them. She opened her mouth to talk but couldn't find the words.

"Anyway, this is my stop. I'm off to have a drink," he said, as the train came to an abrupt halt, causing her to loosen her grip on the grab handle. Crowds of people with shopping bags and briefcases brushed past her as the doors of the overcrowded carriage slid open. The smell of wet coats and umbrellas polluted the small space with an oppressive damp smell. "Stacey already told me you can't make it. You probably have to plan which claim you need to work on early on Monday morning, straight after our meeting, right?" He smiled as he got off the train.

Stacey had invited Julie to come along for a drink, but Julie had declined, feeling relieved that she had made dinner plans with her friends. "So, do you have a hot date? You do, don't you? Who is he? Do I know him?" she had

16

grilled her. The last thing Julie needed was to have a drink with her work colleagues.

Julie stared after George, watching as he manoeuvred through the crowd. She had to admit, he did command attention. He was tall, lean, masculine and confident.

Julie shook her head. Why did she care how he perceived her? He made her cringe whenever she heard his smug voice, and yet, even though she found him smug and annoying, she didn't want him to think she was someone who didn't know how to have fun. That's not who she was at all! Holding on to that thought, she watched him disappear as the train pulled away from the station. She made her way to the vacant seat that would, on other occasions, have left her feeling victorious in her battle to claim it against her fellow commuters. Sinking into it, she stared blankly out of the blurry, rain-stained window and tried to make sense of her disorganised thoughts. But her mind instead went straight to her first and only true love — Scott Stevenson. She hadn't thought about him for a while. Scott had been everything she desired in a man and more. She recalled his twenty-third birthday. They had been together for almost three years and she couldn't wait to surprise him. She knew his friend James had already planned a huge party for him, inviting everyone he knew. Julie decided to plan a private celebration for just the two of them. Tanya, her best friend since high school, had helped her plan. Bold, flirtatious Tanya, with her act-now-think-later attitude, had always been ready to help her, especially when it involved relationships. Julie always valued her opinion on making relationships exciting. Tanya thought that Scott was one of the hottest and friendliest guys at their university and that Scott and Julie were "a match made in heaven". Tanya always had her back.

Julie remembered how Tanya looked at her as she made the final touches to her make-up. "I can't believe how beautiful you look, Julie! I have never seen you look so happy and confident. It's as though the real Julie has come out from her hiding place. I see it in your eyes. You know what I think? Scott did it, Scott brought out the *real* you."

She's right, Julie had thought, giving in to a heartfelt smile as she admired herself in the mirror. Scott made her feel as though she could do anything.

That evening, Julie and Scott had eaten dinner at a fancy restaurant with views of the city. But the only view Scott had wanted was of her. He gazed at her from across the candlelit table with slightly raised eyebrows. She had felt that she wanted the moment to last forever as she looked deep into his sparkling coffee-coloured eyes. His dimples worked overtime that night.

"You did this all for me?" he had asked, as he took her hand into his and caressed her fingers gently. His touch made Julie quiver.

"So you think this is all I planned for you tonight?" she had teased.

"You mean there's more?" he had asked, looking into her eyes, continuing to stroke her hand.

"Well, there's dessert for one thing!" she had said.

"I can't wait for that," he had responded.

"How do you feel about *crème brulee*?"

"So are we having that in the private dining room?" he had asked, smiling wickedly.

Julie had retorted by messing up his overlong brown hair. "No, silly, we're having it here. I hope you're not disappointed."

"Julie … I could never be disappointed with you. Anything I do with you is magical, that's what you do," he had said, stroking her hair from across the cosy table. "You bring magic into my life. Even the simplest thing becomes fun and exciting with you."

Julie felt so much for him at that moment. Scott understood what she was about. She couldn't imagine another twenty-three-year-old guy being so honest with his feelings.

Moments later, they had finished their dinner and headed back to the car.

"Scott, remember you asked me what else I have planned for you this evening? You also said I bring magic into your life. Well, as it just so happens, I've got two tickets to see a very exciting exhibition, by a talented Spanish contemporary artist, who happens to be in Sydney as we speak! I believe he may happen to be your favourite artist?" she smiled.

"What! You didn't! How? There were no more tickets!"

"Well, I waved my magic wand, but I only do that for people I really care about, people I love." She had looked deep into his excited, laughing eyes. "Actually, I know a friend who happens to work at—"

Before she could finish her sentence, he had picked her up and held her in his arms before slowly and gently placing her down. He had softly told her, "I don't know what it is about you, Julie, but the more I get to know you, the more I want to know about every single aspect of you." He had pulled her close. "I love you, Julie … magical powers and all." She then felt his soft, warm lips on her lips as he began to kiss her. When their lips parted, they locked eyes for a moment before he began to ravish her with quick, urgent kisses on her lips, face, and neck. He had hugged her closer. Julie's heart had felt tight with intense emotion. It ached for him. The connection between them was so real. She could not imagine her life getting better. Scott was all she needed and all she wanted.

The rain tapped on the train windows. Julie jolted as she woke from her memory, realising it was her stop. Slightly dazed, she took her hand away from her neck and grabbed her umbrella. She got off the train feeling depleted.

CHAPTER THREE

Julie was still deep in thought as she walked through Greenwood Plaza in North Sydney. Usually she would linger to window shop. That afternoon, however, she hurried through the crowd without having any interest in her surroundings. Just as she neared the exit of the plaza, a familiar smell stopped her in her tracks. She found the source of the aroma: fresh apple and cinnamon muffins. She bought a packet of six and made her way onto the wet, busy street before any other sweet cakes or pastries enticed her. With the void she felt in her heart, she knew that her willpower would fail her when it came to comfort food.

She crossed the street feeling like a lost soul. The rain had stopped but her confusion continued to torment her. She knew it wasn't just the lack of a love life, although that didn't help, she admitted to herself. The conversation she had with George was also bothering her more than she wanted to admit.

"We all know how much you love your job."

I wish, Julie thought miserably. What happened to all the passion she had in her university days? She used to be so enthusiastic to take on new challenges. An image of herself helping to set up the Fancy Dress Club stand outside the university cafeteria instantly came to mind, followed by another image of herself sipping a cup of tea at the Tea Club, savouring every sip — another one of the long list of clubs she had become a member of, which also included the Adventure Club, the Debating Club and the Rowing Club. She had always felt the need to experience and feel every moment in her life, as opposed to merely just letting them pass her by.

A few blocks away, she arrived at the front door of the Victorian terrace house she shared with her two friends, Maria and Cassandra. The ridiculous house prices in

Sydney meant it was more convenient to rent with her friends than own her own place, not to mention it was also a lot more fun. As she unlocked the door and entered the grand hallway, its original ornate ceiling still intact, she followed the murmuring coming from the direction of the lounge room. The oil heater worked its magic and the front of the terrace house was pleasantly warm and inviting. The smell of apple and cinnamon exuding from the muffins instantly perfumed the air. She threw her bag on the replica Eames chair in the corner of the hallway and placed her umbrella in the umbrella stand, making a mental note to air it out later.

She placed the muffins on the marble table in the hallway, and unclipped her bracelet. She had enough jingle-jangle for one day. Still, she couldn't help but admire the Byzantine-inspired bracelet as she placed it down onto the table, its ruby-red beads shimmering against yellow gold. A contemporary Hurricane vessel, made of a cool grey ceramic with a matte finish, was slightly out of place on the table. Julie straightened it, and stood back for a second to admire the whole display. The contrast and complement between the traditional and contemporary pieces invoked calmness within her.

She unbuttoned her coat as she followed the voices, stopping in her tracks when she heard her name. Julie stood, silent in curiosity as to what was being said about her in such a serious tone.

"I think she's in a rut," she heard Cassandra say. "I mean, all she seems to talk about lately is how much she despises her job. She needs to either accept her situation, or do something about it instead of driving us and herself crazy from whinging."

"You said it, sister," Maria responded in a less serious tone. "Seriously though, I agree with everything you're saying. I mean, she said that she would pursue another career when she gained office experience, but it's been so long now."

21

Her heartbeat quickened as she took a step forward so she could hear every word. As Cassandra was about to continue voicing her thoughts on the matter, Julie took another step forward, only to lose her balance. Her arm accidentally knocked a vase perched on another small table as she tried to hold on to something. Within seconds, Maria and Cassandra raced out to the hallway to find Julie on the floor, trying to salvage what she could from the antique French porcelain vase that was now in pieces on the polished, timber floorboards.

"Where on earth did you come from?" demanded Maria, still looking shocked and frazzled from the interruption.

"What … um … from the front door," Julie stammered. She didn't want her friends to know she had been listening in on their conversation. As she stood up, giving up on any attempt to fix the vase, she suddenly felt betrayed by her friends. "Actually, I was ready to surprise you both with some fresh apple and cinnamon muffins, when I suddenly heard something about me whinging and being in a rut."

Maria and Cassandra eyed the bag of muffins on the marble table. As Cassandra made an attempt to explain the conversation, Maria grabbed the muffins and headed straight for the kitchen.

"I'll just start brewing some coffee. I brought some fresh, organic coffee beans with me from the shop. I'd better start grinding. It'll be divine with the muffins," Maria said, leaving Cassandra to do all the explaining.

Julie watched her friend as she hurried down the hallway, her very long, auburn hair, swaying from side to side. It was almost comical, for in her rush to extricate herself from the uncomfortable situation she nearly tripped over on the rug. Cassandra, however, looked keen to reassure her that they were merely concerned about her. Cassandra was twenty-nine and studying counselling, and was always eager to confront awkward situations, rather than run from them. She took Julie by the hand and led her to the lounge room.

"Now, let's enjoy the delicious muffins that you generously bought for us, and we can talk about everything as we sip the wonderful coffee that Maria was so determined to make," she said with a knowing smile. "If that's all right with you?" she quickly added. "A client and a counsellor always work as a team."

Julie looked into her friend's light blue eyes that shone with concern. Her shoulder length, ash blonde hair was pulled back in a tight bun and her face glowed with an infectious warmth. Julie couldn't fight back a smile.

"How can I resist a free counselling session, especially if an aspiring counsellor thinks I'm in a rut?"

Considering the way she was feeling lately, maybe a talk with her friends was exactly what she needed. She felt strangely relieved that they had acknowledged her issues, instantly feeling that she was no longer alone in her confusion. Her friends knew her better than anyone, and if she was even becoming so transparent with her family, and work colleagues as well, she must definitely be reaching the pinnacle of her despair. She needed to make some serious changes in her life. She couldn't continue living with no direction, no meaning, and no passion.

"I'll just go and freshen up. I need it after the gruelling and unbearable day I had at work," Julie added. "What?" she protested as Cassandra gave her a worried glance. "I have to live up to my reputation of being a whining, boring person," she continued with a smile.

As she headed for the bathroom, carefully avoiding the broken pieces of porcelain, she heard Cassandra call after her. "We never said anything about you being boring …"

"I'll meet you at the couch for my counselling session," Julie yelled back. "I have a lot to tell you. Would you believe I overheard something at work, *also*? Of course, we can analyse why I chose the word 'boring' to describe myself as well. Oh … and you won't believe what George did *this* time … I mean his arrogance is beyond comprehension."

She smiled as she passed Maria, who was cautiously carrying a tray of empty coffee cups, and a plate with the apple and cinnamon muffins. Maria reciprocated the gesture, with what seemed to be relief that Julie wasn't angry with them.

Julie breathed a heavy sigh of relief as she pulled off her coat. Remembering the dinner plans they had made, she quickly glanced at her watch, then down at the shattered pieces of porcelain. They reminded her of how she had been feeling on the inside for so long: shattered and incomplete. However, unlike the vase, she suddenly felt that there was hope that her heart could be fixed, and that she could feel whole again.

CHAPTER FOUR

"Please, can someone pass me the papadums? I'm absolutely famished!" Maria's voice held a hint of desperation. After tossing ideas back and forth, the decision as to where to eat dinner was made for them as they passed their favourite Indian restaurant, nestled in a back street in Crows Nest. The aroma of delicious spices was enough to convince all three that they were definitely in the mood for Indian food.

As Cassandra studied the menu carefully, as though she was studying one of her future clients' counselling files, Maria's protests became louder. "Please, make a decision or else I'll faint."

"Okay, okay! I wouldn't want you to faint," Cassandra responded sarcastically. "I'll have the prawn Malabar, since you both chose a chicken and a vegetarian dish–"

Before Cassandra could finish her sentence, Maria waved her hand hysterically, desperately trying to get the waiter's attention.

Julie looked at her friend and couldn't help herself from laughing. She took a long sip of the chilled Chardonnay they had bought earlier, and sighed. She could finally relax after the hectic pace of the week. She enjoyed the dry aftertaste of the wine as she breathed in the fresh aroma of coriander and the other mixed spices that pleasantly infused the air. Earlier, that afternoon, as soon as they'd had their coffee and a muffin each, Julie had quickly slipped into her favourite pair of skinny jeans, and had complemented her silk cream shirt with a beautiful, burgundy print scarf. She had squeezed her black, ankle, leather boots over her jeans, and then threw on a classic camel coat. She quickly ran a comb through her hair, and was ready in record time. She had admired how the unusual scarf challenged the rest of the more "on trend" clothes when she looked at her five foot five frame in the mirror.

Julie studied her friends, who were engrossed in a conversation regarding whether they should have ordered a platter for three instead of the vegetable samosas they had decided on. Maria, at twenty-eight, was content with her life. She had completed a Bachelor of Arts degree, majoring in English and French, just because she always wanted to. In contrast, Julie had studied English only because she needed another subject to make up enough units for her BA degree. Both Maria's parents were Greek. She had a strong work ethic, which she got from her parents, who worked in the restaurant industry. She loved her shop, Eventually You, which sold organic lifestyle products, and was very driven and passionate about making it a success. She was in a new relationship with Antonio, a young man from Chile who was equally passionate about life and his career as a graphic designer. Unlike Julie, she took life one day at a time, and didn't dwell on the negatives.

Cassandra was also very driven and in control of her life. Although she originally graduated with a Bachelor of Education, she decided to become a counsellor as she realised teaching was not for her. She was now in the middle of her studies and worked full time as an administration assistant at a non-government charity organisation, where she was also able to utilise her counselling skills on a practical level. Cassandra was single at the moment and content with that as she was really focused on her studies.

Julie suddenly realised that although they all had met at university, her friends knew where they were heading with their lives. In contrast, after completing her BA degree, majoring in Human Resource Management (mainly because she didn't know what else to major in), Julie had just settled and taken the safe road, not really knowing what career to pursue. As challenging and interesting as her studies had been, she knew that she secretly had a yearning to explore her creative side. She never took it seriously though. It was just a fantasy.

"Okay, enough about the food," said Maria. The appetisers had finally arrived and she had just taken the first bite of her samosa. "It's time to talk about Julie and the rut we all agree she's in. As I said earlier, you need adventure in your life. I mean, look at how you dress. That scarf is so beautiful and unique, almost cutting edge. It's as though you have a rebellious side to you bursting to come out." Maria took a sip of water. "That and you also need a man to share your dreams and complement your life," she continued.

"I agree, well, with the first part of that anyway," Cassandra said. "That was very intuitive, Maria. Anyway, I think Julie needs to concentrate on herself at the moment. I know that you're the expert in finding out what's important in your life, but can I offer you some suggestions? After all …"

"… the client and the counsellor always work together," Maria and Julie chorused, laughing mischievously.

"Oh my God, what have I become? Have I lost my ability to just be a friend without finding every opportunity to practise my counselling skills?"

"Cass, I welcome your input. You may have learned something that can really help me," Julie said.

"Well … okay then. If you insist! It may be that there is incongruence with your real self and your ideal self. You need to find out what is important to you, and what your values are, so that the incongruence can decrease, and the gap can be narrowed. At the moment, it seems that you are working for a company that is in conflict with your values and what you really want to do."

"I don't even know what I want out of life, let alone my career," Julie responded solemnly.

"Well, I'm in the middle of studying career counselling, so you're in luck. Why don't you complete a Values

27

Assessment questionnaire? It may help you figure out what you want out of your career, and hence, out of life. After all, everything is interconnected," Cassandra continued, becoming more excited as she spoke. "The reason that you're in a rut is because you can't find meaning in your life at the moment. You need to strive for self-actualisation. This means you need to attain your personal potential. It's a drive or need that is present in all of us." Cassandra looked as though she had found the last piece of the puzzle to Julie's life.

"Self-actualisation? Do you think that you can skip the jargon and explain things in more simple terms? I may need a glass of wine, though, except I don't drink that much and I am the designated driver," Maria teased.

"Thank God we have a friend who is so into living a healthy lifestyle. What would we do without you? Maybe you can offer some nutrition advice to Julie. You know, try a more holistic approach," Cassandra added, laughing.

As Julie was about to interject, she was interrupted by the aroma of chicken tikka masala and fresh buttery naan bread. The other two mains arrived straight after. They all thanked the waiter politely and started sharing the food expertly amongst themselves.

"So Julie," Cassandra said, whilst in the middle of a balancing act with the rice and the bread basket. "As I was saying, you need to reach your potential and strive for self-actualisation in order to gain passion and meaning to your life."

"I don't know what I want out of life, though. I don't know what I want to be," Julie stated, knowing that she sounded like a broken record.

"That's a misconception. You don't just become something in life. You evolve and grow, otherwise you get bored and remain stagnant. Correct me if I'm wrong, but do you think that you may be listening to the ifs, shoulds, musts and oughts that you kept hearing from your childhood? These are called inferences and introjections.

They form false beliefs, which can be very debilitating to a person's growth," Cassandra continued.

Julie stared at both her friends blankly as she tried to process this information.

"Anyway, I can see that I have overwhelmed you, so I'll shut up right now and you can think about what I've said in your own time. Besides, Maria seems to have become bored with my counselling jargon; she's mesmerised by the couple at the counter." Cassandra gazed at Maria curiously.

"Isn't that that the annoying guy that you work with? Isn't that George?" Maria asked Julie. "I can't believe he was at it again at your last meeting. I overheard you talking about him with Cass earlier."

Julie almost choked on her prawn. She snuck a glance in the couple's direction, and was shocked to see that it actually was in fact George, accompanied by a young woman who was fashionably dressed from head to toe. She was practically glued to his arm. *He must have met her when he had drinks with the others, or maybe he had a planned date with her,* Julie speculated. She wasn't used to seeing him outside of work. He certainly looked handsome. His short, dark brown hair was slightly gelled, and his blue eyes looked deep and intuitive, as opposed to intimidating, as she often thought they were. She could only see the woman's back.

"It's him, isn't it?" Maria asked inquisitively, talking over the slow, mystical sitar music that played softly through speakers above them.

"Yes, it's George Giveski," Julie responded, grabbing her wine glass as though it would shield her from her friends witnessing her blushing, agonised face. How many times would she run into him?

Julie suddenly came out of the spell she seemed to be under, and directed her attention to Cassandra. "Do you think you could give me one of those Values Questionnaires?" she asked, hoping her friends didn't question her reaction.

"Sure, I've got a few copies at home," Cassandra responded, raising her glass.

"Who wants the last papadum?" Maria stared at her friends hopefully.

"You can have it," Julie and Cassandra replied, in perfect harmony.

Julie took a sip of wine, relieved that her friends had not interrogated her about her unusual reaction to seeing George. She would have no answers. She was getting very used to not having any answers. Perhaps the questionnaire was the beginning to gaining some insight. As Cassandra said, "Everything is interconnected."

CHAPTER FIVE

"Give it back! Mum, John took my iPad. It's not fair, it's mine."

"John, give Elisabeth her iPad, please! Ask her if you can have it after she has a turn with it," his mother commanded.

"No! It's mine and I want to use it all day!" Elisabeth cried.

"Johnny, why don't you play with your car racing game? That other game is a bit girlie, don't you think?" Julie whispered hopefully in her nephew's ear. "The car racing game is cool," she continued hoping her niece could not hear her, or her mum for that matter. Julie didn't want to create negative gender stereotypes, but she was desperate. Her head was aching, and she was in no mood for any drama.

"Yeah, my games are cooler than her games. She just has girlie games," John stated defiantly.

Her niece was too engrossed in the game that had caused all the tears and conflict, and Julie's sister, Christina, just sat quietly in the front passenger seat of the car. Julie was sitting in the back seat, next to her niece and nephew in her sister and brother-in-law's four-wheel-drive, heading north to the Hunter Valley vineyards. Her brother-in-law, Brian, was behind the wheel.

Still tired and sluggish from all the wine she had consumed the night before, Julie had been woken up that morning by the demanding sound of her mobile phone ringing on her bedside table. When she placed the phone to her ear, still half asleep, all she could hear were Christina's angry words. Julie replayed the verbal attack in her mind:

"Do you know what the time is? You were supposed to be at our house at seven o'clock. I woke up the kids so

31

early, and you're still not here. How selfish and inconsiderate can you be? We all got ready early and you're just one person and you can't even be on time. You seriously don't know how hard it is to have a family to look after."

Before Julie could respond, her sister had hung up. Julie had stared blankly at the phone in disbelief and in shock. She had completely forgotten about the planned trip: the trip she desperately tried to get out of. She had successfully found many excuses, but could not commit to any of them when she saw the hopeful little faces of her seven-year-old nephew and her nine-year-old niece. They had practically begged Julie to go with them. She had accepted that she simply did not get along with her sister, and the last thing she wanted to do was to tag along on a weekend family outing.

She was frustrated at herself for agreeing to the trip. She may have been late, but there was no reason for her sister to be so rude to her. There were many occasions when her sister was late for a planned outing, but Julie never spoke to her like that. Despite her apprehension, she would put those feelings about the trip aside and keep an open mind. She was doing it for the kids after all. *So much for that though*, she thought bitterly. The weekend had already got off to a tragic start. *At least there'll be plenty of wine,* she thought, although that was the last thing she wanted with the headache that tormented her.

After she hung up, and with a lot of help from Maria and Cassandra, Julie was dressed, packed and behind the wheel of her silver Volkswagen Polo in no more than thirty minutes. As she drove to her sister's house in the northern suburb of Wollstonecraft, she couldn't believe that she had been so pre-occupied with her problems that she forgot about the trip. *Maybe my subconscious blocked it out deliberately*, she speculated. Her sister hadn't even mentioned it the last time they spoke. She could have reminded her since they had planned the trip a few weeks ago. Grudgingly, she turned up at the doorstep of her sister's double storey federation house. Before she could raise her hand to knock, her sister raced out of the house and headed to the car, carrying a huge bag and drink bottles for the kids.

"By the time we get there we won't be able to get the best apartment!" Christina cried.

"What do you mean? Check in time is at two o'clock."

"Yes, it is, but they sometimes let you in early, and we can choose the best one."

Julie's anger surfaced slowly, and just when she was about to forget all her plans to remain amicable and agreeable, and really tell her sister what she thought about her, Elisabeth raced up to her screaming ecstatically, "Auntie Julie, look at what I made at school!"

Her attention quickly switched to her niece and to her nephew, who had also stepped out to greet her. As they all made their way to the car, she greeted her brother-in-law, who loaded Julie's bag into the boot. She gave him a smile that was as fake as tan from a bottle. She didn't want Brian to see how angry she was with his wife. She knew it would hurt him. He always wanted them to get along.

"That's a nice bracelet, Auntie Julie," Elisabeth said, touching its ruby-red beads.

"Thanks, Elisabeth," Julie replied.

"Oh God! I hope you didn't wear that thing to work," Christina shrieked when Elisabeth was in the car and out of earshot. "It looks like it belongs in a museum!"

Julie opened her mouth to respond but her sister had beat her to it.

"Did you have to get such a big bag?" she questioned with obvious disdain in her voice.

Julie obediently climbed into the car without responding, fearing that the next word that may have come out, in front of the kids, would begin with the letter "F". As they pulled out of the driveway, Julie's headache worsened, helped along by the grinding of her teeth.

This is going to be the icing on the cake, she thought as she realised, once again, that she was doing something she didn't want to do. All the hope she felt the night before was threatening to dissipate until she remembered the questionnaires Cassandra had given her that morning. Hope filled her heart again. Her headache was definitely an indication things had reached boiling point, as she was ready to explode. Pleasing everyone but herself was not working for her. It was only a matter of time before she completely snapped.

Her thoughts were interrupted by the loud din of music blasting from the car stereo, its beat echoing the throbbing pain in her head. *Great!* Julie thought angrily. *Now I have to put up with my sister's idea of music.* Her sister's musical taste hadn't matured since high school. *Yes!* Julie thought, *I am a music snob.* She proudly acknowledged this often. She felt justified taking this stance, because who on earth could possibly call this monotonous sound music? If it were her car, the sounds of rock or indie pop bands would be blaring through the speakers. If she was feeling mellow, jazz would permeate the air.

Of course, if her sister was a passenger, she would demand that she turn the music off, as she would conveniently be suffering from a headache, and she would also make sure Julie knew it. Julie decided to just stare at her surroundings, and not make an issue of it as her niece screamed, "I love this song!"

"Another compromise," she mumbled, feeling deflated.

She stared at the familiar surroundings as they travelled north. She had been to the Hunter Valley many times with her friends, but this would definitely be a different holiday. They passed through the suburb of Wahroonga and were soon heading northwards on the freeway. It would be at least another two hours before they reached their destination. With her brother-in-law focused on finding the best lane to beat the traffic, her sister deeply engrossed in miming to the awful pop song that sounded just like the previous one, and her nephew and niece intensely preoccupied with their games, Julie closed her eyes and tried to think pleasant thoughts. She imagined herself walking in the vineyards, hand-in-hand with someone. She imagined herself in a summer dress with a tall, handsome man next to her. Before she could picture the man's face, her eyes began to shut out the world and its problems, and she fell into a deep, pleasant sleep.

CHAPTER SIX

"Auntie Julie, look! Can you see the cows? And there are horses too! They're drinking water from that lake."

Julie felt a small hand digging into her arm. She opened her eyes as the voice of her nephew became louder.

"Look, you're going to miss them!"

"Oh, I see them," Julie managed, her eyes seeing a blurred vision of what appeared to be some type of animal with four legs.

Julie realised they were approaching the quiet town of Cessnock. *I must have been asleep for two hours*, she thought to herself. At least it allowed her to avoid any conflict with Christina.

"Auntie Julie! Why did you have a smile on your face when you were sleeping? Did you have a nice dream?" Elisabeth looked at her inquisitively.

"Oh, did I? I was actually dreaming of the vineyards," Julie vaguely recalled. She couldn't remember anything else.

"Well, we're nearly there," Brian stated. "You must have had a late one last night, Jules. Were you out on a hot date?" Her brother-in-law awaited her response, looking at her in the rear-view mirror. He had a cheeky look in his green eyes. Leave it to her brother-in-law to always try to calm the tension between herself and her sister. She suddenly felt sorry for him always having to be the mediator.

"It's easy to have late nights when you don't have responsibilities," her sister interjected bitterly.

Julie watched sympathetically as her brother-in-law clenched the steering wheel tightly. She decided to refrain from giving her sister the other end of the rope. She knew Brian was trying to lighten the mood, and he would be devastated if his attempt caused the opposite outcome.

"This place is so breathtaking," Julie digressed as they pulled into the vineyards. She suddenly felt excited at the thought of spending two days in the country, and hoped that she was able to spend some time on her own. She needed to gain a different perspective, and the ambience and beauty that the vineyards embodied was almost magical. Although it wasn't the season to see grapes on green-leafed vines, the brown, freshly pruned vines amongst the background of lush, green hills still created a mystical, postcard picture. Rows of dormant vines slumbered for the winter as the hills awoke with new life, blanketing the valley in vibrant emerald; with promise and renewal. Julie opened the window to breathe in the country air, instantly feeling a light, cool, breeze on her skin. She breathed in its rawness, its dirt and its beauty. A smile crossed her face, but began to wither quickly as Christina snapped at her coldly.

"Are you for real? Can you close the window! We're in the middle of winter. John has had a runny nose all week!" Annoyed, but not wanting to aggravate things further, Julie did as she was told.

After driving along a long dirt road, they passed through a charming entrance which led them to the resort they were booked to stay in for one night. Brian parked the car in the landscaped carpark next to the resort's reception area.

"Well, we'd better check in. I can't wait to relax and then try some gourmet cheese, and, of course, get stuck into the wine tasting," he stated eagerly.

"I'm coming too. All the good apartments are probably taken. God knows what they are going to give us now. The kids have so many allergies, so they'd better not give us one with carpet. Do you know how many dust mites live and breed in carpet!"

Julie watched as Christina and Brian walked at a hurried pace towards the resort's reception area. She studied her sister's tense shoulders. The way she walked reminded Julie of soldiers marching into combat. It was a shame her sister took life so seriously. Oddly, her outer appearance was in complete contrast to her serious attitude. She was a lot taller than Julie, and her youthful dress sense portrayed a picture of a carefree, spontaneous and fun person, adorned as she often was in pastels and floral prints. Like Julie, Christina had hazel eyes, and when she smiled, her whole face, which was slightly olive in complexion, seemed friendly and genuinely content. Christina took after their father, who was of Italian origin, while Julie took after their mother, who had porcelain Anglo features and light brown hair with a slight curl in it. In contrast, Christina usually let her thick, shiny, dark brown hair fall freely and naturally just below her shoulders, hair that, as opposed to Julie's, remained stubbornly straight. Julie always thought that aspect of her physical appearance definitely corresponded with Christina's personality.

As the two figures entered the reception area, Julie examined her surroundings. They had booked one of the three-bedroom apartments, which entailed a separate lounge, kitchen and veranda that overlooked the vineyards. The resort contained two tennis courts and was surrounded by a golf course and two scenic bike trails. Julie stepped out of the car to stretch her legs. She stretched her arms, and inhaled slowly, remembering what she had learned from her beginners Vinyasa Yoga DVD. She slowly exhaled, while stretching her arms towards the sides of her hips. "Back to Tadasana," she said, quietly to herself, just as the instructor had done on the DVD.

"Back to what?" Elisabeth enquired, looking at Julie laughing. Julie practically fell to the ground, as John raced out of the car bumping into her in the process. They both started emulating Julie's moves, breathing in and out. Seeing that no one else was around, Julie decided to show them a few more.

"I know how to do yoga, too!" John screamed out, as he leaped onto the ground and tried to lift his whole body off it, whilst balancing on his hands.

Just then Christina and Brian approached them. A flock of rainbow lorikeets swiftly dispersed from the trees above, making a loud screeching sound as they flew past.

"What are you doing Jonathan? Can't you watch him for me for one minute? He's going to kill himself." Christina glared at Julie with a look that made her feel as if she was the worst auntie, and sister, in the universe.

"He was just trying to show me his yoga moves," she managed. "I would have caught him if he lost his balance."

"Anyway, let's go. They gave us an apartment with timber floor boards."

"They all had timber floor boards," Brian said.

Her sister didn't respond.

Julie smiled as she stepped back into the car. "So, my being late didn't impact on which apartment they allocated to us after all," she stated smugly.

"Well, we were lucky this time. I didn't want to waste the day anyway," Christina responded, with what appeared to be a smile of defeat forming on her face.

She should smile more often, Julie thought to herself. *It brings out the colour in her cheeks.* It also reminded Julie of the times they got along with each other. Back when they were younger, they went everywhere together, enjoying each other's company. Christina wasn't as judgmental then. She knew how to chill out and enjoy herself. It saddened Julie that they had drifted apart so drastically. She vividly remembered ten year old Christina sneaking into her room early on a Sunday morning with a block of milk chocolate and a mischievous smile on her face. Julie was six at the time. They would both sit quietly on the carpeted floor, enjoying the sweet, comforting taste of the chocolate melting in their greedy mouths. They would then plan elaborate excuses regarding how the chocolate disappeared, whispering quietly so their parents wouldn't hear.

Julie also often reminisced about the time when she shared Christina's room one summer, when her own room was being renovated. They would often pretend that they were sleeping, only to wake up moments later when their parents had gone to sleep. They would watch the late night music programme, *Rage*, or turn the radio on and wait for their favourite song to come on. That usually lasted for most of the night as every song turned out to be their favourite. They would both try to restrain themselves from singing loudly or dancing on their beds when the Spice Girls or Aqua's "Barbie Girl" came on.

Memories of their teenage years sharing a tub of their favourite mango ice-cream whilst watching *Dawson's Creek*, talking about which boy they had a crush on, or which shop in the city would have the coolest clothes, always filled her heart with nostalgia. She would never forget all the times when Christina helped her redecorate her room, which she did often. Christina had covered for her when she had accidentally spilled blackcurrant juice on one of the lounge room paintings, as she tried to hang it in her own room, thinking it would look better there, as the lounge room already looked cluttered. "Oh no!" Christina had screamed. "Mum will freak out if she sees what you did. Mind the door. I know how to fix it," she had said. She remembered feeling that her sister would always have her back. She thought they would always be able to talk about anything together.

They had definitely grown apart now, and, ironically, the more they kept in touch, the unhealthier their relationship became. The rift between them had occurred so suddenly. One minute they were partners in crime, the next minute, Christina was shouting out orders as though she was a teacher. "Did you finish your homework?" "Who are you going to the party with?" "Do I even know that girl?" Her sister seemed to thrive in her new role. There were no more conversations about boys, or clothes, or music. Their parents had just started an import business in the food industry, and since Christina was seventeen at the time, she was assigned to look after Julie when their parents weren't around. That's when the dynamics changed, when their relationship disintegrated, just like a democracy does when a dictatorship takes the reins.

They finally found their apartment, which looked as beautiful as it did online. All five of them jumped out of the car, eager to unload their luggage, when Julie noticed her sister looking with indignation at her brown leather boots, which she had proudly purchased on sale during her lunch hour in the city, not knowing, as she was now informed, that her sister had the same pair. She had hurriedly put them on that morning, matching them with a black woollen dress and a denim jacket. Julie had been proud of the fact that she had managed to look smart in the space of a few minutes. However, that feeling had now been erased and replaced with a need to defend herself once again.

Three rainbow lorikeets suddenly flew past, joining the rest of the cheerful flock further ahead. Julie met Christina's accusing glare and wished that she could join them.

"I can't believe you have the same boots as me!" Christina stated melodramatically. "Now I can't wear mine. We'll look like twins."

Before Julie could try to understand how they would look like twins when their appearances were nothing alike, a familiar, aching feeling began to reacquaint itself with her temples. The headache which had miraculously disappeared was back to torment her.

That's all I need, Julie thought miserably, as she made her way into the apartment, grasping her luggage tightly.

CHAPTER SEVEN

"What a beautiful afternoon, considering we're in the middle of winter," Brian acknowledged contently.

Julie, Brian and Christina were all seated at an outdoor café, at a charming place called Pokolbin, inside the vineyards. After spending the day wine tasting and having a picnic whilst enjoying a cheese platter, they decided to spend the afternoon shopping at the many boutique specialty stores in the area. Elisabeth and John were ecstatic as they knew that there were many chocolate and lolly shops nearby, as well as a huge jumping castle. They had patiently spent the day giving into whatever the adults wanted to do, so it was their turn to enjoy themselves. It was also an opportunity for the adults to enjoy a cup of coffee while the kids let out all their frustrations jumping on the castle. Elisabeth and John also had an opportunity to pat the animals that were part of the mobile animal farm. It was a glorious afternoon. Even her sister looked happy as she ordered her cappuccino, "with extra *crème* and less froth." A young man with an acoustic guitar played Pete Murray songs nearby. All the ingredients were there for a wonderful time, if there were no other cruel remarks aimed at her from her sister.

"So where did you go last night? Was it a date?" Christina suddenly asked her, looking genuinely interested in her response. It was the first time that she had attempted to have a conversation with her since Julie awkwardly greeted them that morning.

"Actually, I just went out with Cass and Maria," she responded cautiously, the sweet floral smell of the lavender in the garden bed beside them slightly calming her. It felt strange that her sister was engaging in polite conversation.

"Maria is dating someone isn't she? What's he like?"

Julie heard a bee buzzing nearby as she began to speak. "He's really down to earth and passionate about life. He's not bad in the looks department either."

"I remember you saying that he's South American. Remember that guy from Argentina, in my year, back at high school, the drummer in the school band?"

"How can I forget? All the guys were so jealous of him. I remember he was in the class next to my History lesson when I was in year eight. I loved History that year; I always made an excuse to run into him."

"Why is it that when a guy is in a band, all the girls suddenly treat him like a god?" Brian quipped.

"I'm sure you were popular with the girls too, being in the chess club and all." Christina looked at Brian with a teasing smile.

"I'll have you know that there were a lot of intelligent, attractive girls interested in me. Don't forget, I was also on the basketball team."

"I know, I was one of them," Christina responded, her smile now covering her whole face.

Brian was certainly attractive with his subtle green eyes, light brown hair and strong, chiselled jaw. His slightly crooked nose even added to his appeal, as the imperfection seemed to magnify the handsomeness of the rest of his face. Her sister started dating him in high school when they were allocated to team up for an economics project. They couldn't keep their eyes off each other while studying fiscal policy and monetary policy. Julie witnessed this first-hand, as she passed her sister's room numerous times, when they were in the middle of their so called "studying." When they were actually working, she remembered one of their conversations, where they were comparing macroeconomics to microeconomics. They had obviously rejected the former, and created their own micro world, where they only had eyes for each other, Julie had thought. To be fair, they did come first in their presentation, and they were presented with an award for "Excellent research and team work." That definitely laid strong romantic *and* financial foundations in their relationship. They even took the title of "Couple of the year" at their Year 12 formal. Brian went on to university and gained a degree in business. He was now in charge of the marketing department at his firm. Christina majored in a similar field, but put her career on hold after working for a few years, and was now devoted to raising Elisabeth and John.

Julie was glad to see that affection towards each other still existed. She feared that the stress of raising a family was having a negative effect on their relationship.

"Aren't there any eligible bachelors where you work?" Christina continued in a genuinely interested tone.

"Most are married or in their early twenties. The only thing on their mind is partying."

"It's a shame you and Mark didn't work out. I was just reading about him in the Alumni magazine. He seems to be doing well for himself. You made such a fun couple."

"Well, we were both at different places in our lives. He wanted to travel the world and I wanted to work," Julie responded robotically, not liking where the conversation was heading.

Julie had had a four month relationship with Mark while she was still at university. They had met at a uni party. He had bumped into her near the bar, and her Southern Comfort did actually end up going south, and definitely did not feel very comfortable, all over her white jeans.

Julie remembered feeling humiliated. Mark, with his messy, grungy hair and down-to-earth personality, apologised profusely. The warmth in his eyes helped her from wishing the earth would open up and swallow her at that very moment. After Mark bought her another drink, they both realised there was a connection between them: their dislike of dance music and their love of grunge bands from the nineties. They were both impressed with each other's knowledge regarding the Seattle grunge scene, and he was also amazed at her knowledge of sixties rock bands. They became inseparable, meeting between lectures, seeing live bands together and enjoying their talks about music.

Julie knew that their relationship wasn't serious. It was fun and that was exactly what she had needed at that time in her life. She felt safe with Mark. He couldn't hurt her, as there were no expectations from either one of them. He was the raft she needed at a time when her life had fallen apart.

Julie had also recently read about him in the University Alumni magazine. He was working as a sports physiotherapist with various cricket teams around the world. She knew full well that the reason for their split was due to her taking the safe road and doing what people expected her to do, or as Cassandra so often stated, being influenced by "extrinsic, organismic motivators rather than intrinsic ones." She would have loved to have been bold and spontaneous. Taking time off to see the world was something she had always wanted to do.

"Well, I guess you had to work. You couldn't exactly put your career on hold and irresponsibly travel the world. You had to put your career first," Christina stated righteously, as she eyed the cappuccino the waitress had just handed her carefully.

"What career? After completing my BA degree, I didn't know what I wanted to do anyway. Perhaps a year off would have given me some perspective. Maybe then I would have been in a better position to steer the path I really wanted, instead of taking the first office job I came across," Julie retorted.

"That's true," Brian interjected, staring at the kids playing tips on the jumping castle. "Sometimes a different environment is needed in order to see things more clearly."

Christina suddenly interrupted them, crying, "Do they honestly call this *crème*? This is like a flat white. Even a flat white should have more *crème* than this cappuccino has. I'm definitely going to complain about this."

Brian and Julie looked at Christina's shocked face. Julie felt extremely hurt and dejected that her comment, which came from her heart, had been completely ignored. Julie was used to this scene when going out with her sister, especially over the last few years. There was never a time when they sat and ate their food, and enjoyed a cup of coffee with no drama. Julie crouched in her seat embarrassed at the predictable scene that was about to ensue.

"Anyway, why don't we introduce Julie to that guy William, at your work?" Christina asked her husband, after the waitress left, promising to bring her another cappuccino.

It was as though Christina's diva-like outburst had not just occurred. Julie's previous comment had also been forgotten, filed away for another time. It was ironic that coffee was supposed to invite people to address their inner feelings with someone when all it seemed to do in their situation was to force her to repress them even further.

"There is no way that I am going to be set up again, especially after that whole Michael saga, which occurred from your insistence of 'what a wonderful guy he is'," Julie found herself responding.

"Well, you do have rather high expectations. It's as if you know what you are looking for, but no one fits because they don't have the specific credentials."

Julie felt her face colour. She felt her sister knew something that she herself wasn't even aware of.

"Michael had nothing I could possibly want from a guy. He was the complete opposite of me, and the only reason I went out with him for a few dates was to dispel this reputation I had back then, and apparently continue to have, of being too fussy. For God's sake, he was into bodybuilding and ordered salad with fruit juice at restaurants. Let's not forget the interrogation the waiters or waitresses would have to go through, for the sole purpose of determining how many kilojoules the food contained."

"Do you remember when he raced to the beach and pretended that he had saved those two boys, at that party, at that house in Bondi? They were practically on the sand when he pulled them out. They were *thirteen years old*! The poor boys looked shocked — *and* extremely embarrassed. I mean, he knew that he would have to take his tight, white T-shirt off," Brian commented, almost bursting from laughter.

Julie nearly spilled her coffee as she too began to laugh uncontrollably, causing her teaspoon to make a loud clink as it fell back onto the saucer. "They were also members of the Junior Life Saving Club," she added, her eyes becoming slightly teary.

"Okay, point taken. That was a bad example," Christina said with a smile on her face. "It's just that you're twenty-seven, and by the time you meet someone and get to know them, who knows how long it will be before you settle down."

Julie's smile quickly disappeared. "You make it sound like I've already passed my use-by date. For God's sake, I'm only in my twenties. I feel that this is a scene from *Pride and Prejudice*, except instead of the mother trying desperately to marry off her daughters, the older sister takes it upon herself to carry out this job." Julie struggled to add the last sentence in one breath.

"Mum, I'm so hungry. Can we get some pizza?" Elisabeth suddenly appeared at her mother's side.

Julie was grateful for her niece's interruption. She had put up with as much as she could take. She looked at the young man still singing and playing his guitar. He was singing a song by Pete Murray called "Opportunity". As she listened to the lyrics, she tried to gain strength from them as she always did from music. On that note, she stood up, put her sunglasses on, left some money on the table, and abruptly announced that she was going for a walk.

The only opportunity I need at the moment is to get as far away from this interrogation as I can, she thought to herself, as she started walking at a quick pace, feeling her sister's questioning gaze behind her.

CHAPTER EIGHT

Julie walked for at least half an hour along the dirt paths that wound themselves through the vineyards. Her boots dug into the ground with each defiant step. Anger quickly turned into bold determination so she decided to head back to the apartment, grab the questionnaires Cassandra had given her, as well as a glass of Pinot Noir, and sit at a peaceful hill near the tennis courts at the resort. She needed to gain clarity.

Back at the apartment, she eagerly swiped her access card. She entered the hallway, instantly hearing the patter of little hurried footsteps on the timber floorboards. John ran towards her, holding what seemed to be an attempt at a paper aeroplane in his hands. The heavy door creaked as though it was in agony as she released it, causing it to make a loud bang as it shut behind her.

"I didn't know it was one of your papers," Christina called out from the lounge room. "John wandered into your bedroom and managed to retrieve some paper to make an aeroplane when Brian and I had stepped out onto the veranda. Anyway what are all these surveys about?" she continued impatiently, as Julie entered the lounge room holding the paper aeroplane, finding her sister sitting on the couch with a brochure on her lap.

"Cassandra gave them to me. She thought that they would help me establish what type of career I really want to pursue," Julie responded, feeling as though she was on the witness stand again. She couldn't believe what she was hearing. She should be the one asking the questions, regarding how something that was supposed to have remained private was now open for public discussion. There was no apology for not stopping John from practically destroying all the sheets that had been secured neatly in her folder, and placed carefully in the bedroom closet. She wasn't angry at her nephew, but her sister should have stopped him when she found out. Instead, the sheets of paper were scattered carelessly all over the floor.

All Julie could see when she looked at the scattered sheets was Christina's disrespect for every choice she ever made; all her dreams and hope, left there to be trodden on.

"Should you really be worried about a career right now? I mean, shouldn't your love life be a priority? You already have a responsible job. What's wrong with where you're working now?" Christina asked in a condescending tone that was familiar and insulting.

Julie could not listen to her any more. Her head felt like it would explode. Her heart began to race as the anger that she had kept in check for so long reached boiling point.

"What do you mean, I should concentrate on my love life, and that I shouldn't concentrate on my career? Since when did you become such an expert on what I should and shouldn't be doing in my life? Oh, please let me answer that for you. Most of my life, because I obviously don't have a clue when it comes to making decisions concerning what I need!" Julie fumed.

Christina stood up slowly and crossed her arms. She gave Julie a look that she couldn't recognise. Julie wasn't sure if it was shock, or something else, as she ordered John to go and play in his room.

"I'm so sick of you acting like you're my mother. Even Mum doesn't get involved in my personal life as much as you do. You don't know anything about me. All you do is impose your values and beliefs on me, as if I don't have any of my own. Do you honestly think that I can't think for myself? Well, I've had enough, and I am not going to listen to one more piece of unwanted advice, because all your advice does, when I'm stupid enough to take it, is ruin my life!"

Julie couldn't stop. The words were spilling out of her mouth with surprising ease. Suddenly, she felt that she could do anything, feeling elated and free. Her heart, which had felt heavy, suddenly felt light.

"No! I don't think I should just concentrate on my love life. I'm not happy in my career, if that's what you could call it, and I haven't been happy in that job since I convinced myself that, to quote your words, it's 'a responsible, secure job.' I am so damn sick of doing what you think I 'should' do. I've been taking the safe road for too long, and I'm fed up. I want a career that inspires me, which I feel passionate about. I want to keep growing and learning, and travel. Yes! I want to travel and see the world. I don't just want to work in a mundane job where I feel miserable and wait for a knight in shining armour to rescue me. If a guy I'm interested in appears and I feel he's the one for me, well, that would be great. If it doesn't work out, I'll have my own coping mechanisms in place, as I would be the person I created, not the person you, or Mum, or someone else created."

Christina gave her a blank stare. It was as if she couldn't find any words to make a counter attack. Julie continued feeling as if she was in the middle of a soliloquy, searching for the answers to soothe her soul. As she began to relax more, she could feel the imprint that her fingernails had made in the palms of her hands.

"I don't blame you completely. I blame myself for giving you that power over my life. I could have listened to my heart and followed my instincts, but instead I did what was expected of me. I know it's not too late, and I will pursue my dreams from now on. I want my life to have meaning and purpose."

Julie felt that all of a sudden her retaliation had taken a shift in direction. It was as if she was trying to convince herself.

"What I really don't understand is why you care so much about my love life. I mean, if you're happy in your life, why do you have to meddle in mine? Yes! You were lucky and found someone special. You both knew you were meant to

51

be together from the get go. It doesn't mean that the rest of us, who haven't found that someone special, are miserable. Isn't the journey and the hope of finding that someone special part of the fun?"

Christina's arms were still crossed. Her eyes looked distant as Brian stormed into the lounge room carrying a box full of bottles of wine. "We should book the resort's restaurant for dinner," he announced.

Her sister finally moved from the shocked stance she had been in for the duration of Julie's "soliloquy" and began to take something out of a paper bag.

"We went to one of the homeware shops when you left. I bought you some scented candles. I thought you might want some, even if Maria has so many in her shop. One is citrus, the other is vanilla. Apparently, they are certified organic, and they are also made with fresh, local ingredients from the area." Christina handed Julie the candles as if nothing had happened.

Julie was left disappointed and baffled at her sister's reaction. She found her calmness to be rather odd, considering the circumstances. She was expecting something more in return after having waited for so long to voice her feelings. As free and relieved as she felt, it was an anticlimax. Her sister looked hurt and innocent all of a sudden, as if Julie was the aggressor in their relationship.

"Thanks," Julie found herself saying as she accepted the candles.

As Christina helped Brian find the number of the restaurant, Julie picked up the folder and gathered the papers that were still scattered all over the lounge room. Then she grabbed a wine glass from the kitchen, and a bottle of wine from the box that Brian had left on the dining table. Nothing and no one would stop her! She was more determined than ever to find the answers she needed.

CHAPTER NINE

It was around four thirty in the afternoon, and since it was June, Julie knew that the sun would set very soon. Taking a sip of wine, she took in her surroundings in a similar way that she would look at a painting in an art gallery, analysing every detail. The sun, which was slowly fading, gently stroked the trees, the hills, and the lake nearby, creating a serene, comforting picture. Placing a silky strand away from her face, she glanced at a kangaroo in the distance. She could hear the rustling of leaves as a breeze momentarily disturbed the serenity, as well as occasional laughter from a group of people who seemed to be enjoying themselves at the resort's outdoor restaurant, a fair distance behind her. She glanced back at the group and smiled, feeling their positive energy. Julie's eyes then rested on the rows of pruned brown vines across the lake. The stillness of the vineyards made her feel peaceful and optimistic, which was what she needed after her sister's negative interference in her life.

She was determined not to let *anyone* interfere with her desire to gain clarity in regards to her career. She was determined to become more self-aware and gain some insight into what inspired her. A relationship would have to wait! She had to find happiness on her own. She didn't need a man to save her. She would save herself. Only then would she consider a relationship. Just by looking at the view in front of her, Julie realised that there was a whole world out there, full of beauty. She would be part of that world. She would make it happen!

Eagerly opening up the folder of questionnaires, she looked at the five sheets, all with different titles, waiting to be completed by someone who was searching for at least some guidance, if not answers. As Cassandra had pointed out, "The questionnaires are merely a guide to determine what matters to you when choosing a career."

She looked at all the titles, starting with "How Do You Feel about Your Present Job?" followed by "Value Assessment Test," "Needs Test," "Career Assessment Test," and the last one which Julie seemed to be fixated on: "Who Controls Your Life?" Her heart began to beat fast. As she lifted her eyes from the sheet of paper, an image of herself dressed up in stylish clothes, sitting behind a big desk in an office of contemporary design, entered her mind. She imagined herself sketching something in a notepad, and being distracted by an email reminding her that she had to catch a flight to Milan or somewhere just as glamorous. She smiled to herself, as though she was sharing a private joke. Julie looked at the papers again. She was even more determined to steer her future. This was a chance to initiate change. It would start at that moment!

Leave it to Cass to cover all angles, Julie thought, once again looking at the papers. "Who does control my life?" she muttered to herself. After what had just happened back at the apartment with Christina, she definitely knew who was *trying* to control her life.

Julie frantically started filling in the surveys, circling the numbers she felt genuinely corresponded with her feelings. She tried to be as honest as possible. She was astonished that she was already up to the fifth survey when a gust of wind sent the papers flying. Julie ran after them. It was as if they were leading her somewhere, as though they had mystical powers. As she ran, she noticed that a tall man had left the group at the restaurant and was heading in her direction. She looked away, focused on the airborne papers, only to find herself glancing at him again. She finally stopped running when she reached the papers which were now scattered outside the tennis court where a man and a woman were having a game. She started to gather them. One of the papers slapped her on the face and others threatened to escape her grasp.

"Do you need any help?" She was startled at the sound of a male voice close behind her. It was the man from the restaurant. There was something about his voice that caused her skin to shiver. There was something about it that seemed so familiar …

"Do you need any help?" the voice repeated, more loudly. The man was only a few steps behind her.

It can't be. She dismissed the thought that had just entered her mind. It was absurd. Things like that just don't happen! Still, she couldn't mistake that voice. It was much too familiar. She was almost afraid to find out if her assumptions were correct.

She reluctantly turned around to answer and was left paralysed with shock.

"Julie?" He looked just as stunned as she was. "Julie. Is it really you? I had a feeling it was … but I thought I was seeing things. I … I'm speechless," he stammered.

She took a while to answer. All she could do was stare at him. She felt that she was in her early twenties again, vulnerable and naïve. Her heart was racing and she tried to swallow, but her mouth was dry. She took a slow, deep breath trying desperately to steady her heart rate.

"Scott, I'm surprised to see you here. How … I mean what are you doing here?"

She was trembling, her legs weak in the leather boots which had caused such controversy that same morning. It seemed a lifetime ago. She dared herself to look into his eyes. He was staring at her searchingly. He held the intense stare but she couldn't reciprocate. His brown eyes were almost black, emotional and intense. He still looked the same, except more like a man than a boy.

She looked down as the hurt she felt all those years ago resurfaced. She dug deep within herself to find the strength to gain her composure. Sudden anger began to take over. How could he look at her like that with such intense emotion, as if he needed answers? He was the one who had betrayed her.

Julie's mind was back at the university cafeteria. She remembered the scene vividly. She'd just finished an exam and was standing in the lunch crowd. R.E.M.'s "Losing My Religion" was playing in the background. She scanned the room, looking for someone to chat to, when she saw Tanya, her closest friend, with Scott: the guy who had made her feel as if she was the only woman in the world, the guy who stared at her with meaning and intensity whenever she entered a room.

She had first seen him in her Government lecture. They had been discussing the Non-Proliferation Treaty. She had noticed him glancing over at her. Their eyes had met for a second or two. Then she noticed him in the library, as she passed his desk, feeling his stare as she walked by. She had instantly been drawn to his deep, coffee-brown-coloured eyes. He smiled a lot, revealing two dimples that made Julie's heart skip a beat. She recalled confiding in Tanya that she couldn't get him out of her mind. Julie remembered pointing him out to her friend at one of their lectures. Tanya had agreed that he was adorable, and that she thought that he and Julie would make a wonderful couple.

They had finally talked to each other while waiting in the photocopying queue in the library. Julie had been holding at least six heavy books, which she desperately needed to answer the essay question that had been plaguing her mind for that past week. They had fallen to the ground, revealing page after page on the Cold War and its demise. She had leaned down to pick them up, only to find he had intercepted and was already picking them up. As they both stood up, his hand had accidentally brushed hers. It was as if every muscle in her body awoke.

"Thanks," she had managed.

"No problem," he said, smiling. "What's your name?"

"My name is Julie, Julie Canei."

"Hi Julie Canei. My name's Scott, Scott Stevenson."

Her thoughts were interrupted by the papers still circling her feet in the wind. The awkward silence between them was broken as Scott bent to help her collect them. The scene felt so familiar. How ironic that they were once again leaning over to gather papers that belonged to her. They both stood up slowly. Julie's hair briefly stroked Scott's face in the wind. Scott gently placed the disobedient strand of hair behind her ear, staring into her eyes as he did so. He then touched her bare forehead affectionately and smiled. "It suits you," he said, his smile becoming warmer.

"Thanks," Julie awkwardly responded. Julie was shocked that he remembered that she had a blunt, short fringe back then. The anger she felt seconds ago had subsided. She was flattered, and was positive that there was some affection behind it.

The guy gives you a compliment and you're ready to embrace him with open arms, as if he didn't break your heart? She shamed herself at her sudden weakness.

Meanwhile Scott was examining the pages he had collected. "Who Controls your Life?" he read aloud.

Julie grabbed the sheet abruptly from his hands, embarrassed at the thought of him knowing how uncertain and confused she was. It was too late. The title said it all.

"The Julie I knew definitely controlled her own life. When she wanted something or someone, she went for it," he said, staring at the survey. His brown eyes then looked at her so intensely Julie felt he was staring into her soul.

She once again broke the stare and looked down at the paper that she was holding so tight; it was almost torn.

"What do you mean by that?" she finally asked. How dare he stand there, looking as if he had nothing to apologise for!

"I just meant that you didn't let anyone stand in your way when it came to getting what you desired. Anyway, I'm curious to know what you're doing here."

So, he just plants a bomb and then wants to make small talk with me, Julie thought. *Is he seriously trying to act like he did nothing wrong, after I caught him red-handed in a passionate embrace with my so-called best friend?* They had been all over each other. She'd been kissing him so passionately, caressing his hair so vigorously, that Julie was surprised she didn't pull a strand off. He had been into it as much as she was, reciprocating with the same passion. What Julie couldn't really understand was that they had been in broad daylight, in the cafeteria where anyone could have seen them. Tanya would have known that Julie would be in the middle of her English exam, but any one of their friends could have spotted them.

He was still looking at her now, awaiting her response. Anger again started to take over her body. She would not allow herself to become that twenty-two year-old girl again.

"I'm here with Christina, Brian and the kids. We thought it would be great to get away for the weekend, and what better place to do that than here," she replied with a confidence that surprised her.

"You should be a spokesperson for this place. 'What better place to get away is there than here!' I can see you holding your arms up emphatically, walking amongst the vineyards saying that."

There go those dimples again, Julie thought as she gave in to his smile. She too could not help herself from smiling.

"What brings you here?" Julie followed his cue, and continued the lightness of the conversation.

More to the point, who is he with? Is he here with his girlfriend for a romantic weekend? Perhaps, he is here with his wife and kids, or with ... Julie refused to continue her train of thought, as it would only cause her heartache.

"I'm actually here with some friends from work." He glanced at the group at the restaurant. "It's one of the guys' birthday and he invited us all to play some golf, and of course, taste some wine."

Julie followed his glance, noticing that a few women had joined the group of men. "So, is it one of those boys' weekends?" she asked, feeling vulnerable as she looked into his searching eyes.

"No, some female colleagues are also here. They thought it would be fun to challenge us guys in a game of golf. In fact, we've been coming here often for different occasions. My manager even had his wedding here. You're right, it's also a great place to unwind." He was looking at her with a cautious smile, his eyes studying hers. "Anyway, you're here with your sister and Brian. They were high school sweethearts," he said thoughtfully. "It's great to see that they're still together, and have children as well. Maybe they should teach the rest of us something," he added.

Every time he said something, it created a labyrinth of questions for Julie, and she didn't know what answers they would lead her to, or how scary and hurtful they would be. All the feelings she felt all those years ago suddenly re-surfaced.

Why *did* he betray her the way he did, in such a cruel manner, with her closest friend? How could she have been so wrong about his feelings for her? There must be a reason that he was back in her life. From what he had told her so far, it seemed that he wasn't in a relationship, or with *her*, but she couldn't be sure. She didn't want to assume anything anymore. She made that mistake before, when she assumed that he loved her and her alone.

She was also confused about his comments, regarding her knowing what she wanted out of life and how to get it. Shouldn't she be throwing comments like that *his* way?

A ball came flying at them from the tennis court. It was now getting dark and the lights had been switched on at the court. Julie hadn't even realised that the sun had fully set. She found herself staring at Scott as he retrieved the ball for the man and woman who were waiting patiently, even though they looked as though they were playing an intense game.

What game are we playing? she thought sceptically to herself. Questions and answers were being passed back and forth, but unlike a tennis match, there was no clear score. She managed to catch a glimpse of Scott's toned arm, revealed by his rolled up sleeve as he reached for the ball. She stared in admiration as he threw it back to the grateful couple. She imagined that same arm, fully bare, offering her coffee in bed, as she awoke tired and sleepy from a night of intense passion.

"I didn't realise it was getting dark so quickly," he said. "Why don't we catch up later at the bar? We can have a drink. You are staying here, aren't you?"

"Yes I am," she answered, a blush starting to creep up on her face, as she snapped out of the fantasy she was having about him. She was definitely glad that the lights weren't that bright where they were standing. She was about to agree when she remembered she was having dinner with her sister.

"Oh, hang on," she said. "I can't. I'm having dinner with Christina and her family."

"Okay, well why don't we meet tomorrow for a coffee?"

Julie took a while to reply. She didn't want to seem eager, and she didn't want to give the impression that she was letting him off the hook so easily. She also needed time to re-think her whole strategy. They were being so amicable to each other. She had promised herself that she wouldn't let him have the last word. She imagined what she would say to him so many times in her mind, but he was being so charming and irresistibly sexy that she found it hard to find the words.

"I promised my niece and nephew that I'd go to the Hunter Valley Gardens tomorrow morning. Perhaps after that … around eleven thirty? We have to check out by one o'clock," she responded, thinking of what excuse she would give to her sister. The last thing she wanted was another interrogation regarding her love life, that is, of course, if Christina dared to go there again. She had always kept the details regarding their breakup hidden from her family. The last thing she needed was judgment and lectures. She didn't want them to think that she was clueless, not having seen the signs, after having being with him for almost three years. It had become a taboo topic. Surprisingly, they had given up on trying to drag more information out of her. Julie knew that they could sense her uneasiness whenever his name came up in conversation.

She definitely deserved some answers. It was so strange that he didn't look as if he had a guilty bone in his body.

"That sounds great. We have a lot to catch up with." He paused. "Would you agree with that?" He was now staring at her seriously. "How about we meet here tomorrow and we'll take it from there. I still can't believe that I ran into you like this. I don't really believe in coincidences."

"Sure," she answered, mesmerised by his gentle, hesitant smile.

"Bye, Jules," he said in a hoarse voice. He kissed her softly on her forehead, as he stroked another strand of her hair that had set itself free. He parted from her slowly, as if he was savouring every moment.

She watched him walk away, still in a trance from what had just transpired. Nothing had changed. She still longed and ached for him as she did back then. He had called her *Jules*. Could he still have feelings for her after all those years? She could still feel his warm, soft lips on her forehead. His kiss felt so intimate, as if there was so much feeling behind it. Julie stood there for a while processing every detail before walking to the hill, the same hill that she had planned to have a relaxing afternoon on in order to try and gain some clarity, the same hill where she decided that men and relationships would have to wait.

She gathered her things and placed the bottle of wine in her bag. She picked up the empty glass, which had been tossed over by the wind, and walked back to the apartment holding it, whilst hugging the folder close to her rapidly beating heart. Although she walked with a dazed look on her face, she was wide awake, all over.

CHAPTER TEN

The sun's rays strengthened as the day progressed. Julie felt that it was as though she had a warm blanket covering her, protecting her from the chill in the air. It was close to eleven o'clock in the morning, and they had spent a pleasant morning at the Hunter Valley Gardens, the pleasantness only achieved by Christina and Julie not having uttered a word to each other. After walking around the beautiful property, they came across a section comprised of gardens that represented different nursery rhymes. Brian must have taken at least a hundred photos of Elisabeth and John with all the characters, including one with all of them seated at the Mad Hatter's table in the Alice in Wonderland garden, joining the rest of the characters for tea. Elisabeth and John were very excited and enthusiastic as they explored each garden, eager to see which nursery rhyme would follow the previous one. This excitement nearly ended in disaster when John was so eager to emulate Jack in the Jack and Jill garden that he really had "come tumbling down" the steep hill. Fortunately, Elisabeth did not come "tumbling after," and after a few tears, John was content again, enjoying an ice cream, which seemed to have magically erased any memory that the incident had ever occurred.

As beautiful as the gardens were, Julie was preoccupied with the unexpected encounter she'd had with Scott. She still couldn't believe what had happened, especially when she had just been thinking of him just the day before. Why would he just appear so unexpectedly? What really surprised her though, were the feelings that seeing him had evoked. She thought that she would feel nothing but anger towards him, but a familiar, intense need had taken over her instead. It had to be fate.

Julie was excited and nervous about seeing him again. She had been thinking of a plausible excuse to tell the others all morning, and hoped she could make an easy escape without any questions. She had to remain calm. The tranquil atmosphere helped with the task of steadying her heart rate, but she felt that she couldn't keep her nerves at bay for much longer. The tension between Christina and herself wasn't helping. Julie couldn't believe how innocently her sister was acting. She hadn't even flinched the day before during her tirade. She was even on her best behaviour throughout dinner, choosing to only speak to Julie when it was absolutely necessary. Despite this odd reaction, Julie was glad that she had voiced how she felt. She needed to do it. She had already begun to feel empowered and free, even if it wasn't the reaction she was expecting. Julie had more pressing issues on her mind though and, ironically, these had to do with the very thing she had profusely insisted she didn't need to focus on — men.

"Why don't we go and have a coffee and something to eat?" Brian asked, looking at both Julie and Christina, expecting them to jump at the idea.

"I'd love a decent cappuccino right now. I'm so sleepy," Christina replied, avoiding eye contact with her sister.

"I can't possibly do another thing. My feet are killing me. I might just head back to the apartment and lie down," Julie interjected, almost too quickly.

Christina looked at Julie.

"We'll drive you back to the apartment. There's a nice coffee shop we wanted to try nearby anyway," Brian offered.

"Auntie Julie, why can't you come with us?" Elisabeth gazed up at Julie with a sad look on her face. This was going to be harder than she thought.

"Auntie Julie isn't feeling well. You don't want to play when you're not feeling well, do you?" Brian intervened.

"I guess so. Anyway can we go and play on the jumping castle?" Elisabeth asked excitedly, suddenly not the least bit saddened that Julie would not be joining them.

Julie rushed frantically to freshen up before meeting Scott. She examined herself in her bedroom mirror one final time. She had decided on black straight jeans, with ballet flats, a simple white top, and a terracotta woollen wrap thrown casually around her. Together with her earthy, peach-coloured lipstick and her pearl stud earrings, the look was simple, yet elegant. A bit too elegant, she had thought, so she quickly added one of her unusual copper bracelets — a beautiful piece from Istanbul. Maria had gifted it to her as she had so many pieces that Greek relatives had bought her from Greece, Turkey and other neighbouring countries. Feeling confident in her choice of outfit, she grabbed her black leather tote bag, put her sunglasses on her head, and made her way to the tennis courts.

Her heart started beating quickly as she reached the courts. She found a bench and sat down, taking deep breaths.

She was lost in the memory of hurrying out of the cafeteria, tears rolling down her cheeks, having seen Scott with Tanya. She had walked not knowing where she was heading, walking without noticing anything. Her vision was blurred from tears that wouldn't stop flowing. They had stung her soft, warm face. She needed a tissue. Her stomach was in agonising pain but she had to keep moving. The pain had become excruciating and she began to feel light-headed. She needed to sit somewhere, far away from what she saw — from *them* – to curl up in a ball and cry herself to sleep. She bumped into a tall girl. It was Maria. She didn't know her personally at the time, only by her face, as she was in one of her lectures. Maria had been with another girl who was slightly shorter than her, with a warm smile. They had both asked her if she was all right, and she had looked at them blankly through tears.

The other girl had introduced herself. "My name is Cassandra," she had said.

"I'm Maria," the familiar girl had said. "You're in my English lecture."

Her thoughts were interrupted as a golf buggy passed. She looked at her watch. Julie took another deep breath and made her way to the tennis courts, debating if she made the right choice in her decision to wear flats, as a tall image of Scott entered her mind.

There was no one in sight when she got to the courts. As she glanced at her watch, which read 11:35, she had a sinking feeling inside her. What if he didn't show up?

If he cheated on her so easily, why would he care about her feelings now? Was this some kind of cruel joke, leading her on again with that affectionate kiss, only to stand her up?

It all felt too familiar, the humiliation and betrayal, the feelings of confusion and disbelief, except this time she blamed herself for giving him another chance to hurt her. She was older, and she should definitely be a lot wiser when it came to Scott Stevenson.

She sat down on a bench outside the tennis courts. It was where he had given her that soft, gentle kiss. *How dare he kiss me like that? How does he know if I've got a boyfriend, or if I'm even married?*

She looked at her watch again. Another five minutes had passed. She decided to wait. He had to be here for a reason. He couldn't just be sent to her only to be taken away, without even gaining some insight, some clarity, perhaps even an apology for hurting her. She desperately needed him to prove her wrong and not stand her up.

The image of him with Tanya entered her mind again. She had been exhausted from studying the night before and had left the last night for revision. Only things hadn't gone according to plan. She remembered having an early dinner with Scott at one of their favourite Italian restaurants, both of them needing a break from studying for their mid-year exams. They could barely concentrate on the food however, as they gazed into each other's eyes. He had leaned over and kissed her gently. She could sense he wanted more. She definitely did.

They hadn't spent much time together that last month. At Julie's insistence, Scott had tried to keep his distance as they would easily get distracted when they studied together. Prior to that period, they were inseparable — spending many magical, intimate nights together. Sometimes, they wouldn't even realise that the sun came up, as they would spend the early hours of the morning talking about almost every topic under the sun, or just lying in each other's arms, enjoying the stillness of the morning and not wanting it to end.

Scott would often give her a questioning look every time she became consumed with worry. She knew what the look meant. She couldn't hide anything from him. It was as though he was asking her if she was doing it again — if she was doing what was expected of her. He would always encourage her to live in the moment and follow her heart. "Just wear it, Julie," he had told her when she was hesitant to wear an eccentric looking jacket to a family outing one day. "If you like it, that's all that matters," he had continued, looking intensely into her eyes. She loved that he challenged her to follow her instincts in all aspects of her life.

When it came to studying, Scott had a much more balanced approach. He knew that she would get slightly neurotic during exams, studying the same things over and over again, to the point of exhaustion.

"So where is she?" he had asked her one night, slightly raising his voice. "Where's the Julie that's so fun and enjoys every moment of life? It's as though she runs off

67

somewhere every now and then. Tell me Julie, what is she afraid of?"

"What do you mean?" she had asked. "I just want to do well. What's wrong with that?"

"Nothing's wrong with that, if that's what you're really worried about. I don't think you're just afraid of failing your exams, though. I think you're afraid of failing other people's expectations. I think you're afraid of being you." Julie had been so hurt. But she knew he was right.

The chemistry between them that night at the restaurant had suddenly become unbearable. He had a serious look on his face. He kept caressing her face and didn't pay attention to a word she said. He had leaned over the table and kissed her again. This time it was more passionate. They almost knocked over the bottle of water the waiter had just served them, causing curious diners to look in their direction. There was a sudden urgency in his eyes. Her heart was beating fast. She wanted him so bad. He hastily left two fifty dollar notes on the table, even though they had hardly ordered anything, and he definitely could not afford it, being a student. They went back to his studio apartment, which was situated near the university.

When they had just met, they had decided to take it slow. Her first time with him had been pure bliss. Her only previous experience had occurred one night, when she had just turned nineteen, at a high school one year reunion, with a boy she hardly liked. She wanted to find out what the fuss was all about. When it was all over, soon after they began, she was still wondering what the fuss was all about. Julie had promised herself that she wouldn't make that mistake again, knowing she needed to be with someone special.

It was definitely worth the wait. He was always so patient and gentle with her. That night, it was just as magical. She wanted to stay in his arms all night but her mind kept telling her she should be studying. "I have to revise my notes, Scott," she had told him as he kissed her neck with soft kisses. She began to look for her dress and her shoes. He had pulled her towards him, and playfully placed both of his bare, toned arms around her bare waist. He kissed her lips and then her neck again, tempting her with more soft, gentle kisses. Her knees felt weak.

"Stay," he pleaded as he pulled her close to his chest, with his strong arms firmly around her waist.

"Scott, you know that I have to ..." she began to protest as his soft sensual lips caressed hers.

"You know what we just did was just the appetiser," he had teased, as his lips moved towards her bare shoulder.

After a few more playful attempts, sensing her guilt, Scott had agreed to drive her home. "It's okay, I understand. I know how worried you'll be if you don't revise your notes, Jules. I can't say that my ego isn't hurt though." He had tried to resist a smile as he pretended to look hurt. "I'll see you tomorrow, after your exam. I can't wait to have you in my arms again," he told her, as he looked deep into her eyes, suddenly becoming serious. "I want you so much," he had said in a hoarse voice.

She couldn't wait either. She had rushed into her flat to revise her notes. However, the only thing she managed to revise were her thoughts of Scott and how he had made her feel, as she replayed every magical moment they had spent together.

Julie felt a tear stream down her cheek at the intimate memories. Every detail came back to her. It was as if she was watching a mini-series unfold, episode by episode. That night had been so sacred to her. She had felt so content and secure in his arms. How had everything changed so dramatically the following day? She had thought he felt the same about her. She was so wrong.

She was obviously wrong again, she acknowledged, standing up from the bench. Her watch showed that another ten minutes had passed. She started heading back to the apartment, forcing herself not to look back.

"Julie, Julie, wait!"

She turned around as soon as she heard her name. It was him. He was running frantically towards her.

"Julie! I'm glad I caught you," he managed between breaths.

She realised he was struggling to talk. He must have run a fair distance.

"I'm so sorry I'm late." He was about to continue, but he suddenly stopped, as if he had to say something important. He was looking at her strangely, still slightly breathless. "I forgot how mesmerising your eyes are in the sun … with their green and gold tinge … they're like gemstones," he said, looking at her as if he was studying an artefact.

"Oh," was all she could manage. She had a sudden warm feeling in her heart. She tried to play it cool, to hide the elation she felt inside her at his observation.

"I'm so sorry for being late. I was so worried you had left." He forced himself out of the momentary trance he seemed to have been in. "I was on my way to meet with you when I got an SMS from work. I ignored it, but my phone kept on beeping. I'm in the IT industry these days, it can be incessant. Anyway, I'll try and spare you the boring details, but it turns out that it's an emergency. The server is down, and the guy on call has some family crisis to deal with. Anyway, since I'm second on call, and everyone else from our team is here playing golf, I have to cut my weekend short and head back to work. It turns out the problem can't be fixed from my laptop," he ended, still trying to catch his breath.

Julie looked at him feeling relieved and disappointed at the same time. She really needed some answers. When would she see him again now?

"I couldn't leave without saying goodbye to you and exchanging contact numbers. We have so much to talk about, Julie. I must have run into you like this for a reason."

70

Before Julie could respond, he handed her his business card. Julie scanned it, noticing his mobile number and email address. Next to them, she noticed his home number scrawled in blue ink. Her eyes then instantly went to the job title section, which read: "Senior Systems Analyst."

Since when was he interested in IT? He had once wanted to work for an NGO. He was always an idealist.

"So, now it's your turn," he said, leaning until his face was level with hers. He looked at her curiously, before a mischievous smile began to slowly appear on his face.

"My turn for what?" Julie responded, still deep in thought.

"For your contact info," he answered, smiling.

"Oh!" she responded. She felt so strange being around him. It was a surreal experience. She gave him her mobile number and, just to cover all bases, blurted out her home phone number as well, perhaps a bit too eagerly. She didn't want him to have any excuses when it came to him calling her.

"I'll call you very soon. I'm going to Paris in a week with some friends, so it would be great if we can try to get together before that. Actually, the friends I'm referring to are James and Jenny, from uni. You remember them?"

"Yes, I do actually. You three knew each other from high school," Julie responded. She was intrigued at his mention of Paris. He was obviously doing what he wanted with his life. He had pursued another career, and he was travelling as well, while she was still confused and lost.

She couldn't help but remember when they would talk about travelling to different parts of the world. Julie had been amazed by the fact that as a child Scott would also read about different countries and cultures, and fantasise about visiting them one day. He would often pass his spare time in the travel sections of bookshops, enthusiastically flipping through the pages, unable to decide which one to purchase.

Julie had told him that she too would immerse herself in the old encyclopaedias that her father still had since he was a child. They would challenge each other, comparing facts that they had learned. She remembered when Scott couldn't stop laughing when she had a heated debate with him regarding which countries made up Scandinavia. She was appalled that he didn't know that Finland wasn't one of the Nordic countries included. This had occurred after she had watched a Swedish movie and had fallen in love with the landscape. Scott had kissed her passionately after she had told him that as a child she would look at her backyard and tell herself that one day she would instead be staring at the mountains of Peru, or the sunset in Santorini, or the Eiffel Tower, or the streets of Morocco. He had looked at her seriously, and asked her if he could be part of that dream. They had been so close and optimistic about spending the future together.

"You should come with us, if you don't have any work or personal commitments," he said, looking at her seriously, interrupting her thoughts. "I remember you loved all things French. In fact, I recall you loved anything to do with travelling."

She couldn't believe what she was hearing.

"I remember we both did," she replied, tears suddenly forming in her eyes. "Anyway, it's impossible. I have work commitments," she continued, quickly taking control of the situation. She didn't want him to see the hurt in her eyes, so she pulled her sunglasses from her head and covered her eyes. "I better not keep you any longer. You have to head back to work," she continued, business-like. "It's been great seeing you again," she said, extending her hand out for a formal handshake.

"It has definitely been great seeing you again … Julie." He reciprocated, placing his hand in hers, but instead of shaking it, he gently pulled her close to him and gave her a small, gentle kiss on her cheek. "I think we could do a lot better than a formal handshake, don't you?" He gave her a knowing smile, stroked her hair, and parted from her as he did the day before, slowly and hesitantly.

Julie couldn't move. What was happening? She was supposed to be angry with him! The strange part was that she felt that she was seeing the Scott she fell in love with — not the one that betrayed her. The way he had kissed her was so intimate.

"I'll call you," he called out, as he glanced at her one more time. "Think about Paris."

"Bye, Scott," Julie managed, shocked and weak at the knees from the effect he still had on her.

How strange, Julie thought as she sat in the back seat of the car as they made their way to the freeway, heading home. It was odd that the papers which were supposed to aid her in taking control of her life had actually contributed to change occurring without serving their original purpose. They had led her to Scott. Deep, repressed, unresolved feelings had been uncovered from his reappearance in her life. In a similar way, they had also led Julie to voice all the unspoken words she wanted to say to her sister on so many occasions.

The tension in the car between Julie and Christina was once again palpable that Sunday afternoon, so they both sat quietly, avoiding making conversation with each other. However, unlike before, the dynamics had now changed between them, and it seemed they both didn't know which roles they were supposed to now play, or how to play them. Julie still couldn't believe that the very weekend she was trying to get out of had turned her life around in such a dramatic way.

Julie's mobile beeped. It was a message from Cassandra in reply to one that Julie had sent her the day before. Julie had informed her and Maria that something really strange had happened, but it was nothing to worry about. She also had stated that she would fill them in when she got back, and that they'd better be seated when she did, because they would not believe who she had run into. Cassandra had responded by saying that she couldn't wait to hear about it, and that she and Maria were already placing bets on who that person could be.

Julie reached for her phone again, planning to listen to music while her nephew slept soundly and her niece sat contently reading a book beside her. Brian and Christina were having an intense conversation regarding where John's reading level was at, and whether they should get both of the children into tennis, so Julie scanned her phone and found the song that always inspired her: "Drive", by one of her favourite bands, Incubus. A smile emerged on her face as the lyrics began to soothe her with their optimistic message. It reflected how she felt. She so wanted to steer her own path. She would find a way to do it!

CHAPTER ELEVEN

"Sorry," Julie looked apologetically at the older woman she had clumsily bumped into. The woman gave her an unforgiving stare and continued walking hurriedly. It was Monday morning and Julie had just made her way out of Town Hall station, and was now walking frantically amongst the crowds in the Queen Victoria Building. It was pandemonium, as everyone seemed to be in the same predicament that Julie was in: late for work and, in Julie's case, also late for the dreaded "8:30 am sharp" meeting. Julie had spent most of the previous night reiterating every detail of her encounter with Scott to a shocked Cassandra and Maria.

Cassandra had also found it ironic that her Career Counselling surveys played a part in Julie's unexpected encounter with Scott. Both her friends knew how much Scott had hurt her all those years ago, and even Cassandra, who didn't believe in fate, tried to rationalise the encounter as a coincidence, only to find herself saying, "But how could this be? You're practically at the crossroads of your life, and he appears out of nowhere!"

Cassandra had also analysed the scores from the surveys Julie had completed. In between the analysis, being baffled at Scott entering her life again, and his impending phone call, coupled with the physical and emotional fatigue the trip had caused, she had completely forgotten about the meeting that her manager had planned. Friday seemed like a lifetime ago.

Julie tossed and turned all night, barely sleeping. She recalled hearing the birds chirping at around 4:00am, and was panic stricken at the realisation that she hadn't fallen asleep yet. She somehow felt as if she was a different person. The woman walking home, without any purpose on Friday afternoon, almost seemed like a stranger. She was just as confused as ever; however, all of a sudden she felt that she wanted to make things happen. She wanted to use all the energy she had inside her to change her life in a positive way.

As she made her way to Market Street, manoeuvring her way through the crowd, she suddenly remembered what she had overheard that Friday morning. It was only a matter of time before they would find out, assuming that's what the meeting was about. She crossed the street and entered the high-rise building she had dreaded entering for the last five years. She walked through the foyer and headed towards the lifts, showing her security card to the security officer who acknowledged her without smiling, even though they had made eye contact for the last few months. Julie always wondered if they had learned to remain serious at all times as part of their training, in order to be alert and ready for any suspicious activity.

She robotically pressed level twenty-two in the lift, and held her breath for a few seconds as she always did, to stop her ears from blocking. When the doors finally opened, she felt that the foyer looked different, perhaps because her attitude was now different. As she placed her security card in front of the security access box, the doors opened, revealing a buzz of activity, even though it was just after 8:30am. Telephones rang continuously. People looked stressed and extremely busy. A fax machine beeped impatiently from one corner of the floor, and the different conversations emanating from numerous sections across the floor sounded like one big murmur. This was mostly prevalent in the Accounts section, which had a reputation for being an unpleasant, stressful section to work in. An air of seriousness always enveloped that particular corner of the floor. The Claims Division's reputation was somewhere in between. Their workload was always daunting. There were also times when everyone looked as stressed as an obstetrician called upon to perform an unexpected delivery. However, there were also times when someone, usually Stacey, would turn on the radio and people could be heard laughing.

Julie smelled burnt toast coming from the kitchen as she headed towards her desk, glancing at the clock, hoping she wasn't too late for the meeting. She was ten minutes late, to be exact. She threw her bag on her desk, marched quickly to the meeting room, and took a deep breath before opening the door.

"Oh, hi Julie, so glad you could make it!" George remarked as she entered the small meeting room.

"I'm sorry for being late, everyone." Julie brushed George's remark aside, feeling powerful and in control that morning. She looked calmly over at him as she sat next to Sarah. George looked surprised and amused that Julie had not responded. Despite his arrogance, he looked smart in his dark blue, crisp-looking shirt.

"Anyway, now that we're all here, we can begin our meeting. First of all, I'm sorry to drag you in here so early on a Monday morning, but an urgent and unfortunate matter has come up which will impact all of you in this room."

Julie was stunned. Colin Ferguson never apologised for anything. He also didn't make any unpleasant remarks regarding Julie's lateness. As she scanned the round table, she realised that everyone looked just as surprised. It must have something to do with what she overheard.

"Unfortunately, I have been informed that due to the economic instability of the current climate, we will need to make some cutbacks. After numerous meetings, it has been decided that we will need to outsource some of our divisions. I'm sorry to say that the Claims division will be taken over by our central Melbourne office."

Colin continued in the same tone for a while. Julie vaguely heard parts of the conversation as she wrestled with her thoughts. He went on to explain that one person would remain as the contact person between Sydney and

Melbourne as they would be needed to deal with doctors on a face-to-face basis regarding clients' medical details. The part of the conversation she definitely heard was that they would all be retrenched. The contact person had already been selected and would relocate from Melbourne to Sydney.

Julie switched off for a while. She couldn't believe that her whole team would be retrenched! She was surprisingly calm, and excited at the same time. It was the clean break she needed; an opportunity to strive for fulfilment in life. The timing couldn't have been better, especially since she had a new burst of energy that needed to be utilised in some way. One thing was for sure: she wouldn't settle for another job like the one she had. She would not hide behind excuses anymore!

"Each one of you will have a meeting set up with HR, and they will discuss your settlement package and entitlements with you. This will take place this week, as the last day for all of you is actually Friday. I know this is all very abrupt, but I personally have no say in the matter. I myself will be taking over the call centre as the manager in charge there has resigned. Although, it isn't my first choice, when times are tough, adaptation is required."

As Julie listened to her manager's last words, she surprisingly felt sympathetic towards Colin, as he seemed to be convincing himself to accept the unexpected change in his circumstances. Julie was very familiar with that tune. As dismayed as everyone else in the room seemed, she couldn't believe how content and excited she felt: a complete contrast to how she felt a few days ago when the word "cutbacks" made her feel as though the world was coming to an end. She was more than ready to move on. She would be free at last. It was almost like she was given permission to shine. Of course her excitement was heightened by the fact that she was entitled to a retrenchment package. Her options were now even more flexible than if she had resigned. She didn't have to rush to find another job. *Maybe I should travel,* she pondered. It would be the right time to take the gap year she had missed out on having before uni. This was exactly what she needed!

After some questions, especially from Sarah, they were free to continue the rest of the day "carrying on as usual", whatever that meant.

As Julie made her way to her desk, Stacey came charging after her.

"Can you believe it? What are we going to do now? I have so much credit card debt to pay off. Now I'll never be able to purchase the designer bag I've been eyeing for so long. My retrenchment payout won't even be able to cover half of my debt."

"Don't worry Stace! I'm sure with your vibrant personality and confidence, that you'll be able to secure a job somewhere else in no time at all. I think I heard Colin mention that you could even apply for some of the internal positions," Julie offered.

"He also mentioned that it would be quite difficult, as any internal job is very scarce, and that they are looking for the most qualified candidates," Stacey muttered.

Julie had missed that part. Her heart went out to Stacey. Her own financial situation wasn't as bleak. But she was confident Stacey would land on her feet again. Julie gave her a sympathetic smile.

At that moment George appeared beside them. "Cheer up, Stacey. I'm sure you'll find a job somewhere. Any employer would be lucky to hire you." George smiled. "You'll be all right. You, on the other hand," he turned and looked at Julie. "You must be devastated to leave this fine establishment and our beloved leader, Colin. I'm really surprised that you're not crying your eyes out. You seem surprisingly calm for someone who has just been told that they will never work at a job they love so much."

"Oh, I'll be fine, George. Despite what you think, I do have other interests and I'm glad to have some time off to pursue them," she finished, as he looked at her as though someone had just slapped him on the face. "Anyway, from where I'm standing, I'm thinking the same thing about you."

He looked at her intently. His eyes were smiling.

"George, I know its short notice but you're first for your meeting with Human Resources," Colin called out from his office.

"Okay, I'll just get some water," he responded, still looking at Julie as he spoke, before making his way to the water cooler.

"I know what will cheer us up: caramel lattes! I'll run down and get some. It's my shout," Julie stated happily to Stacey.

"All right, Stacey responded, cheering up slightly.

The rest of the day passed quickly. Julie felt like a child in the last week of school before the Christmas holidays. As she tidied her desk, grabbed her bag and headed to the lifts, she felt free. The company didn't own her any more. The atmosphere felt warmer and kinder. This feeling continued as she made her way into the busy city streets. She took a deep breath to take it all in. Even the noise of the traffic and the dank haze of pollution didn't dampen her mood. Instinctively, she headed towards George Street, and made her way into one of the main department stores. As she did this, she thought over what had happened and a sudden bout of nerves momentarily made her feel anxious about the future. However, remembering what Cassandra had once told her about challenging "automatic negative thoughts", she began to replace those thoughts with positive ones and told herself to remain present-centred. Of course she could change her life. Her current circumstances weren't working for her; therefore, change was definitely needed.

She felt like rewarding herself. A new scarf would do the trick. She decided on purchasing a fashionable royal blue, striped scarf. She headed to the counter and handed her credit card to a young lady with flawless make-up. As she headed towards the escalators, her attention was diverted to a beautiful display. She walked over to it, admiring every detail. The gold wallpaper was so opulent. The chair in the display complemented the stunning wallpaper so cleverly. However, she felt that something was missing. If she had put together the display, she would have added a touch of black to accentuate the gold, or even added a really contemporary lamp, thus making the display more avant garde. Julie stared in awe at the decadent display, feeling inspired as she turned to take another glance while she made her way to the escalators. She continued her journey feeling content and at peace.

Comfortably seated in the train on the way home, Julie stared out of the window, proudly holding her purchase in her hands as she admired the majestic view of Sydney Harbour as the train crossed the Harbour Bridge. Usually, she would ignore the view, her mind racing with thoughts of unfinished work issues, planning what needed to be completed the next day. That afternoon, she wanted to take in everything. The beauty of everything around her led her thoughts to the career surveys she had completed.

After having analysed the scores, Cassandra, Maria and Julie all realised that three things really stood out. The first was that Julie was living her life and making decisions based on other people's beliefs and values. She had stopped trusting her instincts. The second was that her job satisfaction with her current employer was very low. The finding that jumped out of the "Values Assessment test", which could be instrumental in facilitating change, was that her aesthetic dimension score was very high. The results had validated what Julie already knew about herself, but seeing it on paper highlighted it more. Maybe that was what she needed: more beauty in her life, and a career that brought out that side of her. The results were just a guide to aid her in self-assessment, but they did ring very true in her situation. She had known it all along but simply ignored it.

Her thoughts were interrupted by the ringing of her mobile phone. She frantically searched for it in her bag, not having had time to place it in its sleeve that rushed morning. She finally found it, but had missed the call.

What if it was him? What if it was Scott wanting to organise to meet me? Her thoughts raced.

She looked to see the number that was displayed on the screen, only to be disappointed to see it black. Her phone needed charging. All of a sudden, she was anxious to get home in case he rang her home phone number. The only thing on her mind was Scott. Her career plans would have to be temporarily filed away. She still needed answers from him and she wouldn't be able to settle until she got them.

CHAPTER TWELVE

"Oh, hi Mum. How are you?"

"Hi Julie, were you expecting someone else?"

"Someone else? Oh no, I'm just surprised that it's you. I mean, I wasn't expecting to hear from you." Julie stumbled to find the right words, trying desperately to hide her disappointment. She was out of breath, as she had run to answer the phone as soon as she opened the front door.

"Anyway, I called you earlier on your mobile, but it made a strange noise. I'm really concerned about Christina. She called me yesterday and she said that you spoke to her really abruptly and she is really upset."

Julie couldn't believe what she was hearing. "*She's* upset?! Do you think I'm not? Just because I've kept my mouth shut every time she insults me and my life choices and now I finally defended myself? I've been silently upset for so many years. She's shocked because she can't believe I would speak up for myself. She always thinks that she can tell me what to do with my life. She acts as if she's my mother and I'm her teenage daughter."

"She just cares about you. She wants you to be happy."

"I knew you would take her side. I mean, you always think that I can't make my own decisions as well. Dad is the only one that has faith in me. You never trust that I know what the best thing for me is. Did any of you ask me what I want out of my life? Just because I'm not married and I don't have children, it doesn't mean that I'm clueless!" Julie was on fire. She'd had enough. She had finally told her sister how she felt. It was her mother's turn.

"I never ever thought you were clueless about anything," her mother responded, after pausing for a few seconds, seemingly shocked at the accusation. "In fact, I always knew that you were always confident in your abilities. You were always a happy child, full of hope and passion for life. You refused to conform. You would treat each day as though it was your birthday, finding different ways to make each day exciting. I knew that you could achieve anything you set your mind to do from when you were a little girl. All your teachers would agree. "

Julie was taken aback by her mother's words. She hadn't heard anything positive like that for a long time. She suddenly felt like she was a little girl again, needing her mother's approval.

Her mother continued. "If you're referring to my enthusiasm about you meeting someone, I just feel that you ... well, that you've shut yourself off from relationships ... you know since ... I mean, it's almost been five years since your last serious relationship. I know finding a career that inspires you is just as, if not more important to you at the moment."

"I know it's been a while, Mum. But you really don't have to worry. I have been rather standoffish with men over the years, but I'm starting to realise that maybe being in a relationship and finding meaning in life aren't mutually exclusive. I just feel that you always tell me to ask Christina before I make any decisions about anything, especially about my career."

"I only say that because I think you and Christina have a good relationship and that you can discuss anything. In my heart though, I know you are quietly confident in your abilities and that no matter what anyone tells you, you will follow your heart and not let them sway you."

"Yes, I was always confident ... back then," Julie acknowledged.

"I'll never forget the time when you refused to paint a picture the way your Year 6 teacher instructed you to paint it," her mother continued. "Do you remember? You insisted that you should only use a touch of the bright colours to reflect nature because it would create a more dramatic contrast amongst the warmer colours. Too much would not be as interesting. You even reminded your teacher that art was subjective. Let's not forget your choice of outfits — always refusing to wear what everyone else was wearing. When denim was in, you'd choose to wear suede, when green was in, you'd wear yellow. You were always so confident and determined to be yourself. I'll never forget the time you painted your room. We found you with blue paint all over your hair and even on your school uniform. You would always say …"

"… that different colours reflected different aspects of me. Yes, I remember." Julie smiled at the memory. Blue always had a comforting effect on her. She even had the lounge room in the North Sydney terrace painted a pale blue colour, while the walls in the rest of the house were Arctic White. It was the ideal space for honest expression and reflection. "Well, unfortunately, I did let people sway me. You're right, Mum. I did have a lot of passion and confidence for life. I was determined to pursue my dreams, but somewhere I got lost along the way. I kept on hearing things like, 'It's the responsible thing to do', or, 'Shouldn't you do that instead?' I stopped listening to my instincts, and I started taking other people's advice. I stopped believing in myself and lost my inner self-confidence. I never wanted to settle."

"Perhaps it's my fault to some extent. I thought you were always confident and sure of yourself. I could have told you how much confidence I had in you more often. Even now you always look happy and you never complain, so I assume that everything is okay. Maybe I gave Christina a lot of power over you when you were little. Your father and I worked long hours. I guess she took her role too seriously when we told her to look after you, and felt that she had to also be responsible for your decisions, even now."

"Mum, I don't blame you. I don't even blame Christina that much. I realise I have to take responsibility for my actions. I guess I was lost for a few years, but now I have hope that I can find my way again. It's never too late to follow your dreams, right?"

"Of course not Julie, you're so young. You're only twenty-seven, and it's never too late. I have to admit, I've been guilty of not following my dreams as well. I think I let my insecurity get the better of me. You're right about something. It's not much fun living one's life doing what someone else thinks is right. I always did what was expected of me. I definitely don't want my girls doing the same thing, and living their lives with regret. Who cares about what you should and shouldn't do? Nothing is written in stone after all. We're all in charge of our own lives. As for Christina, I think she may be lost as well. If she does interfere where she shouldn't, which I know she often does, it's only because, deep down, she's scared. She only wants the best for you. She just goes about it the wrong way."

Julie's heart warmed. These were the words she'd wanted to hear for so long. Her mother did have faith in her after all. If she had spoken up before, she would have known that already. Her mother did understand her and she was right. She did have passion and optimism for life from when she was young. Julie still remembered the time when she was eleven and they couldn't go on a family picnic because of bad weather. She had spent that afternoon decorating the veranda with citronella candles and flowers, and insisted they all eat dinner outside to make up for their loss. "Wow!" her mother had said. "It must have taken you hours to decorate this. It's really lovely, Julie," she had told her with wide eyes as she observed the beautiful space. Julie had smiled with pride. They all enjoyed their dinner so much that they ate dinner on the veranda every night that winter, and had different dinner themes each night. Her parents had even invested on an outdoor heater.

"Anyway, Julie, I've got to go. Some women that I met from my art class are coming over. Just remember, it's never too late. Come over for dinner one day and we'll chat more. I'm glad we talked. Bye!"

"What art class?" Julie queried, but her mother had already hung up. Julie smiled. So her mother had a secret desire to be an artist. *Maybe, her aesthetic dimension would also be high if she did the Values Assessment Test?*

She automatically walked over to retrieve the scarf she had purchased, just to admire it. As she did this, she realised that she hadn't told her mother anything about being retrenched. *Oh well*, she thought. *By the sounds of it, Mum knows I can land on my feet again.*

CHAPTER THIRTEEN

Julie woke up at 7:30am the following morning, confused by a strange dream. Usually she didn't remember her dreams, but this time she did. She was at a busy restaurant, and she had seen George Giveski with a young woman, just as she had at the Indian restaurant a few nights ago. However, in her dream, the woman turned around and smiled at her. *It was Tanya.*

Julie was so confused. She didn't know what the dream meant. There was no obvious similarity with the woman in the restaurant and Tanya, so why did she appear in her dream, with George's arm around her of all people?

That afternoon, after spending the day in a daze, Julie walked into the terrace house, looking forward to a cup of Maria's organic herbal tea to aid her in gathering her thoughts. As she approached the kitchen, she heard Cassandra and an unfamiliar male voice coming from the dining room. *It must be her new study partner*, she thought as the conversation became clearer. Julie heard words such as "Gestalt therapy theory" and "unfinished business" being reiterated over and over again.

"So, one of the aspects Gestalt therapy theory deals with is unfinished business. Something has to be complete before something new begins. In a person's life this means they cannot start something new if they haven't resolved unfinished business. In order to do this, that unfinished business needs to come out into awareness, otherwise it hangs around in the background and doesn't allow the individual to be in the here and now."

"That's right," Cassandra responded. "It makes perfect sense, doesn't it? We all need closure in our lives, whenever possible, otherwise we can't focus entirely on the here and now, and move on in an effective way. We can't grow as individuals and strive to reach our potential if we don't complete the uncompleted."

"So, it says here that Gestalt is a German word and it means 'a whole': a configuration or pattern. It's all starting to make sense now. It's great studying with you, Cass."

"Well, you helped me understand Cognitive Behaviour Therapy, so I guess we're even now. I don't know when we are going to do the next practical though. We'll have to organise a time."

Julie suddenly wanted to find out more about Gestalt therapy theory. It did make sense. She definitely had unfinished business with Scott. Is that why she hadn't been able to move on with another guy? Christina did have a point to some extent, not that she would ever admit that to her. She did dismiss any mention of a relationship without even considering if there was any potential. Well, apart from the "Michael saga", as she called it. The relationship between her and Scott had not even officially ended. The "unfinished business" was always in the background so it was disallowing her from being present-centred. The first time she'd even talked to him since she saw them together was at the Hunter Valley resort.

Christina had also commented on her wanting to find someone that matched specific criteria. Was she comparing every potential relationship to the one she had with Scott? She suddenly felt that it might have been wise to see a professional counsellor all those years ago. For the moment, having a friend who was a counselling student had to do. Sometimes Julie felt that she was studying with Cassandra, as she had learned so much ever since Cassandra commenced her course. Julie decided to walk into the dining room and meet this new, mysterious study partner of Cassandra's. He sounded very charming.

"Hi Cass, I hear you're busy studying. Don't mind me though. I'm just off to make a cup of tea."

"Hi Jules, come and meet my new study partner, Connor. Connor, this is my wonderful friend Julie."

Julie shook hands with the tall, handsome man by Cassandra's side. His grip was firm and his intense aqua-blue eyes sparkled with good humour. "Hi Julie, nice to meet you. We'll probably be seeing a lot of each other. We've got a lot of units to get through." He ran his fingers through his curly light brown hair and smiled at Cassandra.

"I'm sure we will," Julie responded, with a cheeky grin. They both seemed to be enjoying their studies way too much.

"Before I leave you two to your studies, would you both like a cup of tea or coffee? We have a huge selection of organic teas and coffee. I'm sure Cass has filled you in on Maria's abundant selection of anything organic."

"No thanks, Julie," Connor replied. "We just had a coffee. Actually, I met Maria a while ago and she went through the whole product range from her shop with me. She was really excited about the new organic exfoliator that's exclusively for men."

"Yes. She's very passionate about her store and anything in it."

"What do you do, Julie? You must be in a creative field?"

"Why do you say that?"

"Well, Cassandra was telling me that you've decorated most of this house. It looks great. You have quite a talent."

Julie was about to modestly brush the compliment aside and say that it was nothing. However, she quickly remembered that she was dealing with not one, but two counselling students and they were sure to make some type of observation about her inability to accept a compliment.

"Thanks," she simply replied. "Well, I'm actually in the Insurance and Superannuation industry at the moment. However, a week from now I'll be officially unemployed."

"You can always take up Maria's offer and work part-time at her store while you work out what you're going to do next," Cassandra offered. "That is, if you're brave enough to hear her go on endlessly about all the ingredients that are found in her products."

"I'll think about it. I better let you get back to ... what was it? Oh, that's right, Gestalt therapy theory."

They both smiled at her as she left the room. Connor had a very nice smile. *He must be in his late thirties*, Julie estimated. He also had the bluest eyes Julie had ever seen. *Cass must have a difficult time concentrating when she had to look into those eyes!* Julie thought with a smile as she headed towards the kitchen.

Soon, she was settled in the lounge room, in her favourite white armchair, which faced the garden. Julie loved admiring the pink roses and charming white camellias that could be seen from the French doors, especially in the morning when the sun would light the whole room, and fill it with warmth. The sun was setting now, but despite this, she still enjoyed sitting in her favourite spot, nursing her cup of tea while the warmth of the heater blanketed the air in the pale blue room. It was the perfect environment to try to make sense of her dream.

She realised that Tanya may have appeared in her dream because she couldn't stop thinking about her the night before. Memories of their friendship, and how close they had been for years, came flooding back. Tanya would flirt with a lot of guys, but Julie always thought it was innocent and part of her charm. She always had plenty of guys seeking her attention, mostly due to her extroverted, charismatic personality, not to mention her glamorous looks. She herself was slightly more reserved compared to Tanya.

"Julie, can't you see that the guy is into you?" she had asked at one of their high school discos, during their senior years, when one of the popular boys flirted with Julie.

"I can, but we have nothing in common. Why should I pretend that I'm interested?"

"Lighten up, Julie. Any girl in our year would jump at the chance to go out with him."

"I just don't see it … yeah, he's hot, but so are many of the guys in our year. I'll admit, I did say he was gorgeous and I couldn't keep my eyes off him at first. I need more though. There's no spark."

"Well, in that case, I'd better make sure he's not too let down by you. You don't mind do you?" She didn't waste a moment.

"Go for it," Julie had said as she watched Tanya stride towards the other side of the room, flicking her silky, dark tresses and swaying her hips ever-so-confidently. She had become accustomed to Tanya's ways, even if she couldn't relate to them. Julie's rejected "hottie" had quickly become Tanya's trophy.

Despite their differences, they both looked out for each other, and had a lot of things in common. Tanya had been in a relationship with a guy named Steven for a few months, just before she decided to make her move on Scott. She had just broken up with Steven – actually Steven had broken up with her — on her birthday. To keep up with the theme of being an "obnoxious bastard", as Tanya called him, he had also made sure that she knew that he had met another girl, straight after he had wished her "happy birthday". Tanya wasn't used to anyone breaking up with her, especially in such a humiliating and hurtful way. Usually, she lost interest first. She still couldn't understand how Tanya would betray her like that though, knowing how she felt about Scott. She knew she always found Scott attractive. "You're so freaking gorgeous, Scott. I mean, with those dimples, you could definitely be a model," she would tell him with a vivacious smile that amplified her own gorgeous dimples. However, she would always support their relationship, and do anything in her power to ensure their relationship was romantically exciting: surprising them with tickets to see the symphony as a birthday gift; limousine rides around the city for no reason at all; a romantic weekend getaway as a one year anniversary gift. In fact, Julie couldn't believe how much she cared about their relationship, at times finding it a bit too selfless, only to feel bad for her friend later, thus accepting that maybe Tanya was just that: a truly good friend.

The only reason that made sense to Julie, apart from Tanya finding Scott "irresistibly sexy", was that she wasn't used to Julie being the one in a relationship — a serious, beautiful relationship with a wonderful, sexy guy. Tanya had never had a true connection with a guy, not the way Julie had with Scott. Scott had also been slightly frustrated at the time with Julie's plan for the two of them to focus on their studies and not see each other for a while. She obviously took advantage of the opportunity. However, she still couldn't believe Tanya would betray her like that. She still didn't understand it. At the time, she didn't even want to try.

Julie took a sip of tea. The fragrant ginger and lemon cleared her senses. Its warmth soothed her throat as she took another sip. The more she thought about it, the more sense it made. She still wouldn't be able to completely move on if she didn't have closure with Tanya as well. She was her closest friend for many years. Living life with uncertainty and no control had made her anxious and rigid; afraid to take chances and move forward. She couldn't see things clearly in the present because her past wasn't clear. She was sick and tired of feeling helpless! She had been willing to accept the past, but now a chance at gaining clarity had practically fallen in her lap. She was still puzzled, however, as to why she saw Tanya in her dream with George, instead of the woman he had actually been with.

It was just a dream and most dreams were weird, she reasoned. What she was certain about was that completing the incomplete could only be achieved if she talked to both

Scott *and* Tanya. First she would confront Tanya, and then she would call Scott, if he didn't call her first, that is. She owed it to herself to take the initiative from now on. She had to move on in all areas of her life. The only problem was how she would find Tanya. She hadn't seen or heard from her for years.

Of course! She jumped up, almost spilling her tea as she raced out of the room with one thing on her mind: closure.

CHAPTER FOURTEEN

"I can't believe I'm doing this."

"You're right, Julie. It's the best thing to do. Like you said, she owes you an explanation," Maria said.

"I can't believe she has been working so close to me for all these years and I never ran into her in one of the coffee shops, or even by chance on the street."

"At least it was easy to find her. It's amazing what or who you can find by just searching a name online."

"I know. All I did was type her name and her business details just appeared. She sounds very successful. I mean, she's a nutritionist and she has her own practice. She always said she wanted to switch to a Bachelor of Science. She must have done that the year after she betrayed me and I stopped talking to her. It's strange. I lost focus and direction when I did nothing wrong, and she had the willpower and courage to change courses, right after she betrayed her best friend."

"Julie. Remember what you said. You know the thing about not being a victim. As for being true to yourself, that's why you're here now." Maria looked around, musing, "I wonder what's keeping Antonio? I closed the shop early so we can go out. We're going to miss the movie."

Julie and Maria were both seated in a cosy booth in one of the city's wine bars. It was five thirty in the afternoon, and Maria had decided to offer Julie some moral support as she waited for Tanya to arrive. Maria's shop, Eventually You, was situated nearby. She was also meeting Antonio there as they had plans for dinner and a movie.

"I can't believe Antonio is late. I hope he doesn't have some last-minute creative breakthrough. I can't keep him away from his laptop when his graphic design juices start flowing. Now I'll have to exchange pleasantries with

Tanya, and if there's one thing I detest, it's being fake. The plan was for Antonio and me to make an exit before the bi—, I mean Tanya arrives."

Julie looked at her friend, slightly amused. She found it funny that Maria embraced the organic and present-centred lifestyle. She was also into yoga, pilates, aromatherapy and meditation, and even dressed in Bohemian-inspired, free-flowing clothes with an array of colours and prints. However, when it came to confrontations, she was anything but calm and subtle. That's why she would avoid them altogether, as her emotions would get the better of her, and she would say exactly what was on her mind. With Maria, there was no medium ground. It was either flee the scene, or retaliate with all guns blazing. Julie suddenly realised that she herself may be in that category as well. When confronting someone, she found it difficult to say what was on her mind without bursting into tears, or insulting the specific individual with personal attacks and accusations thrown haphazardly at them, sounding more aggressive than assertive.

Maria's presence had a calming and soothing effect on her nerves, and she was secretly glad Antonio was late. She had been so nervous when she called Tanya the night before. Tanya had, naturally, sounded surprised to hear from Julie, but she welcomed the meeting as soon as Julie hesitantly uttered the words. In fact, she immediately agreed to meet at the wine bar, which was conveniently situated between Julie's office and Tanya's practice.

The wine bar was starting to become busy as more people entered. A lit fireplace in the corner of the room greeted customers who took off their gloves and coats, feeling the warmth of the cosy room immediately, a complete contrast with the winter chill outside. A suave young man skilfully stroked the keys on a grand piano in the centre of the room, filling it with soft jazz melodies. The crystal chandeliers which hung from the ornate ceiling complemented the room perfectly. The grand atmosphere was juxtaposed cleverly with contemporary works of art that were hung up on the white walls, amongst numerous chalk boards which listed countless selections of wine. Prized bottles were on display and the lighting was dim. Every booth and table contained a candle housed in an elegant gold lamp strategically placed in the centre, welcoming conversation.

Julie inwardly congratulated herself for choosing one of her favourite venues. The atmosphere would definitely help with the difficult task of calming her nerves. Her gaze fixated at the glass doors as they were opened by a beautiful, tall woman with long, glossy, dark brown hair. She was smartly dressed in a white skirt and a black suit jacket. Her blue eyes searched the room for a moment before she smiled at Julie.

She began to make her way towards them, as Maria quickly announced: "It's her. I'd remember her smug face anywhere."

Julie found herself awkwardly smiling back at the familiar looking woman, who she once upon a time called a friend.

"Hi Julie, I'm so glad we could meet again. You look great."

"Hi Tanya, do you remember Maria from uni?" Julie asked, trying not to look too shocked at the fact that Tanya now greeted her with a kiss on each cheek. She looked so sophisticated and cosmopolitan. *She must be well travelled*, Julie thought, feeling slightly envious.

"Hi Maria, I remember you. It's so great to see another familiar face."

"Hi." Maria responded in a matter of fact way, still remaining in her seat. "I'm not staying," she continued. "I'm meeting my boyfriend here. We have dinner plans."

"Oh. That's a shame," Tanya replied politely, settling herself in the vacant seat. "It's always wonderful to see people from uni. It seems so long ago that we were all eager students ready to learn and explore life."

Julie gave Maria a knowing stare. She knew that her friend would snap if Tanya continued to be so cordial, acting as though the three of them were best friends. This was especially the case when they all knew that the only topic that was on the agenda for discussion was how eager Tanya had been to "explore" Scott.

"It's such a charming spot here. I come here often. I'm rather surprised that I haven't run into either of you before. I mean we work so close to each other," Tanya continued, steering the conversation after the awkward pause.

"Yes. It is surprising," Maria flatly acknowledged.

Julie couldn't find any words. She had so much to say to the woman sitting opposite from her who was now almost a stranger, but her voice failed her.

"Hi Maria, I'm so sorry that I'm late," a breathless Antonio interjected, breaking the silence between the three women. "I just came up with the most brilliant idea and had to make some notes in case I don't remember it later. You know how it is. Ideas sometimes appear in people's heads at the strangest times. You've got to grab them while you can."

"Well, we'd better hurry if we're going to make the movie," Maria stated much too hastily, dismissing Antonio's explanation, obviously eager to escape the awkwardness of the situation.

"Hi Antonio, this is Tanya. We use to go to uni together." Julie introduced Antonio as Maria gave her a look that clearly asked, *"How could you?"*

"Hi Antonio, it's great to meet you," Tanya greeted him with a flirtatious smile. "Why don't you join us for a glass of wine?" she offered, once again taking the lead.

"I guess one glass of wine won't hurt. It's always great to meet people from Maria's past," he responded innocently.

"Actually, Tanya was Julie's friend," Maria stated with a tight jaw. "I'm sure they have a lot to discuss. In fact, I'm positive about that." Maria's voice became louder and clearer as she spoke. Her ability to maintain a façade hadn't even lasted for ten minutes. She was speaking as if she was talking to a class of pre-schoolers.

"One glass won't hurt." Tanya decided to intervene. "Grab a seat. Although, I wasn't directly friends with Maria, she was Julie's friend and it will be fun to reminisce together about the people we knew," she responded with a smile and placed an arm on Antonio's shoulder, as though she'd known him for years.

Julie couldn't believe her audacity. She was acting as if she had nothing to feel guilty about. She also couldn't believe how flirtatious she was being with Antonio, touching her hair, smiling continuously with her luscious, rosy lips. She realised Maria had also noticed this, as she looked at her with a look of disbelief. Julie knew she had to do something before her friend exploded. Tanya had obviously not changed. She was still eyeing men that were clearly not available. Was it some kind of power game? Or did she truly not want to see anyone else being happy? With her stunning looks, she could clearly have any man she wanted, then and now.

Julie chipped in. "Actually, you better go now if you want to catch the movie. Besides, they offer some of the best wine at the restaurant you're going to."

Antonio looked at his watch. "You're right, Julie. I didn't realise what time it was. We better go. I know Maria closed the shop early so we can spend some time together."

As Maria grabbed her bag and coat, Antonio pulled her gently towards him and gave her a passionate kiss on the lips. Julie smiled and looked at Tanya, curious to see what her reaction would be. She was smiling as well, as if she applauded their public display of affection. Just what game was she playing? She had done the same thing with her and Scott. One minute she was Scott and Julie's loyal supporter, and then out of nowhere she made a play for him.

"Bye all," Maria said with a confident smile, eyeing Tanya suspiciously.

Maria and Antonio had left arm in arm, after Maria had leaned over, whispering in Julie's ear, "Don't let her off the hook."

It was time for business. "What would you like to drink?" Julie finally asked, deciding that she should be the one to take charge of the situation since she was the one who organised the meeting.

"I think I might have the Shiraz from the Barossa," Tanya responded, studying the menu.

Eager to get the conversation on the track she wanted, Julie eyed the waitress, and quickly ordered Tanya's Shiraz, and a Merlot from the Yarra Valley.

"So, you really do look great, Julie. Slightly more conservative than I remember ..."

Julie gave her a questioning look.

"But you look just as great," Tanya quickly added. "You always did have fabulous taste though," she continued.

"You look great too, Tanya, as you always did."

"Well, my taste was never as original as yours," she said, eyeing Julie's blue striped scarf.

"I have to admit though, I was very surprised that you called me. I mean, from what I can remember, you didn't want anything to do with me," Tanya said.

Julie had enough of formalities. It was time to get the answers she needed.

"Do you honestly blame me, Tanya? I mean, would you want to talk to me if I did what you did to me?" Julie felt that she was communicating in Morse code.

"Well, actually I would have Julie. Maybe not straight away, but eventually I would have talked to you. I was very hurt with what you did. I mean, you wouldn't return any of my calls and you avoided me. I've replayed the situation a thousand times in my mind, and I still can't understand

100

how our friendship could have been destroyed so abruptly. I mean, I considered you to be my best friend."

Julie couldn't believe what she was hearing.

At that moment the waitress interrupted. "One Shiraz from the Barossa Valley, and a Merlot from the Yarra Valley. Enjoy!"

Julie and Tanya thanked the waitress, as they both sank back into their chairs. The interruption had eased some of the tension for a moment, as they both took a sip of wine. Julie took this time to regroup and plan her words carefully.

"Just what do you mean when you say you need closure? You're acting as if you did nothing wrong. If anyone needs closure, it's me. I'm the one who was hurt by your actions."

"Julie. It's taken us so long to get to this point and as nervous as I was to see you again, thinking that you hated me all these years, I was also relieved that I could finally understand why you chose to avoid me, instead of confront me. Do you know what a brave face I had to put on when I saw you sitting with Maria? I mean, you became her friend as soon as you started avoiding me. Before I knew it, you became a stranger to me. The few times that I ran into you, I felt so hurt when you all looked at me as if I had the scarlet letter sewn on my clothes."

"Wait a minute. I'm confused. I can't believe you're acting so innocent. You know what you did. I saw it with my own eyes. You must think I am an idiot if you're denying what I witnessed. You say that you considered me to be your closest friend at the time. Well, can you please explain to me how a so-called best friend can betray her friend the way you betrayed me? Please tell me. You must know what I'm talking about. You owe me an explanation after the heartache you put me through; the heartache that you both put me through."

"You saw it with your own eyes? Well, then please tell me what you saw? I need to hear it from you, to see it from your perspective. If you did that back then, our friendship and your relationship with Scott wouldn't have been ruined. It was really unfair that you didn't give me a chance to explain. I thought our friendship meant more to you than that. I would never have treated you with such contempt and disregard."

Julie tried to calm her anger. She couldn't believe that Tanya was acting so hurt, and so self-righteous. She tried to compose herself when she noticed two men in business suits sitting on the table next to them looking at them inquisitively. Tanya looked genuinely upset, as she managed to take another sip of her wine.

"Look, Julie. Just tell me. We're here now. I just want to know how you could avoid me like that after being friends for so long. I mean, we'd known each other since high school. Scott was just as hurt and confused. Before we knew it, you were with Mark. Scott was so devastated. I have to admit. I never thought you were the type of person who could move on so quickly. I mean, I thought what you and Scott had was sacred. I have to also admit, I was jealous of the new friends you made. I would often look at all of you, sitting and laughing on campus, and would think that we used to be like that."

Julie couldn't listen to any more. She felt her stomach turning. "I just can't believe what you're saying. How can you sit there and accuse me of hurting both you and Scott? Do you honestly think I didn't have a good reason not to *ever* speak to you again? You stole the only man who ever meant anything to me. You betrayed me in the worst possible way. I saw you that day at the cafeteria. You were both kissing passionately, oblivious to anyone around you. That's why I couldn't speak to you! Does that ring any bells to you? Is it all coming back to you now?"

Julie was shaking all over. She sat back in her seat, after realising that she was practically standing over Tanya in an aggressive stance.

"Julie. I can see you're angry with me. You need to allow me to explain everything. It was all one big misunderstanding. What you think you saw wasn't what really happened. I know I'm speaking in riddles and what I'm saying sounds so cliché, but you have to give me a chance to explain. I was certain that someone we knew had seen us. I didn't know you saw us with your own eyes though. What really hurt me is that you didn't give me the benefit of the doubt. How could you think that I would betray my best friend in such a cruel way? How could you not have confronted me and given me a chance to explain? Before I knew it, you had moved on with your life, and it seemed that you despised me so much."

"Okay. Explain to me why you were kissing my boyfriend in broad daylight without any concern for my feelings. Was it too hard for you to accept that I was happy? Did you have to ruin my relationship just because you were miserable after Steven had hurt you? Please. I can't wait to hear this. What possible excuse could you have?"

"Okay." Tanya cleared her throat. "I went to the cafeteria that day feeling miserable. You're right about that. I was devastated after Steven had broken up with me. You remember how cruel he was to me? He had made me think that we were exclusive, and that our relationship was growing into something real. I finally thought that I should end the games, and try being in a mature relationship ... like the one you and Scott had. I couldn't believe it when he told me, *on my birthday*, that he didn't want to see me anymore. It was as if he had changed the script on me without giving me any signs. Remember how heartbroken I was? He had told me that he was seeing someone else right after he gave me my birthday present. I sure knew how to pick them. Anyway, I desperately needed a coffee. I ran into Scott. He seemed really happy and he asked if I'd join him. I told him that I wouldn't be good company, but he insisted. He couldn't stop talking about you. He was so happy. He told me that he had a great time with you the night before, and that you were the girl of his dreams. I remember feeling so happy for the two of you. It gave me hope that there were good guys out there."

Tanya paused and took a sip of her wine. Julie was listening intently to every word that came out of Tanya's mouth.

"You have to believe me when I tell you that I was so genuinely happy for you and Scott. I mean, I had never heard a guy express how he felt about his girlfriend so honestly. He was absolutely crazy about you. I knew from the moment you met him that he was the perfect guy for you. I always made sure you knew that. To answer your question that you asked earlier, or should I say the accusation you made, the last thing I wanted to do was to jeopardise what you had. I would never intentionally do something so callous, and why would I be so blatant about it? I mean, anyone could have seen us."

"If you were so happy for us, then why on earth would you kiss him?" Julie was beginning to think that she may have made a huge mistake. Tanya wasn't off the hook yet though.

"Julie, I know this still doesn't make sense to you, but it will soon. As Scott was going on and on about how happy you made him and how he couldn't wait to see you again that night, I noticed Steven walking towards us, hand-in-hand with another girl. As you can imagine I was devastated. I didn't know what to do. Although I had only gone out with him for two months, I had really lost my self-esteem for a while. Without thinking, I pulled Scott towards me and started kissing him. Scott backed away, but I pulled him closer to me and I just kept kissing him. Steven hadn't even met Scott, so I wanted him to think that I had moved on too, and that he didn't break my heart at all. Scott was so shocked when I finally let go of him. So was Steven when I looked at his smug smile disappearing. After it was over, I realised it was a stupid and childish thing to do, but at that moment, I was acting on instinct. Steven had humiliated me so much. I didn't want him to have that power over me."

"So you did all that just to seek revenge on Steven?" Julie asked, speaking slowly. "I can't believe this. You mean to tell me that this was all a tragic misunderstanding?"

"Yes. You had every right to be upset with what you saw, but I thought you would at least give me a chance. You know how stupid and impulsive I could be back then. I mean, I would have never hurt your relationship intentionally, and I never imagined you would think that of me. I always supported your relationship with Scott. Why would I suddenly do that? I realised that you had found out, and I desperately wanted to explain. I understood that you needed space to deal with your emotions, but you kept avoiding us and we tried desperately to reach you. I couldn't believe that I was responsible for destroying what you and Scott had."

"But weren't you and Scott and item after? I mean you were always together."

"No. We were both devastated. You wouldn't accept our calls. We left you numerous messages explaining what had happened, but you severed all ties with us. After Scott saw that you and Mark were an item, he was in terrible shape. I guess you could say we leaned on each other, purely as friends. I remember feeling so confused at the time. Scott understood what I was going through, as he felt the same way. That's all it was. I wonder how he is now? I haven't seen him since uni."

Julie couldn't breathe. A sinking feeling took over her, and she felt like she would be sick. What had she done?

She remembered deleting any messages she received from Scott and Tanya as soon as she heard their voices. She should have known better. She should have given them the benefit of the doubt.

Her whole body felt numb. What if she had listened to those messages? What if she had let them explain? Three lives had been affected just because of a misunderstanding and her selfish indulgence in her own self-pity. She should have listened to Cassandra and Maria. Even they had asked her on numerous occasions if it was a misunderstanding. Julie had convinced them that it wasn't.

"Julie. All we could do was move on. That's what you had done. The next year I had decided to concentrate on my studies. I was lucky to be able to change to a Bachelor of Science degree. I realised that I really wanted to be a nutritionist. I had already fulfilled some of the requirements, but I had to study for another two years. I was determined to succeed though. It was all I had at the time. My studies gave me focus and a direction. That year had taken a huge toll on me."

Julie sculled the rest of her wine, even though she had an awful feeling in her stomach. She needed another drink. She needed time to process all of it. She looked at Tanya. She suddenly looked different to the stranger who had opened the glass doors of the wine bar almost an hour ago. She couldn't believe that she had so little faith in her friend, and in Scott.

"Julie. Do you want another drink?" Tanya asked, as she eyed the waiter near their booth. "We'll have two of the same," she told him when Julie hadn't replied. "To be fair to you, I can see why you would jump to conclusions. Through your eyes, the writing was on the wall. I just wanted you to allow us to explain. I so valued our friendship."

"I thought you enjoyed stealing other people's boyfriends. I even thought you were flirting with Antonio today. Somehow I formed this image of you that I kept with me ever since."

"That was just me trying desperately to look friendly; I didn't quite know how to act around Maria, or you for that matter. I knew that your new friends didn't like me. I wanted you both to see that I'm not the callous bitch you all thought I was. My nerves got the better of me though, and I obviously appeared too friendly. Besides, I'm happily married with a child, a little three-year-old girl."

Julie found herself smiling. She thought that Tanya looked so self-assured. Now that she saw things through her eyes, she realised how intimidated she would have felt with both her and Maria waiting there. She was also surprised that Tanya was married and was now a mother. She never imagined that she would settle down and have a family.

Julie's thoughts were interrupted by the waiter, as he served them their wine. Tanya raised her glass and made a toast. "To closure," she said. "And to moving forward, forgiving, and rekindling old friendships?" she asked.

Julie raised her glass as well, still in shock, and reciprocated in kind. Perhaps it was time to make amends and learn from past mistakes.

"To rekindling old friendships," Julie added, her glass raised.

CHAPTER FIFTEEN

Julie's mobile phone vibrated. She took a look at it still in a state of shock. She was sitting on the train, heading north on her way home. The train was approaching Milsons Point. Soon it would be her stop, but she desperately wanted the ride to be longer so she could clear her head. She looked at her mobile which was charged this time, in case she received a message from Scott. After the conversation she had with Tanya, she didn't want to wait any more. She had to make amends and change her ways. Why was she once again waiting? She would call him. If she had been more eager to confront people back then, who knows where she and Scott would be now?

All those wasted years, she thought with regret. As she glanced at the messages on her phone, she realised they were all from Scott.

He must have called while she was in the wine bar. As much as she had wanted to hear from him, Julie didn't want any interruptions during her talk, so she had put her phone on vibrating mode, and had placed it in her handbag. The last thing she wanted was Tanya finding out that Scott was back in Julie's life, especially when at the time Julie thought that Tanya was the woman who intentionally broke them apart.

"Julie, I've been trying to call you all afternoon. I figured you would be in a meeting or something. I also called on Monday, but your phone mustn't have been charged. I tried your home phone, but it was engaged. Anyway, can you please call me on any number so we can plan when we're having coffee? It's been a hectic week. I have a lot to get through before the trip. Please leave a message if I'm not there. I really need to see you before I leave! Bye."

So he had also called when my mobile needed charging, and when I was on the phone with Mum? Julie thought sceptically. Her conversation with her mother had been so intense she didn't even realise there was another call on the line.

Julie thought of Scott: his face, his deep coffee-coloured eyes, his sexy dimpled smile, his overgrown, wavy dark brown hair, his slightly stubbled, strong jaw, the look he gave her when he recently ran into her. Their relationship could have grown so much if it had been given a chance. Now, they'd never know. So much time had passed. They were two different people. Julie suddenly felt so sad. Her heart ached at the pain she must have put him through.

Julie's mind went back to that moment when he accidentally ran into her: the moment he saw her with Mark. She had been seeing Mark for a few weeks. She hadn't planned on dating anyone so quickly. After weeks of avoiding Scott and Tanya, and hardly going out at all, except to her lectures and tutorials, Julie remembered suddenly feeling an extreme need to get out of the house. She had moved back in with her parents. They too were concerned about her. Christina and Brian would often visit but Julie felt unable to confide in any of them.

It was a Friday night, three weeks after she had witnessed them in that passionate embrace. Cassandra, Maria, and a group of other friends in her human resources class had insisted she go with them to a party. She had protested profusely at first. Her attitude completely changed when her sadness was suddenly replaced with extreme anger at the thought of their betrayal. Empowered, she had worn her most flattering white jeans, her most provocative gold high heels, and a shimmering gold top. She had thrown on some gold jewellery to complement the look, and a small brown leather jacket. She remembered thinking that she looked like a glamorous pop star. She was ready to face the world again, high heels and all. However, her sudden burst of confidence hadn't lasted long. The moment she had arrived at the party, she felt that she didn't belong. She was surrounded by couples and happy people, dancing, drinking, and laughing. She remembered thinking that she used to be one of those people. The group that she was with was also happy, as they joked and danced to the trance music the DJ was playing.

She had tried desperately to cheer up. She remembered feeling silly in her choice of outfit, as it suddenly didn't match her mood, and it definitely wasn't her taste. She had also started feeling anxious at the realisation that *they* might also be there. The thought of Scott and Tanya on the dance floor together had sent shivers down her spine. She thought she was ready, but she was far from it. She suddenly couldn't take it anymore and decided to go and get a drink. She had walked through the smoke-filled room to the bar, then back through the crowd at the bar with her drink intact, when it happened. It was that night — the night she met Mark. He appeared out of nowhere, spilling the drink which she had, until then, successfully carried through the thirsty crowd.

She had been aware that she shouldn't get involved with anyone so soon. However, she felt that she needed someone like Mark. Besides, Scott had moved on with her so-called best friend, she had rationalised to herself. They went on a few dates and realised that they connected on other levels as well, not just in terms of their taste in music. Then it happened. She finally ran into them. It was a Saturday night. Julie and Mark had decided to go and see one of the uni student bands that were performing. Mark knew the lead guitarist as he was in one of his lectures. They were playing at the university. They both had a fun night and decided to have a late dinner in one of the many restaurants in Newtown, as it was nearby and Julie loved looking at all the boutiques, and homeware and furniture shops.

As they were walking along King Street, arm in arm, Julie remembered her jaw dropping at the sight of him. Scott was walking towards them with his best friends, James and Jenny. There was another woman walking amongst them who she couldn't make out at first. Her heart sank when she realised it was Tanya. There was no escape. Pretending that they couldn't see each other, or fleeing the scene, was not an option.

Julie had told Mark everything that had happened. She felt that it would be the fair thing to do. Julie, being Julie, naturally froze. However, Mark being Mark, with his easy going nature, smiled at the group as if there was nothing strange or awkward about the situation and politely said, "Hey, how is everyone?"

It turned out that he knew James as they had played soccer together. Meanwhile, all Julie could do was stare at the ground and avoid making eye contact with any of them. The one time she did look at them, she saw the look Scott gave her. His eyes looked so sad and hurt, as if someone had taken the air out of him. Every muscle in his face and body looked tense. At the time Julie hadn't understood his reaction.

Before Julie knew it, she had heard Mark saying: "Bye, enjoy the rest of the night!"

She had walked away holding Mark's hand tightly. She took one final look at the group and noticed Tanya had the same look in her eyes as Scott.

Mark had tried to comfort her. He had tried to cheer her up as they shared a Spanish paella and sangria. She got through the night, and then the next day ascribing to Mark's "let's make the most out of life" mentality. They had started the morning by going jogging. He had insisted that the only way to clear her mind would be through fitness. It had worked. Mark wasn't Scott, but he was full of so much positive energy. She needed positivity back in her life. One month then became two, and two quickly became four.

Julie had already arrived home. She couldn't even remember how she had managed to reach her street so quickly. Her mind had been transported to another world

– one five years ago. It felt like it had all occurred yesterday. Julie suddenly wondered if it really was too late, as she opened the front door of the terrace house. Maybe they hadn't changed that much. Maybe their sudden reunion hadn't only occurred for much needed closure, but for another chance as well. Julie's mind was suddenly working overtime. She had a lot to do if she wanted to find out if their relationship could be given another chance. Scott was still talking to her, after all that he thought she had done to him. Tanya was still talking to her after she had bad-mouthed her to so many of their friends. It must have been awful for her. She had been ostracised from all her close friends, as they had sided with Julie. No wonder she needed Scott in her life. Julie threw her bag on the sofa, and headed to the phone. She had to do it. She had to find out if everything could be made right again. She picked up the phone in the hallway and dialled his home phone number. She would work down the list of numbers and email addresses until she reached him.

"Hi Scott, it's Julie. So when's a good time for that coffee?"

CHAPTER SIXTEEN

Friday came around quickly. Most of the day consisted of packing desks, sending goodbye emails to colleagues from other departments, and clearing out email inboxes. The radio in the corner had been on all day, playing music to assist with making the tedious task a little less painful.

It was lunchtime, and they were all seated at a Greek restaurant in the city. Lunch had been organised by Colin as a way of saying thank you. The mood was light and playful. Everyone was reminiscing about the old days and the people they had worked with. Stacey kept everyone informed on what past colleagues were doing now, as she had many friends in other departments who were somehow well informed about such matters. The fact that she had been the president of the Social Club for so many years had also helped with her abundant knowledge. Everyone was surprisingly in a jovial mood. Even Sarah was smiling at all the jokes, especially the ones that came from George, as he was the one who attempted to say the most. Julie too was in a mellow mood. They were all enjoying the Greek delicacies that were on offer, from *haloumi* cheese, eggplant dip, stuffed vine leaves, to spinach triangles and *souvlakia*. They had opted for a good Australian white wine though, declining the waiter's recommendation to try their selection of Greek beverages. There was even a *bouzouki* player in the corner for the lunch time crowd.

Julie, and nearly everyone in the restaurant, couldn't stop laughing when George took Colin by the arm and tried to dance the *Zorba*. She saw a different side to George. He really did have a fun sense of humour. She wondered why she was noticing this now, not that she often voluntarily socialised with him, or any of her work colleagues, especially in the last couple of months. Colin was also generous taking them out for lunch at his own expense. He occasionally joked about some of the mishaps that had occurred over the years. Of course at the time it was no laughing matter. As they were reminiscing however, it all seemed quite funny. George and even Sarah admitted to a few blunders, and Julie also pitched in, highlighting her own. She caught George looking at her with an amused smile on his face. Everyone refrained from sharing any more when Colin announced that if they needed a reference, he would need to be honest with their contribution and their work performance. After looking at them with a serious look on his face, he burst into laughter. "Who said I don't have a sense of humour?" he said. "Relax. I know that you have all been dedicated employees, and if there's anything I can do to help you gain employment elsewhere, I'm your man." The light mood continued for a while as they ordered desserts.

"I'll try the *galaktobouri*," George stumbled.

"I think you mean the *galaktoboureko*," Julie interjected, familiar with the word as she had known many friends with Greek backgrounds over the years, including Maria, of course.

"Yes, that's the one," he said eyeing Julie suspiciously. "Thanks, Julie, for coming to my rescue. It's not often that something like that happens."

"Well, do you blame her?" Stacey intervened. "I mean, you've been giving her grief over the years."

"It was just some healthy office fun. Julie can handle it, especially with all those witty comebacks she always hits back with."

"Healthy office fun? Is that what you call it? I would call it something else and I think you know what I'm talking about." Stacey smiled at George.

Julie, on the other hand, didn't have a clue what they were talking about.

"Anyway, what are you doing now that you're unemployed, Julie? Any job offers yet?" George asked.

"No. I think I might use this time to unwind and regroup. It's a good opportunity to think of what I really want to do," Julie responded.

"What you really want to do? I thought insurance was your thing. I'm really surprised at your *laissez-faire* attitude though. I thought you would be updating your resume as soon as you heard the news."

"Well, there's a lot you don't know about me, George."

"I know more than you think," he said, becoming serious. His blue eyes suddenly looked so deep, as though he was thinking carefully. He then looked down at his glass of wine.

"What I know is that I need a job. My credit card debt is growing while I'm sitting here," Stacey interjected.

As Stacey continued talking about her financial woes, Julie glanced at George when he wasn't looking. Before she could look away, he caught her looking at him. She too had no option but to look down at her empty glass.

Back at the office, everyone congregated around Justin Jones, the senior manager of the entire Superannuation Division. He was in the middle of his speech, thanking everyone in the Claims and Redemptions Division for their contribution over the years. He also emphasised how regretful they were for having to make such a difficult decision. He explained that there was no other alternative, and that times were tough.

It was Colin's turn now. He thanked his team for their dedication and commitment, and reassured them, once again, that his doors were open if there was a need for any references. He also stated that he would miss every single one of his staff, and that it would not be the same without them. Julie thought he would start crying as he said that. He then called them up one by one, and presented them each with a gift: a huge bouquet of flowers for each of the

115

women, and a gold plated pen enclosed in a small gift box for the few men in the team. The flowers were beautiful, and she pictured which room she would place them in and in which vase as soon as they were handed to her.

After much applause from everyone, many hugs and tears and questions from other still-employed colleagues regarding what they would do next, Julie felt overwhelmed by the emotions that surprisingly emerged from somewhere deep within her heart. The feelings she felt were bittersweet, as she looked at all her colleagues who had become a second family over the years, albeit a dysfunctional one. She realised that, in a weird way, she would miss seeing them every morning and finding out what they did on the weekend. Were they really as bad as she thought? She would even miss Stacey asking her if she wanted to "join them for a drink," or relentlessly grilling her for information on her love life. She would even miss George's smug remarks. Now that everyone was in the same boat, there was no need for pretences.

As she walked back to her desk, she felt sad at how empty it looked. Usually it was full of post it notes, coffee mugs, and files scattered everywhere. Her PC was shut down, and her phone was eerily quiet as the number had been disconnected. It was empty, except for a beautifully wrapped gift sitting on its own. She had received a few gifts from her colleagues in her team and from other departments.

She placed the sweet, fragrant flowers on her desk and began to pack the gifts and the "Goodbye" cards that she had placed on the credenza. Just as she was about to pack the last gift from her desk, she felt someone's hand on her back. It was Sarah.

"Julie, it's been great working with you. Thank you for all the support you gave me over the years, especially when I was new. I don't know what I would have done without you."

"That's okay, it's been great working with you too," Julie responded, taken aback by Sarah's sincerity.

"I have to admit. There were times when I couldn't keep up with you. I mean you were always so into your work. I felt that Colin would think I did nothing compared to you," Sarah added, smiling as if she felt relieved to get it off her chest.

Julie was shocked. She'd always thought that Sarah was competing with her, and that she came a disappointing second. George mentioned something similar in another note. Julie realised she may have been wrong about his intentions too. It was funny they thought she loved her work and even thrived on it. She looked at Sarah and smiled at her. She was beginning to see things more clearly now, as the animosity and resentment she held in her heart slowly melted away.

"To tell you the truth, Sarah, I felt just as vulnerable as you apparently did. I hope we keep in touch."

"Don't worry about that, Jules. I'll make sure of it," Stacey said, as she heard Julie's words. "I've got an excellent idea for a reunion already. I'll keep in touch and fill you in on the time and place, and I will definitely not take no for an answer!"

"Neither will I," George added. "No more excuses. I mean you won't be that busy now, unless you find another job where you could immerse yourself in mountains of work and deadlines."

"I'll miss you too, George," Julie responded.

"Don't be a stranger!" he added, and gave Julie a hug.

Julie felt his cool, smooth hand as it accidentally brushed her face, causing her eyes to instantly meet his. She quickly looked away, only to look back up at him when she felt his eyes still on her.

"Julie," he said, "I ... I just wanted to say ..."

"Yes, George?" Julie asked when he didn't speak, giving him a warm, slightly awkward smile.

"I ... just wanted to say good luck with everything."

"Thanks. You too. Good luck," she said, feeling her face becoming warm as she once again met his thoughtful, intense blue eyes.

"Hey George," Justin Jones called from the corridor. "Get yourself over here. I heard that you beat the CEO playing tennis at the company Sport's Day."

George was still looking at Julie. His face gave way to a half-smile. He then turned, and slowly walked towards Justin's office.

"Bye, George," she said with a surprising feeling of regret.

As Julie made her way to the elevators, she instinctively knocked on Colin's door. She felt that she couldn't leave without one final farewell. After all, they had worked side by side for five years. It wasn't his fault that she hadn't been happy with her job.

"Hi Colin, I just wanted to say one final goodbye."

"Ah yes, Julie. I'm glad you did. You've been a godsend. You've helped me out so many times. I could always count on you to ensure that the work was being done. Although, I did suspect that you may have been a tad too dedicated. I mean, no one likes superannuation and insurance that much."

"I guess I felt that it was all I had for a while."

"And now things are different?"

"You could say that. Let's just say that I'm on the verge of finding a new purpose to my life."

"I always thought you would. You have so much passion. I can see it when you argue your point in our team meetings. Anyway! Get out of here. You have a whole world to explore. Remember my door is always open if you need help with seeking further employment. Well, if I'm still here that is. You know I don't thrive on this work as much as people think I do, either."

"Bye, Colin."

"Julie," he called out, as she headed for the door. "I hope you find what you're looking for."

"I will," Julie confidently responded.

There is a whole world to explore, and the sooner I explore it the better, she thought to herself. But she had a lot to do before she could do that.

Later that afternoon, Julie walked into the terrace house, lazily throwing her bag on the sofa in the lounge room. A small parcel fell out. Recognising the gold wrapping paper, she curiously picked it up. It was the gift that had been left on her desk. She carefully unwrapped the gold paper and opened the elegant box, revealing a small figurine of a white bird on a branch. It instantly brought a smile to her face. Her heart began to beat fast as she read the words:

Hi Julie, I just wanted you to know that I have truly enjoyed working with you over the years. I wish you all the best with your future endeavours. I hope you achieve everything you set your mind to. I know you will. If anyone can make it happen — it's you!
All the best,
George

She couldn't believe it. *George?* she thought. The beautiful gift with the kind words was from *George*.

CHAPTER SEVENTEEN

It was Monday morning. People were frantically dragging their luggage to the various terminals. Julie waited anxiously, anticipating Scott's arrival. They had planned to meet at the airport. He had told her everything had been organised. All she would have to do is pack and ensure that she had her passport. He had also asked her to meet them at 6:00am, so that they had enough time to check in their luggage. Jenny and James would also be meeting them at the entrance of the international terminal.

Julie took a deep breath. She couldn't believe that she was doing it. In the past it would usually take weeks, if not months, to plan a trip. Yet here she was at the airport waiting for Scott, ready to head to Paris! Who would have thought that a family outing with Christina would lead to this? She would never have imagined that she was capable of being so spontaneous. Yet, something about it seemed natural. As anxious as she felt, she also felt excited about where she was heading. She felt proud that she was following her heart — her instinct, and not just settling for another office job just because it was the safe thing to do. She couldn't move on with her career while being in a haze, carrying the baggage of "unfinished business" with her. She couldn't focus on one and ignore the other. She felt that every part of her being was wide awake, even though her eyes were struggling to stay open.

Maria had also woken up early. She had offered to give her a lift as she wanted to open up the shop early anyway, even though the airport was out of her way. She had seemed just as excited as Julie was, telling her on numerous occasions that she wished she could join her. Julie hadn't been sure if she could do it. She only had three days to pack and organise everything.

Thank God I splurged on a whole new summer wardrobe last summer, she had told herself repeatedly, as it would be the peak of summer in France.

She was also relieved that she actually had a passport. "Thank God for that conference I had to attend in New Zealand," she had told Cassandra and Maria continuously all weekend. "If it wasn't for that Superannuation and Insurance Conference Colin ensured I attended, I wouldn't have a passport."

After some last minute shopping, a Saturday morning trip to the hairdressers and the beautician, ticking off items from her long list, and a few calls to Scott ensuring everything was organised, she was set.

There was one thing she still needed to do when Sunday night came around. She made a quick call to her mother and informed her that she would not be around for the next three weeks, and that she would call her "as soon as I get to where I'm heading."

"So you won't be able to make it to the barbecue your father and I have planned for Sunday afternoon?" she had asked.

"No, Mum," Julie had replied, admiring the bouquet of flowers from Colin which she had placed in a beautiful crystal vase on the writing desk in the lounge room. "I don't think I'll be able to attend," she had said, her excitement growing as she spoke. "I'll be in Paris!"

Julie had met Scott for a quick coffee on Thursday. It had turned out that he was working for a company at Wynyard, a train stop away from her own work. They had sat down at a busy coffee shop at first, and then continued their conversation at Hyde Park when it got too noisy. There was no time for any revelations on what Julie had discussed with Tanya. There was too much to do if Julie was to take up his offer and join them in Paris. Scott seemed very eager to make things happen when she told him on the phone that Paris seemed like the break she needed as she would be unemployed for a while. He had told her that she could share rooms with Jenny and he would share with James, looking at her intently as he said this.

Julie didn't even have time to think about what she would tell him. She didn't have time to think at all. All she knew was that she had to take advantage of the opportunity they were given.

Before she knew it, she was in Maria's brand new hybrid car, heading to the airport. "If it wasn't for your abrupt nature, you'd be a walking stereotype," Julie had joked that morning, commenting on her friend's choice in vehicles.

Now, standing alone at the busy and noisy airport, it suddenly dawned on her that the reunion with Scott's friends may be awkward. After all, in their eyes and Scott's eyes for that matter, Julie was the one who did all the betraying.

"Hey stranger, long time no see," a relaxed male voice addressed her.

Julie turned around, coming face to face with two familiar people. It was James and Jenny. They were easy to recognise, not having changed much. Jenny still dressed in athletic attire, as she did back then while she was in the middle of her physical fitness degree, and James was dressed like he was ready to explore the Himalayas instead of Paris. He was always the adventurous type.

"Hi James, Jenny," Julie cautiously responded.

"Glad you could join us. The more the merrier, I always say," James continued. He was the type that would make people feel at ease, and that part of his nature fortunately had not changed.

"So are you ready to be roommates, Julie? Before you respond, I must warn you, that I'm not a morning person, so don't take my moods personally first thing in the day," Jenny looked at Julie.

"Well in that case, we should get along just fine. I'm definitely not a morning person either."

"Don't worry," said James. "The French breakfast that's included in our hotel package should change all that. I myself cannot wait to wake up early and jog around the streets of Paris. That's the best way you can get a real feel for the city. Early in the morning, when the shops are opening, when the people are slowly starting to emerge and start their day. Did I mention that you can buy the freshest baked bread then as well? When I'm travelling, that's the part of the day I love the most." James took a deep breath, as if he was breathing in the crisp morning air from the streets of Paris at that very moment.

"Didn't we just tell you that we don't like early mornings? I haven't even had a cup of coffee yet and you sound like you're about to recite a poem," Jenny interrupted grumpily.

Julie smiled at James, as Jenny rolled her eyes with a wry smile on her face. They had known each other so long that they sounded like a married couple. As well as being dressed casually, they each had only one small suitcase and a carry bag. They definitely looked like smart and experienced travellers.

In contrast, Julie had a large suitcase, her handbag and a carry bag, despite the warning Cassandra had given her about packing lightly so that she could be able to fit any new purchases from Paris back to Australia. Similarly, she had opted to look casual but stylish and wore a pair of skinny beige chinos, a tomato-coloured trench coat, and a pair of cool, black, studded flat shoes that slightly clashed with the elegance of the outfit.

"I'm surprised you could join us. I mean, I'm surprised you haven't got any other commitments such as work or family. It's very spontaneous and even brave to decide to come along with us," said Jenny.

James clarified. "She means it's brave of you because a lot of people wouldn't dare take time away from their routines. That's all she meant by that."

"I think I know what I meant. You don't need to speak for me, James. You know, Scott was right. We are beginning to sound like a married couple. Where is Scott anyway? He's the one who told us to be here early. I hope he didn't have to do any last minute changes to the system again. He's always on call."

"You're definitely right about not being a morning person. Somehow I don't think Julie's moods will be as bad as yours. If she gets too difficult to live with, feel free to join me for those early morning walks," James offered, looking apologetically at Julie.

"Anyway, Julie, back to my question. What I meant to say was that we're all at some juncture in our lives. Well, apart from James. The main reason he wants to go to Paris is because of the Tour de France. He made sure our plans coincided with the race. You must be going through some type of transition in your life as well, to take Scott up on his offer."

"I just felt that ..."

"Stop grilling the girl. We have three weeks to catch up. Why she's here isn't important now. Where the hell is Scott? Now *that's* important. We'll never even get there at this rate."

As if on cue, Scott appeared. "I'm right here, James my friend. I'm sorry to say, but you are beginning to sound a lot like Jenny."

"That will never happen. I have too much optimism and I see only the good in the world. I wasn't worried about you being late. Mate, you know me. I always know I can count on you to be on time. It's that job of yours that worried us though. They expect you to carry your mobile 24/7. Humans aren't supposed to be chained up like that. They need to be free and come and go as they please."

"Don't worry about me, James. I don't mind getting called every now and then, as long as the whole system doesn't crash. Anyway, for the next three weeks, I'm officially on holidays, and that means no work interruptions." He suddenly turned and looked at Julie. He automatically put his arm on her shoulder and looked at his friends. "So, I see you've reacquainted yourselves with m—, I mean, with Julie?"

Julie looked at James and Jenny as they awkwardly looked at Scott. She was sure that they were thinking what she was thinking. She was almost positive that Scott was about to refer to her as "my Julie". She also noticed that he still had his hand on her shoulder, and she was conscious that James and Jenny were also aware of it. For that moment, it felt like old times. It was as though Scott and Julie were together, and James and Jenny were joining them. The reality however, was that it was really Scott, Jenny and James going somewhere, while Julie was joining them.

"Well, we better go and check our bags in. Julie I've got your ticket right here." He waved the ticket in the air and gave her a warm smile.

How was he still able to do that to her? How was he able to make her heart flutter with just one smile?

James and Jenny expertly took the lead and headed towards the specific terminal which indicated that it was for all flights to Singapore.

Scott eyed Julie's luggage and started laughing. "I forgot how meticulous you are. I remember when we went to the Australian Open tennis finals. Your suitcase was nearly as big as this one, and it was only for two days," he said.

"Well, it was in Melbourne, and you know how the weather changes so sporadically there. One minute it's forty degrees, the next thing you know, the temperature is in the low twenties." Julie replied. He smiled at her as she finished her sentence. Although he was smiling, his eyes became deep with thought. She realised that he would often look at her in that way.

"Scott," she found herself saying. "Scott. There's something I want to tell you."

125

"Not now, Julie," he said, gently. "We have three weeks together. We can talk then. Now let's go and make this trip finally happen. We owe it to ourselves. It's what we had planned."

He grabbed her luggage before she could talk. "Interesting choice," he added, catching a glimpse of her shoes. "I love that," he continued with a smile, as he leaned up and led her towards the terminal. "It will be okay," he reassured her as they made their way to James and Jenny.

"Please, Scott. I hope everything turns out to be more than okay. We do owe it to ourselves and I am so sorry for ever doubting you, for doubting us." They were the words Julie desperately wanted Scott to hear, but she would have to wait until they had some privacy. At least for the meantime, Jenny and James were being very amicable and accepting of her, and they didn't seem to harbour any resentment towards her.

Julie's heart was racing. There was a familiar feeling in her heart, a feeling she hadn't felt for years but one that she was recently being reacquainted with, as it persistently made its welcome presence in her life. She knew exactly what it was. It was passion for fun, adventure, for life and for striving to achieve what she wanted out of it.

There was another feeling that had also been missing in her life. That feeling was hope. She felt optimistic about the present and the future. She also felt optimistic about love. She felt that she could have it all. The difference was that her heart was now open to the possibility. A few weeks ago, she would never have accepted Scott's offer, convincing herself that he didn't really mean it: that he was just being nice. She was sick of doing the responsible thing.

She looked over at Scott, sitting next to her. Their seat belts were securely fastened. He had kindly offered her the window seat. Jenny was on the other side of him. James, over the aisle, had also volunteered his seat to Julie with a cheeky smile covering the entirety of his face. They were about to take off. The A380 commenced its departure, going slowly at first then suddenly picking up speed. She could feel the wheels rolling on the runway. Julie's heart was beating with excitement. She wasn't sure if it was due to the aircraft moving so vigorously as it picked up speed, or if it was due to Scott suddenly squeezing her hand. He was looking at her. This is what they had talked about all those years ago, as they spent countless precious hours in each other's company. With one sudden jolt, the plane took off and was airborne.

Scott was still looking at her, his smile fading for a second, and then re-emerging when Julie's smile grew wider, as she surrendered to the adrenalin.

She looked outside the window and rested her head back into her seat. She could now leave everything behind her and begin a whole new journey, literally and figuratively. The world was awaiting and it was full of endless possibilities. It was up to her to embrace them.

CHAPTER EIGHTEEN

They landed in London after having changed planes in Singapore. Scott informed Julie on the plane that they would also stay in London for two days.

"Sorry, I can't believe I forgot to tell you. There was so much to do and so little time. I'm sure you don't mind, though. I mean you always had the travel bug and a sense of adventure. I'm glad to see that you still haven't lost that about you. It was obvious when the plane took off. Your smile said it all Julie … I remember you always thrived when you embarked on something new. I mean you joined practically every club back at uni," he said, looking at her affectionately, gently stroking her hair away from her face as he spoke. Julie's heart felt as though it was melting. His touch was so soft and sensual; his eyes so deep with emotion. He had observed her reaction on the plane. Julie could feel that there was still something there between them: the way he touched her, the intense look in his eyes — it was all slowly coming back to him, the way it was for her.

The streets of London were full of traffic and packed with pedestrians crossing busy roads, waiting at bus stops, or at crossings. As they sat inside the hired car on their way to their hotel, they had a chance to see different aspects of the city. The first thing Julie commented on were the old chimneys on the roofs of buildings and houses. There were so many chimneys. James explained that people back in the 17th and 18th centuries used to have a fire place in every room, and that they were actually taxed for how many chimneys they had. She also looked with interest at all the red double-decker buses, and the many black cabs.

James had been to London on many occasions and took on the role of tour guide. "Our hotel is situated in the West End, in a street called The Strand, in the heart of London. It runs from Trafalgar Square to Fleet Street, so it will be easy to see the many tourist attractions in two days on foot, without the need for public transport," he stated. "That's the best way to get a feel for the place anyway," he added.

Julie felt that she would be hearing that a lot throughout their trip. She marvelled at the beauty of the city. The enormity of the statues and buildings was humbling. She wondered where Buckingham Palace and Hyde Park were. She quickly took her camera out of her handbag, suddenly feeling as though she might miss capturing something significant if she didn't have it on hand.

"Isn't this exciting, Scott?" Julie asked, looking at him, genuinely wanting to know his thoughts. "I mean, we're actually in London. Can you believe it?"

"What I can't believe, Julie, is that I'm sitting here with you," he responded, looking at her with a serious expression. He quickly looked away again, clearly not wanting to stay with the moment. That sadness in his deep, brown eyes seemed to be there again.

Oh Scott, Julie thought. *I'm so sorry for having doubted you and moving on so quickly.*

"Well, this is your hotel," the driver stated as they pulled up. "You chose a great spot. It's easy to walk to all the tourist attractions from here."

"I know," James said, proudly.

They had pulled into another busy street which was buzzing with activity. Boutique shops stretched up both sides of the road. Crowds of people clustered upon the footpaths and roads, all looking extremely busy, talking on their phones, carrying shopping bags or walking fast to get to their destination. There were so many people. Julie felt that they were walking even quicker than they did in Sydney. A cab beeped impatiently as commuters crossed the road after exiting one of the many double-decker buses that was once again full with people — many having filled the narrow spaces within seconds of it being empty. The noise of the buses filled the air. Julie breathed in the city — the smell and noise seemed to keep it alive, feeding it with energy. She could feel its energy. It did look like a great location. She couldn't wait to see the hotel. As much as she loved contemporary settings, she hoped that it would be grand and full of history.

Julie's impression of the hotel lived up to her expectations. It was grand and opulent. "Nothing but the best," James boasted. "We're not uni students anymore."

"This is your room, ladies," James announced in an English accent.

"Why, thank you, kind sir," Jenny responded.

"We'll meet you both downstairs in around an hour, if that's all right with you. We can start by taking a walk and …"

"… getting a feel for the place," Julie and Jenny chimed in, while Scott tried to suppress his laughter as he handed them their key.

"See you in an hour," Jenny and Julie called out as they opened the door to what was to be their home for the next two days.

It was a glorious day. Julie expected grey skies and rain, but in contrast, it was a sunny day and quite hot. They decided to commence their tour of London by walking towards Buckingham Palace, and then see where that would lead them. Before they knew it, they were in yet another busy street.

"Wow," Julie marvelled. "It's Big Ben!" She quickly took out her camera, ready to take a photo.

"You're one of those people, aren't you?" James asked.

"Which people?" Julie asked, defensively.

"The ones that want to capture every moment of their trip."

"James believes that stopping to take photos ruins the flow of the experience. It ruins the moment, so to speak," Scott volunteered.

"But what if I want the moment to last forever? I mean, what if I'm enjoying the moment so much that I want to capture it, so I can remember it on a long-term basis? Besides, it's not as though I'm addicted to taking selfies."

Scott looked at Julie and laughed. Meanwhile, James and Jenny continued walking as a vintage car caught their attention.

"Why are you laughing at me?"

"I don't know. I just feel like laughing when I'm with you. Your enthusiasm is amazing. In fact, it's infectious. Give me the camera. I'll take a photo of you."

"I'll take a photo of both of you. It's difficult to take photos as a couple when you're on vacation," a woman dressed in cargo pants and a backpack, standing nearby, volunteered.

"Okay," Julie awkwardly said. They both stood on the busy street, people scurrying hastily around them. Scott moved close to Julie and wrapped his arm around her waist. She instantly felt his strong arm around her. The slightly loose, cotton fabric of the summer dress she had changed into caressed her skin with every slight movement of his hand. He had changed into a grey T-shirt, exposing his toned arms. As Julie continued to look at the camera, she felt Scott's arm brush the skin of her own. Her knees felt weak from his touch as the woman tried to get as many angles of Big Ben as she could.

"There, that one should be great. Big Ben is definitely in the photo and you two look great in it as well. You look good together."

"Thanks," Julie said slightly embarrassed, as the woman handed her camera back to her and walked off. Julie looked at the photo and couldn't help but agree. "We do look good together," she acknowledged. Scott was leaning his head close to hers, and was hugging her tightly. They both had smiles on their faces.

Scott and Julie picked up the pace as they tried to catch up with James and Jenny.

Before they knew it, they were at St James Park. They walked through a path lined with rows of old-style, cast iron lamp posts. Julie gasped with surprise as she noticed a few squirrels scurrying along the lush, freshly mowed, green grass.

"We might as well walk through this park, since it's named after me," James said with a laugh.

It was a beautiful looking park, and a beautiful day. Julie still couldn't believe that this was all happening. She was in London and she was with Scott. As they stepped onto the slightly moist grass, they all began to comment on the variety of bird life, including geese, pelicans, and ducks. The ponds were lovely and peaceful. Shadows from tree branches were reflected in the calming ripples that were created by elegant swans and ducks. All of a sudden she felt like enjoying a picnic lunch, and basking in the gentle sunlight, as many around her were doing.

"Why don't we sit and have a picnic? This park is so peaceful and beautiful," she suggested.

"That's a great idea," Jenny stated, without hesitation. "I need to rejuvenate before I get a feel for the city."

"Okay …" James said, with apprehension in his voice. It was as if he was in a race and the pace he had set for himself had been abruptly interrupted.

"James. Since you're feeling so energetic, why don't we go and buy some lunch? You know the city anyway. I'd love to try an English pie," Scott said.

Before too long, James and Scott returned, carrying trays piled high with sandwiches, pies, wedges, salad and drinks. It looked as if they had bought the whole shop.

"How much food did you get?" Jenny gasped.

After the formalities had been finalised, they all sat back and enjoyed the scenery of the park. It was glorious. Children were playing in a play area nearby. Sweet-smelling, fragrant flowers were in full bloom all around them, and they could hear music from a marching band, which seemed to be coming from the direction of Buckingham Palace.

"So Julie, what have you been up to with your life?" Jenny asked.

Before Julie could find the words to answer, she caught Scott's attention abruptly being diverted from his task of opening his bottled water, to her.

"Nothing much, to tell you the truth," Julie answered modestly, looking at her turkey and cranberry club sandwich as she spoke. "I've been working for an insurance company for a few years, living in North Sydney, and now I'm officially unemployed." She couldn't believe how simple and pedestrian her life sounded in one sentence.

James and Jenny seemed to be oblivious to her sudden feelings of vulnerability. That all changed when she met Scott's gaze. Julie was positive that she heard a "mmm" sound emanating from his mouth. It was as though he could sense how vulnerable and exposed she felt.

Unable to look at him anymore, her eyes became fixated on the children playing. She somehow felt that she had let him down. It was as if the wide-eyed girl she was at uni had been replaced with a toned-down version who was far less interesting.

"So what are you going to do now?" he asked, gently. "It's a great time to explore your options and think about what you really want to do."

"Yes, I guess it is."

"Not what *others* want you to do," he stated, with a serious look on his face. "I mean, after all, *you* control your life, don't you?"

The atmosphere suddenly became tense.

"Everyone controls their own life. That's the motto I live my life by. It's the only way to truly be free," James interjected, breaking the intense atmosphere with his light-hearted tone.

"What about relationships? Are you seeing anyone at the moment?" Jenny continued.

She was obviously not going to give up. Unlike her sister, though, Jenny's directness had no agenda.

Julie instinctively looked at Scott. He was now looking into the distance. His jaw was tight, and the flexed muscles in his arms were tense.

"No, I'm not in a serious relationship at the moment. In fact, I haven't been in a serious relationship since …" Julie paused and swallowed, "… for a while."

She looked at Scott. He was now looking down at the grass. He wouldn't meet her gaze.

"So, what about you, Scott? What made you get into the IT industry?" she found herself asking. She was genuinely interested in his response, and had wanted to ask him on the plane. However, their time had been taken up with small talk, watching movies, drinking Martinis and listening to music. After a long pause, he finally answered.

"I guess I liked the certainty that came with computers. I mean, there's always a way to alleviate problems by using specific commands and programs. You always know where you stand with computers. There's no ambiguity."

Julie was taken aback by his response. "So what happened to working in a non-government organisation?"

"I did for a while. I worked for an organisation that dealt with human rights. It was challenging, but it was also frustrating. I found it difficult to tear down walls that had already been built. Besides, I didn't feel that I was at a good place myself to fight for justice. I mean, I sort of lost hope for just causes for a while. Anyway, when an opportunity came my way to join the IT industry, I took it. I was self-taught, but I also completed a few training courses. I find it challenging. The money isn't bad either, I guess."

A sense of guilt tore through Julie's heart. She looked at her iced tea not knowing how to react.

"I enjoy what I'm doing now. It's good to keep things fresh and challenge yourself. Nothing is set in stone. We can change direction whenever we choose. That's what you're doing now, aren't you, Julie?"

Julie couldn't answer. She was holding her iced tea as if it would shield her from the hurt.

Suddenly, she felt Scott's hand on her shoulder. "Julie, I guess what I'm trying to say is that IT was the right move for me at that point in my life."

She finally looked at him. "Scott. Many people feel the way you do. They spend years looking for answers and lose their way in the process. Sometimes, the answers they find are not what they expected."

He was now looking at her with a puzzled expression on his face. He finally spoke. "Perhaps they won't be. There's always an explanation, I guess. People need to be given a chance before anyone jumps to conclusions," he continued, the meaning behind his message becoming more obvious as he spoke. "That's the only way to find justice."

For a moment, no one said anything. Julie broke the awkward silence by diverting her attention to Jenny and James, who had clearly finished their lunch, and were now staring at them. James suddenly made a strange sound, as he made an attempt to speak. He cleared his throat, and awkwardly decided to take charge of the situation.

"Okay. Does anyone want any more salad, or wedges, or half of the fish pie? They're the only answers I need right now."

"No thanks," everyone replied.

"We'd better get going. We don't want to waste the rest of the day. Do you think you feel rejuvenated now?" James continued, starting to pack all the trays, whilst looking at Jenny.

"Oh. I don't think we wasted any part of the day. In fact, I think it has been a very productive lunch. Thanks for your concern, James. I feel very rejuvenated. Don't you guys?"

Scott and Julie looked searchingly into each other's eyes. They didn't reply.

CHAPTER NINETEEN

They spent the rest of the day doing touristy things. They took many, many photos outside Buckingham Palace, much to James' dismay. First, they concentrated on the gold and black cast iron gates, which were enormous to say the least. They looked so small standing next to them. Julie gazed in awe at the impressive gold statue of Queen Victoria that stood in front of the palace. Then they stared at the palace's countless windows, hoping they might see a glimpse of royalty. They were all amazed at how patient and focused the guards were, and tried to be just as patient when they waited for the changing of the guard. They also took a walk around nearby Hyde Park, which was just as lovely as Julie expected.

A huge, magnificent, white marble structure with intricate carvings stood alone, encapsulating grandeur and empowerment, commanding attention.

"It's the Marble Arch!" Julie cried.

"That's the one, and it's right at the western end of Oxford Street," James replied.

"Oxford Street! One of the most popular, crowded streets in London — famous for its shopping!" Julie cried again. She knew all about the big name chain stores, most of them being of the high street variety, not to mention a few of the big department stores.

Scott was looking at Julie as though she was from another planet.

"What?" she asked. "Don't think I don't know about your sneaky expedition to Tottenham Court Road while Jenny and I were freshening up. I know the type of shops that are found there — those of the electronic variety perhaps?" she teased. "James said he couldn't get you out of there."

"Not to mention the many pubs," Scott interjected, smiling.

They continued their tour and took photos outside Westminster Abbey. Scott had laughed when he saw how many photos she was taking.

The mood between them had once again become playful and light. The tension from lunchtime had subsided. They were all tourists and behaved as such, marvelling at everything they saw from the pristine parks, to the beautiful buildings that still had their original brickwork intact. They laughed like teenagers as they took individual photos in the old red telephone booths. Even James began to embrace the tourist mentality, giving in and agreeing to be included in the many photos they all took together.

They all finally acknowledged that they were exhausted, and agreed to go back to the hotel and unwind, and then go out to dinner at one of the many nearby pubs.

The break gave Julie an opportunity to call home.

"Yes, Mum. I'm all right. Don't worry, it's wonderful here. We had to stop over in London, so James thought it would be a great chance to see some of the city."

"James! Who's James? Who are you actually with? Do you think it's wise to travel with people you don't really know Julie? We are all so worried about you. This isn't like you."

"Actually Mum, it's exactly like me. You're just not use to seeing the real me. I even forgot who that person is. To answer your question, yes, I do know these people. Didn't I tell you they are friends from uni? You don't need to worry. I know what I'm doing. Remember what I said about you trusting me, and having faith in me?"

"Well, yes, of course I trust you … actually you're right. You know what you're doing. I'm sorry. I know you wouldn't do anything foolish. It's just that it was all so sudden. You're right, however. You need to follow your dreams and why should anyone stand in your way?

Actually, I'm really proud and excited for you, Julie. I always wanted my girls to follow their dreams, and embrace the world."

Julie's frustration towards her mother once again turned into surprise. Her mother's encouragement was touching. Julie suddenly wondered what Christina would be thinking about her being overseas. She would definitely have an opinion on it, considering that not only was she without a husband, but also to her dismay, out of work as well. Julie decided that she didn't care what Christina or anyone thought. That was the old Julie's mentality.

"I can't believe you're in London with Scott. How is he? Did you tell him what happened yet? Be sure to tell us everything when you do. Before you hang up, Stacey called and she wanted to know where you were. She said she wanted to plan a work reunion. She couldn't believe you were overseas. She said that she couldn't wait to tell George. She said something about him not believing her. Anyway, bye Julie. Make sure you keep in touch."

Julie hadn't been able to get a word in edgewise when she had talked with Maria. She was puzzled by her mention of Stacey telling George about her being overseas. Julie found it odd that she would be a topic of conversation. Surely, they would have other things on their minds, such as finding a job, especially Stacey, with her financial woes. She then began to think of the gift that George had given her. She couldn't understand why he chose the beautiful bird as a gift. In fact, she still couldn't believe he had bought her a gift in the first place. Was there a message in it? Current trends in home décor did focus on nature, she reasoned, remembering an article in one of the many interior design magazines she had recently purchased. The kind words he had written to her in the card … she couldn't believe they were from *George* of all people. Julie made a mental note to thank him.

"Are you ready for another heavy meal? I can't believe how much we're eating already. I was planning to eat healthy on this trip. The last thing I want is for my students to think I'm a hypocrite. At this rate, I'll go back to work looking like I haven't exercised at all."

"Don't worry, Jenny. We can eat healthy in Paris," Julie responded with a smile, knowing full well that that would be almost impossible to achieve.

"Yes. There's nothing tempting to eat in Paris. No fresh pastries, bread with chocolate, and the French don't use much butter in their cooking," Jenny added, sarcastically. "We'd better be off. I'm sure Scott can't wait to see you."

Julie looked at Jenny. Jenny hadn't mentioned Scott to her during their time alone.

"Don't look so shocked. You know what I'm referring to. I'm sure you two have a lot to discuss. I know it has been difficult so far, but I'm sure you'll get your alone time. James will be obsessed with the race when we get to Paris. I'm sure he'll expect me to tag along."

"Jenny, did Scott say anything to you?" Julie asked, matching her directness.

"Look, Julie, I'm sure Scott will tell you everything when you get the chance to be alone with him. I was just stating the obvious, which is that you do have a lot to talk about after what happened between you two. James and I know that so many things were left unsaid. Anyway, we'd better go and meet the boys. If you haven't noticed, as carefree as James thinks he is, he does get impatient when it comes to waiting."

"Sure," Julie responded, her mind working overtime. It was almost like Jenny didn't want to reveal anything she wasn't supposed to. She had mentioned that "Scott will tell you everything" but wasn't he waiting for *her* to tell *him* everything?

Julie closed the heavy door of the hotel suite behind her, taking a deep breath. "Just go with the flow," she told herself. She would not go back home without having a chance to explain everything to him.

Julie's heart suddenly ached as she followed Jenny down the blue-carpeted, grand corridor. She came to a halt as she saw a familiar, beautiful face, with warm caring, deep brown eyes walking slowly towards her. She just stared at him. She was about to grab his hand and take him somewhere private to tell him how sorry she was. He was looking at her, oblivious to everything around him. It was as though they were communicating without words.

"Mark, Mark! You forgot your keys."

The intimacy between them was gone, replaced by an awkward silence as they both watched a woman waving and calling out frantically to a man heading towards the elevator.

"Mark. You forgot your key. I might go for a walk while you're gone."

Scott looked down at his feet, his jaw tightening the same way it had tightened that afternoon.

"Let's go. I'm hungry," he said to no one in particular, as he eyed the elevator and the man in front of him, whose only crime was that he shared the same name as the man from Julie's past.

"Let's go," James said, patting Scott on the back.

Julie walked towards the elevator with heavy legs. She hoped the mood would change quickly. For the first time she felt like an outsider. If that wasn't bad enough, the stranger named Mark was also innocently standing next to Scott, key in hand, acknowledging all of them as he questioned if they were going to the ground floor.

Yes. We are definitely going down, way down, Julie acknowledged to herself, realising it may have been wise to have had that talk before they had agreed to vacation together.

Jenny's reassuring smile eased the uncertainty she felt for a moment, but then she took a look at Scott's square raised, broad shoulders, and his sullen mood, and she

141

knew that it would take a lot more than a pint to alleviate the tension between them. She was finding out that the carefree and forgiving Scott that she had run into a week ago had a lot of built up anguish embedded deep within his soul. The façade was beginning to reveal a few cracks, and there was no telling when the first big piece would break. As they made their way out of the elevator, out of the hotel, and into the busy London streets, Julie hoped that once that hurt came to the surface, there would also be room for forgiveness and understanding.

CHAPTER TWENTY

It had been another adventurous day in London. They started the day walking along The Strand, the street where they were staying, and stumbled upon Australia House, which they found hiding behind a row of trees. James, their self-appointed tour guide, also thought it would be a good idea to venture into Trafalgar Square since it was close by and they didn't have much time left. They walked slowly through the massive space. Water flowing from the fountains created a tranquil atmosphere, as many enjoyed the morning sunlight, looking extremely chilled. Julie took photos of Nelson's column, and the four gigantic bronze lion statues which guarded it, as well as the National Gallery. "Come on Julie!" they all had shouted, as she walked back to take another look at the lion statues. She hurried back to the rest of the group, and continued looking back. There was definitely a relaxed atmosphere in the centre of Trafalgar Square as office workers, tourists and Londoners took a break, sitting on the huge steps as they listened to a woman singing and a musician playing a violin.

As they walked from Trafalgar Square, along the Strand, they ended up in Covent Garden. The streets and buildings reminded Julie of The Rocks in Sydney, where a British influence was prominent. Similarly, there were markets selling creative, beautiful things – including artworks – and many street performers welcomed crowds. It had a relaxed feel to it. Julie had once again fallen behind from the others as she admired the unusual homewares. Scott had walked back to her when he had noticed this: "Julie, I don't want to lose you," he whispered in her ear and then gave her a warm smile as he took her hand in his. "You won't," she said, looking up into his sincere, almost vulnerable eyes. She felt her heart beating fast when the smooth skin of his fingers touched hers, and they continued walking on the cobblestone footpaths hand in hand, keeping their eyes on James and Jenny in front of them. *You won't lose me, Scott*, she repeated to herself; *Not this time.*

They walked to the River Thames, where they took countless photos of the London Eye, and caught a glimpse of the business district on the other side.

"Isn't that the Gherkin building?" Julie asked, with excitement building up in her voice.

"It's really called 30 St Mary Axe," Scott answered, with a warm smile. Everything was all right between them again. The tension they had felt back at the hotel was gone, for the time being anyway.

Similarly, the mood at dinner the night before had been jovial and light. Julie couldn't help but notice that Scott had touched her hand affectionately several times, when she made a comment on certain topics which made all of them laugh hysterically.

"Julie, I forgot how witty you are. I can't stop laughing!" Jenny had commented, as Julie convincingly imitated one of their government lecturers. "You look so innocent but you have such a wicked wit, in a good way that is."

"I remember how she made me laugh during our uni lectures. She would comment on everything the lecturer was saying, picking on how boring his tone was, or how his tie didn't match. I was about to get kicked out one day when I started laughing uncontrollably," Scott had added, laughing as though he was back in the lecture theatre. "Remember when you offered me Maltesers in one of our Government lectures, and the whole packet fell to the floor? Everyone was looking at us as they rolled down the steps of the lecture theatre, and some of them landed at the feet of the lecturer!"

"We were both in stitches from laughing. What did the lecturer call us then?" Julie had asked.

"He actually called us juvenile delinquents, and told us that we should still be in high school," Scott replied, laughing hysterically at the memory, while placing his hand on her knee.

"I was humiliated at the time, but I couldn't stop laughing. We both had to leave the lecture because we couldn't help ourselves," Julie had stated, matching Scott's laughter.

"We had great times together, you and I," he had replied, giving her a look that made her feel warm all over.

To her surprise, she had found herself stroking a strand of hair out of his eyes, the same way he had done when he ran into her. He looked just as surprised. Scott's face had instantly become serious. Julie remembered feeling embarrassed after having realised how intimate her gesture had been, and she had tried desperately to digress by commenting on a man wearing a strange hat near them. The only problem was that the hat wasn't so strange. Julie had caught Scott looking at her with a knowing smile on his face. He had definitely felt something when she touched his face. She had too, but the more she tried to be direct and proactive, the more afraid she felt when she received any kind of signal from him.

So much for taking chances, she had thought to herself. She didn't even know how to initiate the conversation she wanted to have with him. Part of her knew that she was procrastinating. If she really wanted to, she would have already organised to spend some time with him alone. Deep down, she knew she was afraid to get her answers. It would all be too real and final if things didn't turn out the way she wanted.

"Why don't we go to Piccadilly Square?" James suggested, interrupting Julie's thoughts, as they all sat on a bench to rest for a while.

"We just sat down," Scott protested.

"I'm disappointed with you, Scott. What happened to the active, adventurous Scott I used to know?"

"That Scott didn't have many responsibilities, except an exam here and there. I've had so many things I had to take care of before I left Sydney. I was also working flat out at work."

"I told you, they work you too hard. You should get a freelance job like me. I write when I feel like it. It keeps me creative."

"James, I told you I like my job. I know it can be demanding at times, but I love challenges."

"I think you are definitely protesting too much," James retorted.

Scott just grinned, and then held his arms up. "Okay, I give up. I can't stand my job. You're right. I should get in the freelance game like you."

Julie laughed at Scott's attempt to get James off his back. She was curious however as to what the "so many things'" he was referring to were.

"Why don't we go for a short walk around Piccadilly Square, and then we can relax for the day?" Julie suggested. "Well, after we also go to Oxford Street that is."

"We could also go to Regent Street," James added.

"We could have organised to stay longer," Jenny interjected. "Then, we wouldn't be so tired, trying to fit in everything in the space of two days.

"Yes, we could have, Jenny, but do you really want to miss one of the best sporting events, which is happening as we speak?"

"That's right! You're not even seeing the entire race because it's spread out into many regions of France, and its neighbouring countries. They'll cross the finish line in Paris, at the Champs-Elysées, in the final stage, which is on the last week of our trip anyway."

"Yes Jenny, but do you know how exciting the atmosphere in Paris will be, as everyone waits to see the final stage of the race? It's intoxicating!"

"Well, in that case, let's see how intoxicating Piccadilly Square is. Maybe we'll be able to taste the atmosphere and get drunk on it," Jenny said, teasingly.

"You can tease me all you like, but you will all thank me later. You'll all see what I mean. It all happens in Paris!"

CHAPTER TWENTY-ONE

Julie stepped out of the hire car and onto the narrow footpath of the Parisian street. Wide-eyed, she gazed in wonderment at all the old cream-painted apartment buildings with their identical wrought-iron Juliet balconies. Scott and James helped the driver unload the luggage. Julie grabbed one of her bags and began to walk up the ascending street, noticing a charming cafe at the top end corner as she walked.

She had been caught up in the excitement of it all. She felt like crying from joy when they were waiting for their driver at Charles de Gaulle airport.

"*Merci*," she heard Scott say to the driver behind her.

"Well, here it is, our home for the next few weeks," James said as they stood in front of the entrance of the grand, cream-coloured building. They followed him inside as a doorman opened the heavy, gold-handle, glass door. The delicate scent of French pear immediately welcomed them, perfuming the hotel foyer. Everything made an impression on Julie, from the old paintings on the walls, to the polished marble floor, and the elegant chairs: the whole provincial French look. It was the look she had tried to emulate in the terrace house that she shared with Maria and Cassandra. She had successfully blended French antiques with some contemporary pieces, and it somehow worked, as everyone who visited would tell her.

Julie looked over at the old elevator that would take them to their hotel suite. Its black, cast iron door had so much character. She then walked over to the tea room and admired the cerulean blue panelled walls, and elegant heavy curtains that draped the old windows. Paintings in antique gold frames covered the walls.

"Beautiful, isn't it?" Scott asked her as he entered the opulent room. James was right behind him.

"Looks like there's a mix up with the rooms," he announced. "There's no point for all of us to wait. It will be a while. They haven't even cleaned the rooms that we've booked yet. You guys can go. Jenny and I will sort it out," he added, quickly. "Just go and enjoy Paris," he insisted.

"Well, in that case, why don't we go for a walk and explore the neighbourhood? We're right near the Champs-Elysées, you know?" Scott suggested, turning to Julie when James left the room.

"Why not?" she said, happily.

Julie was amazed when she found out how close they were to the Champs-Elysées, one of the most famous shopping strips in the world. As they walked slowly, taking in everything around them, she couldn't help but notice how many dogs had left evidence that they had been around. A cabbage had escaped from one of the many over-filled bins, its rotten leaves spilling onto the footpath. Julie didn't mind the smell. She thought it added to the authentic charm. The street they were walking in contained a humble little grocery shop, and a few small coffee shops.

Soon they had realised that they weren't walking in the direction of the Champs-Elysées, but into a beautiful street lined with many traditional French luxury boutique apartments which led to a lovely park called Parc Monceau. They walked past a group of women pushing designer prams, and made their way into the park from the second massive black and gold wrought iron gate, which contained a section that also housed a few more boutique apartments. They walked casually and admired some statues and Ancient Greek-influenced columns near the sunlit pond.

"Remember how excited we both were when we had planned to visit the Louvre one day," Scott asked. "Now, we finally get our chance to see it together," he added, looking at Julie, his eyes squinting slightly in the warm sunlight.

They walked towards a quiet, shady area and sat on a bench near a flower bed full of white roses. "It was our dream," Julie said looking at him as they sat. "I wonder which paintings we'll see. I've always loved Renoir. You know I actually went to a Renoir exhibition in Sydney. I like a lot of the French impressionist paintings," Julie continued, her smile growing wider, as she imagined how exciting it would be to stand in the actual museum.

Julie looked at Scott when he didn't respond. His expression had changed. Julie could tell that he wasn't in the mood to talk about impressionism, expressionism, or anything else about art. He was silent and thoughtful as he looked at her. He then looked at her bracelet, and gently placed his hand around her wrist. Julie instantly felt the smoothness of his skin on hers.

"I bought it here," she said.

He continued studying the unusual piece, touching each gold-plated charm, half-smiling to himself. He then looked deep into her eyes.

"Is everything okay Scott?" she asked him, as his smile slowly faded. "Why are you looking at me like that?" she continued nervously when he didn't respond.

"It's just … I don't know, hearing you talk with such passion … it brings back memories … sweet, beautiful memories. I remember everything about you Julie, who you always strived to be …" he glanced at the bracelet again before looking back at her. "Your smile … it's so freaking beautiful. *You're* so beautiful Julie, and sweet, and smart," he said, caressing her face with his hand. "It's as though time has stood still … that five years didn't pass between us."

Julie couldn't speak. His brown eyes almost looked black as they looked at her with intense emotion. They looked slightly teary, as they stared searchingly into hers.

"I … I just love talking about things that inspire me …" she stumbled, speaking quickly, her nerves taking hold as her heart raced.

He took his hand away from her face as she completed her sentence and stared at the ground, his demeanour changing instantly. "You like things that inspire you …" he said, as his face gave way to a half-hearted smile. "Who do you think you're talking to Julie? I mean, you'd think we were strangers." He turned again and looked straight into her eyes. "Didn't you hear a word I said? I know so much about you … how could I not? I mean, how did we even get here Julie? One minute you're in my bed …"

Julie looked down at the grass. She couldn't look at his intense, questioning eyes anymore.

He then abruptly stood up and took a few steps away from her. He vigorously combed his fingers through his hair and pulled it away from his face, as if he was bothered by it. He then turned around, his whole body tense with frustration. Julie couldn't believe what was happening. Without a second thought, he walked towards her. She stood up without thinking. He pulled her towards him and began to kiss her passionately. Julie responded with the same urgency, kissing him intensely, as his slightly hard lips guided hers. Feeling lightheaded, she ran her fingers through his soft hair as she felt his hands stroking the sides of her waist. Her heart was beating so fast. Their lips finally parted. Julie felt tears streaming down her face, as they both stood there taking quick, heavy breaths.

He abruptly broke away from her and stood with his back towards her and his arms on his hips, breathing deeply. Julie felt afraid of what he would say to her. He finally turned around and looked at her.

"What happened, Julie?" he asked her, his voice slightly loud. "What happened?" he asked her again. "Why Julie? Why did everything go so wrong? Why? I don't understand it."

He was shouting now, but he lowered his voice slightly, as a few passers-by glanced their way, interrupting their quiet space. "For years I tried to make sense of everything, but I'm still just as confused as ever. All I know is that one minute everything was fine between us and then …"

"Scott, please let me explain everything. It was all a tragic misunderstanding. I felt the same as you did for years but I got the answers I needed. Please just, sit down and let me explain."

Scott interjected. "I keep replaying the last night we were together. We were so happy together. I felt so connected to you. I couldn't wait to see you again. All I kept thinking the next day was when your exam would be over so that we could see each other again. I trusted you so much. I thought you felt the same way. How could I be so wrong about you? How could you have betrayed me so easily?"

"Scott. I can explain everything. I know I hurt you, but at the time I thought you had hurt me too. Tanya explained everything to me. It was a misunderstanding. You knew that I wasn't the type of girl to jump into a relationship without being sure that I was making the right choice. You were the only guy that I felt sure about. I wanted everything to be feel right, and it did, for over two and a half years, it was wonderful … it wasn't what you think with Mark, I thought you had betrayed me!"

Scott looked perplexed. "When did you speak to Tanya? That doesn't matter. I can't believe you just said you felt so close to me. You moved on with another guy in the space of, what was it, two, three weeks? You looked like you were so affectionate with each other. What I never understood is how I could be so wrong about you. When we had met, you took it slow with me and I respected that. So please explain how the hell you could jump into another relationship so quickly? I wanted to hate you when I saw you that night in Newtown. I tried so hard to hate you, but then I kept remembering how good we were together. I couldn't believe you were the same person."

"Scott. Please. Listen to me. Tanya explained everything to me. I got in touch with her after I ran into you." She reached out and held his hand. "Please, just sit and let me explain," she pleaded.

He looked at her and slowly followed her cue, sitting beside her. "I know what you're going to tell me. It's what both Tanya and I knew all along. Someone saw us kissing at the cafeteria."

Julie stumbled for a second, not knowing how she would explain what she saw in a way that would justify her actions. "I saw you, Scott. I saw you with my own eyes." Julie suddenly started feeling angry again at the memory of him and Tanya. She remembered what she felt at the time. "You were both kissing each other so passionately." Her voice got louder. "I had never seen a man so into a kiss. You were holding her hair so firmly, as if you couldn't contain your desire for her. I saw it with my own eyes Scott," she added, her voice becoming softer.

"You saw us kissing? You had an exam."

"It finished earlier than I thought. The point is, I saw you, Scott. I couldn't believe my eyes. I was trembling all over. I didn't know what to think. I couldn't believe that you would hurt me so cruelly with my best friend, especially after the night we spent together. Through my eyes, the two people I trusted had betrayed me. I felt so stupid and naïve. I saw you kissing my best friend! I mean, what was I to think? All sorts of things went through my mind. I even thought you were hurt and frustrated because I wanted to focus on my studies instead of being with you. I just wanted to run from what I had witnessed and never look back."

Scott was now deep in thought. He was staring at her. His expression had become gentler. "Okay, Julie. You saw Tanya and me kissing. I get that. You must have been so hurt and angry with both of us. What I don't understand is how you could have had so little faith in me, and in your best friend. I mean, it didn't make sense. You and I were so connected the night before. Didn't it seem strange that I would just kiss your best friend? I mean, I knew Tanya for a while, for years. If I wanted to kiss her, I would have had plenty of opportunities to do so. You never gave me the benefit of the doubt. You never let me explain. You just gave up. You should have tried harder, Julie!"

"Scott. You were kissing her so intensely. I didn't know what game you were playing with me. I was young and inexperienced when it came to relationships. You were my first serious relationship. I didn't know how to deal with what I saw. Your boyfriend is never supposed to kiss your best friend! I felt like you both had been fooling me throughout our relationship and I was too innocent to see it. I even accepted your playful relationship. I trusted both of you and then … the way you were holding her … I couldn't let go of that image. I didn't want anything to do with both of you. It was too painful."

"The reason I was holding her like that was because I was so shocked at what was happening. I was trying to push her back. I didn't know what to think. What you thought was wild passion were my impulses fighting Tanya off me. I was dumbfounded. One minute I was talking about how happy I was with you and how much I cared about you, the next thing I knew your best friend was kissing me. Tanya then later explained that she wanted to make her ex jealous. She didn't know what came over her. Anyway what sort of a person do you think I am? What does it say about me as a person when you concluded that I was upset because you wanted to study, so then, feeling frustrated, I made moves on your best friend, after just having been intimate with you the night before? I'll tell you what it said. In your eyes, I was a complete bastard."

"No, Scott. I was just confused. After seeing you both, I thought you were a couple. You were always together, so when I met Mark, I thought I might as well move on, since you and Tanya did."

"What? You thought we were a couple? I can't believe that. We were confused. We tried desperately to explain what happened. You had moved on with new friends, and you weren't even living at your apartment for a while. We both had the same goal, so we joined forces. We needed to explain what had happened but you closed yourself off from us. We were both ready to knock on your parents' door and ask them to talk to you, until I saw you that night. Seeing you with Mark was the only answer I needed. I felt that it was as though you were looking for an excuse to break up with me, and move on with him. I didn't even know if you had just met him, or if you had been with him while we were together. All sorts of things went through my mind. I thought that he was the reason you had pushed me away, and your studies were the convenient excuse. I mean, even if someone had seen us kissing, you never questioned the absurdity of it knowing what type of guy I was. We had been together for almost three years, Julie! How could you believe that about me? You obviously didn't know me at all though. I realised that I was wrong about us as a couple. You didn't really know me, and I didn't really know you."

"Scott. I know now that you weren't a couple. Tanya told me everything. I can't believe I hurt you both so much, but try to understand that I was hurt too. For years I've needed answers. It changed me as a person. I had only started dating Mark because I genuinely thought you and Tanya were a couple. Mark knew everything about us at the time. Yes, it seemed that I moved on with him, but I didn't. Even when I was with him, all I thought about was you. I felt that I was being unfair to him. That's why I broke it off with him eventually. When I ran into you at the Hunter Valley, I couldn't believe it. I wanted to be angry with you too, but when I looked into your eyes, I couldn't. I felt that we were being given a second chance to gain some clarity and perhaps … I don't know." Julie looked at the ground, embarrassed. She suddenly felt

155

drained and exhausted. She realised a woman had sat on a nearby bench, and was reading a book, trying to seem uninterested but evidently eavesdropping. But Julie didn't care who was listening, as she normally would. They needed to have this conversation.

Scott sat closer to her. He placed his arm around her shoulder. "So what happens now?" he asked her.

"Scott, I just want you to know that I never meant to hurt you. When Tanya explained everything, I knew that I was wrong not to have given you both a chance to explain. I never wanted to give on us. I … I loved you."

"Julie, I loved you too. That's why I was so hurt to see you with Mark. The fact that he was a nice guy didn't help. I guess the only consolation was that because of this, he would treat you well. I cared about you too much. I never wanted you to get hurt."

"I can't believe how wrong I was about everything. Had I been more brave and confronted you both, things might have been very different now. Scott, I should have trusted you. Can you ever forgive me?"

"Julie. We all contributed to this mess. Talking to you now, I realise that you've suffered just as much as we did. I could have also questioned your relationship with Mark. I should have known that you only started seeing Mark because you felt hurt and betrayed. I mean, I said that you should have trusted me, but the same applies to me. I was too proud and stubborn. I wanted to believe the worst about you. I thought that would make losing you less painful."

"So, what do we do now? Here we are in Paris, after so many years. It's as if it was meant to be. Is this a second chance? I mean, is it fate intervening? This is exactly what we talked about. It's as though we have come full circle. Do you think we can try again?"

"I don't know. A lot of things have changed. I do know that for years I've been a mess, and even though I was with someone, something was always missing. I never quite knew what it was. It didn't let me enjoy the moment. I felt that I needed to be on my own to sort myself out. I realised that I couldn't completely move on with anyone until I sorted through my feelings. Then you came along. I was in shock. It's as though you came at the right time, when I was alone, and in need of feeling whole again. The instant I saw you, I realised that I had to make things right with you. I couldn't move on unless I did. I wanted to feel anger towards you, but all I felt was a deep affection."

A buzzing sound interrupted them. It was Scott's mobile. The interruption made Julie feel as dazed as she often felt when she walked out of the cinema, after having been engrossed in a two-hour movie. Scott answered the phone. She looked at him affectionately. She then looked at two white roses standing together, away from the rest; their pure white petals gently moving in the momentary breeze. Her heart felt light.

"It's James. He says that everything has been sorted out. Our rooms are ready. I guess we better go."

"So, everything is sorted out … with us?" she asked.

"Yes, it is. There was nothing to really sort out in the first place … that's the tragedy in this whole situation, but we both now know that we never meant to hurt each other. I guess we can only take one step at a time and enjoy Paris together, just as we had planned. All I know is that when I saw you again, part of me felt that nothing had changed. I still felt connected to you."

"I felt the same way. Anyway we'd better get back. I really am sorry for hurting you, Scott."

He placed his finger on her lips. "There's no need to apologise. I can't believe you carried all that hurt around with you too. Let's go and enjoy this beautiful city. We deserve this time together."

They walked back to the hotel hand in hand, not saying anything. The silence was comforting, not awkward as it had been before their talk.

CHAPTER TWENTY-TWO

It was their first official day exploring Paris. James was right. The atmosphere was intoxicating. People filled the long and wide, tree-lined footpaths along the Champs-Elysées. Some were locals. Others had travelled from around the globe. Many of course had chosen to follow the trail of the various stages of the race throughout France, such as the Pyrenees, Burgundy, Champagne, and other small towns. Others, however, seemed quite content with remaining in Paris and soaking up the atmosphere of the city.

The famous avenue was engulfed with noise from pedestrians, scooters, cars, and buses. It was a complete contrast to the narrow streets and peaceful gardens surrounding the hotel at which they were staying. They were now heading towards the Arc de Triomphe, located at the western end of the Champs-Elysées. Julie felt as though she had to pinch herself when she saw the imposing, white historical structure with its golden hue. It was enormous! The lane-less roundabout surrounding the arch with its noise and commotion, added drama, as motorists tackled to get around it with Napoleonic bravery. Despite the commotion, the Arc de Triomphe commanded full attention from people standing near or far as it towered over the avenue as though it was guarding it.

Julie placed her sunglasses on her head, and walked slowly as she studied the reliefs sculpted on the arch which depicted scenes from the French Revolution. A tear began to roll down her cheek and she took a deep, heavy sigh.

"Julie, are you okay?" Scott softly whispered in her ear.

She stopped walking. "I don't know what came over me. I just feel emotional, being here. It's strange how life turns out."

"I know. I feel exactly the same," he said looking at her and wiping the tear away with his hand. He moved close to her and put his arm around her waist, sneaking a quick kiss on her head as they continued walking arm in arm.

They walked by many of the shops at the famous shopping district and the big names stood out. Their eyes feasted on clothes, accessories, shoes, and luxury items displayed creatively behind freshly polished shop windows. Julie felt that she was in scarf heaven when she eyed all the scarves in the boutique windows, wrapped around mannequins in numerous different ways.

Before too long, they had walked to the Eiffel Tower. James had seen it before, and was enjoying watching everyone's reaction. Even Jenny, who was a seasoned traveller, was excited that they were there. In contrast, Julie and Scott couldn't stop talking about how spectacular it was, and both took photos of every angle of the huge tower. They admired the River Seine, and imagined what it would be like to have a flat in Paris overlooking the Eiffel Tower.

By the end of the day, they were exhausted and hungry. They queued at one of the crepe stands, and Julie trembled as Scott, standing close behind her, placed his hands on her shoulders. The air was infused with the smell of cooked butter. When their crepes were finally ready, they sat at a nearby bench and ate in silence, surrendering to the activity around them, as they listened to the music which came from the children's carousel ride in front of them. Before they knew it, the lights from the ride came on as night started to set in. A young woman, who was with a group of people nearby, started dancing to the French music of the carousel ride, laughing hysterically as the sounds of an accordion took over. Julie was surprised that she didn't assume that the woman had one too many drinks, as she normally would. Instead, she went with the flow of the atmosphere. There was a magical and festive feeling in the air, which seemed to bring out a childish innocence in everyone in its presence.

"Wow! How spectacular. Look, Scott. The Eiffel Tower is lit up!" Julie screamed with excitement.

"Later on, the strobe lights draping the tower might begin to flash," James added knowledgeably. "Do you want to go on the tower tonight or should we do it another time?'

"Let's go now," Julie responded, eagerly. "There's something about this place that just makes you want to … I don't know, just do things."

"This city is amazing. It does make you want to go outside of your comfort zone and just live life to its fullest. I guess travelling does that to people. Let's go." Scott agreed, deciding to take charge, as he grabbed Julie's hand and led her to the long ticket queues at the Eiffel Tower.

Julie was conscious of his hand holding hers, and felt the same tingling she always did when he made any kind of contact with her. She hadn't felt that electric sensation for a long time. The only person who really made her feel like that was Scott. If it was another man, she would have been irritated, refusing to be led so boldly, always feeling the need to prove her independence. But it was different with Scott. She liked him taking charge. She felt safe and protected with him.

James and Jenny also obediently followed. Julie could tell that they knew that something had changed between her and Scott. It was as though they somehow planned for them to spend time alone, sensing that the air had to be cleared, especially after the awkward elevator scene in London.

"I can't believe we're on top of the Eiffel Tower, looking down at this majestic city. I can't believe that I ran into you and now I am in Paris with you, Scott. How could things change so quickly? It's all so surreal."

"It is surreal," he agreed as he moved closer to her and placed his arm around her, protecting her from the night chill. He looked at her for a while and then looked at the view.

As she rested her head on his chest, she felt his smooth hand caressing her bare arm as the chill became more intense. Suddenly, he took off the brown bomber jacket Julie had admired him in, and placed it on her shoulders, noticing that she was shivering in her sleeveless summer dress. She looked at him with an appreciative smile. "Thanks. It smells like cooked butter," Julie said, wrapping herself in its warmth, as the wind tousled her hair.

"As does your hair," he said, kissing her head gently. "The last thing I want is for you to catch a cold," he added, looking at her, his dimples appearing slowly. She noticed that the stubble on his face was becoming a slight beard. It continued under his chin, and ended at the upper part of his neck. It made him look rugged and sexy, yet soft and youthful. It reminded Julie of the shoreline: rough waves from the ocean fiercely breaking onto the sand, yet capable of seducing it with their sensual swaying, and to caress it with natural purity. She then looked into his light-filled eyes and noticed her reflection in them. Scott gave her another warm smile as the wind messed his hair and then turned to look at the peaceful view again.

Julie looked out across the city, at the Notre Dame in the distance. The cacophony from the traffic was far away from them; only the occasional faint car horn or siren could be heard from the streets way down below. Murmurings from different segregated groups of people on the tower were like comforting background music as they peered down at the illuminated city. All the ingredients were there for them to take their relationship further. She was staring at one of the most romantic cities in the world with the only man that she had ever given her heart to.

She felt a feeling of peace come over her as Scott hugged her closer to him. Wrapped in his warmth, she rested her head on the soft cotton fabric of his T-shirt which covered his taut chest, and they stared at the view in silence, his strong arms holding her close. She felt his chest moving gently while he breathed. The crisp night air caressed Julie's face, and as she felt Scott's heart beating, the city continued to move her, evoking intense needs and emotions from a place deep within. Julie felt that words could not disturb the gentle beauty of the moment. As she momentarily lifted her head from his chest, noticing how content Scott looked from the corner of her eye, she was positive that he felt the same.

CHAPTER TWENTY-THREE

They had been in Paris for a week and a half and Julie was enjoying every precious moment. Life and the world appeared different. She realised how much there was to learn and explore, and how foolish she had been thinking that she had to be a certain way in life and not venture in any other direction.

With her sudden burst of enthusiasm and appreciation for what the world had to offer, Julie decided to take James' advice and to join him every morning for his walk. Jenny and Scott decided to also join in.

"I guess you don't want to be outdone," Julie teased.

"Well, I am the fitness teacher in this group," Jenny responded. "Although, at 70 metres in width, crossing the Champs-Elysées could be considered a workout in itself."

"Well, I'm definitely not going to be the odd man standing. Besides, that's the only way to get a feel for the city isn't it, James?" Scott asked his friend, laughing.

"Well, it is, Scott, but I must warn all of you, that I take my fitness seriously, so if anyone can't keep up, they'll have to go it alone. Once I set my pace, there is no stopping me."

Jenny rolled her eyes in disbelief. "You honestly think I can't keep up with you? We'll see about that. Do you know that I beat half the boys in my year at the athletics carnivals in high school? Oh, of course you do, James. You were one of the boys I beat," she retaliated with a smile.

"Okay, we'll see if you can put your money where your mouth is. Are you up to the challenge?"

And so began their morning walks. Jenny and James did end up taking it seriously, while Scott and Julie set their own pace, one that gave them an opportunity to get fit and admire their surroundings as well, not to mention the opportunity to spend more time with each other. Julie loved watching the natural flow of the city, seeing the cosy looking shops opening up for business and watching Parisians heading to work at a much more leisurely pace than Sydneysiders would as they stopped to buy a coffee or sit and enjoy a pastry.

She also loved exploring the narrow streets that were reminiscent of old Paris near their hotel. They were amazed at the ability the Parisians had when it came to parking their cars in the narrow streets which would be a challenge to any driver. That also explained the many scooters parked throughout the city, and the many Smart cars that were prominent in the narrow streets. She would have in depth discussions with Scott about such observations. They were also amazed at how many play areas existed in the many parks, and how well maintained they were.

On one such morning, Julie stood next to Scott in one of the most decadent and beautiful patisseries she had ever seen. The aroma of fresh coffee greeted them as they stepped inside the opulent space. Everything looked so grand, from the ornate ceilings, to the expensive looking parquetry, the beautiful leather booths, the extravagant cake stands which displayed cakes that looked too impressive to be eaten, to the smartly dressed waiters standing behind the polished glass counters that displayed cake masterpieces in every corner. Scott and Julie decided to order a box of macarons, having heard so much about them, and because Julie could not decide on which flavours she preferred, Scott ordered an assortment which included one of nearly all of them. The colours of the macarons looked so beautiful in the elegant box they were carefully placed in. "*Merci*," they said in unison.

Julie walked outside the patisserie feeling proud of their purchase and looked forward to tasting the different flavours. Scott was amused with her as he caught her admiring the elegant box on numerous occasions. "You make me laugh, Julie," he commented. "You really know how to appreciate things, don't you?"

Yes, I do, Julie thought to herself as she looked at him, appreciating every angle of his beautiful, handsome face. "I wonder what the green macaron tastes like?" she mused, glancing at the box again.

"There's only one way to find out," Scott said, as they sat on a bench facing the Arc de Triomphe.

"Shouldn't we wait for Jenny and James?"

"We're only trying macarons, not stealing secret service information," Scott replied with that same boyish, mischievous smile he always gave her.

"Okay. Maybe we'll try one."

Scott was looking at her with amazement.

"What!" Julie questioned.

"You're looking at the box as if it is a box full of expensive jewels."

"I'll try one of the green ones."

"Don't you mean the emerald one?" Scott asked, laughing.

She carefully opened the box and invited Scott to make his choice.

"*Je voudrais un macaron au chocolat*," he replied. "Sorry, I thought I'd try and see if I remember any of my first year high school French."

"I just remember *J'ai faim*, and *j'ai soif*, meaning I'm hungry and I'm thirsty."

"Don't forget *Je m'appelle* Scott."

"This is delicious *Je m'appelle* Scott," Julie teased as she took her first bite. "It's actually mint and it tastes so fresh. I've never tasted anything like it. What flavour is yours?"

"It's coffee, and it's delicious. You're right. It's so unique and you can tell they use real flavours, not artificial ones. Here. Try some," he offered, casually extending his arm out for her to taste the coffee-flavoured macaron.

She could feel his presence as he moved closer to her. His knees touched hers as she took a bite of the temptation in front of her.

Very tempting, she thought when she looked at him, not solely referring to the macaron. The coffee macaron was so sumptuous she couldn't hide her appreciation. She realised Scott was staring at her longingly.

Julie couldn't move. All she could do was stare at him. It was as though she was locked in the moment. His serious eyes revealed so much feeling. He leaned over to her. She could feel his warm breath. Julie was drunk with excitement for what was to ensue. A rush of anticipation took over her. She could almost feel his lips on hers …

"You have something on your lips," he said softly as he reached his hand over to her lips, and gently wiped a crumb away.

"Oh," Julie managed. She quickly looked down at the box of macarons, trying to hide her disappointment.

As she began to turn to reach for the box, she felt Scott's hand on her hand. The smoothness of his touch instantly made her shiver. Scott moved even closer to her. He touched her warm face gently and looked deep into her eyes. "You smell so nice Julie, what scent is it?"

"Vanilla …" she began to say but could already feel his soft, sensual lips on hers as he kissed her. She looked into his eyes searchingly when their lips parted. That was only for a second. He began to kiss her again; this time it was faster. She responded with the same intensity, running her fingers through his soft hair, and holding onto the back of his neck as his hands worked their way from her hair, to her shoulders, right down to her waist, every stroke sending tingles all over her.

Their lips parted. "Just so you know, that was what I really wanted to do," he said, gently touching her face, then tracing her lips with his thumb, speaking between heavy, short breaths. "I'm crazy about you, Julie, I always have been. The time we spend together is precious. I

167

thought we would never get another chance." His intense brown eyes studied every aspect of her face; of her lips, until they met her eyes again.

Julie just smiled. Her heart beat fast. A deep, familiar lingering desire overtook her whole body. His touch, his smell, the way his chest moved as he breathed, the softness of his hair between her fingers, the slight roughness of his face brushing against her skin … It was all coming back to her. She finally looked away and picked up the box in a daze with slightly trembling hands. Scott placed his arm around her as she stood up, almost losing her balance on the stone paved footpath.

"Take it easy," he said, giving her a warm dimpled smile. With Scott's arm around her, the beautiful box in her hands, surrounded by the magic and beauty of the most romantic city in the world, Julie felt delightfully and blissfully content. Her heart felt tight, but at the same time, she felt that it was dancing, swaying freely to the music that was playing inside her. Scott's fingers intertwined with her own and they continued to walk slowly, intermittently glancing in each other's eyes, sinking deeper into each other's hearts.

CHAPTER TWENTY-FOUR

Exhaustion began to take over as Julie took another glance at the building behind her. The Louvre was one of the largest museums in the world and, despite her fatigue, she felt honoured and elated to be in the presence of historical greatness. The Louvre Pyramid that sat beside it, juxtaposed with the traditional architecture of the Louvre, gave it an air of confidence. Julie loved how it boldly challenged convention. They had all spent the last few hours trying to see as much as they could, only to realise that it was an impossible task, as a few weeks would probably still not be enough time to ensure that every painting, statue, or piece of furniture on display had been viewed. She applauded herself for choosing to wear comfortable sandals with her mid-length, tangerine summer dress.

The walk to the Louvre in itself had been pleasantly exhausting as they walked down the long avenue of the Champs-Elysées to the eastern end at the Place de la Concorde. Julie couldn't stop looking at all the fountains, monuments, and arches as they walked through the busy square that was surrounded by another huge, noisy roundabout with no lanes. Sounds of buses, car horns, scooters filled the massive square. They all had to drag her away from the famous Fontaine de la Concorde. Julie studied it in case she missed anything. She was entranced by the statues that glistened in the sunlight in emerald green, black and gold, and by the fountain from which clear water flowed gently and melodically. It was like watching a symphony of flowing water as the surrounding fish sculptures began to also spray water onto the centre of the fountain in a dramatic way. There was just so much beauty and history to absorb! Her senses were in overdrive, and she kept glancing back at all the famous monuments as they continued walking.

"I can't believe how big this place is! I mean, it's almost impossible to see everything. At least we managed to see some of the most famous paintings," Julie commented.

"Yeah, we can't go to the Louvre and miss the Mona Lisa. That would be almost sacrilege. We also got to see the Venus de Milo, some more of Da Vinci's work, and Monet's Water Lilies," James added.

"Not to mention the many paintings depicting the French Revolution and Napoleon," Jenny added. "What!" she protested, as everyone including Julie looked at her with astonishment. Jenny usually took no interest in art or anything in the creative field.

"I guess the Louvre has that effect on people. It can bring out an appreciation for art in just about anyone! "

"What the hell is that supposed to mean?" Jenny beckoned. "As if you're so creative James! All you've talked about since you've arrived is sport."

"Oh Jenny, what am I going to do with you?" James asked, as he placed his arm around her. "I was only joking. I know everyone has different sides to them. I mean, look at Julie. She has genuinely taken an interest in cycling. She can't stop asking me questions about the Tour."

"Yes, I must have been the only person that didn't know that 'peloton' refers to the main group of cyclists." Julie laughed. "Anyway, what stage is the race up to now? I'm surprised you're not covering it."

"It's up to stage nineteen. Soon they'll cross the finish line at the Champs-Elysées, so we better not miss it. To answer your second question, Jules, I always base my holidays around sporting events, even if I'm not working. I guess sport is always with me. I don't consider it a job."

"It must be great to have an occupation that you feel so passionate about. I still don't know what I really want to do!"

"I'm sure you'll find out soon enough!" Scott gave her a gentle smile. "Maybe you'll have a different outlook when you get back home. Did the surveys that you completed help you in any way?"

"They did help me to confirm what I already suspected about myself. I need beauty in my life, as my aesthetic need is high."

"And did you establish who controls your life?" Scott asked.

"I do, Scott. I mean, I do from now on, and nothing is going to stand in my way."

"Way to go, Jules," Jenny joined in. "It would have been more dramatic if you were standing next to the Arc de Triomphe though."

"I guess this structure will have to do," James said. "It's the Arc de Triomphe du Carrousel," he continued, pointing to an enormous white arch monument with gold and rose hues, which resembled the Arc de Triomphe.

They walked around the charming and unapologetically grand Tuileries and Carrousel Gardens and headed towards an outdoor café. Everything looked so beautiful in the enormous, wide open spaces, from the cream concrete pathways, to the magnificent statues, the elegant fountains, the beautiful flowers that were in full bloom, and the lovely pond, upon which a few children raced toy boats. The huge, impressive statues were intricately detailed. They would have made the most fastidious person seem disorganised. Julie found herself sighing when she gazed at them; a liberating exhilaration would take over her, making her chest tight with intense feeling and passion. "How can humans build such greatness?" she kept thinking aloud.

"Maybe after lunch we could go back to the western end of the Champs-Elysées and be part of the atmosphere. I mean the race is nearly over," Julie suggested.

"No problem," James said. "We could even have a beer at one of the beer stands and enjoy it in the sun."

All in agreement, they walked to the café. *This is the life*, Julie thought, sighing contently as she heard the familiar drumming sound of a woodpecker on a nearby tree. It amplified the beating of her heart; she was finally feeling life again. She felt comfortable; at ease in her own skin. The intimate kiss she shared with Scott added to that feeling. The pleasant, burning ache in her heart felt familiar.

After a long walk back, and a beer at one of the stands, they sat on a bench and languorously observed the action around them. As lazy as she felt, Julie wanted to keep moving. She decided to buy a few Tour de France jerseys that were being sold at a number of the stands. Jenny decided to join her as she too wanted to make a few purchases for family and friends. Julie bought jerseys for Brian, her father, Jenny, James, Scott, and one for herself. "My shout," she insisted as Jenny offered to pay for the jersey. "I want to buy it for you. If it wasn't for all of you deciding to go to Paris, I wouldn't have been here having the time of my life!"

They then ventured into the many boutiques situated nearby. Julie purchased a few scarves for Maria, Cassandra, Christina, her mother, and of course, herself. There were so many to choose from. She felt like a kid in a candy store. Julie also purchased a studded belt that reminded her of the eighties from one of the more alternative shops, and some daring beaded shoes with a unique block heel.

As they made their way back to Scott and James, proudly satisfied, Julie couldn't help the strong feelings that emerged from within her when she glanced at Scott as he talked on his mobile. His dark brown, overlong hair was lighter than usual, highlighted by the sun. She sat on the bench next to James, still looking at Scott, who seemed to be having a serious conversation. His broad shoulders looked tense.

"So you two did a bit of retail therapy I see!" James stated, eyeing the bags carefully.

"Yes, we did. James, this is for you. I knew you would end up buying one anyway." Julie handed him the jersey, while she quickly glanced over to Scott, who was heading back to the bench.

"Look what Julie bought for me, Scott. Isn't she sweet?"

"So what did James do to deserve a gift?" Scott asked as he placed his mobile in his pocket, deep in thought.

"I bought you one as well," she said as she stood up.

"Thanks Julie," Scott said, and kissed her lightly on the lips. "You didn't have to though. "I'll think of you whenever I wear it," he said, hugging her affectionately, instantly coming out of his trance. James and Jenny gave each other a knowing look. Julie felt that he was updating them about their relationship status.

"Why don't we all make the most of the remaining days of our trip?" Scott suggested. "I took the liberty of making reservations at one of the most upmarket restaurants in Paris."

Everyone agreed that it was a wonderful idea. Julie felt excited at the mere suggestion of it. She already began to plan what to wear when she realised that she wasn't the only one.

"What am I going to wear?" Jenny asked, in bewilderment.

Julie smiled at her. "Let's go back to the hotel and plan our outfits," Julie suggested excitedly.

"To tell you the truth, I don't know what to wear either," James admitted.

Scott nodded in agreement. "Well, we better get back to the hotel. We've got serious decisions to make!"

CHAPTER TWENTY FIVE

The atmosphere was infectious. There was noise everywhere, from the crowds that had gathered, to the announcements that were being made every minute adding to the urgency of the race. This was it — the finish line at the Champs-Elysées. Stage twenty, as James had informed her. Julie was surprised at how excited she felt. She once again felt that she was part of something. However, she suddenly realised that it would all be over soon. Just as the race was nearing an end, so was their stay in Paris. Julie felt teary at the thought of it. She wanted to keep travelling. She enjoyed feeling free and living from a suitcase in a hotel.

She looked at Scott, Jenny and James who were standing beside her, waiting to catch a glance of the first cyclist. She had become so close to them over the last three weeks. They had welcomed her with open arms despite the fact that there were a few awkward moments between her and Scott. She then looked solely at Scott. She couldn't believe how far they had come.

Her mind drifted to the conversation she had with her mother earlier that morning as she sipped her tea in the hotel's opulent tea room. She had savoured every sip in the perfumed, curtained room, and admired the pink roses in the crystal vase which decorated the elegant round table where she sat to have her breakfast. It had been her time alone — to pause, to ponder and breathe in all the beautiful changes in her life. As she looked at the gold-framed artwork around her on the blue panelled walls, she thought of her mother. She had been eager to talk to her about all the art and beauty around her. It was nice be able to share her thoughts and passion with her. She had filled her in on how beautiful and spectacular the Louvre had been. They had discussed the trip, and everything seemed okay with the world for a while, until her mother mentioned the barbecue she was planning for the following Sunday, having postponed the previous one. Julie didn't know why, even with her new perspective, she was still uneasy at the thought of seeing Christina again. She hadn't had a proper conversation with her since the outburst at the Hunter Valley. She knew that Christina would have something to say about her spontaneity. She always had something to say. *More unfinished business*, Julie thought.

"They're coming!" James shouted at the top of his lungs. I think its team …"

Julie couldn't comprehend what James was saying. She couldn't hear anything as people cheered frantically. In fact, she could hardly see anything, just a few helmets going past extremely fast. Just as she was about to ask Scott if he had seen anything, she realised he was no longer next to her. She searched for him as she scanned the crowd, which had congregated around her. She finally saw him. He was frantically texting someone. Julie couldn't believe it. What or who could be so important that he would miss the end of the race? She knew that he was interested in seeing who the winner was, maybe not as much as James was, but enough to ignore his mobile.

Jenny grabbed Julie's hand as James led them out of the crowd, which was going wild. He led them to Scott who had finished texting.

"It was just as I predicted," James told Scott.

Julie vaguely heard the rest of the conversation. She heard some European sounding name but lost interest in who had won. All she wanted to know was why Scott was being so mysterious.

***

Julie's ears were ringing. Did she hear him correctly? His voice was very clear at the time.

She entered the taxi at Sydney airport feeling numb. Scott was seated next to her. Jenny and James had said their goodbyes and had caught another taxi. Julie didn't know what to say to Scott. She had been waiting for her luggage when she had noticed Scott's on the conveyor belt. She had walked over to him to alert him, not realising that he was talking to someone on his mobile phone again. Just as she was about to tap him on the shoulder, she heard him saying goodbye to someone. He didn't address her by her name. He called her "sweetie." He then continued saying the words that Julie didn't want to admit she heard. "I love you sweetie. I can't wait to see you again and spend time with you. You're my world."

"Julie, are you okay?" Scott was asking her, tapping her on her leg. "You haven't said a word since we left the airport."

The taxi driver interrupted. He began telling them stories of the days he spent in Paris. Julie kept quiet, oblivious to everything around her.

"Julie, we're here. This is your street, isn't it?"

Julie woke from her trance. She looked at the street. Its familiarity brought her back to reality and suddenly she felt that she was where she belonged.

Scott walked out with her and helped her with her luggage. "Julie, I'm already missing you and I haven't even said goodbye yet."

The words would have sent her heart racing earlier that same day.

He then hugged her. "I can't wait to see you again. I enjoyed the time we spent together. I'll call you tomorrow and we'll make plans. How does that sound to you?"

"Whatever."

Scott stepped back to the taxi as the taxi driver stated that he had another stop to make, and then rushed back to where Julie was standing and kissed her gently on the lips. "I really enjoyed the time we spent together," he said again lifting her chin up, forcing her to meet his concerned eyes. He then stepped back into the taxi, as the driver persistently beeped his horn.

"Who's 'sweetie'?" she suddenly called out.

"What?" Scott looked at her with a confused look on his face.

"Who's 'sweetie'? You said you love her and that she's the world to you."

She saw he understood what she was talking about. The driver pulled out of the parking space. Scott leaned his head out of the window. He looked desperate to explain.

"She's my daughter, Julie. She's my daughter."

CHAPTER TWENTY SIX

Julie was lying down on the cream sofa back in the terrace house. She was in her pyjamas, staring at the ceiling. It was nearly midday and she had slept in as her body tried to adjust to the new time. After handing gifts to Cassandra and Maria, discussing the trip over a nice vegetable casserole Cassandra had prepared, they settled in front of the computer and looked at some of the hundreds of photos that Julie had taken. Of course all eyes were on Scott.

"The Eiffel Tower is interesting as well," Maria had added.

They all agreed that Scott looked just as handsome as he did back at uni. Cassandra went a step further. "He looks like a handsome, sexy polo player!" she commented.

Julie realised that Cassandra appeared different. She seemed excited. It was as though her mind was at times floating contently somewhere else. In contrast, Maria wasn't as carefree as she usually was. In fact, Julie realised that she looked as if she was worried about something. Although she attempted to mask her feelings with jokes, Julie could tell that her humour was forced.

Her friends deserved to know about the talk she had with Scott. Julie filled them in on what had transpired. "He couldn't understand why I didn't trust him and why I hadn't given him a chance to explain," Julie told them.

"Poor Scott," they both commented.

"It seems that he has suffered over the years as much as you did," Maria added sadly.

"Are you all right Maria?" Julie had asked her friend, not used to seeing her so empathetic.

Maria had digressed, looking at the photo of Julie and Scott in front of Big Ben. "You really look good together," she said and then began to cry.

"Maria, are you sure you're all right?" Julie had asked, while Cassandra looked at Maria knowingly.

"No I'm not all right," Maria confessed. "He's leaving," she said, covering her face with her hands. "Antonio, he's going back to Chile."

Apparently, Antonio had to go back and help his parents rebuild their lives as their house had been destroyed in the recent earthquake. Julie tried to offer her support to Maria by asking her if there was anyone else who could help, but apparently Maria had already explored every possibility. Julie wasn't used to seeing her friend in such a state and felt that she would need all the support she could get from her and Cassandra. Maria admitted that she had developed deep feelings for Antonio. "Maybe he won't be gone that long? I mean, he admits that he loves living here and I know he loves being with you," Julie had offered.

"I don't know how long he'll be there for. It's just so unfair because we were finally starting to become more serious. What if this trip ruins everything and he decides to live there?"

The night continued with questions and speculation until Maria told her friends to go to sleep, and that she would be okay. Julie was not convinced and agreed to have lunch with her the next day, jet lag or no jet lag. "I'll have plenty of time to sleep," she had told her. "I'm unemployed, remember?"

Now Julie just stared at the pale blue walls around her, and then at the garden outside which looked so beautiful. Not wanting to take away from her friend's concerns, she had not mentioned those final words from Scott, the words that had shattered Julie's world in the space of a second. Part of her didn't want to deal with it. It felt too familiar.

"She's my daughter." Julie replayed the words over and over in her mind. Now she understood what he was referring to when he had told her that things had changed. What else was he keeping from her? Was her mother still

in his life? Was he married? Even Jenny and James hadn't mentioned anything. Did he specifically tell them not to? That was why Jenny tippy-toed around the subject of her and Scott, and had told her Scott would explain everything. It all made sense now.

What did he want from her? He got his closure. Why didn't he tell her that there was no chance for them to try again? She had felt so close to him at the trip — the way he had kissed her — it was so real. He reassured her that he was crazy about her. Now that had all changed again and he seemed like a stranger, someone she knew nothing about. As she got up and headed to her bedroom, realising that she should get dressed for her lunch in the city with Maria, she heard the phone ring. Too exhausted to talk to anyone, she ignored it and hurried upstairs to her bedroom. Deep down, she had a nagging suspicion that it might be Scott, but she didn't allow her mind to go there. She had to concentrate on her friend now. Her problems, which seemed only to unravel into new ones the more she tried to solve them, would have to take a back seat for a while. Besides, if it was her mum calling, she was in no mood to talk about the impending barbecue, which she was certain would be the primary reason for her calling.

Everything felt so familiar. The frantic commuters; the smell of fresh coffee brewing from numerous coffee stands; the men and women dressed in executive work attire heading to lunch as they left busy office buildings. Julie felt strange that she was no longer part of that life. She had just made her way out of St James station, deciding to take a longer train trip as she desperately needed to rest. She walked towards Pitt Street Mall. As she did so, a tall structure caught her attention. It was the building that she felt had taunted and teased her for five long years. Now, with no ties to it, it just looked like another tall building. Usually her stomach would turn when she looked at it. Now she just continued walking, no longer feeling threatened by it. She knew in her heart that she had nothing else to offer the company if she was still employed there, and therefore things were as they should be when it came to work. She continued walking, not taking another look, and headed to Maria's shop. For now she was one of the people who were there to enjoy a day shopping, or to take in the sights of the city, or to simply enjoy a leisurely lunch. It felt strange that two days ago she was in Paris; she was expecting to see the Eiffel Tower at any moment. Instead, the Sydney Tower caught her attention as it cast a shadow on the streets, standing with just as much pride and conviction, even though it wasn't half as famous.

She caught a glimpse of Eventually You from afar, and felt proud of her friend's charming and inviting little shop. Julie had always enjoyed visiting Maria at work, especially when her own day had been the opposite of relaxing. She would be welcomed by the scented candles, the little water fountain which stood in the middle creating an ambient atmosphere, the smell of organic teas, and the beautiful, exotic incense burners which would be carefully placed on display. Julie also loved looking at the various products: exfoliators, face masks, organic soaps, hand and body moisturisers, bath crystals, and so many other healing and pleasant offerings.

Maria obviously knew what she was doing. Julie was positive that everyone who walked into her store felt the same way she did: content and at peace. It was a little sanctuary in the middle of the busy and demanding city. Julie suddenly imagined herself working there. Maybe it wasn't such a bad idea to take Maria up on her offer and work there for a few hours a week until she worked out what career to pursue. As she looked at the store, she remembered the decadent patisserie that she and Scott had visited, where they had purchased the delectable macarons. Her heart ached. All the time they spent together was under false pretences. Scott had intentionally kept the truth from her. He was right. Everything had changed between them. He had a daughter — with someone else.

Maria was serving a customer, looking very professional and focused, dressed in black pants and a black top. Her long auburn hair was tied back in a ponytail. She usually wore it down when she wasn't working, and it flowed freely as she walked. Although she usually wore vibrant or earthy-coloured bohemian clothes, at work she felt that she didn't want anything to take away from the products. The products in the shop were simple and pure. She didn't want to confuse things with colourful clothes. Julie agreed wholeheartedly with her friend that plain black clothes worked best to offset the products.

Maria noticed Julie from the window and made her way to the door. "Thank God you're here," she said as soon as she saw Julie. "The last thing I want to do today is work."

Julie realised that Maria was more devastated than she originally thought. She always loved working in her store and took pride in it. As she grabbed her rose-pink coat, she led Julie out into the street.

"I must be coming down with something. I feel so tired," she continued.

They walked towards the Strand Arcade, a grand old building which housed numerous inviting coffee shops. Maria sat at the first coffee shop they saw. "I hope you're okay with this one," she checked with Julie. "I just feel so exhausted."

"That's okay. They're all as good as each other. To tell you the truth, I feel exhausted as well. I don't know where I am. I feel as though I'm at the Champs-Elysées and that I'm about to see James and Jenny any second."

"And Scott," Maria added, looking at Julie curiously.

"Yes, and Scott," Julie quickly corrected.

After ordering two focaccia, two flat whites, and a bottle of sparkling mineral water to share, they sat back in their seats and stared at the activity around them.

"Julie! Your phone is beeping. I'm surprised you haven't noticed. It might be Scott calling to plan a romantic evening with you."

Julie looked at her friend as if to say that she doubted that was the case.

"How do you know? Just because my relationship will soon be non-existent, it doesn't mean you and Scott can't work out."

"Just because Antonio is going back home for a while, it doesn't mean your relationship is over."

"Well, I'm not a believer of long distance relationships. Once he leaves, so much time will pass that he won't remember anything about me or what we had together. Besides, the earthquake was so devastating, it could take over a year for his parents to get their lives back in order. They also have a lot of health problems. What sort of a bitch would I look like if I protested about how long he stays and helps?"

"It may not be as bad as you think, Maria."

Julie looked at her phone and realised that there were so many unread messages. They were all from Scott. How would he explain himself out of this one? She decided to ignore them, feeling too mentally and physically exhausted to deal with him just yet.

As she placed her mobile back into her bag, she realised that she was doing it again: avoiding confronting Scott. She was appalled with her behaviour. *So much for being proactive*, she thought with disgust. Right then, she made a mental note that she would face him after she dealt with Maria's issues. It was definitely going to be difficult to change old habits, Julie acknowledged.

"So who was it?"

"It was just my mum wanting to see if I can make it to the barbecue she's having on Sunday."

"Don't forget, Stacey has been going on about some work reunion thing. She said that she'll call you when you get back. She was thinking of organising a cruise around the harbour."

"That's Stacey, always wanting to socialise. I have to admit, she does have passion and drive. When she wants something, she puts her heart into it."

"She was keen to make sure everyone could make it, especially you and George."

Julie instinctively thought of George. She found herself wondering what he was doing with his life now. She was still surprised with the gift he had given her, not to mention his kind words.

"So Maria, have you talked to Antonio recently? Did you tell him how you feel about him going to Chile?"

"What am I supposed to say? 'Antonio, please don't leave me! I can't do without you!' You know that's not my style."

"You don't have to beg him, but you can be honest about your feelings for him. Does he even know that he means a lot to you, and that you have developed genuine feelings for him? I mean, he may think that you don't care that he is leaving. Maybe if he knew, he would make other arrangements."

The food and coffee arrived at their table. Maria took a sip of her coffee. She then took a bite of her food and pushed the plate away.

"I don't even feel like eating."

"You're obviously more upset than you realise. If you're true about your feelings, and you're honest with Sco—, I mean, with Antonio, you may be able to work it out." Julie slightly coloured as she completed her sentence.

"What about you? What happens between you and Scott now?" Maria asked studying Julie curiously.

Julie was about to avoid mentioning what Scott had told her about having a daughter, when she realised that she couldn't lie to Maria, especially when she just told her to be honest with her feelings regarding Antonio.

184

"I wouldn't have a clue, to tell you the truth. I thought everything was going okay, until ..."

"Until what?"

" ... until I heard him talking to someone on his mobile. He called her 'sweetie' and said that she was his world."

Maria looked at Julie with her mouth open from shock.

"It wasn't another woman." Julie quickly ended her friend's speculation.

"Was it a man?"

Maria's shocked expression almost looked comical for a second to Julie.

"No, nothing like that, I already mentioned that the recipient of his affection was a 'she'. He was actually talking to his daughter."

Maria's shocked expression returned. "I can't believe it. When did you find out?"

"Just when the taxi pulled out of our street, the minute I got home."

"You mean all that time you spent together in London and Paris, he didn't tell you anything?"

"No. I don't even know if he's married. I'm just as confused as I ever was."

"How many times is this guy going to do this to you? I mean, even if it wasn't his fault back then, he should have known better this time. He should have been honest with you after all the years that were wasted on false assumptions." Maria appeared really angry. "It doesn't seem fair. Nothing seems fair any more. Why can't everything be black and white?"

"I didn't mean to upset you, Maria."

"I know. I don't know what came over me. I just feel so jumpy and irritated. I hate not being in control of my life. It makes me anxious."

"I definitely know what you mean. Not being in control can cause a lot of anxiety. Believe me: I know that feeling of uncertainty too well. I guess the next step is to take control back. Although, that's what I thought I was doing.

Anyway, how about we both make a conscious effort to do that? I know you're the last person who likes to dwell on things."

"Usually, I'm not so emotional. I haven't been myself lately. You're right. Enough of this feeling sorry for myself stuff. First, let's go home and light one of my organic candles, one that creates a space full of peace so that we can unwind. I feel tired and I told Denise, one of my part-timers, to look after the store for the rest of the day."

"Sounds good to me, I think the jet lag is starting to really kick in now."

"We better check if Cassandra has other plans though. She may be 'studying' with Connor again," Maria emphasised with a grin.

"What do you mean? Are Connor and Cassandra more than study partners? What are you both keeping from me? I go away for three weeks …"

"Let's just say that Cassandra has been very happy lately. I think she is more smitten than she is admitting. Maybe she needs to practise what she preaches and be more true and genuine with her feelings."

"Maybe she should." Julie agreed, as she sipped her mineral water and took her last bite of the smoked salmon and cream cheese focaccia.

Later that evening, Cassandra burst into the lounge room where Julie was trying to relax and fight the exhaustion that had taken over her body. She had been contemplating whether she should have a warm bath when Cassandra sat on the cream couch across from her, smiling to herself.

"So how's the jet lag?" she asked innocently.

"Oh, it's still punishing me …" Julie began to respond, stopping when she realised that Cassandra was staring into space with the same smile still plastered on her face.

"This candle smells so nice. What scent is it?"

"I think it's neroli oil. It's supposed to create a peaceful atmosphere. So, how's Connor?" Julie decided to be direct. She wasn't used to seeing Cassandra so dreamy eyed. She usually looked so focused.

Cassandra suddenly looked at Julie curiously, as if she was taken aback by her abrupt question. "He's fine. Why do you ask?"

"No particular reason. I was going to tell you when I first met him that he has the bluest eyes I have ever seen. How can you concentrate with those eyes staring at you?"

"He does have nice eyes," Cassandra agreed, staring at the ceiling with a smile that covered her whole face. She quickly straightened her posture and tried to look professional when she caught Julie smiling at her. Julie suddenly burst into laughter as she looked at her friend who was trying desperately to conceal her feelings.

"What's so funny?" Cassandra asked.

"You are."

Cassandra looked at Julie with a shocked and hurt look on her face. Julie continued laughing.

"Julie. What has gotten into you? Is it the jet lag? Did you have too much wine at lunch with Maria?"

"None of the above," Julie answered cheekily. "It's just that you would be the first to tell us to be honest with our feelings and to acknowledge them."

"What are you talking about? Feelings for what?" Cassandra asked trying to look perplexed.

"You know, the feelings that you feel when you are totally falling for someone; in your case, a male who has striking blue eyes and knows a lot about Gestalt therapy theory, thanks to your help, and whatever therapy you're up to now!"

"Solution Focused Therapy. We're up to Solution Focused Therapy, and don't look so proud of yourself. I'm totally aware of my feelings for a certain male with blue eyes and yes, before you say anything else, I know I always say that it's preferable that people try to be honest with their feelings, but I haven't felt this way before. This is new territory for me. Besides, just because I'm becoming a counsellor, it doesn't mean I'm not a human being first. I get just as awkward as other people do when discussing my feelings, especially when I feel like a love struck teenager who can't focus on anything else but how I feel when I am in the presence of those sexy, deep blue eyes."

"I know you're just as human and vulnerable as the rest of us mortals. I guess I should be more sensitive and offer you the same empathic understanding and positive self-regard that you offer me."

"I'm impressed. You have learned some of the essential ingredients that can create a non-judgmental atmosphere to facilitate Person Centred Therapy between a counsellor and a client. But enough of that for now though. I just want to talk to someone about this before I burst from happiness. I couldn't talk to Maria as she is dealing with a lot right now. You were having the time of your life in Europe with your brown-eyed polo player look-alike. Julie, I feel so excited and happy. I can't stop thinking about Connor. Every time I see him, I can't help but fantasise about being with him, so much that I don't hear a word he says when we study together. I am definitely acting like a teenager."

"Well, it's about time I helped you with your love life. I mean, over the years, I have greedily spent hours talking about my problems and my confused love life or lack of it."

"That's not true. You always listen to my problems, especially when I'm confused about my studies. I mean you nearly know as much as I do, the way I go on and on about each different therapy."

"Not without using the information to help myself with my own life."

"There's nothing wrong with that. After all it's a practice that deals with human emotions, and who can't relate to that?"

"So, Cassandra, before this becomes about me again, what's happening between you and Connor?"

"Well, I can tell from the way he looks at me that there is a connection between us. We talk for hours and don't even realise how late it is. The more time I spend with him, the more I want to be with him. He always surprises me. He's into everything. The way he embraces life is so inspirational."

Julie listened to her friend with intrigue. She knew exactly what she was talking about. That's how she had felt about Scott. She loved the connection she had with him. She had felt that she could look into his soul once upon a time. The more Julie listened to her friend, the happier she felt for her. No wonder she couldn't talk to Maria about her feelings. It would just emphasise what Maria would be missing when Antonio left for Chile. Cassandra's whole face lit up when she talked about Connor.

"The thing is," Cassandra continued, "I don't know why he won't make a move. I mean, the atmosphere is always so right. The only thing I can think of is that he doesn't want to ruin our relationship as study partners. Maybe he doesn't know where I stand." Cassandra looked sceptically at the candle on the glass coffee table, as if it would give her the answers she needed, when they both looked towards the entrance of the lounge room where a shocked Maria was standing holding something in her hands.

"I can't believe this, I can't believe this is happening to me, especially now. We were so careful."

What's wrong, honey?" Cassandra asked.

"I can't believe it!"

"Believe what?" Julie asked struggling to conceal her worry.

"I'm pregnant. I can't believe that I'm pregnant."

Julie instinctively looked at Cassandra hoping that she would have some trained response from her counsellor's tool bag, but she was just as shocked. Julie and Cassandra walked up to Maria and put their arms around her. Julie could feel her fear and uncertainty, as her body trembled all over. Maria burst into uncontrollable tears as the shock of her revelation started to sink in.

CHAPTER TWENTY-SEVEN

It was Friday night. Sydney Harbour looked breathtaking as Julie headed towards the pier at Circular Quay. She had been home for a few days, and although she was beginning to settle in her usual surroundings, her mind was at times still in Paris. As she headed toward the pier where she would meet Stacey and everyone else for the one-month reunion, Julie stopped to admire the majestic view of the harbour. Paris was definitely magical but as she took in the view, she had to admit that she too was living in one of the most glamorous cities in the world.

"Hey, stranger,"

Julie recognised the man behind the voice almost instantly. She was surprised by the warmth that filled her heart when she heard it. She turned around and gave George a warm smile.

"Hi George, nice to see you again."

"Likewise," he replied and greeted her with a kiss on both cheeks. "That's the European way, isn't it?"

"I guess. So I gather you've heard about my trip to Paris?"

"Yes, I have and I must say I was pleasantly surprised."

"You didn't think I could be so carefree."

"That's not what I said. I just thought you needed someone or something to unleash the rebel inside of you."

"Oh," Julie stumbled to find her words. George appeared different. He looked warm, boyish and playful. Although she had seen him in casual clothes on dress down days, she never really paid that much attention to his style. He looked very down to earth in his bomber jacket, black chinos and shirt which bore a youthful print. His hair was cut short but was slightly messy in the front. His blue eyes were happy and approachable.

"You look great in your scarf and black leather skirt, very French."

"Oh thanks." Julie responded, surprised that he was also checking out what she was wearing. "I actually bought the scarf in Paris. It's true. The French really love their scarves. In fact they love anything that has beauty in it."

"Well, in that case, I'm sure they loved you."

Julie found herself staring at him. She couldn't believe the compliment he just paid her. She began to feel self-conscious as they both stood there, looking at each other.

"Hi guys. Glad you're on time."

Julie turned around and saw a beautiful, slim, and very tall Stacey standing next to them in the coolest high heels Julie had ever seen. She was obviously keeping up with the trends despite her credit card debt.

"Hi Stace," George greeted her with a kiss.

"Julie. Look at you! You look so rejuvenated. You're so lucky to be able to jet off to Paris. I'm in such financial strife that the only holiday I'll be having is a day or two on the south coast. Good for you I say! You deserve a holiday after all the hours you put in at work. Anyway, we better head to the pier. We don't want to miss the boat. I've got to make sure everyone is here. By the way ... cool belt, Julie," she finished, looking at Julie's eighties-style belt before dashing off.

"Thanks!" Julie couldn't keep up with Stacey sometimes. She was always so energised and enthusiastic. It was amazing to see her switch from "social Stacey," to "professional organised Stacey." She knew how to take charge of things and looked like a person in control as she stood on the pier, marking people off her list. Julie was surprised that she couldn't use her organisational skills to sort out her finances.

Julie was seated across from George. If it wasn't for the elegant surroundings of the small cruise ship, the rectangular table, and of course the floor moving under her feet from the swaying of the boat, it almost felt that they were back at their morning team meetings. Stacey had made all the seating arrangements and she was very particular about people sticking to her plan.

"Just like old times," George commented from across the table, as if reading her mind.

"Yes it is," Julie acknowledged. *Except in the old days, you would be challenging me on any issue I raised and I would be looking at you with contempt*, Julie thought to herself.

"So, is Colin coming?" Sarah asked as she sat next to Julie and greeted her and everyone on the table with a smile.

"I sure am!" Colin emerged looking very debonair in an elegant suit jacket, jeans and a crisp light blue shirt.

"You can sit at the head of the table for old time's sake," Stacey instructed.

"Okay. Don't worry everyone. There's no need to take the minutes. I won't be discussing any customer complaints or how we can work more efficiently."

"Just to make sure, what will you be drinking?" George volunteered, eyeing the bottles of wine and beer on the table.

"A beer will be fine for now, George."

"What about you, Julie?" George looked at Julie inquisitively. "There's no French wine here, but I'm sure our renowned Australian wine is to your liking."

"I'll have a glass of Pinot Noir," Julie responded, smiling.

"Yes, you'll have to tell us all about your trip," Colin interjected. "It didn't take you long to pursue your dreams. I'm curious. What made you jet off to Europe so quickly? Did we work you so hard that you just couldn't wait any longer?"

"Or did someone special whisk you off for a romantic holiday?" Jasmine, from the Redemptions team decided to join in on the conversation, as she made her way past Julie to her seat on the next table.

Julie tried desperately to hide the fact that Jasmine's question had some merit. She took a sip of wine to gain strength. As she looked up, she noticed George awaiting her response with a serious look on his face.

"Was it a romantic holiday?" Sarah reiterated the question, looking at Julie with her eyes wide open.

"No," Julie finally said, feeling all eyes on her. "It was just a holiday with some old uni friends. I always wanted to travel and the opportunity presented itself, so I jumped on it."

"I'm sure you did," Jasmine added from the other table, with a wicked smile.

Julie felt a blush creeping up on her face. She had responded much too hastily, trying to sound convincing. She had obviously chosen the wrong words. Any thought of Scott made her feel uneasy and anxious. Jasmine hadn't helped matters. She caught George still looking at her curiously from across the table.

"Well, I'm sure we'll hear all about your trip throughout the night." Stacey intervened, looking at George.

They finished their main course. The music was blaring, and people were taking to the dance floor. A band entertained everyone for a while and then the DJ took over. Everyone on the table started laughing when "Rock the Boat" came on.

Julie suddenly felt like dancing. "Who wants to join me on the dance floor?"

Stacey was about to get up, but she stopped when George stood.

"Come on, Julie. Let's show them how it's done and rock this boat." He reached for her hand and held it firmly as he led her to the dance floor. Surprisingly, she didn't mind.

Most people on the dance floor were singing the lyrics to the song and Julie decided to join in as they found a tiny spot on the crowded dance floor. George laughed and also decided to sing along.

Julie didn't know if her relaxed mood was due to the three glasses of wine that she had, or the fact that she had no immediate life plans. The fact was that she felt free. She danced as if she was the only person in the room. George twirled her around and tried to emulate some dance move he had seen, which didn't work out as he planned. They both nearly fell to the floor.

"Sorry," he said. "My sister's staying with me and she insists I watch *Dancing with the Stars* when it's on," he explained as they bumped into a woman next to them. They both started laughing when the woman next to them gave them a "how dare you" stare.

As the night progressed, they danced to some eighties pop music and some nineties dance music before they both agreed they were tired and headed outside to get some fresh air and enjoy the views of the harbour. As they headed towards the exit, they noticed Colin dancing enthusiastically with Stacey and Sarah.

"I think Colin is a party animal at heart," George remarked.

"This is so beautiful," Julie cried out as she made her way onto the deck of the cruise ship. "Sydney Harbour lit up at night is always breathtaking," she exalted, as the sea-salted night air gently caressed her face.

"So, George, what have you been up to lately? Have you looked for another job yet?" she asked, feeling the boat rocking underneath her feet. Julie could see George's stubble in the moonlight as he looked at the view. She noticed a few fine hairs moving on his bare taut chest, as a button became loose on his shirt. George noticed her looking as he turned to face her.

"No, not really. I already have a job. I've been working part-time on the weekends for a while and now I've extended my hours." He looked down at his loose button, and looked back at Julie.

His smiling eyes shimmered under the moonlit sky. Julie gazed into their kaleidoscope of blue. Feeling slightly embarrassed, she began to tidy her wind-blown hair. Her embarrassment quickly turned into curiosity. Why would George be working part-time? He was such a dedicated employee, always wanting to climb the corporate ladder. When would he find the time?

"What type of work is it?" she asked.

"I coach children to play tennis. It's one of my passions, playing tennis. I've always enjoyed the outdoors and being active. I can't stand being stuck in an office all day."

Julie's jaw dropped. She just stared at George not knowing how to respond.

"Don't look so shocked. Is it so hard to imagine me out of an office?"

"No," Julie stumbled. "Well, I guess I am used to seeing you in the context of an office setting only. Anyway, you also have false assumptions about me."

"I do? Okay, since you know what I think, indulge me. What pray tell do I think about you?"

"Well, you think I'm this uptight office worker who loves administration and hasn't got a life outside of work. You know, it's rather ironic because I thought that about you. I actually thought that you were so ambitious and that all you cared about was climbing the corporate ladder at the expense of other people's feelings. I mean, why else would you always try to humiliate me in our team meetings whenever I raised an issue, or just entered a room? You always seemed to challenge me on everything."

Julie's expression became serious. At the time, she had dismissed it and told herself that he wasn't worth worrying about.

George seemed concerned. "Is that what you thought? You actually thought that I wanted you to look bad so that I could further my career? That's the last thing I wanted to do. Although, I must admit, I did enjoy listening to your replies. Hearing you speak made me realise that you were a person with strong convictions and one who would do anything to stand up for her choices."

196

"You mean not just some conformist who crawled to her manager?"

"Julie, I know that's not who you are."

Julie looked up at George. He had a serious expression on his slightly rugged, tanned face. "So you mean that all those times you humiliated me, it was just for your personal entertainment? I can't believe you, George."

"Well, not exactly. I simply wanted to get your attention. It wasn't some calculated plan or anything like that. I didn't realise it was humiliating. Sorry, can you ever forgive me?" he asked, laughing slightly.

"Well, I'm glad you think my suffering is amusing," Julie continued, staring at the ocean.

"Julie, look at it from where I was standing. From the moment Stacey introduced you to me, you didn't want to have anything to do with me. You kept pushing me away. You seemed to be focused on something all the time … at times it seemed that you were focused on something else, something that wasn't in front of you. Of course, on most occasions, I just wanted to help you. You kept agreeing to do everything. I was genuinely trying to be a team player, which you shot down, at our last meeting."

"Well, do you blame me? You and Sarah wouldn't stop emphasising that I had too much work. It looked like I couldn't cope," Julie responded, avoiding the former part of his response, feeling embarrassed that he had uncovered her agenda.

"Oh Julie!" he said with a smile on his face. "When are you going to realise?"

"Realise what?" Julie asked.

"Hey Julie, George, come and have a look at Colin. I think he's had too much to drink. He's dancing with everyone on the dance floor, even some German tourists." Jasmine screamed. Julie looked at Jasmine who looked like she had one too many herself. She then looked back at George. He was looking at the ground. He was no longer smiling.

Julie and George made their way to the dance floor to witness their ex-manager in action. Whilst approaching the dance floor, Sarah came up to her and mentioned that her mobile which was placed in her bag at their table, had been ringing non-stop.

"Thanks," she responded and made a mental note to check her messages as soon as she could. She hadn't called Scott back since he had left her the original messages. She knew that she was avoiding him again. The more she thought about him, the angrier she felt. He hadn't considered her feelings at all. Keeping that information from her was cruel, especially, when she had been honest about her feelings for him.

All of a sudden, she felt overwhelmed with emotion. She had wanted their relationship to finally work. How could he let her down like that when he had kissed her so passionately? Didn't he know how hurt she would feel? More to the point, didn't he care about her feelings?

"Julie. Are you all right?" George asked her, his eyes revealing genuine concern. "You seem like you're a world away. Is it because of my being such a nuisance at work?"

"No. I was just thinking about Paris, something that I have to deal with."

"Well, I hope it isn't anything too serious. You did get away to gain a new lease on life, didn't you?"

"Yes, and travelling did help me immensely with that, especially in finding out what I don't need in my life."

"Oh, and what's that?"

"Unfinished business!" she yelled over the music.

They both looked at a figure that was approaching them. There was no mistaking it. He was heading their way. Before George could respond to Julie's comment, Colin grabbed both Julie and George, and before they knew it, they were officially part of the long line of dancers doing the La Bamba.

"Looks like the DJ has gone back to eighties music," George shouted on top of the music.

Julie smiled at him as she struggled to hold on to the line that was threatening to be broken in two halves. They had no choice but to dance to the remake of the original classic. It was either that or to get trampled.

The rest of the night was taken up with everyone sitting around the table reminiscing about work. Julie also answered everyone's questions regarding her trip. However, by the end of the night she felt that she was talking too much as she had more wine to drink than her usual maximum of three glasses. She always knew when to stop before she made a fool of herself. Although, she wasn't drunk, she felt pleasantly tipsy, and she knew that she was being loquacious as she recounted every minuscule detail about London and Paris, of course leaving her reunion with Scott and what the hell was happening with their relationship out of the conversation. One thing she did realise though was that she had mentioned Scott more than she had mentioned anyone else. Julie had explained that they were all friends from uni. She had mentioned the macarons she shared with Scott, the walks she had with Scott, the time she spent at the Louvre with Scott.

When Julie finally stopped talking, realising that she was hogging the limelight, she caught Stacey looking at George who was walking towards the door. As he stepped out onto the deck, he stopped and stared at the view for a while, finally coming back to the table as the cruise ship had made its way back to the pier. They all agreed to continue the night and have more coffee and dessert at one of the many restaurants at Circular Quay. Julie and George had fallen behind from the others.

"So, George, tell me more about your role as a tennis coach. That must be so different to working in an office. What made you get into that?"

"I've always been interested in tennis. I played since I was a child and played competitively as a teenager. I realised that it took a lot of work to turn professional, and

199

I wanted to have a few options. I studied finance at uni, but I realised that when I'm on the court, I feel alive. Sport can give you focus and discipline and make you fit as well. I guess I find it rewarding when I impart all that to kids."

Julie was moved. "That's very inspiring. So are you going to concentrate on being a coach on a full-time basis?"

"To tell you the truth, I'm in the middle of negotiations to become a co-owner of the tennis coaching school. It's what I always wanted to do. Working in superannuation was just to earn a bit of extra cash."

"I'm impressed."

"How so?"

"Well, it's very inspiring when someone pursues what they're really interested in, even though they have studied something completely different. I think it takes a lot of courage and insight regarding what makes them happy as individuals."

Julie felt that she had once again gotten carried away. George was looking at her.

After a long pause, he spoke. "That's very wise Julie. So what makes you happy?"

"I don't know. I know I wasn't happy before. I mean, sure, working in superannuation is okay for some people but I realise that I have no aspirations to be a manager, and I know that I want to do more than admin. I don't even think I have a corporate bone in my body. I somehow convinced myself that I did. Now that I've had time to think about it, I realise that I always wanted to be in a creative field. It may sound silly, but I love creative and beautiful things. That's why I felt at home in Paris. The appearance of every room, hotel, restaurant or museum had been given a lot of thought. I honestly believe that the environment people are in can make them happy. You don't have to live in a mansion to be happy. All you need is to create the right space, something that says this is who you are, and you can always change who you are, just as you change your environment. I think sometimes there are no rules to design. People have many aspects to their true self. They evolve and grow. That's what I'm realising. You can incorporate the different sides of yourself into your environment. They can reveal the 'right' you." Julie paused. "Sorry, I'm waffling. It must be the wine."

Julie looked down at the ground slightly embarrassed at how honest she was being with George.

"I get it," he suddenly said. "That's sort of like what you do … isn't it?"

"What do you mean?"

"The way you dress. You strive to create the right space, with your clothes, with your accessories: the 'right' you?"

He studied her eyes, as they tried to resist his stare. She could feel her heart beating fast. They had stopped walking.

"Well, I guess," she managed. "You mean with some of the things I wear?"

"Yes, I do, Julie."

His eyes were still locked with hers; she could feel her vulnerability revealing itself slowly.

"Although, the way you were talking earlier, you didn't need anything to help you with that. The light in your eyes revealed a lot, about the 'right' you … just like they are now," he continued.

Julie continued to look at him, her vulnerability disallowing her from moving. The salty, night air stung her eyes, making them slightly teary.

George was looking deep into them. "Hey," he said with a soothing voice. His face became lighter. It slowly gave way to an affectionate smile that had started from his eyes.

Julie smiled back at him, slowly coming out of her moment. "The salt just got to my eyes," she said with an awkward laugh. She then continued walking.

George walked by her side, looking at the ground thoughtfully.

"Anyway, sounds like there's an interior designer in you," he then said.

Julie stopped walking again. Many people had complimented her on her ability to transform a room, and she had even imagined how exciting it would be to work in such a field, but that's as far as it had gone. It was just a dream, one that other people pursued, but not her. It made sense, though. All her life she had admired how different houses and buildings were designed. She always enjoyed redecorating her bedroom as a child, and now the terrace. She bought as many design magazines as she could get her hands on. That's what she loved doing. It made perfect sense. Her aesthetic need was high and she needed beauty in her life. What career could offer all that? Interior design! She couldn't believe that it took George to highlight that it may actually be a valid possibility, not just a dream. The way he said it somehow made it sound plausible, as though she could really do it. She could really be an interior designer. It had been staring her in the face for so long and it took a former work colleague who she thought had been her enemy to clarify it for her.

Julie's thoughts were abruptly interrupted, not by any response from George but from the familiar figure that was approaching her. Her elation at the realisation that she had just made had changed to uncertainty.

Scott looked as if he was on a mission, focused. He soon reached them.

"Are you okay Julie?" George asked as he placed his hand on her shoulder with concern.

Scott stared at both of them, and especially at the hand that George had placed on her shoulder. Their eyes finally met.

"Just like old times, isn't it, Julie?"

"What do you mean, Scott?" Julie asked, genuinely confused.

"I was wrong about us changing. Nothing has changed. First you jump to conclusions, then you avoid me, and now you find another man to lean on. Is this a pattern with you? Don't try to work anything out, just move on with someone else?"

"What's going on, Julie? Who is this guy?" George asked.

"This guy is her ex-boyfriend, her first true love, the guy she went to Paris with, the guy who wanted to give their relationship another chance. The only problem is that she heard something that upset her and she didn't give this guy the benefit of the doubt."

George looked confused.

"Is everything okay?" Stacey walked towards them eyeing Scott as she approached them. She then looked at George inquisitively.

"I think these two need some time to talk. There has obviously been a misunderstanding," George said as he headed back towards the rest of the group, who were now looking at a menu outside one of the popular restaurants.

"George," Julie began to explain.

"It's okay. I'll catch up with you at another reunion, unless you ever want a tennis lesson." He began to walk away until he stopped and turned around. "So I was right," he said. "I was right that someone helped you to unleash the rebel in you."

Julie stared at him as he walked away and witnessed Stacey putting her arm around him. Then Julie looked at Scott who was looking at her with the same look he gave her all those years ago in Newtown. "So here we are again," he said.

"Yes. Here we are again," Julie responded, staring at him blankly.

CHAPTER TWENTY-EIGHT

After what seemed like eternity, he spoke. Julie didn't know what to feel as she stared at him thinking that this scenario between them was becoming all too familiar.

"I've left numerous messages on your mobile as I'm sure you're aware. I called you countless times on your home number. I finally had enough. I went to your house and Cassandra and Maria told me you were here. I'm sick of these games, Julie. Didn't we learn anything from the last time?"

"What? I'm playing games with you? You're the one who wasn't honest with me. When were you planning to tell me that you had a daughter? How stupid of me! Here I was thinking we had another chance and you can't even be honest with me. So tell me, Scott. Are you married? Do you have someone else in your life?"

Julie's voice was getting louder just as her desperation to find out the truth was getting stronger. She peered over to where George and the rest of the group were and she caught George looking at her. Scott also witnessed this. "Why don't we find somewhere quiet to talk?" he suggested. Julie walked by his side. Still fuming, she released her arm from the smooth touch of his hand.

"And for the record, I have not moved on. Talk about jumping to conclusions. George is a former work colleague. How dare you accuse me of lying to you when you're the one who wasn't honest with me? How dare you turn this around?"

"Julie, please calm down. I didn't mean to upset you." Scott stopped walking and faced her. "I just wanted to explain everything to you. I know I was being childish about that guy and you, but you looked really close when I saw you together. I guess the past came back to me."

Julie looked into his confused eyes. He was standing close to her. She didn't know if it was the wine, the fact that she hadn't stopped to relax since she had arrived back in Sydney, or the fact that she felt so hurt by Scott again. She suddenly burst into tears. She could feel her tears streaming down her face. She was shaking all over. Exhaustion kicked in and she felt that she was about to collapse.

She felt Scott's strong arms around her. She didn't resist, allowing her whole body to surrender in the safety of his arms. He began to caress her hair. "It's going to be okay, Julie," he told her. She could feel his heart beating fast.

"I just want to know …"

He pulled her face away from his chest and looked into her eyes. "What do you want to know?"

"I want to know where we stand. I need to know if there is any chance that we can try again. I just want you to be honest with me and tell me everything."

"I will, Julie. I promise that I will tell you everything."

All Julie felt then were his lips on hers. He began to kiss her intensely. When their lips parted, she remained in his arms for a while, resting her head on his chest. She finally pulled away from him and began to wipe the tears from her face.

"I don't know what came over me," she managed.

"I hurt you, again. That's what came over you. It's the last thing I wanted to do but I did it."

Julie could see that Scott's remorse was genuine. She also realised that they hadn't walked that far from where George and the rest of the group had decided to continue the night. She took a quick glance and noticed that they were deep in conversation. She hoped that they hadn't witnessed her sudden melt down and Scott kissing her.

"Let's go and grab a coffee," Scott said.

Soon after, they were seated in a beautiful restaurant overlooking the Sydney Harbour Bridge and the Opera

House. Julie was stirring the flat white Scott had ordered for her.

"I think the sugar has dissolved now," Scott commented, looking at her with a cautious smile. "Okay, are you ready?" he asked her. "Are you ready to hear everything?"

"Ready as I will ever be, I guess."

"Okay." He leaned over to her and cleared his throat. A serious look crossed his face. "I have a daughter. A beautiful three-year-old little girl called Victoria." He reached out for her hand before he continued. "The thing is Julie, I'm also married."

Julie froze. She was about to pull her hand away from him but he held it tighter and leaned closer to her.

"I'm separated. I've been separated from my wife for eight months now. We were having problems for a while and things only got worse. I've had a lot to sort out. It's been complicated, especially when it comes to Victoria and when I can and can't see her. It's been the worst year since … well it's been really difficult. I'm trying to keep everything amicable for Victoria's sake because as you heard me tell her on the phone, she is the world to me. Anyway, that's why I've been all over the place. It had nothing to do with work. My wife, Ashley, has been very difficult lately. I don't blame her though. I feel that I have let her and Victoria down. She really didn't deserve this. She is a really nice person but she was making me feel so bad about leaving Victoria behind, even though Ashley had already made arrangements for Victoria to spend time with her grandparents before I even decided to go to Paris. I had to make sure she was all right before I left. I think the separation is making Victoria very fearful. She thought that I was leaving forever and that I wouldn't return. I guess she found out Paris is far away and somehow got the impression that I wasn't coming back."

He paused for a while and looked to see how Julie was reacting. Julie listened to every word. She felt numb all over.

"Anyway, I didn't want to play games with you. When I ran into you, I couldn't believe it. For years I've thought about us and how my life would be if we were still together. You have always been on my mind, Julie. I needed answers. I didn't want to go on thinking that you could intentionally hurt me the way I thought you did. I honestly thought we were given another chance and you came into my life at the right moment. I was separated. Ashley and I had been in trouble for a while. I knew you came into my life for a reason."

"So, that's what you meant when you said that things had changed."

"Yes, although I knew we were given another chance, the reality is I'm still married. I wanted to find the right time to tell you. One thing I was certain of though was that my marriage wasn't working and I know that the reason I couldn't make it work was because I felt that as much as I loved Ashley, my heart was always with you. I never got over you. I felt that I was cheating on Ashley because I kept thinking of us and what could have been. I felt that my marriage was a lie. So, I left Ashley to clear my mind and gain some clarity."

Julie didn't say anything for a while. "You know, Scott, I guess we're not so different."

"Oh, how do you mean?"

"I haven't been able to move on either. I've seen a few guys, but it has only lasted a few months, even less. I always compared every guy to you. I guess the difference with your situation though is that you're married and you have a daughter. It's a lot more complicated."

"When I found out that you and Mark had broken up, I felt that we had wasted our opportunity. Part of me felt like contacting you to see if we could fix things. I guess my pride got in the way. I met Ashley at a seminar when I changed to IT. She's a computer programmer. In a way, she reminded me of you. She had the same warm smile and a real passion for life. We dated for a while, and then she fell pregnant. That's when I proposed to her. I had convinced myself that I had to move on, and she was the only woman, other than you, that I could do that with. The fact that she was expecting my child had made me realise that I had to take responsibility. I was going to be a father. I had to get my act together. For a while, everything was great. Until I realised that I had a lot of repressed feelings when it came to you. Everything had happened so quickly. It was too soon to be involved with someone else. As much as I had developed feelings for Ashley, I felt that my life had taken a direction I hadn't anticipated. Deep down, I felt lost and confused. I wasn't sure if I had married Ashley too quickly. I started to take it out on other people, on Ashley. I didn't want Victoria growing up in an unhappy home. Julie, I really want to give us another chance. Tell me. Do you think that's possible?"

"I don't know. I guess the question to ask is: do you love her?"

He looked at his coffee for a moment.

"I want to be honest with you. I will always love Ashley. She has brought a lot into my life and she is the mother of my child. I just feel that there has been something missing in my life. I know it sounds selfish, but I feel that we've been robbed of our chance to be together. I don't know about you, but I don't want to live my life with regrets. Don't you think we owe it ourselves? Haven't we suffered enough?"

"Oh Scott, I don't know. I just need to know that Ashley knows where she stands. I don't want to be responsible for another person's pain. If you weren't trying to reconcile with her before I came back into your life, then maybe we can try again."

"I left her because it had all happened too fast. It was too soon. You and I hadn't really broken up. We had deep feelings for each other: a connection. Then, because of false assumptions, we abruptly stopped seeing each other. The feelings we had didn't go away. They stayed with me, and from what you've told me, they are still with you as well. It wasn't supposed to have ended. Even though I was only twenty-three at the time, I really thought you were the girl for me, the girl that I could envision spending my life with. Do you think we can start from the beginning and see where we end up? Try to get to know each other all over again, the way we did back then, now that everything is out in the open?"

"Maybe we can start from the beginning and take it slow. Like I said though, I want you to be honest with me about where you stand with Ashley. I don't want her waiting by the phone for you."

"You don't need to worry about that. We already did the compulsory counselling, and we need to remain separated for a while. She knows that it's over. She knew for a long time that my heart was somewhere else."

"Okay then. So, where do we start? Do we go back to the library and retrace our first meeting?"

Scott suddenly looked sceptical. "Oh, you mean when you clumsily dropped your books on … what was it? Oh, I remember, the ending of the Cold War. You were obviously so into me that you couldn't control yourself."

"Well, as I recall, you couldn't wait to help me pick them up. It's as if you were waiting for an opportunity to talk to me and when the opportunity arose, you pounced. I guess *you* couldn't control yourself around *me*."

"Is that so? Well, nothing has really changed then because I still find that I can't control myself when I look at your mesmerising hazel eyes. You can't begin to imagine the fantasies that have filled my mind since I ran into you at Hunter Valley," he said as he caressed her face.

Julie looked down at her coffee feeling Scott's gaze on her. He was holding her hand again. Each smooth, sensual stroke sent goose bumps all over her body. She remembered the fantasy she had about him when she ran into him but she knew they couldn't rush into anything.

"So, when's our first official date now that everything is out in the open?" she asked.

"How about dinner tomorrow?"

"Sounds good to me, but now all I want is to go straight to bed," Julie responded sleepily.

Scott looked at her, smiling with intrigue. "That sounds like an interesting proposition to me."

"I mean I want to sleep! I don't know about you, but I still feel exhausted from the trip."

"I guess I didn't help with that. You were probably thinking the worst of me."

"Actually, now that we're being so honest, that didn't help. I've had a headache all week. Now that we're on the subject, I didn't avoid you, well not entirely. In my defence, I also had a lot of issues to deal with. I have made a vow to myself that I would face any obstacles that life throws at me and not procrastinate. I was also jet-lagged and I needed some time to clear my mind. As for tonight, well, I forgot to look at my phone."

"So you were going to call me back?"

"Yes, eventually. Avoiding things only leads to living in fear, and I definitely don't want fear to rule my life."

Scott was looking at her the same way he would often look at her back when they were a couple. "I'm glad for you. I always felt that you held back sometimes. It was as though you wouldn't allow yourself to thrive or to say something out of line. I knew you wanted to though."

They both looked at each other for a while.

"Come on. I'll drive you home," he said.

As they left the restaurant, Scott's arm around her, Julie noticed that another woman had joined her ex-work colleagues who were now also leaving the nearby restaurant. The woman was walking alongside George, and she was laughing with Stacey. She looked very familiar. After a few minutes, Julie remembered it was the blonde who was with George at the Indian restaurant.

Well, they must be a couple if she's still in the picture, she thought to herself.

Scott looked at her as he walked by her side, his arm shielding her from the chill in the night air. "Is everything okay?" he asked.

"Yes, everything's fine," she replied. *Everything is as it should be*, she then told herself.

CHAPTER TWENTY-NINE

"So, Maria, have you had a chance to talk to Antonio?"

Maria stared blankly at the birdbath in the middle of the garden, which had enticed a few brave birds even though Maria, Cassandra and Julie were sitting a few steps away at the outdoor table. It was a sunny Sunday morning, and they all thought it would be a great opportunity to have their breakfast in the garden.

Julie was also eager to find out how Maria was feeling about her situation, and if she had told Antonio the news yet. It was very hard to talk to Maria when she shut her feelings off, and Julie thought being outside may encourage more honest expression. Julie herself wanted to savour every moment of peace before she went to the family barbecue her parents had planned. She was apprehensive about seeing her sister again. Too much had happened since she last saw Christina, and Julie didn't have time to think about how she would handle her encounter with her until that morning. She had spent the whole of Saturday finally unpacking her bags, which took a lot longer than she had anticipated. Everything she pulled out led to her reminisce about where they were when she wore a particular outfit, or bought a particular souvenir.

The fact that she had a lot of laundry to get through in between unpacking didn't help to speed up the process, and when she finally completed both tasks, she helped Cassandra with some much needed household chores before getting ready for her dinner with Scott, which had taken place at a French restaurant in Paddington. They both felt their hearts were still in Paris, as were their taste buds.

"By the way," Julie digressed, seeing that Maria wasn't responding to her question. "Don't forget, my parents also

212

invited Cass and you to the barbecue. I know Cass can't make it, but it would be great if you could join me. My mum said that you can also bring Antonio along," she added, hoping that would open up the lines of communication.

"Nice try, Jules," Maria responded.

"So, who wants coffee?" Cassandra offered. "Oh," she quickly corrected, looking at Maria. "I forgot. You can't drink too much caffeine now, can you?"

"That's okay. I don't even feel like drinking coffee. The thought of it makes me sick." Maria finally looked away from the birdbath and took a sip of her orange juice.

"Maria, I can see you're still feeling uncertain about telling Antonio because you don't want him to feel obligated to stay with you. You also seem to still be in shock about being pregnant. Is that right?" Cassandra added.

Julie knew what Cassandra was doing. She was trying to reflect Maria's feelings. She would often use this counselling technique and other similar ones, such as paraphrasing and summarising. It seemed to have become engrained in her dealings with her friends, not just her clients. Julie was usually impressed with how effective such techniques would be.

"You're right. I'm still in shock. I just can't see myself as being pregnant. I feel stupid for not being careful. I don't know how I'm going to deal with everything: the shop, being a single mother. I never expected myself to be in this situation."

"You do feel that you need to tell Antonio, though?" Julie intervened, not being able to contain herself. The way Maria was talking, it was as though she was planning to keep it from him.

"Of course I plan to tell him. I just feel ... I don't know what I feel."

"Afraid? Do you feel afraid to tell him?"

"Yes. I feel scared."

"What do you feel scared about? Do you think that Antonio wouldn't want the baby?"

"No. He would definitely want the baby. That's the type of guy he is. It's just that, to tell you both the truth, I'm angry that he decided to go back to Chile just when everything was looking so promising. I know it's selfish, but I feel that he has chosen his family instead of me. I mean, if he really loved me, wouldn't he want to try and let our relationship grow? We're still a new couple and the distance that this trip would put between us can be detrimental to the relationship. It's still new and fragile. I mean, nothing lasts if there are no strong foundations."

"Well, Maria, if you feel this way, why don't you tell him?" Julie suggested. "Tell him everything. Tell him that you don't want him to leave and that you have developed strong feelings for him. Tell him that you love him and ask if there is another way he can help his parents. I don't think that's selfish. You love him. What's so selfish about that? You can't help how you feel. Trust me. You don't want to live your life feeling that you avoided telling someone how you really feel. Things can change, and it may be so difficult to go back."

"Wow! What's come over you?" Cassandra looked at Julie.

"I just think that we sometimes need to stop running and start being brave and facing things."

"You mean, like facing this barbecue that you don't want to go to because of some spat you had with your sister?" Maria enquired, now smiling.

"Well, yes, that's one issue I want to stop running from."

"What's the other?"

Julie took a sip of her coffee and looked at both her friends. "It's Scott. You already know he has a daughter. What I didn't tell you yet is that he's actually married, but before you both start attacking him, he has been separated from his wife for a while. Now, everything is so different. We've both decided to start from the beginning and take it

214

slow again, but just think how easy it would have been for us back then. Had I confronted him, everything may have worked out differently. Of course, he would never regret having his little girl, but it's all so complicated now."

"So you still intend to see him?" Cassandra asked.

"Well, for the time being. He said that their relationship had been over for a while."

"Well, he's definitely still crazy about you, the way he came looking for answers about where you were on Friday. It was really brave of him to face us like that. He even made a joke when he introduced himself stating that he was 'Scott, the guy who broke Julie's heart'," Maria added.

"How do you feel about going out with a man who's in the middle of a divorce?" Cassandra asked, not wanting to shift the direction of the conversation.

"I don't know. All I know is that I wouldn't be in this mess if I had spoken up." Julie looked at Maria, not liking where the conversation was heading. Cassandra always tried not to be judgmental with clients, but she often found it more difficult with her friends. "So Maria," she continued, "Please tell Antonio how you feel. It's like Gestalt therapy theory," she said, turning to Cassandra. "You can't move on without completing the incomplete."

"That's right. Everyone needs to do that when they can, and sometimes when they do, they realise that a different path awaits them than the one they had anticipated," Cassandra added, as though she was on the same page as Julie but reading a completely different book.

"That's right," Julie added, not knowing if she understood what Cassandra had said but at the same time, not wanting to find out either.

"Okay, okay. You're both driving me crazy. I feel sick. No food appeals to me all of a sudden, and I can't listen to this philosophical counselling talk on an empty stomach. I'll talk to Antonio. I know I have to anyway. I know that I have to deal with the situation. I'm just letting the fear take hold. You're both right. Now you, Julie, can do the same and go and fix things with your sister."

"Yes sir!" Julie smiled at Maria, happy to see her friend snap out of her temporarily paralysed state of mind. "What about Cassandra?"

"Well, Cassandra can find out where she and Connor stand."

"And how do you propose I do that?"

"I don't know. Listen to your heart and stop analysing everything," Maria stated wisely. "It's about time I offered some advice," she added, and she left with a proud grin on her face, knowing that she hadn't let Cassandra have the last word on the subject.

***

Julie took a deep breath, as she often did when she felt tense about something. She was standing at the doorstep of her parents' double-storey, newly renovated brick house, holding a blueberry baked cheesecake and a bag of gifts from her trip. Just as she had summoned enough courage to ring the doorbell, the door flung open revealing her mother and little John trying to pass his grandmother to greet Julie first.

"Hi Julie, you look wonderful. You obviously got some sun in Europe."

"I want to say hi to Auntie Julie." John pushed his way through the small space between his grandmother and the door.

"Okay, John. Don't worry. You'll get your chance to see your Auntie."

Just as Julie was about to lean down to give her nephew a big kiss, his little hands reached into the bag that she was holding. "What's in the bag? Is it a toy?"

"Mum, you'd better get the cake before it goes everywhere. I think it would be wise to get the formalities out of the way and hand the gifts out now."

She quickly snuck a kiss on her nephew's soft cheek and then led him into the house, reassuring him that she did get him something special from London and Paris.

"What did you get me? Is it a toy? Elisabeth, Julie got me a present!"

"Hi Elisabeth, you look so beautiful in your red coat. John's right. I did get him something, and I got you something as well. Let me say hello to everyone first and then you two will be the first to receive your gifts."

The smell of balsamic vinegar led Julie to the kitchen where she found her sister adding salad dressing to one of the many salads that were placed on the table. Her mother always went to so much trouble when she invited them for lunch or dinner.

Julie, Christina and Brian would often protest, saying that a few lamb cutlets and a salad would be more than enough. Her parents would agree until they would host the next lunch or dinner where the same formula would be applied: food, and lots of it.

"Hi Christina," she greeted her sister.

She had told herself that she would try her best to be fair with her sister but she would remain strong and assertive if any sarcastic or judgmental comments were made.

"Hi. Dad's outside with Brian tending to the barbecue," she said flatly.

"I'll go and say hi, and then I have a few things from my trip I'd like to hand out. John is trying his best to be patient so I'd better hurry," she said feeling like a deflated balloon. *So much for being assertive*, she thought. She would need all her strength to endure this lunch.

"Julie, don't let Christina get to you. I'm sure she'll come around. She's just being stubborn. She seems really unhappy lately, more than she usually is. Don't let it bother you," her mother whispered in her ear when Christina was out of earshot, placing her hand on Julie's shoulder. "I'm so proud of you for following your heart," she added, and headed back to the kitchen.

Julie stepped outside. Gaining some strength from her mother's words, she walked over to the rest of her family. She could already smell the smoke from the barbecue in her soft curls. John and Elisabeth walked beside her, eagerly waiting to see what she had in the bag.

"Hi Dad, hi Brian."

"Hi Jules, how's my beautiful daughter? Did you have a good trip?"

"I had a wonderful trip. I've got plenty of photos to show you all."

"So, which did you enjoy more, London or Paris?" Brian asked.

"I guess it's hard to say. They are both so different and special in their own way. I didn't have that much time in London. James, one of the guys in the group, was eager to get to Paris as the Tour de France was on."

"I can't wait to hear about the race. You know I love cycling. I used to ride my bike to work every day. I can't believe you were there. I've watched it on TV every year and it's been one of my dreams to actually be part of it."

"Maybe you and Christina can plan a trip there with the kids? You'll have so much fun, and Paris is very child friendly. They'll learn so much."

"I wish we could. I'm sure Christina wouldn't want to ruin any schedules that the kids have," Brian responded, looking down at the barbecue.

"Yes, Daddy, can we go to Paris?" Elisabeth asked, happily.

"Yeah, I want to go on the Eiffel Tower," John chimed in. "Look. I can look like the Eiffel Tower."

Everyone laughed as John emulated the shape of the Eiffel Tower with his body.

"Very impressive," Julie commented, smiling.

"I hope you're all hungry. Looks like the cutlets and the sausages are ready. I don't want to burn them. I've got some prawns we can cook after, and we can have some cold," her dad added cheerfully. He knew how much they all loved prawns.

Julie's heart suddenly filled with regret. Why couldn't she and her sister work things out? It was a shame that they couldn't really let their hair down and enjoy each other's company without any tension or anxiety.

Julie quickly handed out everyone's gifts. Of course John and Elisabeth were first. John was so excited with his London toy cab and Big Ben sharpener. They both loved their plates, adorned with pictures of the Eiffel Tower and the Arc de Triomphe, as well as the pencil cases, T-shirts and glow in the dark Eiffel Tower souvenirs. Brian and her father were ever so pleased with their T-shirts, and her mum couldn't stop admiring the scarf she bought for her, which was enclosed in an elegant box. She also gave Christina a scarf, which Julie was sure she would like, and a pair of earrings for both of them. Christina was obviously happy with her gift but all she could manage was, "Thanks," as she quickly placed them back in the bag that they came in. Julie then caught Christina looking at the shoes she was wearing: the ones that she had purchased in Paris with the unique block heel.

They gathered around the outdoor table on the patio. Julie answered questions about the trip. Her mother was interested hearing about the Louvre and began a whole discussion on art and what she was doing in her art class. Just as she was about to launch into another topic, she realised that Christina was oddly quiet. She was playing with her food, looking rather agitated.

"Mum, can we go and play now? We've finished our food!"

Christina nodded. John and Elisabeth took advantage of their mother's unusual response, as she would normally make a big fuss that they should eat more. They immediately stood up and ran off laughing.

"Good on you, Julie," her father said. "It sounds like you had a wonderful time and you learned a lot. Travelling is great. It broadens the mind."

"Well, it's easy to travel when you have no responsibilities such as raising children, or care about anything like getting a job," Christina commented, obviously fuming as she spoke.

"Oh, I don't know," her mother interjected. "Everyone can find the time to travel, even when they have children to raise. It can bring people closer together, as they experience new things together." She gave Julie a knowing smile.

"It's hardly the same, though," Christina continued angrily. "I mean it would be a completely different type of holiday. I would still have the same responsibilities. It wouldn't make a difference if I were in Paris or Lisbon. I would still be worried about what the kids will eat, if I've packed all their toys, if they're bored. How relaxing would that be? Not everyone can sleep in and spend hours at the Louvre without a care in the world."

Brian finally spoke, choosing his words carefully. "I think it's what you make it. You can make an experience a positive one depending on what you as a person put into it, or what outlook you have."

"Oh, so you're saying that I don't have a positive outlook, that I'm too pessimistic?"

"That's not what I said," Brian said, colouring slightly. "I just mean if you really want something, you can find a way to make it work."

"So you're saying that I don't try to make things work? I can't believe all of you. Julie is the one who irresponsibly travelled to the other side of the world when she just lost her job. She has no house to her name, no family responsibilities, and you're all acting like she did the most amazing thing. She travelled to Europe with a group of people she hasn't seen for years. Meanwhile I try and do the right thing for years raising my kids, making sure they

220

go well at school, and now I'm made to look like I'm selfish and I'm holding everyone back. I've had enough. All my life I've been treated like this, like I'm the boring rigid sister, the one who doesn't know how to have fun. I'm sick of it."

Everyone around the table looked on as Christina stormed into the house, slamming the door behind her. Brian stood up but Julie felt that she and Christina needed to talk.

She found Christina staring out into the street in the front lounge room. The freshly pressed, cream-coloured linen curtains were drawn open. As Julie entered the light-filled room, she suddenly became anxious. She was worried that the conversation would turn into a screaming match. She walked in and sank down near Christina on the brown leather couch.

"So, what was that all about?" she asked Christina, who was still staring out into the street. She seemed to be a million miles away. Her mother was right. She genuinely looked unhappy. "Christina, can we just try to talk to each other? We obviously have a lot of repressed feelings. I know what you think of me and my life choices. Now you also revealed that we all think you're boring and rigid. Shouldn't we talk about what we feel once and for all? Aren't you sick of all the pretending?"

"What I'm sick of is you always judging me!"

"You think *I'm* judgmental?" Julie tried to remain calm.

"Yes! You think I judge you? You're the one who assumes you know everything about me. You think I have it all figured out, that I have a formula for my life and other people's lives. If you thought about someone other than yourself for a moment, you would see that I hate this role that you all expect me to play. You think that I don't have aspirations for myself other than being a wife and mother? Do you honestly think that I don't want to live an adventurous life and travel? It isn't easy trying to balance it all. I don't even know who I am anymore, so don't place

221

me in a box and label me. You accused me of wanting to force my beliefs onto you and to tell you how to live your life. Well, did you ever think that I'm just as confused about life as you are? Just because I got married early and had kids, it doesn't mean I'm content."

Julie was shocked. Part of her wanted to dismiss the allegations as ludicrous, but the other part of her saw some truth in them. She had been consumed with her own problems and inner conflict lately.

"Why didn't you ever tell me you felt this way?" Julie asked.

"How could I? I'm always supposed to be the responsible married one with kids, who shouldn't complain because I apparently have everything I want out of life. When we were young, I was the responsible one and you were the spontaneous, carefree, creative one. I was supposed to take care of you. I always felt that I would let them down if you didn't do your best at school. I know Mum and Dad had no choice at the time. I mean, they had just started a business in the food industry, which at first they knew nothing about. It took a lot of years for the business to finally pay off, and they needed to feel that we were okay, but I always resented the fact that I was supposed to be the responsible and wise one."

"I always felt that they thought you were wiser and smarter than me, that I was incapable of making my own decisions, that I couldn't make it without you holding my hand. Mum always told me to ask for your advice when it came to making decisions."

"Mum always thought we were close and that we respected each other's opinions. I guess we were at one stage, until I was promoted to 'person in charge of the house when they weren't around'. The thing is, I always resented you because you could be yourself. You never worried like I did. You were always optimistic about life. I felt that I had to be studious and responsible. I guess I projected that onto you and I still tend to do that. I felt that we would fail in life if we didn't do things a certain way. Even now, I feel so lost and confused. I don't know what I want for myself."

"Aren't you happy with Brian? I mean. You and he were the 'it' couple at school, and John and Elisabeth are adorable."

"I am happy with them. I love them so much. I just feel that something is missing. It's as though I want something that is completely mine. I feel that I'm projecting my fears onto them as I did to you. I look at you and although I lecture you about finding the right guy, I envy the fact that you can come and go as you please. I feel that if my routine or the children's routine is ruined, that I'll lose control of my life. I'm just so confused about everything. I don't even know what I'm trying to say."

"No, I understand. You want to find something that ignites your passion as an individual. You love being Brian's wife and a mother, but you need to do something for yourself. That's not selfish. In fact, if you're happy as an individual, you'll be a happier wife and better mother as well."

Christina looked at Julie. Julie hadn't seen her sister look at her like that since they were close. She was really looking at her, not pretending to be. "You really do understand how I feel," she said, a sincere smile forming on her face.

"Yes. I do understand because that's exactly how I feel. I know I'm not married and I don't have kids, but I know that I need to do be true to myself and do something that ignites passion into my life. I think you need that in order to be happy in a relationship, or as a mother."

"Exactly! I want to feel proud of myself. I want to wake up in the morning and look forward to accomplishing something for myself. I also want my children and Brian to be proud of me and not just look at me as the person who takes care of them."

"That's why I wasn't happy in my job. I felt that it was sapping away my creativity. I've always wanted to do something creative." A liberating sense of relief took over her whole body. Julie suddenly laughed.

"What's so funny?"

"You and I are. Here we both were thinking that we were so different when we really are quite alike. Our circumstances might be different, but we definitely feel the same about life and what's important."

"I never wanted to tell you because I felt guilty. I always felt that I shouldn't complain. I'm financially secure and I have a great family. I do miss working though. I miss the challenge and the excitement."

"Why don't you go back then? The kids are older now."

"To tell you the truth, I don't know if I want to work in marketing anymore. I'm not sure about what I want to do, but I know I've always wanted to be my own boss. I always dreamt of having my own business, but I don't know what type."

"You do have the business and finance knowledge to help you with that, and you can always talk to Maria, or Mum and Dad. In fact, maybe the career surveys I completed can also help you in finding out what sort of business you want to get into."

"You mean the ones that John nearly destroyed? Sorry about that. I was going to stop him but he had already taken them all out. I was about to get off the couch and pack them up when you came in the room. I felt embarrassed that you caught us with them scattered all over the floor. Anyway, to tell you the truth I was tempted to look at the one titled, 'Who Controls Your Life?' I was wondering if that would have been me."

"Well, maybe just a little bit, but I came to realise that I control my own life."

"Julie, since we're being so honest, can you answer something for me?"

"Okay," Julie answered, taken aback by the sudden change of mood.

"Was that Scott, the guy that was talking to you at the Hunter Valley, near the tennis courts?"

Julie couldn't believe what she was hearing. How did her sister even see her with Scott?

"We all saw you talking to him. The coffee I had bought wasn't up to scratch, so we went to get another one. I saw you talking to a tall, attractive guy, and from a distance, he looked exactly like Scott. You were looking so intimately at each other, and then you didn't mention anything to us. I could tell you were acting mysteriously that Sunday morning, after you blasted me the day before. I knew it wasn't just you being angry with me."

"I can't believe you saw us!"

"I didn't tell you that I saw you together because I knew it's such a touchy subject. I mean, you went to great lengths to hide that you were meeting him. I know you don't want to confide in me about him. You didn't then, so why would you have wanted to now? I can see how uneasy the subject has been making you for years. When you two broke up, I was going to ask you about him but you had closed yourself off to everyone. You were a wreck. I felt so hurt because I knew he meant a lot to you and you didn't even feel that you could talk to me. "

"I didn't tell you because …"

"… because you thought that I would impose my opinion and that I would be judgmental instead of supportive about why you broke up. I know what you think of me, Julie, and it really hurt me because I just wanted the best for you. I was so happy that you found someone you felt so passionate about. It's hard to find that. As for your job, I didn't want you to travel with Mark because I knew your heart was still with Scott. I thought you needed to gain some perspective so that you could be with the guy that was right for you. I knew you could get another job. I mean, it wasn't even what you studied. Deep down, I thought you might rekindle your relationship with

Scott. I knew that you really loved him. That's the type of passion I felt with Brian."

"So why did you say it was a shame that I had broken up with Mark?"

"I knew the subject of Scott was still a no go zone. As for Mark, I guess I was sussing out if you were letting what happened with Scott affect any potential new relationships. It was my indirect way of finding out about Scott. I thought that you might finally admit everything to me."

"So that's why you also said that I match guys to a certain criteria?"

"Guilty as charged," Christina said, smiling.

"You know, he was with me in Paris. Scott was with me in Paris and I am still seeing him now. We're dating and taking it slow. A lot of things have changed."

"I suspected that might be the case. So where do things stand?"

"It's a very long story." Julie looked at Christina, who looked disappointed. "It's not that I don't want to confide in you about it. I'm just exhausted from all the uncertainty. It's a story that requires a lot of coffee and a few hours of your time. Do you think we can arrange that?"

"You mean, do what sisters do and go and have a coffee together and talk about men?"

"I'm game if you are."

"Just promise me something, though." Julie suddenly looked at her sister with a serious expression on her face.

"What?' Christina asked puzzled.

"Please, don't complain about the coffee, unless it's really shocking."

Christina sighed. "I know I always complain, but a good cup of coffee is the only thing I look forward to sometimes. It sounds sad, but it's like my own little reward during the day. I guess I complain a lot because I feel that sometimes I can't control parts of my life and I need to control something. Does that make sense to you?"

"More than you know. My escape is in music and …"

"Music *can* be freeing. Don't look so shocked. You'd be surprised and impressed with the different genre of music stored on my phone. Despite what you think, my taste in music has matured over the years. Excuse the dance music in the car though. Elisabeth can't stop listening to it, and I guess I know all the songs now. Anyway, they make me feel young again. Being a teenager feels like it was a lifetime ago, the way I've been feeling lately."

"In that case, maybe we can go and see a rock band together, or listen to some live jazz. Anyway, I don't care what music you listen to. To tell you the truth, I love all types of music. I guess I'm also growing, and I'm trying to be more open minded. Creativity and talent can be found everywhere. I just felt that you judged all my choices in all aspects of my life, including the music I listened to. You always say that you have a headache whenever I play any music."

"That's because I hated that you thought that I was so rigid. A lot of the songs you played also emphasised the need to follow your dreams and screw everyone and everything else. Don't think I didn't pick that up! It was very explicit in some cases. The more you emphasised how rigid I was and how cool and alternative you were, the more I rejected your interests, even if they were also my interests. It's really childish when I think about it, I know."

Julie smiled. "You must be referring to some of those retro punk bands." Julie gave Christina a cheeky smile. "I guess we're both just as childish as each other. The more you resented my choices, the more I felt I had to repress my true self. That would explain my passive-aggressive responses, I guess."

Christina suddenly looked at Julie's shoes. "Cool shoes, by the way."

"Thanks. I got them in Paris," Julie said. "They don't look like they belong in a museum?"

"No, that was my resentment rearing its ugly head again … sorry Jules."

"Forgiven," Julie said, with a slight smile. "Anyway, I remember you used to love going to all the alternative shops as well. We used to have so much fun together."

"I guess, I've allowed myself to become the person I thought others expected me to be … and the one I desperately tried not to be … just like you."

"Anyway, getting back to our previous topic, I think that you need to find your niche, something that inspires you. We both need to strive for self-actualisation. I've learned a lot from Cassandra and her counselling studies."

"So did her surveys help with your quest to find a career that inspires you?"

"It basically highlighted what I've always suspected, that my aesthetic need is high."

"I could have told you that. Your clothes are a giveaway but you also always admired beautiful things like art, furnishings, and architecture. When we were little, you went crazy redecorating your bedroom. You always changed it. I still can't get that image of you out of my mind, when you had streaks of blue paint all over your hair. Anyway, I always thought you would be an interior designer when you grew up."

"I can't believe that you're the second person in the last few days that has made me realise that there might be a future for me in interior design."

"I'm your sister. I grew up with you. So who else highlighted that for you?"

"Just George from work."

"George Giveski. I know him. I met him once when I ran into you in the city. I thought he was really attractive."

"He's okay." Julie shrugged off her sister's observation, slightly colouring.

"Anyway, do you think you could ask Cassandra for some more of those surveys? I'd love to gain some insight. Looking at you going off to Europe and taking time to try out a new career has inspired me. I know that I've become grumpy over the years because I feel that I've let myself down, and everyone else around me. Poor Brian has been suffering in silence for so long. I can tell he's walking on eggshells around me."

Just then Brian walked into the lounge room with a worried look on his face. "Is everything okay in here?"

"Everything is fine," Julie and Christina replied in unison, both smiling.

"In fact it is better than it has been in a long time." Christina added. She turned her attention to Julie. "I'll have to hear all about Scott another time. I'm curious to learn what really had happened between you two and where you're at now."

"We'll do lunch one day and maybe some shopping," Julie offered. "It's been a while!"

"That sounds great. I'd love some new clothes to inspire me. It has been a long time." Christina said, still smiling. She stood up and walked over to Brian, who appraised them with a baffled look on his face. He finally began to speak. "Look, Chris, about what I said earlier, I didn't mean that you're holding us back …"

"Don't worry, Brian," Christina said, messing his hair in an affectionate way. "I was angry with myself because there was some truth in that. I've come to realise that I'm the one who's holding me back. Don't look so worried. It's all good. I just needed a push to get me back on track. Let's go see what the kids are up to. They've been strangely quiet. That usually means that they're up to something."

"Is everything okay?" Julie also heard her mother enquire, as Christina and Brian made their way to the kitchen, where her mother was preparing the desserts.

"Don't worry, Mum," said Christina. "Everything is okay. I just needed to get my feelings out. I'm entitled to indulge in a tantrum now and then aren't I?"

"Of course you are and just for the record, we think you're doing a wonderful job with the kids, and we know you have so much to offer as an individual as well."

"Don't worry, Mum, you don't have to say that."

"I want you to know that. It never hurts to remind both my daughters just how proud your father and I are of both of you."

Julie listened to the conversation that was coming from the kitchen feeling content. She was also pleased to see that the affection between Brian and Christina was still there. Christina was right: it was all good. Christina actually understood her and she understood Christina. Who knew?

CHAPTER THIRTY

Julie yawned as she scrolled down the screen to find what she was searching for. She had woken early, not having been able to sleep, too excited to begin her quest realising her dream of working in interior design. She couldn't wait to get started, although she didn't know where to begin. After showering, she slipped into the most comfortable clothes she owned: a pair of black yoga pants, a matching top and a warm oversized tracksuit top. She pulled her hair back with a scrunchy and made herself a pot of coffee after finishing her bowl of oats and juice. Then she made herself comfortable in front of her computer desk, eager to begin her search on interior design courses. She felt inspired about her future.

At that moment the porcelain bird that George had given her caught her attention. She had placed it on the desk, deciding that it belonged there. "Oh no!" she gasped. She hadn't thanked George for the gift he had kindly given her. She had a perfect chance on the cruise, but once again, her mind had been pre-occupied. She had to thank him. How could she have been so inconsiderate after he had gone to all that trouble for *her* of all people! Rejecting his friendship all the years they worked together was bad enough, but to not even acknowledge the gift he gave her — that was just cruel! She would call him straight after she completed her research. She once again looked at the screen, trying to regain her focus.

"Bye, Julie," Maria called out from the hallway. "Try and enjoy your day off. Remember tomorrow you'll be starting early at the shop with me, and you'll need to be alert for training. You won't believe how many different ingredients are found in the products. Customers always want to know the exact ingredients, being organically conscious and all. Have a nice day."

"Don't worry. Once I look up some courses, I'll study the brochures that you selected for me. I can't get enough of how wonderful the few samples that I have in front of me smell. They are definitely magic to the senses. Can I test them as part of my training?"

"Knock yourself out. It's great to see my employees being so enthusiastic to learn," she added teasingly, before heading to the front door.

Julie had asked Maria the night before if her offer for her to work part-time at Eventually You was still open. Maria jumped with joy, screaming at the top of her lungs, "Of course it is!" She had hugged her so tightly and said that she had made her day. "Just think of how much fun we'll have," she had added, "not to mention that you've accepted my offer at the best time. Now that I'm pregnant, I need all the help I can get. This morning sickness is really sapping my strength. To tell you the truth, the different scents from all the products are really making me feel sick. I can't exactly say that to the customers though."

She had continued like that for a while and began making plans straight away, handing out products and briefing Julie on some of them. It was great to see Maria so excited and happy again. It seemed that she was starting to accept the fact that she was pregnant. Just hours ago on that Sunday morning, she hadn't even been able to talk about it. Everything had changed however, when she finally gained the courage to be honest with Antonio. While Julie was having a heart to heart with her sister, Maria was doing the same with Antonio. Both conversations had similar positive results. Maria had walked into the terrace house with Antonio. He had his arm around her and was smiling proudly. He had obviously taken the news well. It turned out Antonio had felt hurt that Maria didn't show any disappointment that he was leaving. Once again, it was a typical

232

misunderstanding. Julie had a lot of experience on the subject herself and she felt by now that she could run workshops on it.

Antonio had felt obligated to go back to Chile just to see how he could help. He too had felt that it was the worst time to be leaving Maria, as he felt that their relationship was progressing smoothly. It turned out that his brother who lived in America had decided to go back and live there anyway, and he had insisted that Antonio remain in Australia. Antonio had agreed to offer his parents financial help. When he finally heard about the pregnancy he had picked up Maria and kissed her "nearly one hundred times," as Maria had emphasised.

"You have made me so happy," he had told her in his rich accent. "I can't imagine having a baby with anyone but you. Believe me, when my parents hear the news, they will scold me for ever having thought of leaving you to help them. I wouldn't be surprised if they spend every last coin they have on airfares, and come over here to make sure you and their future grandchild are okay."

Maria and Antonio had slipped out of the kitchen with a bottle of non-alcoholic white wine, and then they went to pack some of Maria's things so she could spend the night at Antonio's apartment, after Maria insisted that she wouldn't be jealous if Antonio drank alcohol in front of her.

"You know I don't drink much even when I'm not pregnant," she had reassured him. He was planning a romantic home-cooked meal for her, and they obviously needed to make plans.

Maria had placed her hands on both Cassandra and Julie and given them each a big hug. "Thanks," she had said. "Thanks for making me face my fears and giving me the push I needed to be honest with Antonio. I know we both still need time to adjust to the change, and at times it won't be easy, but at least now I know that he always wanted to stay with me. Isn't it silly how people waste time, hiding how they feel from each other?" she had added, before running towards the door where Antonio was waiting, also holding a bag of fresh, organic ingredients for the lavish dinner he had promised.

Julie had decided that it was time she took charge of her career again. Cassandra looked relieved that Julie had finally realised that interior design might just be the career change she needed.

"Why didn't you say anything before?" Julie had asked.

"I wanted you to figure it out for yourself. I thought even Connor would have inspired you when he complimented you on your taste, but you seemed to have wanted to dismiss the obvious. A lot of people do that. They concentrate on something that they aren't interested in or even not that good at, instead of doing what they are really good at," she had responded.

Julie had just begun to read information about interior design courses online when her phone rang. She hesitantly went to answer it, not wanting to lose her focus.

"Hi Julie," Stacey's voice greeted her.

"Hi Stacey, how are you?" Julie responded, wondering why Stacey was calling her at home. Stacey hadn't really socialised with her outside of work, although she had emphasised that she wanted to keep in touch with her.

"I'm fine, Julie. You're probably wondering why I'm calling. Don't worry. I'm not planning another work reunion just yet. We're all still recovering from the cruise. It turned out really great don't you think? Did you enjoy yourself?"

"Yes I did. The cruise was a great idea. I think everyone enjoyed it."

"You and George seemed to be having a good time. Colin also proved us all wrong. He isn't the uptight boss we all thought he was. Anyway, I didn't know you were seeing someone. Who was that guy you were with after?

He was really attractive. You both seemed to have a lot to talk about."

Julie couldn't believe Stacey's directness. Is that why she was calling? This was typical Stacey, needing to know everything regarding who was dating whom. Pursuing a career in the tabloid industry may be a great career move for her, perhaps as a gossip columnist, Julie speculated.

"Well, I wasn't seeing him exactly. He's actually my ex-boyfriend. He was in Paris with me and two other friends. We're dating again, but we're taking it slow."

"Oh," Stacey replied, sounding disappointed. "I didn't know you were on the verge of dating someone."

"It just happened so quickly. I don't know where it's heading. I guess we'll just take it one step at a time. Anyway, I've been meaning to ask you, have you found another job yet?"

"Would you believe I'm actually working in a shoe shop? I really needed a job, so as I was about to spend more money on the nicest pair of boots I have ever seen, I decided to ask to work there instead. It stopped me from purchasing them, and helped me earn some money to pay off my credit card. I can't stand looking at feet all day though. Administration sounds so glamorous compared to this. I guess everyone has different ideas on what makes a good job and what doesn't. Have you found anything yet?"

"I'm just going to work in my friend's shop for a while. You know, the charming one that sells organic products. Remember I showed it to you during our lunch hour one day?"

"I love that shop. I've been there often after you took me there. I envy you. You'll be working amongst beautiful scents, and I'll be working with feet."

"There are some healing foot creams you might be interested in. Perhaps you could recommend them to your customers," Julie suggested, laughing.

"Very funny Julie! Anyway, keep in touch. Maybe we can organise lunch one day since we're both still working in the city. Maybe we can even ask George to come along, for old time's sake. I'm sure he can spare an hour from his tennis coaching. That's impressive isn't it? Imagine how sexy he would look in his tennis shorts?"

"We'll try to organise it," Julie responded, trying to imagine George in tennis shorts. He did have a good body. "Nice to catch up with you again, Stacey."

"Bye, Jules. I might come and visit you in your little oasis. God knows I'll need to purchase something soothing."

Julie hung up the phone. She still didn't know what the phone call was really about, other than to find out if she was dating Scott. She shrugged it off, remembering that Stacey always gave her a hard time about her love life or anyone else's. She sat back into the leather chair in front of the computer. Her heart beat faster as she realised that she was so close to taking action. The course was definitely what she was looking for: self-paced, offering a variety of subjects leading to accreditation as an interior designer. It all sounded so exciting.

After carefully reading what the course had to offer, and spending a few hours comparing it to other courses, Julie finally went back into the original website. She clicked on the enrolment form and read about the course commencement dates, knowing that she was taking the first step in changing her life. All she had to do was complete the form and the rest would follow. She finished entering her details and without hesitating, submitted the form. The wheels were in motion and it would only be a matter of time before she commenced a new journey, one that would involve a lot of creativity and much needed excitement. With one click of the mouse she would change the course of her life, and steer herself to a new path, a path she was choosing for herself.

Moments later, she nervously dialled the number of George's mobile, which she found in a list of contacts that

Stacey had handed to everyone for future social events. It was ringing. She cleared her throat.

"Hi George, it's me, Julie … you know, from work."

"Julie?"

"I know it's weird that I'm calling you, but I just wanted to thank you for the gift you gave me." Julie couldn't believe how nervous she felt. She was talking so quickly. She could practically feel him smiling on the other line, if that was possible.

"That's okay, Julie. I just wanted you to know that contrary to popular belief, I actually *did* enjoy working with you. I saw the porcelain bird at one of those contemporary homeware stores. I had to buy it. It reminded me of you."

"Oh?"

"There was something about it I guess; the way it was holding onto the branch, caught in the moment before taking flight. I always thought that you always seemed focused at work, yet at the same time your mind was wandering somewhere else. Anyway, that reminds me, how is everything with that guy you ran into? Did you work everything out?"

"Um … yes, we worked it out eventually," Julie answered, remembering that George had mentioned something similar at the cruise.

"I hope he didn't think we were more than friends? I wouldn't want to get in the way of love."

Julie didn't know how to respond. She couldn't believe how direct George was being.

"That's who that guy was, your first and only true love, right?" he queried.

"Well, yes, he was, I mean he still is … I don't know, we'll see," Julie stammered.

"Well, I hope everything turns out for you anyway. I really hope you find what you're looking for."

"Thanks, I hope you do too, George."

"Thanks, but in my case, I may have to keep looking. A word of advice though, if I may, that is? You didn't want my advice back when we were colleagues," George continued in his usual cordial tone. "Although, you were more … open to it at the cruise."

"You may, George," Julie responded in the same formal tone. She felt her face becoming warmer.

"Just don't hold on too tightly to the branch. If it's too difficult to hold onto it, it may not be the right branch. It may not be strong enough. It's your call."

"Okay …"

"Anyway, if you need a tennis lesson, you know where to find me."

"I know, or maybe I'll see you at another reunion. Bye George, and once again, thanks for the gift," she added, while trying to analyse what he had just said.

"Bye Julie."

CHAPTER THIRTY-ONE

It was like walking into a different world. Immediately, Julie's senses were engaged in a blissful, invigorating relationship with the aromas that permeated through the air. Aromatherapy was not just a word. It actually did have the means to invite a person into a world of calmness and contentment. The citrus scent of candles created a healing and delightful atmosphere.

"No wonder you love working here. What a difference to deadlines, phones always ringing, customers complaining about fees, urgent last minute meetings."

"Shh, be quiet! Those words are blasphemous in here," Maria teased.

It was Julie's first official day of training, and Maria thought it would be a good idea to start work earlier than usual so that Julie could familiarise herself with some of the products and find out where they were displayed in the shop. For the moment she would try to learn as much as possible about the products and help customers with any queries. Then she would move to the register for training, and Maria would also brief her on the privileges that customers had by becoming members.

Julie had already studied the brochures and was eager to see if she recognised the products on the shelves. She already felt confident when she spotted some of the products that she had seen in the brochures. She had also learned all the benefits of the products. Everything in the store was certified organic. There were moisturisers, cleansers, soaps, shampoos and conditioners, deodorants, healing plant masks, facial scrubs, essential scented oils, teas, coffees, scented candles, perfumes, and many more products which prided themselves on being made with natural, plant derived, organic ingredients. After around thirty minutes of being shown around the store and the back storeroom, Maria made a cup of tea for both of them. It was ten minutes before the shop's doors would be officially open.

"Yes, all our products are certified organic," Julie found herself informing the fifth customer in a row. Maria was right. Her customers really wanted to know everything about the products, and to be reassured that they met the Australian standards for organic goods. After a while, the words began to roll off her tongue without much thought. She was beginning to enjoy talking about the healing properties that many of the products offered, as opposed to talking all day about superannuation. It was a welcome change.

"Excuse me! Can you please show me some of the moisturisers for men? You see, I just came back from Paris, and I didn't use much sunscreen ..."

Julie turned around, immediately recognising the voice belonging to the handsome man staring smugly at her.

"Oh, you went to Paris?" she enquired. "Well, even though the sun's rays aren't as strong as they are here, they can still cause a lot of damage to the skin. We actually have a big selection of moisturisers for men. Perhaps you would also like to try one of our facial scrubs which exfoliate the skin. Now let's see how smooth your skin is!" Julie placed her hand on Scott's face and gently stroked his skin discreetly, in case any of the other customers saw. "Now I don't think there is too much damage. Your skin is actually quite soft."

"So tell me, do you offer such friendly service to all your customers?"

"Not really, only the extremely handsome ones," Julie responded, smiling.

"What's going on here? First day at the job and you're already flirting with my customers?" Maria was looking at them both, trying to remain serious.

"Sorry, Maria. I guess I shouldn't have distracted her. I forgot she can't control herself when an attractive man is in her presence," Scott laughed.

"Actually, you have distracted her at the right moment. Julie has finished her shift for the day. She has agreed to work on a part-time basis for the time being, and I give her full marks for effort."

"Well, thank you, Maria but I can't believe my work day is already over. It all happened so quickly."

"You must have been enjoying yourself," Scott remarked. "This is a great business you've got here, Maria. I already feel tempted to purchase something. Everything is so relaxing."

"You mean they don't have scented candles and water fountains in the IT department at your work? Surely it must be a breach of some Occupational Health and Safety requirement," Julie said.

Maria laughed. "Well, at least you know that you're not too far away from this wonderful oasis. Remember to tell your IT colleagues. Anyway, I'd better get back to work. See you at home, Julie. Nice to see you again, Scott."

Julie grabbed her trench coat and handbag from the back room, and headed out with Scott beside her.

"So, you seem to be enjoying yourself," Scott remarked.

"I am. It's what I need at the moment. So, are you on a break?"

"Actually, I have time for a coffee before my two o'clock team meeting. You remember those don't you?"

"Vaguely," Julie replied happily.

They seated themselves at one of the coffee shops in the Queen Victoria Building.

"You smell so nice, Julie. What scent is it?" he asked as he leaned close to her.

"It must be a combination of scents. I tried so many of the organic perfumes. They're all so beautiful."

Scott smiled at her from across the table.

Julie couldn't wait any more. Although she had managed to tell Scott about her plans to work with Maria, she hadn't revealed her plans to commence an Interior Design course.

"Anyway, you won't believe that I finally know what career I want to pursue. I've decided that I want to be an interior designer. Isn't that amazing? It's the perfect job. I don't know why I didn't think of it before." Julie couldn't control her excitement. She still couldn't believe that she was doing it.

Scott smiled. "I'm so glad for you. I can really see you as a designer. It will give you the chance to creatively express yourself. So, I'm curious. What made you realise that interior design was the field you wanted to get into?" He took her hand in his, and moved closer to her.

"I couldn't believe that of all people Geo— I mean my sister pointed it out to me." Julie cleared her throat. "I was always interested in design, but I never took my interest seriously enough to consider it as a possible career."

Suddenly Scott's mobile rang. "Sorry, I'd better get this," he said. He stood up from the table and took several steps away. "Hi Ashley," he said.

Julie's heart skipped a beat when she heard the name. It was his wife. Julie couldn't even call her his ex-wife because she wasn't. For a moment, she felt uneasy. Yes, he was separated, but the fact that he was still legally married made her feel as though she was the other woman. Julie looked at Scott as he spoke to Ashley. It was Scott, her first and only true love. She had carried this image of him in her heart for so many years, choosing at times to avoid visualising him as someone who had betrayed her. Here he was in front of her. He hadn't betrayed her, but he had moved on with his life. He now had a family and she was the reason that he couldn't commit to them.

"I'll definitely be at the birthday party. You know that I wouldn't miss that for the world. How could you think such a thing?" He shook his head and bid Ashley farewell, returning to the table.

"Sorry about that. It's Victoria's birthday and Ashley thought that I wouldn't attend her party."

"It must be difficult not being there for her on a full-time basis."

"It is at times," Scott replied, cautiously looking at Julie. "Please, you don't have to feel bad. I'll always make sure that Victoria is part of my life. I don't want you to feel guilty about it. I told you, I've been separated for almost a year before you miraculously re-emerged back into my life."

"I don't want to be responsible for a little girl being upset that her dad isn't there for her."

"You're not. Even if I didn't run into you, I would still be in the same situation. Anyway, you were telling me all about your new career plans. You seemed so excited. I want to hear more. I'm so happy for you."

She filled Scott in on the details of the course and told him that she was awaiting a response for an official interview. They then sipped their coffee and talked about their holiday and the early morning walks they used to take in Paris.

"Oh, by the way, James and Jenny say hi. James called me the other day and he said that he wore his T-shirt, and it reminded him of you."

Julie felt as though a cloud came over her when he mentioned their holiday.

"Julie, are you okay? I seemed to have lost you."

He took her hand in his again. She felt a rush charge throughout her whole body when she looked into his kind eyes.

"You look so beautiful, Julie," he suddenly said, his eyes studying her. "There's something different about you," he continued. "You look different to the girl I ran into at the Hunter Valley. You seem stronger, more focused. This coat … it's so unusual," he touched the silk fabric of her trench coat.

Julie looked at her coffee. She had become bolder with her style of late, the way she used to be. Scott was right! She did feel different. Over the past few weeks she had taken more chances than she had in years, and even though things were complicated, she felt that she was living her life, as opposed to hiding from it. She looked up into his eyes. They were so sensual, so emotional.

"Julie." He caressed her hand with his fingers. "I want you so much." His voice was hoarse as he stared searchingly into her eyes. She was slightly reluctant to let herself be drawn in by them.

Her reluctance quickly turned into an intense need. She could feel his eyes combing her face, her lips. Julie could hear buzzing. "What is that?" she asked, slightly irritated at the intrusion. It was Scott's phone again. They instantly unlocked their eyes.

"Oh! Hi Ashley, okay I'll talk to her," he responded obediently. "Hi sweetie …"

Julie felt awkward sitting there listening to Scott talking to his daughter. She observed his body language, the tone of his voice. She couldn't believe how quickly he switched his mood from wanting her so bad, to playing the dutiful husband and father. He seemed uneasy as she looked on from across the table.

"Julie?"

"Yes?" Julie jolted. She had been deep in thought.

Scott placed his phone on the table. "Sorry that I took so long. I can't believe how quickly the time passed. I've got to attend that meeting I told you about. I'll call you later and we can plan a dinner night. How does that sound?"

"Okay," she responded, not knowing how to act. This was all new to her. She didn't know what the rules were.

He kissed her quickly on the lips as he rose to leave. "God, you smell so nice," he said. "I can't wait to see you again."

"Bye," she said, forcing a smile.

After watching Scott slowly disappear into the lunchtime crowd, she finally stood up and began walking aimlessly around the shops.

Eventually she decided she needed to talk to Tanya. She felt that she had to fill her in on what had happened between herself and Scott. Tanya had deep remorse for what she had done and Julie felt for the friend she had lost.

Julie rang Tanya as soon as she stepped into the terrace house. She was sitting comfortably on the cream couch in the lounge room, feeling that she needed a quiet place to talk, knowing that she may have to answer a few questions regarding Scott and his being married.

"Hi Tanya, how are you?"

"Julie. It's so good to hear from you. It's such a coincidence because I was just thinking about you. I wanted to organise lunch or something. I was also meaning to talk to you about Scott. Did you end up talking to him about everything? If you did, it must have been an intense conversation."

"I did. He explained everything and I explained how I felt. It was a very intense conversation. He was also surprised that I got in touch with you. I'm sure he'll eventually want to see you again."

"That would be great. So where do things stand now between you? Are you going to try again or has he already moved on? I hope you've been given a second chance. It would be a pity if that isn't the case."

"Well, I have been seeing him, but we've decided to take it slow. Did you know that I went to Paris with him? James and Jenny from uni were also with us. I've been meaning to call you and fill you in on everything."

"Wow! I can't believe it. How did everything happen so quickly?"

"They had already planned the trip and Scott asked me to come along. I thought, why not? I felt that this might be the second chance that we needed to make things right."

"Is that what happened? Have you made things right?"

"To a point. I mean, a lot has changed. It's complicated now." Julie struggled not to convey her disappointment.

"How complicated? Is there someone else?"

"Yes. I was meaning to discuss it with you in person, but since we're on the subject, he's married and he has a daughter. He's been separated from his wife for at least nine months now. When I ran into him, he was living on his own and was trying to sort out his emotions. He felt that he couldn't commit to the marriage. However, he is completely devoted to his little girl and the Scott I remember would definitely make an exceptional father."

Julie heard Tanya breathing on the other side of the line. She was obviously in deep thought. Finally she spoke.

"How do you feel about this, Julie? I mean, it must be really difficult for you to once again not know where you stand."

"It is difficult, especially knowing that he can't always be there for his little girl. Scott has reassured me that the marriage is over, and that he felt that he could not completely commit to his wife. He feels that they rushed into marriage as Ashley was pregnant and they were still at the early stages of their relationship. He was still attached to our relationship."

"So he needed closure?"

"Well, yes, I guess we all did. But now that he knows the whole story, he told me that he wants to be with me. He said that it would be unfair to remain in the marriage, that he would be living a lie."

As Julie spoke, she felt that she was on the witness stand. She began to feel defensive and decided to shift the direction of the conversation and focus on the other reason for her call.

"Anyway," she continued. "I was wondering if you would like to come out for dinner with Cassandra and Maria on Friday night. Are you available? I know you have a husband and a little girl who will miss you."

"I'm sure they won't miss me for one night. If it was more than that, my daughter would manage I'm sure, but I know she would be miserable. Even when I work, I sometimes feel so guilty that I'm not with her to capture every moment. I work long hours and the time I have with her is precious. I want to savour every moment. I make up for it in the evenings. But now and then I deserve to treat myself, so, sure, I'd love to have a girls' night out. I can finally meet Cassandra and Maria as your friend, I hope, and not the man-eating bitch they thought I was."

"It was very unfair of me to paint that picture of you without giving you the benefit of the doubt. They know everything now, and they also want to meet the real Tanya." Julie's words came out but her thoughts were still fixated on what Tanya had said about her daughter. It seemed that Tanya was trying to make a point.

When she finally hung up the phone, she realised that she didn't feel as content as she thought she would. She was glad that she had organised a night out with Tanya, but she couldn't get her words out of her mind. "*If it was more than that, my daughter would manage I'm sure, but I know she would be miserable.*" She tried to fight the words from taking root in her mind.

By the end of the night, she had the most terrible headache. Cassandra's words also came back to her. "*Your real self and ideal self, need to be congruent or else there is inner conflict and anxiety. People need to be true to their values.*"

What were her values? Everything seemed fuzzy as she headed upstairs to sleep off her headache. When she finally got into bed and closed her eyes, she knew that whatever her values were, one thing was for sure. She never expected to be dating a married man who had a daughter. She would not have chosen to steer herself in such a direction. Julie closed her eyes with that thought. She felt that she was driving blindly and that the windows were

247

fogged up. She needed to see clearly again. Feeling consumed with uncertainty, she fell asleep.

When she awoke the next morning she decided to face the uncertainty and see where it would lead her. Julie told herself that she was over-analysing and she and Scott had to make things right. They had to have another chance — they deserved it.

CHAPTER THIRTY-TWO

The last few weeks of August passed. September arrived bringing with it all the hope that spring embodied. Julie kept herself busy working at Eventually You. She found herself looking forward to work every day. She couldn't get enough of the scents and felt rejuvenated every day. Maria was very appreciative, as her morning sickness didn't seem to be improving. Julie was also looking forward to commencing her interior design course at the beginning of October. She had already attended the interview and the orientation day, and she was convinced that it was the right career move for her when the outline was explained to her.

Her relationship with Scott was also progressing smoothly. They had discussed many of Julie's concerns and Scott had reassured her that he would talk to Ashley about their relationship when the time was right. They spent a lot of time together, attending art galleries, the theatre, taking long walks on the beach, and simply enjoying each other's company.

Julie still felt the same rush throughout her whole body whenever Scott touched her, and whenever he looked into her eyes. He seemed to be fighting the urge to take her in his arms and show her what she meant to him. At times she felt that they were in their early twenties again and that they were both free, with no responsibilities.

The dinner with Tanya had also gone well. Cassandra and Maria declared that they were totally wrong about her, and that she was really down to earth and quite warm. The subject of Scott was of course one of the main issues on the agenda. They all agreed that he was extremely attractive and that Julie and he made an adorable couple, "If only …"

Scott had made a surprise visit to the restaurant in Woollahra before anyone of them could complete that sentence. He lived close by at Bondi Junction and joked that since he would be the topic of conversation, it would only be fair that he represented himself. By the end of the night, Cassandra, Maria and Tanya were so mesmerised by his charm and his devotion to Julie – demonstrated by his arms constantly making their way around her waist – that any comments regarding his marital status were left unsaid.

Julie had also planned a shopping and lunch day with Christina. As promised, she told her everything about her and Scott, including what had happened at uni.

Christina was surprisingly supportive about everything.

"That's why you had shut down like that. You thought that your best friend and your boyfriend had betrayed you," she had commented.

Julie even went so far as to telling her sister that he wasn't just her boyfriend, but her first true love, her first real connection with a man. Christina listened carefully as Julie conveyed how she felt; that she couldn't connect to any other man as much as she had connected with Scott. Mark had been there for her and he was the only other guy that she allowed herself to become intimately involved with, needing someone to make her feel special again. It definitely wasn't like her to get involved so quickly. It had been years since she had been intimate with another guy. She really had been in a rut. She finally dated someone she met at a work training course for a while but she couldn't allow herself to take it further, until she convinced herself that she couldn't live like a nun. She soon ended it after a spending a few nights with him. It didn't feel right. Then there was Michael …

"Okay, okay," Christina said defensively. "I know. He was a walking cliché with his muscles and extreme exercise regime. How far did that relationship go?" her sister had asked, trying to restrain from laughing.

Julie couldn't believe she was being so candid with her love life to Christina, of all people. "To tell you the truth, I nearly did sleep with him, mostly because I had convinced myself that I'd never find the intimacy that I was looking for. I nearly did walk in that minefield again, until I caught a glimpse of him and I in the mirror. Would you believe he was admiring himself in the mirror instead of looking at me? Not to mention the way he pinched my skin as though he was analysing how much fat I had, the same way a fitness instructor would."

Julie felt closer to her sister than she had in years. Since the mood was so light and non-judgmental, Julie had told Christina everything regarding Scott being married and having a daughter. To Julie's surprise, Christina remained non-judgmental.

"It's not really fair is it? Just because of a misunderstanding, now it's all so complicated for all of you. I can see why you want to continue seeing him. You feel that you've been robbed of an opportunity. At the same time, I feel for you because it can't be easy. I know what type of person you are and I know that you will feel terrible for his family. Who knows? Maybe, you'll get your answers if you continue to take it slow and continue seeing each other. I think you will realise what you need to do. Just try and take it slow. A lot of peoples' feelings are involved, including yours."

Who would have thought that her sister would be so open-minded? Her input made Julie feel a lot better.

All in all, everything had been going fine. Even though there were uncertainties, Julie came to realise that was part of life and what made it exciting. The only advice she could offer herself was to remain positive in her thinking and true to herself. Just as Julie was contemplating being okay with uncertainty, the inevitable conversation happened. Scott had finally had the talk that he had been meaning to with his wife. Julie had learnt about it one Sunday afternoon, just as they were having a relaxing lunch at Bondi Beach. At first he had seemed really drained from the intensity of the conversation. Julie felt for him. He had looked as if he hadn't slept for days. His hair was unkempt and his T-shirt was rumpled, as if he had just thrown on anything he had found from the washing basket. He had admitted that Ashley did not take it well.

"Why would she, though?" he had asked, more of himself than Julie. "I mean, she had felt that we were happy together until I shut her out and became so irritable and distant. She thinks that I was overwhelmed by the responsibility of being a father and that I was just anxious."

Julie didn't know how to be sympathetic, or what possible advice she could offer.

"Well, now that everything is out in the open, it might be a good time for you to meet my daughter. I really want you to meet her. She means the world to me, and so do you Julie."

Had she heard correctly? Julie had felt panic begin to creep all over her body almost instantly. She felt hot and agitated. Her palms were sweaty and she felt that she would collapse at any minute. She tried to remain cool, speaking positive thoughts to herself. *She's just a little cute girl. Of course she'll like you. You're friendly; look at how much Elisabeth and Jonathan adore you*, she tried to reassure herself. Why was she so afraid of this meeting?

"I'm sure you and Victoria will get along just fine," Scott had commented.

"I just don't want her to think of me as the evil witch who stole her daddy. I'm sure she's miserable now that you're not around."

"I think she would be more miserable if I was always around and she saw that her dad was sad."

"From what you just told me, Ashley assumes that you were overwhelmed with your new situation. Maybe things weren't as bad as you think. Maybe you can salvage your marriage with her now that you know what really happened between us," Julie found herself saying.

"Julie! What is it going to take to convince you that you're the only one for me and that I need you in my life?" he had asked her.

Now Julie sat in the kitchen, still in her Parisian robe, nursing her cup of coffee and pondering how the initial introduction would go. It was Saturday morning and she had planned to meet Scott and Victoria at Darling Harbour for ice cream. Perhaps they should go to a fun park. That might reduce the possibility for awkward moments.

She looked at fresh flowers in a crystal vase placed carefully on the corner of the kitchen bench. They were for Cassandra from Connor. Julie admired their elegance and simplicity.

Right then the recipient of the beautiful flowers strolled into the kitchen, looking as though she hadn't a care in the world.

"Morning Cass."

"Hi, Jules." Cassandra poured herself a cup of coffee. Julie thought that she looked as though she was floating on a cloud.

"You seem really happy Cassandra; not just happy, content."

Cassandra's smile became wider as she sat beside Julie at the kitchen table. Maria also waltzed in. She had spent the night at Antonio's apartment, as she often did lately.

Julie knew that it was only a matter of time before Maria moved in with Antonio. It wasn't very practical going from one place to another. Her severe morning sickness — or in her case, all day and night sickness — added to the difficulty. Julie sensed that Maria felt that she would be abandoning them, or perhaps she would even miss living with them and sharing all the girlie talks they had grown accustomed to.

"I certainly am happy, and content," Cassandra sighed.

"Looks like I arrived just in time," Maria stated, heading towards the fridge and reaching for the orange juice. "Are we about to hear a revelation?"

"Actually, you are," Cassandra stated with obvious excitement in her voice.

Julie suddenly felt that they were in high school, and that they were about to talk about who was going out with whom.

"Well, I've been observing both of you, and I've come to realise that you're both making things happen. So, last night, I had enough of waiting for Connor. I decided to practise what I preach and become more proactive. So as we were discussing how many units we still had to complete before we officially become qualified counsellors, I pulled him close to me and I kissed him, in front of everyone in the restaurant."

"Wow!" Maria and Julie exclaimed.

"Anyway, one thing led to another and before we knew it we were back at his apartment."

"Judging from your satisfied looking smile, you spent the night with him, right?" Maria curiously enquired.

"Yes I did. I've never felt so wanted in my life. It was so incredible. I haven't felt like that with any other man. Had I known it would be that good, I would have made the first move a long time ago. He really knew what I wanted. It was as though he was looking into my soul."

Maria and Julie were staring at Cassandra as though they were reading a romance novel, wanting to know what happened next. Julie realised she was smiling as well. It was what every woman wanted from a man: passion, excitement and an intense connection. Julie had that with Scott. She wondered if it would still be the same between them.

"I feel like that with Antonio. I guess in your case though, both being counsellors has really allowed both of you to express yourselves. He's probably so observant and can read what you need. Being a counsellor, he would also be more prone to expressing his feelings in more ways than one," Maria added with a mischievous smile.

"I just feel so happy. I want to spend every moment with him. It's so unexpected because I wasn't looking for a relationship."

"So you're officially a couple?"

"Yes. We're having dinner tonight, and then we have tickets to see the Sydney Symphony at the Opera House."

Julie felt envious. She wished that she and Scott had plans to see the Symphony. Feeling guilty about not wanting to meet his daughter, she brushed her feelings aside and focused on Cassandra.

"I'm really happy for you, Cass. You deserve to be with someone who really understands you. You're a truly an intuitive and warm person. Connor is so good for you."

Cassandra nodded emphatically. "I feel that we can talk to each other for hours. All the walls come down when I'm with him. I can delve into any subject."

Julie's heart suddenly felt heavy. Cassandra and Connor's relationship was untainted. It was new, fresh and pure. That's the type of relationship Julie always wanted to be in, one where she could express herself freely and not feel that certain topics were taboo.

"I'm so happy for you, Cass. I want to hear more, as much as you're willing to tell us, that is. But first, I've got to go and call my Saturday employees at the shop. I want to make sure that they know about the new promotion we're doing." Maria looked at the clock on the wall.

"I'd better get ready as well. I have to meet Scott and Victoria at Darling Harbour."

"That's right." Cassandra looked at Julie, her smile fading. She looked as though she knew something Julie didn't. "Well, good luck with that. I know it can't be easy."

"I'd be lying if I said it was," Julie stated hastily, marching out of the kitchen before her friends noticed how nervous she really was. She quickly walked upstairs to her bedroom to commence the usual "what am I going to

255

wear?" regime. She wanted Victoria to like her and she knew how brutally honest kids could be when it came to how adults looked.

Julie was behind the wheel of her car, enjoying her time alone. She needed to gather her thoughts before she met with Scott and Victoria. It was a fairly warm spring day, and she wore a beige linen casual shirt-dress that fell just above her knees, and a pair of gold, flat Roman sandals. She complemented the look with aviation sunglasses, and let her silky, light brown curls fall loosely below her shoulders. She passed the Sydney Fish Markets, which were full of people shopping or having a bite to eat at the pier, and waited at the lights. Julie looked at the boats swaying lightly with a heavy heart. Her mind instantly went to the cruise. It had really been a fun night!

She had planned on meeting Scott at one of the coffee shops they both knew. He had to pick up his daughter from Ashley's place, so they both thought it would be better if she met them there. Apparently Victoria was shy with new people and he didn't want her to feel intimidated.

"I know how you feel," she said to herself, feeling that she too was a shy little girl meeting a stranger.

Scott eagerly waved at her. Julie suddenly felt a strange feeling of sadness for him. She felt guilty for not wanting to meet his daughter. He didn't know how she felt, and that made Julie feel as though she was betraying him. She told herself right then that she would try to think positively.

"Hi Scott," she greeted him with a smile, not wanting to upset the adorable looking girl who was standing behind him, hiding behind her dad. She looked at the little girl. "Who could this pretty little girl in the beautiful dress be? Could it be Victoria?"

Victoria looked at Julie from behind her father, unsure if she should reveal herself completely.

"Is that a magic wand you're holding? Which storybook is that from?" Julie continued.

"I'm a fairy princess," Victoria finally gained the courage to speak.

"Victoria, this is the friend that I've been talking to you about. This is Julie. Do you want to say hello to her?"

Victoria said nothing and hid behind her dad again.

"That's okay," Julie responded. "We have plenty of time to get to know each other. Do you feel like eating something yummy?"

"Dad said that we're having ice cream." Victoria looked up at her dad with a hopeful look on her face.

"We'll have something to eat first and then you can have ice cream for dessert, okay, Vicky?"

Scott bent down, picked up his little princess and placed her face next to his. "Maybe you can play on the rides after. How does that sound?"

Victoria began to laugh uncontrollably, as her dad kissed her on the nose and lifted her up in the air. Julie couldn't help but admire Scott. He was definitely a good father to Victoria, and she couldn't help but feel sad that the little girl he was proudly holding up in the air didn't belong to both of them. The connection between Scott and his wife would always be strong. They shared a child together.

"So, how are you, Julie?" Scott asked looking intently into her eyes. He gave her a quick kiss on the cheek when Victoria wasn't looking.

The afternoon had passed pleasantly enough. There were no major dramas. After eating their lunch, followed by the promised ice cream, they took a walk around Darling Harbour. They finally sat down on a bench and watched Victoria chase the seagulls near the water.

"I'm so glad you agreed to meet Victoria. This year has been really difficult for her. I think she really likes you. You're very good with kids. I always suspected that you'd be a wonderful mother."

Julie looked at her gold sandals glistening in the sun. Victoria had been drawn to them and had told Julie that she looked like a fairy princess in them. She suddenly felt his hand on her bare knee.

"Julie. Can you please be honest with me? I know this can't be easy for you. Just tell me what you're thinking. I've noticed that you've been distant with me. That's not what I want for us. I want us to be able to be honest with each other. That means a lot to me in a relationship and I know it does to you too."

Julie was still fixated on her sandals. She didn't feel like confiding in Scott. She felt like she would burst into tears if she did so. She felt Scott's hand on her face. He gently lifted her chin until her eyes met his. A tear started rolling down Julie's face. Scott gently wiped the tear away with his hand and kissed her cheek gently. "We're in this together. You don't have to hide your feelings from me."

"I guess I'm just scared."

"Scared of what?"

"Scared of us."

"You do want to try to make our relationship work, don't you?"

"Yes, but I'm scared of being with you, and at the same time I'm scared of not being with you. Does that make sense to you?"

"It's because of Ashley and Victoria. You think that you've destroyed my family or that I may go back to them."

"Well, how do you know what will happen? I just don't want to get seriously involved with you and then you start regretting breaking up with Ashley. I don't want either of us to live with guilt. I don't know what I'm supposed to be doing or how I should act. I never thought of myself as being the reason a family had broken up. How do you know you'll never go back to your wife? I mean, you obviously felt something for her if you married her. I don't think you married her only because she was pregnant. It

258

seems to me that she's a nice person who just wants her family back together. It's not her fault that you and I had missed our chance at being a couple. Can you guarantee that you are one hundred per cent sure that you won't regret divorcing her?"

"Julie, please, calm down," he said, gently placing his thumb on her lips. "I know that Ashley is not to blame for any of this. I just feel that we owe it to ourselves to have another chance. Looking into your beautiful eyes, touching your soft skin, being able to run my fingers through your hair ... it has brought back so many memories. I would always lose myself in your eyes. Do you remember how right it felt waking up in each other's arms? Surely you haven't forgotten what we had. Just give us a chance. We can have that again." He stroked her hair, intermittently ensuring that Victoria wasn't looking. He then touched her face, his thumb making its way to her lips again. He looked into her eyes searchingly.

"Scott, should we be doing this here, next to Victoria?"

"It's okay, Julie. I know I have to be sensitive to Victoria's feelings. It means a lot to me," he said, "you, agreeing to meet Victoria. Thank you."

"You don't have to thank me Scott. Victoria is such a sweetie. She has your eyes, you know?" Julie said, and then looked at the city skyline in the distance.

He placed his hand on her arm, and caressed her bare skin slowly, sensuously.

Julie looked at his handsome face. He hadn't shaved. He looked so sexy, and his eyes conveyed so much desire. "Scott, what are you doing? Victoria might see ..."

"There's that look again," he interrupted, a smile suddenly appearing on his face. "I know that look so well. I'd see it in your eyes when you were consumed with worry, when you felt that you weren't doing what you should, just like the last night we spent together. You had insisted on studying and I wanted you so much ..."

"Daddy, Daddy, there's a merry-go-round. Can I go on it?" Victoria asked, running towards them eagerly.

Scott quickly diverted his attention to Victoria, taking his hand away from Julie's arm.

Julie looked at Victoria. She wasn't just any little girl. She was Scott's little girl. Her heart went out to her. She was so innocent and adorable. How could Scott want to deprive her of anything when he looked into those hopeful brown eyes?

Julie felt the heat from Scott's hand as he gently grabbed and led her to Victoria, who was running excitedly towards the merry-go-round. He stopped walking for a few seconds, turned to face her, and kissed her softly on the lips, his fingers were intertwined with hers, as he reassuringly held her hand tightly. "I love you, Julie." His eyes looked almost teary as he looked into hers with intent. "I never thought I'd ever get another chance to look into your eyes and tell you that ... but here we are ... surely, this all happened for a reason."

Julie's heart felt like it was melting. "I love you too, Scott," she said softly. She walked hand in hand with him, basking in the glorious warmth of the sun. She decided to live in the moment. She had to think positively if she wanted to give their relationship another chance. Scott was right! They must have been reunited for a reason. They would find a way to make it work, and they would ensure Victoria was okay as well. She and Scott also had a bond — one that should never have been broken.

CHAPTER THIRTY-THREE

Julie awoke the next day confused by the dream she had. It was the same dream she had been having ever since Maria had noticed George with the blonde mystery woman in the Indian restaurant. She was the same woman that was with George at Circular Quay, the night of the work reunion. The last time she had the dream, the woman had turned into Tanya.

However, in the dream she just had, there was no Tanya or even Scott. In fact, she couldn't even remember who the man and woman were this time. Feeling too sleepy to analyse the dream, Julie closed her eyes again and fell back asleep. When she woke up again, feeling worse than before, she remembered having another dream. She was walking hand in hand with a tall man. That was all she could remember. *It was Scott*, she thought to herself. He must have been fresh in her mind when she fell asleep. The dream had left her with a warm feeling all over her. The confusion she had felt was obviously no longer with her.

The intimacy they felt on their last date had definitely eased her uncertainty. Once again, too exhausted to further analyse the dream, she forced herself out of bed and headed to the bathroom to shower. That would help the fuzzy state her head was in, as would a strong cup of coffee.

***

The following weeks passed quickly. Julie was busy working at Eventually You. Towards the end of September she was also becoming more and more excited about her design course, which would commence in a few days' time. She had spent hours looking at interior design magazines and at the course outline. The modules appeared rather daunting at first. The two-year course entailed a variety of subjects ranging from applying colour theory and design principles, to developing and drafting skills, soft furnishings research, to marketing and dealing with clients, and becoming familiar with different architectural styles. The list was extensive, but as daunting as it seemed at first, Julie felt excited.

The weather was getting warmer, and Julie could practically taste the possibilities of new opportunities in the spring air. As she stood behind the counter of the store on a Friday afternoon, just having lit some scented vanilla candles, Julie thought of Scott. She felt that something had to change in their relationship. She could sense that Scott felt the same way when she was with him. He had called her earlier from work, and had asked her if she wanted to have a bite to eat at one of the local restaurants in his area.

A few hours later, Julie was in her bedroom preparing for her date. She felt oddly nervous, and felt the need to look her best. She put a lot more effort into her appearance, feeling that something would happen that night. Scott would be there any minute, having volunteered to pick her up. She took one final look in the antique mirror and headed downstairs where she waited in the lounge room for the doorbell to ring. Feeling like a teenager waiting for her date to pick her up for the high school formal, Julie reached for a travel book on France which she had hastily purchased the Saturday before her trip, and began to browse through it.

She remembered how excited she had been at her decision to drop everything and go to Paris. It had all started from that moment. She had proved to herself that she could do whatever she wanted in life. She had placed the travel book next to the many counselling books Cassandra needed for her course. *Soon the shelves will be full of books on interior design*, Julie thought to herself. There would be two students in the house. Just as she was about to open the book and find out if she recognised any of the buildings in Paris, the doorbell rang. Julie jumped at the sudden intrusion, and her heart raced uncontrollably.

Get a hold of yourself, she lectured herself. She couldn't understand why she was so nervous.

Scott appraised Julie approvingly at the front door. "You look beautiful, Julie, not to mention sexy."

Julie realised that she did look sexier than usual. She wore a stunning green above-knee dress, and her tanned shoulders were bare. Suddenly Julie felt the urge to wear a jacket to cover her bare skin. She didn't want to entice him. Feeling excited and nervous, she stepped into his Volkswagen Tiguan. She could smell his cologne, subtle but masculine, as he expertly reversed out of the parking spot in two quick motions. Julie couldn't help but look at his strong, tanned arms. The smell of his cologne and his hands on the steering wheel, and the gorgeous smile he gave her as he caught her looking at him, made her feel tempted to jump into bed with him at any moment. That all changed however when he uttered the words, "Victoria and I are going to the zoo on Sunday and I was wondering if you wanted to come along."

The feelings of pleasure were almost instantly replaced with feelings of guilt, as Julie envisioned herself walking hand in hand with Scott and Victoria, looking at the giraffes and the elephants. *What was wrong with that picture?* she asked herself. *Oh, I know. I would feel like the biggest elephant of all as one crucial person would be missing: Ashley*. But she couldn't think like that. They deserved their second chance.

Julie slowly breathed in the air. She loved this time of year. Soon it would be summer and the evenings would be balmy, enticing people out of their homes to enjoy the many restaurants and bars or to simply walk along the beach promenades and piers around Sydney. They had decided on one of the outdoor restaurants in Bondi. Just as they were about to be seated, Julie suddenly realised that Scott had insisted on going to a local place to eat. He lived close by in Bondi Junction.

They ordered a bottle of chilled Pinot Gris to match the feeling that summer was around the corner. By the end of their meal, Julie was so full and once again, as she often did, questioned why she stuffed herself with bruschetta before their main dishes arrived.

They were having a wonderful time, reminiscing about their holiday and the time they spent at university. That topic had led to Tanya and how great it would be if Scott saw her again. Julie also wanted to organise to see James and Jenny again. As they talked over wine, Julie had noticed that Scott had stopped drinking. She also realised that when the waiter came round to pour some more of the wine into both their glasses, Scott stated that they had enough for the night without confirming this with Julie.

"Julie, do you want to go back to my apartment?"

"Sure. Okay," she found herself responding. They both stood up at the same time, as though they were on auto pilot. As they left the restaurant hand in hand, there was a silence between them. It wasn't an awkward silence, but it did make Julie feel anxious. She felt that it was her first time again. She knew she wanted to be with Scott, but at the same time she felt like she was driving without being able to reach the brakes. As much as she wanted to take the relationship to the next level, she also felt like running and ending whatever it was she was feeling.

Julie was invariably impressed when she entered Scott's apartment. A replica Cyclops floor lamp always caught her attention from where it stood in the hallway, as though it was leaning over to say hello. Scott's taste was of a contemporary, minimalist style. However, like Scott, it was relaxed and warm at the same time, not clinical or pretentious like some modern furnishings and designs were. He had added some personal touches to the simple furniture, which highlighted his travels and his interest in art.

Julie couldn't help but remember how excited Scott had been when, on his twenty-third birthday, she had surprised him with tickets to the art exhibition, where the current work of his favourite Spanish contemporary artist was on display. They were so close, so in love.

"What are you smiling about? Is it a private joke?" Scott queried, as he walked towards her looking as if he had a plan. He then stroked her hair away from her face.

"Oh, I just remembered the art exhibition we went to see on your twenty-third birthday," Julie responded.

Scott didn't reply. She suddenly felt soft sensual kisses on her neck, and then on her bare shoulders. He gently pulled her closer towards him and she could feel the warmth of his breath as he caressed her bare back. It felt magical. It awoke every part of her. She found herself leaning closer to him, running her fingers through his wavy hair. He began to kiss her sensuously on the lips and she responded with the same intensity. *This is right. This is the man I should be with*, she told herself. She closed her eyes to feel every stroke, every kiss. He guided her to the edge of the bed. She couldn't help but notice that the bed was made very well. The grey quilt cover and matching pillow cases looked as though they were made with the finest cotton. Before she knew it, Scott was sitting on the edge of the bed. He pulled her gently towards him. He placed his hands on her waist and Julie felt as though she was in heaven. *I want this*, she told herself. She wanted it … until she saw them.

He had a photo of himself and Ashley right next to his bed. She saw them smiling at her. Their eyes said it all. Something was emanating from them. Julie instantly knew what it was. It was happiness. *And why wouldn't they be happy?* Julie asked herself. They had a beautiful little girl and they had each other.

As much as Julie didn't want to admit it, she had to start being real about the situation. She was being realistic about other aspects of her life. Now it was time to face the reality of how Scott really felt about his wife. As much as he denied it to himself and to her, the truth was staring her in the face. She knew it and now Scott had to acknowledge it as well. How more obvious could it be? They looked so happy together. It was hard to believe that their marriage was ever in trouble.

"Julie, are you okay? Isn't this what you want?" Scott said gently.

She remained fixated on the photo. Suddenly she couldn't breathe. It was the same type of feeling that she felt all those years ago at the university cafeteria. The only difference was that she felt that she was the one doing the betraying. She felt that she was betraying that innocent little girl that she had got to know and love over the last few weeks. She felt that she was betraying the kind looking woman. She obviously brought something into his life when he had first met her, something that made him want to marry her. She had also brought a precious little girl into his life. They had to give their marriage a chance, otherwise Scott would regret it. He had his closure now, so he could focus on what he already had in his life — a family he loved. Julie couldn't be that person. She couldn't be the other woman. She couldn't break up a family that wasn't really broken.

"Julie. Where are you going?"

Julie couldn't stop. She ran out of Scott's apartment. She desperately needed fresh air. She couldn't breathe. She had to let all her repressed emotions out. She had to be honest with herself and with Scott.

"Julie! Please slow down. Why are you running? Did I do something wrong? Was I rushing you?" Scott asked her with a concerned look on his face.

"I can't do this anymore, Scott."

"Do what?"

"I can't live this lie any more. I wanted it to work between us. I was in denial because I had such high expectations for us. I was scared to admit that it couldn't because I might never experience what we shared with anyone else."

"Julie. Stop. You need to slow down. Just breathe."

"I can't breathe. That's the problem, Scott. I can't breathe because this isn't right anymore. We're trying to relive the past and it's just not possible. I've tried to give us a second chance and to go with the flow, but I can't be that woman."

"What are you talking about, Julie? What woman?"

"The one who breaks up a family! You know me, Scott. You know that I wouldn't be able to live with myself. I also know what type of person you are and you wouldn't be able to live with yourself, either. You're in denial right now because you think that it's what you want. You feel that you have wasted all these years thinking about us and why things went so wrong. Now you want to make something of our relationship, otherwise it would mean that you wasted all those years thinking that I was the only girl for you."

"Julie, I shouldn't have rushed you. You're obviously confused. You need to calm down."

"No, I'm not, Scott. Everything is making sense to me now. As much as I would have liked for it to work out, I'm being honest with myself about the situation. It can't work because we both wouldn't be true to our values. Although our circumstances have changed, our values are still the same. I honestly believe that you still have feelings for Ashley and that you can make it work. I mean, you have a photo of her next to your bed. The only thing that was keeping you from fully committing yourself to her was not knowing what happened between us. You had unfinished business. You needed to complete the incomplete just like Gestalt therapy theory suggests."

"Julie, what are you talking about? What Gestalt therapy theory?"

"Scott, I know we were good together back then, but what you have with Ashley is real. What we had together was special but it isn't real any more. We're desperately clinging on to a memory and a possibility. You need to give Ashley another chance. You said so many positive things about her. You can make it work now that you have your answers. You can move on now. You owe it to her now, and to your little girl."

Scott was staring at her with a serious look on his face. "Can I have a chance to talk now?"

"Sure," Julie responded.

"First, I just want to tell you that Victoria placed the photo of Ashley and me on my bedside table. I was so excited about seeing you tonight that I forgot to put it away. I guess she's trying to tell me something. Anyway, I would never be that cruel to you Julie, to place a photo of me and Ashley while I was planning on spending the night with you. As for everything else you just told me, you're right."

"What?"

"You're right. I am trying to recreate the past, especially the last night we shared together before it all went wrong. I wanted to feel close to you again. I felt like we were drifting apart these last few weeks. I wanted to be with you so much. I wanted it to work out between us. I haven't been able to let it go for so many years." He placed his hands on her shoulders. "Julie, I will always love you but you're right. Things have changed between us. I tried to ignore how I felt, how you felt."

Julie looked into his eyes. Was she that transparent with her feelings? Of course she was. Scott could always see through her.

"I noticed that you've been distant with me lately. I tried to ignore it, telling myself that things will change. I also tried to hide the guilt I felt when I spoke to Victoria and Ashley. I feel that I have let them down. I took them on a ride with me and abandoned them halfway. I was just thinking of myself. I genuinely felt that we were owed another chance. I wanted this night to work out. It's how we left things. The reality is that I've been denying the truth to myself. As much as I love you, Julie, I will never feel comfortable if I don't give my marriage a chance now that I've got the answers that I needed. I do feel for Ashley. Everything had happened so fast and I was confused. I've been very unfair to both of you."

After a moment, Julie settled her conflicting thoughts and looked at Scott. "I know us, Scott. I know we both couldn't live with ourselves, and our relationship wouldn't have a chance. I tried to deny it as well. The result was feeling anxious around you. I've made a vow to be honest with myself from now in all aspects of my life, and I don't want to live with uncertainty. I want to be in control of my life. I want to remember our relationship for what it was, something sacred and special. You were my first true love and thanks to you, I now know not to settle for anything less. I hope I find that again with someone else. I don't want to ruin what we had together by living a lie and end up resenting each other. We're both different people now. We're not students any more. We were looking at things from those young, untainted eyes. We've seen different things now and we need to view our relationship clearly."

"You're right about seeing things more clearly, but you're wrong about something. It will never happen. I will never resent you. I couldn't even resent you back then when I thought you betrayed me, as much as I tried. Anyway, when did you become so wise and aware of your feelings? You were always analytical, but now you've taken it to a whole new level."

"It helps when you live with an aspiring counsellor."

"Is that where the Gestalt therapy theory comes in?"

They both cautiously smiled and then looked at the ground. "So where do we go from here?" Julie finally built up the courage to ask the question. Was it possible to remain friends with him, or was she just being selfish and naïve?

"I would like to remain friends with you. James and Jenny are already planning a reunion night. They both really enjoyed seeing you again. How does dinner at an English pub and a French film sound to you?"

"It sounds great."

"Oh, and by the way. Maybe you can come over for a barbecue and meet Ashley?" Scott said, looking at Julie with a casual expression on his face.

Julie tried to remain cool and relaxed, but could feel her fake smile crumbling from the extreme force.

"You're so transparent, Julie," Scott laughed. "I was only joking. I know it's too soon to meet Ashley. Let's try and crawl before we walk. Besides, I need to do a lot of damage control. I just hope she forgives me."

"I wasn't so opposed to the idea. How did you know I didn't want to meet her quite yet?"

"It was the same smile you gave me when I asked you to meet my daughter, except this time I didn't think I had to call the paramedics."

"I was just nervous," Julie responded, suddenly matching Scott's smile.

"I know. Just don't ever become a poker player."

"I don't plan to. After years of searching I know exactly what career I want to pursue."

"I'm happy for you, Julie. I'm happy you're finding out what a spectacular and talented woman you really are. I always made sure you knew that."

"I know. You always tried to bring out the best in me. Ashley is definitely a lucky woman and from what you told me about her, you're a lucky man to have her in your life."

As she completed the last words of her sentence, she was surprised at the warmth that took over her. It was the right thing for both of them — for all of them. Julie had found the missing piece to the puzzle. She felt complete. As content as she felt, part of her still ached for the relationship that had finally ended. She looked at Scott. She was certain that he felt the same as she looked into his sad brown eyes. He gave her a half-hearted smile. The realisation that she wouldn't look into his eyes the same way again overwhelmed her with melancholic regret. A tear streamed down her face, followed by another, then another. Scott pulled her close to him and hugged her tight. She could feel his heart beating as she leaned on his chest.

"I'll never forget what we had," he whispered in her ear and hugged her closer to him. "Things could have been so different."

"I know, but everything is as it should be," she said with tears in her eyes. They held each other for a while, savouring every bittersweet moment. "I won't forget what we had either, Scott," she said softly.

CHAPTER THIRTY-FOUR

The day had finally arrived. Julie was excited as she walked the corridors of the Design Institute, crowded with eager students rushing to attend lectures and tutorials. She could taste anticipation in the air. It was the taste of embarking on something new; of learning and knowledge; stationery and books; the means of gaining an education.

A chic looking young woman appeared by Julie's elbow. "Hi, you were in my Introduction to Design tutorial. What did you think of it? It was pretty cool wasn't it?"

Julie nodded. "It was exactly how I thought it would be, inspiring and very exciting."

"It was so interesting to learn about the different styles of design from classic to contemporary and how they can both work together, and on their own. I can't wait to look at our first unit of work. I wonder what our first practical assignment is. By the way, my name's Cathy. Maybe we can team up for a practical if we need to work in teams? You seemed to be as enthusiastic as I was in the tutorial."

"My name is Julie. You're right, I was very intrigued in the tutorial. I can't believe I'm doing something I love. It all seems so exciting. I'd love to work with you in the future."

"Cool. See you tomorrow." Cathy waved farewell and scurried down the corridor.

Julie hugged the folder containing the first unit of work, smiling at the thought of having a new friend. It felt great to meet new people who shared the same interests. Cathy seemed really passionate about becoming a designer, as was evident by her enthusiasm in the tutorial. Julie was glad that she decided to attend the optional tutorials, to learn with other students who were just as excited as her. Julie recalled how Cathy smiled with excitement throughout the tutorial and could not stop asking questions.

As Julie left the building, her mind momentarily wandered to thoughts of Scott. As difficult as it was, Julie was slowly accepting the idea that they could not be an item. Realising that it was getting late, she rushed to her car. Julie had promised Maria that she would work at the store after her tutorial.

An hour later, she was on Pitt Street, walking at a fast and steady pace towards Eventually You. Focused at getting to the store on time, as Maria had a prenatal check up with her obstetrician, Julie was bumped abruptly by a tall, familiar blonde woman. Julie immediately recognised her as the woman she'd seen with George. Behind her was another familiar person – Stacey.

"Hey Julie, fancy seeing you here! How have you been?" an exhausted looking Stacey called out to her. She then turned to greet the blonde woman who was checking Julie out from head to toe. "Hi Toni, I just managed to escape that shoe hell that I call work. If I have to measure one more foot, I'm going to scream. If it wasn't for the employee discount card, I would have left a long time ago. You can never have enough shoes right? By the way, where do you want to have lunch?"

Before the woman could answer, Stacey looked at Julie. "Perhaps you'd like to join us, unless you have to go back to that relaxing, beautifully scented oasis you call work." Stacey was staring at Julie with a hopeful look on her face. "Oh by the way, this is Toni. Toni this is Julie. George and I used to work with Julie in the Superannuation and Investments section. I really miss those days."

"Hi Julie, George has mentioned you a lot in his conversations. I feel as though I already know you!" Toni replied.

"Has he?" was the only thing Julie could manage between gritted teeth, wondering what George could have been saying about her.

She contradicted her thoughts, remembering how much fun and surprisingly down to earth George really was, not to mention kind and intuitive. Besides, she wouldn't blame George if he had anything unpleasant to say about her. She had rejected him from the onset for no reason. He was right. She had been focused at work, but at the same time her mind had been elsewhere. She hadn't really noticed what was in front of her. Deep in her heart, she hoped he hadn't said anything negative. Julie suddenly found herself checking out Toni. It was her turn to take a closer look at the woman who was obviously involved with George. She definitely was stunning and immaculately dressed, but a little too much of a fashion victim, as Julie observed that every single item she had on looked as though it came out of the pages of the "What's Hot" section of a fashion magazine.

Having had a chance to get to know the real George, Julie realised Toni looked a little high maintenance for him. Julie thought that being a tennis coach, he would prefer a more down to earth looking girl. Julie blushed, as Toni caught her staring. She was surprised that Toni responded by giving her a warm smile, making her feel like a complete bitch. Who was she to judge George's girlfriend? They could be really happy together. Considering the state of Julie's love life, she was definitely no expert. Julie also realised that people probably thought she was high maintenance too, as she would rarely leave the house without any make-up and always ensured that she looked her best.

"Anyway, Jules, we've got to run. Toni has to meet George at the jewellers after lunch, and I have to get back to work. Are you sure that you don't want to join us?"

Everything that Stacey was saying blurred into a jumble of words. Julie was still hanging on the word "jewellers". It seemed that Stacey was speaking at supersonic speed, way more than her usual two hundred words per minute. Catching the last words of Stacey's sentence, she told them both that she had to get to work.

"Maybe next time, I've heard so much about you," Toni once again commented.

"Sure," Julie awkwardly responded and began to walk away from them.

"Oh by the way, how's Scott?" Stacey stopped in her tracks and turned to Julie. Suddenly her commitments weren't so pressing.

"Actually, we're not together anymore," Julie replied, feeling no need to keep the information a secret.

"You're not! That's — that's a shame," Stacey responded, and she looked at Toni. "Anyway, I'll call you soon. Don't be a stranger. We should have lunch together, like the old days."

"Bye, Julie. It was a pleasure to finally meet you."

"Sure," Julie stumbled, and she began to walk slowly away from the strange encounter, picking up speed as she looked at her watch. How strange that George's girlfriend or soon-to-be fiancée would be so interested in her. Maybe she felt that she was a threat to her and wanted to keep her enemies close, assuming that George had anything nice to say about her.

As Julie approached the store, she decided that Toni was probably just a friendly person which made Julie feel slightly ashamed in regards to how she felt about the girl she just met. She was puzzled by her reaction to Toni.

"Thank God you're here," a frantic looking Maria, and a more relaxed Antonio greeted Julie at the entrance of the store.

"Sorry Maria. Are you late for your appointment?"

"That's all right," Antonio replied. We always have to wait so long anyway. The last time the doctor was in surgery so we had to wait at least two hours. Having a cup of coffee at the hospital coffee shop gets a bit old after the first fifteen minutes."

"I know what you mean," Julie agreed, remembering the last time she was waiting in her local GP's depressing waiting room, struck down by a nasty cold. All she could do to pass the time and stop herself from becoming depressed was to envision how she could liven up the place by refurbishing it, and therefore begin healing people as soon as they walked through the door. Julie often found it ironic that they had so many home decorating magazines in the magazine rack, yet the place was so dull.

"At least *you* can have coffee!" Maria interjected angrily.

Antonio put his arm around her. He looked at Julie. "I've been trying to get her to relax, you know, make sure her blood pressure isn't too high. She gets anxious when the doctor takes her blood pressure."

"Well, I hate waiting in the waiting room. Of course my blood pressure would be elevated. Anyway, a lot of people can relate to that. It's called 'white coat syndrome'."

"Sorry if I've added to that by being late and making you wait more," Julie apologised again, feeling sorry for her friend. Maria detested going to see any doctor, period. But part of her wanted to burst out laughing as she watched a grumpy Maria and a supportive Antonio make grumpy Maria even grumpier. She suddenly envisioned how the actual labour would be. Other people who saw them together would think that they weren't good for each other. Julie however knew that Antonio adored Maria immensely, and would do anything for her. That's why she couldn't believe Maria couldn't tell him how she felt about him going back to Chile. He always forgave her moods and knew how to make her relax. In turn, Maria would encourage him to be more in touch with his anger. "No one can be so calm," she would often remark. "It's just not possible."

Cassandra and Julie would often joke that maybe Antonio should be the one who owned a shop like

276

Eventually You, as he seemed to embody all the things that the store offered, and its philosophy, espoused upon its product brochures: "An organic life is a healthy and relaxed life."

"Don't worry about it. Just don't forget to lock up when you leave. Tell me all about the design course at home," Maria called out, as she fought her way through the crowd with Antonio trying to keep up with her.

Julie was relieved that Maria's customers didn't see her in her anxious state. No scented candle would have been able to calm Maria, not even the neroli or vanilla one, unless it came in a bottle containing a certain percentage of alcohol, and was served at a stylish booth, instead of a dreary, depressing doctor's office. Considering Maria was pregnant, and that she didn't drink that much anyway, alcohol was evidently not an option, but the stylish booth could help, Julie surmised. As she walked towards the counter, throwing on her black apron with the store's name on it, she marvelled at the display at the centre of the store. She had helped Maria with the presentation of the store the day before when things were quiet. They had both decided that the bottle containing incense oil, which was a replica of a jewel, would stand out on the centre display table, surrounded with a selection of scented candles and similarly coloured soaps. It did stand out all right, Julie acknowledged but not for the intended reason. Julie's heart sank when she looked at the jewel staring at her with its illuminating presence. The only thing that it highlighted was the word "jewellers."

Why were George and Toni meeting at the jewellers? Julie's mind worked overtime, as it often seemed to do lately, when it came to relationships. More to the point, why did Julie care so much? Could she have … ? *No!* Julie laughed at her silly suspicion. *It's just not possible*, she told herself. *Besides, he's clearly not available. It's probably just a rebound thing.* Her heart had other ideas though, a stabbing pain searing through it the moment her eyes fell on the incense bottle, drawing her attention as it shone brightly from every angle of the store. The part of her mind that understood marketing acknowledged that the organic oil in the jewel shaped bottle would definitely be a winner for Christmas sales. The beautiful selection of soaps and candles surrounding it would have customers enquiring about them as well. The products complemented the bottle enticingly.

Julie's mind raced at the thought of Christmas being around the corner, how quickly the year had passed and how much she had seen and accomplished those past few months. She had come so far. She panicked at the realisation that she would have to fit in some Christmas shopping amongst her studies and her job. Her mind drifted to what her niece and nephew would want when they already seemed to have everything. Her sister would not take favourably to any new technological gadget, which would only add to the feuding that takes place between parents and their children in almost every modern household, as homework and chores, as well as their attention span, would always take a back seat.

Julie automatically turned on the store's computer and began to search for some gift ideas, finding a window of opportunity before any customers entered. As she searched for children's gift ideas, an employment agency advertisement flashed on the side of the screen. Without thinking, she entered the site. As her eyes scrolled down the list of available job entries, they stopped and remained fixated at an advertisement for a design company needing a part-time assistant to help the head designer with orders, administration and other office duties. Office experience was essential, as was a professional manner. An interest in interior design was a bonus. Deciding she had nothing to lose, Julie quickly typed a cover letter and attached her resume. The cover letter almost wrote itself, as it was easy to highlight why she wanted the job. She pressed send with a feeling of satisfaction.

She greeted one of the store's usual customers who always appeared happy and excited every time she entered the serene atmosphere. Julie caught the woman taking off her sunglasses and sighing deeply in gratification as she marvelled at the display in the centre of the store. Julie was used to this scene. Most of Maria's customers had smiles on their faces when they entered the store, and if they didn't have one when they entered, they were sure to have one when they left. She greeted the woman with a warm smile. "How are you today? If you need anything, please let me know."

CHAPTER THIRTY-FIVE

"What does it mean? It doesn't make any sense. I mean I've accepted the fact that it isn't possible to be in a relationship with Scott." Julie looked at Cassandra who was watching her every step, trying desperately not to lose her footing on the many steps of Sydney Opera House. It was challenging enough without wearing a recently purchased pair of glamorous high heels.

"I don't know. You definitely seem to have accepted the fact that you can't be with Scott. It is strange that he is constantly in your dreams, unless there are any lingering feelings or hope that it may work out in your subconscious mind. Do you think that's likely?"

"No. It's unlikely. For the first time I feel that I know where I stand with Scott. I finally have the closure that I need and I know that we have both grown and moved in different directions," Julie managed to express her feelings between trying to catch her breath.

"Well, it could also be that in your mind you were a couple for so long and now it's difficult to see things differently. I mean you were carrying the image of you and Scott in your mind for many years because the relationship discontinued suddenly between the two of you without it officially ending. In your mind, you were still a couple."

"You're right about that. Although, as I recently realised, it was the image of Scott and me, the way we were back then."

Maria, ahead of them on the steps, turned back to look at them with a look of impatience. "Come on, you two. We don't have time to analyse dreams at the moment. We're going to miss the show. I don't want to miss a moment of it. It got great reviews in the paper."

Julie and Cassandra looked at Maria in disbelief. She was the pregnant one and she had managed to climb the steps in record time. It was a Wednesday night and they were rushing to watch the Sydney production of *My Fair Lady*, having booked the tickets a few months ago. They had gotten carried away chatting whilst eating dinner at a popular restaurant near the Opera House which prided itself for its delectable food and was usually a place to do a bit of celebrity spotting.

It was a wonderful dinner as they all finally had a chance to catch up. Lately they were all too busy. Cassandra would often go on dates with Connor, study, or work. Maria would spend most of her time at Antonio's as most of her belongings made his place their home, and when Julie did see her at work, they were usually too busy to talk as customers were starting to do their Christmas shopping early.

Julie herself had her hands full as she was getting used to her new role of being a student and working. Of course, there was the Scott conundrum, which she had thought was resolved until she had that dream again. It was the same dream she had previously. Once again she was walking hand in hand with Scott. Julie once again felt confused. Why was she still dreaming of him?

It could be the fact that she still wanted him in her life as a friend. Now that he was back in her life, she couldn't imagine not seeing him again. She just hoped that Ashley wouldn't have a problem with it. Scott had called her the night before and had explained that he and Ashley had worked everything out and that she had forgiven him. Julie was truly happy for them. She wanted things to work out for them. So why was she still dreaming of Scott?

"Yes, that's it!" Julie shouted out, louder than she wanted to, as they handed their tickets to a smartly dressed, serious man at the theatre entrance. People turned to look at her. "I know why I had the dream," she whispered, this time to Maria and Cassandra only. "I was just scared that Scott would not be in my life anymore and

I wanted to hold on to him. That's why I was holding his hand."

Maria looked at Julie as though she suspected she was on some type of hallucinogen. She rolled her eyes and grabbed her by the hand leading her to the theatre.

"Sorry, it's my fault. I should limit my counselling talk at home," Cassandra said, smiling.

"That's okay. Nothing can ruin my mood, even morning sickness, which seems to have dissipated. I can't wait to see the show and I feel so wonderful in this scarf."

"It really suits you, I must say, I chose the right colour for you," Julie said.

"Thank you madam. Now, ladies, please join me to watch this spectacular production! Shall we?"

"We shall," Cassandra and Julie responded and they all walked into the dim room, arm in arm, ready to be taken on a musical journey.

***

The following morning, Julie woke up early, eager to commence her first official assignment for her Introduction to Design unit. She had a tutorial later that afternoon, and she had promised Maria that she would work that night as Thursday night shopping was always hectic, especially leading up to Christmas.

Despite having a lovely night out with Maria and Cassandra, she felt depleted, so she needed something inspirational to bring her out of her solemn mood. Julie opened up her laptop and began by brainstorming ideas. Just as she began to make some progress, her thoughts were interrupted by the phone. Cassandra and Maria were still sleeping so Julie hesitantly picked up the phone in the lounge room.

"Hi Jules, how are you?" It was her sister.

"Hi," Julie mumbled, her mind still full of ideas about space, colour schemes, the personality of the client, and so on.

In the past, hearing Christina's voice would have sent her pulse racing, but they were slowly getting to really know each other as individuals, not just as sisters. The more that Julie got to know the real Christina, the more she respected her.

"How was the musical?"

"It was great …" Julie began to answer, only to be abruptly interrupted by Christina.

"Now, before you get angry, I just want to tell you about this guy I know. I think you and he will really get along. Don't let the Michael thing ruin any other possibilities."

Julie couldn't believe what she was hearing. It was classic Christina wanting to set her up with yet another guy.

"Christina, I thought that we already talked about this. I thought that you understood that I don't need anyone finding a guy for me." Julie tried to remain calm as she spoke. She wanted to give her a chance to explain before she told her what she could do with the guy that she would supposedly get along with.

"I know. Relax! I know you have just gone through a lot with Scott. I also know that the last thing you need is me meddling in your affairs. Trust me. I know all that. I just feel that you will click with this guy. Whenever he speaks, I think of you. All I'm asking is for you to have one date with him. Come on. You said that you want to embrace life and take chances. Isn't this taking chances and living spontaneously?"

Just as Julie was about to protest yet another time, Maria waltzed past the lounge room and headed to the kitchen. She was singing so loudly that Julie couldn't hear a word Christina was saying. All she could hear was Maria's version of "I could have danced all night".

"What was that? I can't hear a thing. I think we left Maria at the theatre. She's still singing the songs from *My*

Fair Lady. Friday night? This Friday? Okay. I guess I have nothing to lose. Okay. I'll meet him on Friday at 7:30pm, for a drink at the wine bar next to the Irish pub after work."

"Okay, great, don't forget. I've gotta go. I have to get the kids ready for school."

"Wait! How will I recognise him?"

"He'll be on his own. And he's very handsome."

Julie hung up the phone in a daze. She couldn't believe she had agreed to go on yet another blind date that her sister had organised. What was she doing? This wasn't her steering her own course. This wasn't Julie being in charge of her own life. Perhaps it was a way of embracing different possibilities and not taking life or herself too seriously, she reasoned. Besides, she was eager to get back to her assignment. She knew her sister wouldn't give up until she accepted. Ironically, now that they were on amicable terms, her sister was even bolder about discussing certain subjects that were taboo between them. The tension that was present in the past was no longer there. It had been replaced by honest expression from both sides.

Julie suddenly felt the need for a cup of coffee, so she headed to the kitchen.

Maria was now acting like Elisa Dolittle, acting out different scenes from the show.

"Thanks a lot," Julie interrupted her accusingly.

"Thanks a lot? For what? What did I do?" she asked, attempting a cockney English accent.

There was obviously no stopping her. "If it wasn't for your singing, I wouldn't have agreed to another blind date that my sister set up. I only agreed because I couldn't hear a word she was saying, due to your singing. The only thing I heard was the date and the place. I don't even know anything about the guy."

"Oops. Sorry about that. You can always call back and cancel. Anyway what happened to standing up for yourself when Christina interferes in your love life?"

"I guess I figured I have nothing to lose. I'm definitely not in the mood to get into a serious relationship. It might be fun just to meet someone new and just have a drink. It doesn't have to mean anything. I do tend to analyse things too much. This is just me living spontaneously."

"Sure. You don't have to convince me."

"I know, I know. I'm doing it again. It's obvious that I'm trying to convince myself. I just don't want to go back to living my life through others people's beliefs and convictions. I guess changing old destructive ways is a daily challenge."

"Don't be too hard on yourself. I think you're doing great. You're taking more chances than ever and you're not letting fear rule your life. You even convinced me to talk to Antonio. I can't believe how proud and stubborn I was being. It's strange how the decisions we make can either improve or hinder our lives. I guess being honest with people you care about is not as bad as I thought. It beats sulking and living in denial. No regrets, right?"

"That sounds good to me. Anyway, I'd better get my coffee and continue my assignment. As much as I loved studying at uni, so far with my design studies, I feel that it isn't even studying. I just love it! I can't wait to get started. It's my baby. You know what I mean? I'm doing it because I want to."

"I know what you mean," Maria responded, looking at her stomach. "Seriously, I really do know what you mean. That's how I feel about my shop. As exhausting as it may get at times, it's mine and I love having something I'm passionate about in my life, other than Antonio, that is. Anyway, I'd better get going. I have a shop to open and most of my things are at Antonio's."

"See you tonight." Julie walked out of the kitchen with her coffee in hand and she laughed as she sat down on the cream sofa, in front of her laptop. Cassandra had just woken up and Julie could hear her singing "Just You Wait" from the top of the stairs.

They had all enjoyed the show so much that they had a post-show discussion at one of the cafes at the Opera House. It was funny how everyone took something different with them as they walked out of the theatre. Cassandra analysed the different personalities, while Maria beamed at every scene comparing it to the movie she had seen a zillion times. Julie took an interest in how the set was designed and what type of period furniture was used for each scene. Inspired, Julie began typing.

***

The next morning, Julie once again woke up confused. It was one of the dreams she had been having for a while. She began making her way to the bathroom trying to figure it out and make some sense of it. She froze. Yes! It was the same dream. She saw George in the Indian restaurant with Toni, the girl whom he was no doubt engaged to by now. The strange thing was that in the past she would see Tanya on George's arm, not Toni. However, the strangest and most shocking thing about the dream this time was that Toni had turned into someone else.

Her.

She was with George in the restaurant, not Toni, not Tanya. It was her, Julie.

She couldn't believe it. The thought had crossed her mind on numerous occasions lately, but she didn't want to admit it to herself. Could it be true? Did she really have feelings for George? Is that why her heart ached? Yet again, was she not being completely honest with her feelings?

Julie went back to her room and sat on her bed. It was as though the dream amplified what she already felt in her heart. The way she felt when she ran into Toni, and when she found out that she and George were meeting at the jewellers could only mean one thing: she was jealous! Why didn't she realise how she felt about George before? Was that why she cared so much about how George treated her at work? For years she had complained to everyone she knew about him. It all started making sense, except for one thing. Why was she still having the other dream about her and Scott?

As she stood up again deep in thought, she spoke softly to herself. *It isn't Scott in the dream!* Suddenly, the image of the guy she was walking hand in hand with in the dream became clearer in her mind. Julie couldn't believe what it revealed. It wasn't Scott at all. Scott had brown eyes. The guy in the dream however, had blue eyes. "It's George," she uttered to herself in shock. "I'm holding hands with George."

"Finally," Cassandra's eyes lit up. "Finally you've realised how you feel about George. I was ready to add my two cents about it, but I wanted you to work it out by yourself."

"You too? You're telling me that both you and Maria suspected that I had feelings for George? Am I that transparent to everyone? More to the point, am I walking around wearing blinders?"

"Well, you talked about him often enough. 'I can't believe how rude and obnoxious George is. I have never met anyone so into himself.' You went on and on about how annoying he was to work with." Maria looked pleased with herself, as if she had uncovered a mystery. "You then went on about how he constantly humiliated you."

"Well, if anyone was too self-absorbed, it was me. For years I played the role of the victim and built walls around me at work and in my personal life. What I still don't understand is, why did Tanya also appear in my dream holding George's arm?"

Cassandra paused thoughtfully before she spoke. They were all seated around the kitchen table having breakfast. "Maybe Tanya appeared because in the past she represented a threat to you. For years you thought she was the one who took Scott away from you. Maybe she symbolised the fear that you have deep within you, the fear that you may not be with someone you truly care about."

"I know that Tanya didn't betray me. I trust her so much now, and I should have trusted her then too."

"Yes, but for years you thought she had betrayed you and she was the reason you and Scott broke up. So maybe she appeared with George because you had feelings for him that you weren't aware of. Now that you're ready to move on, it has all come out into awareness. Toni and Tanya do not appear with him, you do. In fact, you have sorted out your unresolved issues with Tanya so she doesn't need to appear in the dream anymore. The fear no longer exists because you got closure so you can move on with someone else."

"It does make sense to a point. Even though Tanya isn't a threat, Toni is still with him and she may even be engaged to him, so I still can't pursue him. Anyway who said that he has feelings for me?"

"Oh Julie! What are we going to do with you? When will you realise? You were right about wearing blinders. You are so clueless when it comes to realising that a guy is interested in you! How many times does he have to annoy you and try to get your attention before you realise he's into you? I mean, the guy probably gave you so many hints but you probably ignored all of them. He probably thought that you didn't even notice him, so he had to resort to childish antics. I find it hard to believe that a man would constantly try to get your attention like that would not be interested in you."

Julie stared at her friend. Could she be right about George liking her all these years? She just thought that he was competing with her and wanted to make her look incompetent. She knew that the real George she got to know at the cruise wasn't like that. He was passionate about his tennis coaching career. He wasn't trying to compete with her at work at all. And it was her who had the issue — she had ignored him from the moment he met her. It had been just over a year that she had broken up with Scott when she had been introduced to him. Deep down, she knew that he reminded her of Scott. She recognised the flirtatious, sexy smile, the confident walk, his charm, and his intelligence. She had decided that that combination was dangerous. He was too nice, too attractive, and too confident. He could have any woman he wanted, and he *had* to know it. He *had* to be arrogant. It was safer to invent that image of him in her mind, to distance herself from him. She had been there before.

She remembered him looking almost child-like one afternoon when he had asked her if she needed help when she was trying to reach a file that was too high. She didn't want to believe it to be true at the time — that he could be so hurt, so vulnerable. She had flat out rejected his offer for help.

"No thanks, I can manage," she had hastily said.

"Don't worry. I can reach it for you. It's okay to sometimes accept help, Julie. Some of the other women on this floor don't seem to mind when I help—"

"Well, I'm not like the other women," she had blurted out.

"Oh, I can see that. You know what though Julie, I'm not like the other guys either. Well, I'm certainly not *that* guy," he had said as she stepped off the ladder, inadvertently meeting his sad, intense eyes. Julie had looked away abruptly, not wanting to admit that she had hurt him — this arrogant, confident, attractive man. He couldn't possibly be hurt by her. He was too arrogant and shallow to feel such emotions. She didn't want to think of what he meant either — about not being "that guy". He knew her then and he still knew her now. He could feel her hurt; the hurt "that guy" made her feel — that *Scott* made her feel!

"Forget it," he had said, throwing his hands in the air as he walked out of the filing room, after she had said that she didn't have time to chat, avoiding his gaze as she searched through the files. She had looked at him as he walked out. Her heart was heavy. It wasn't like her to be so cold, so vicious.

Perhaps he *was* interested in her. If that was the case, George would have felt so rejected. The modest part of her quickly rejected the possibility. It was bold, confident George after all. He would have just told her he liked her or asked her on a date. Then again, she hadn't just built walls around herself, she built a fortress and even the strongest individual wouldn't have been able to tear it down.

"When will you realise?"

"When will I realise what?" Maria asked Julie with a confused stare.

"When will you realise?" That's what George asked me at the cruise. I was talking to him about how often he humiliated me and that's how he responded. Could he have really had feelings for me?"

"Yes, yes!" Maria and Cassandra both chorused.

Suddenly Julie's heart started throbbing and a burning, sweet pain began to overwhelm it. It was as though the music had been turned on inside her again. In fact, as she placed her hand on her heart, it felt like a whole live orchestra had begun performing; percussion, strings and all. It continued to throb and burn wildly. Could George be the one? Could she feel the same excitement and adulation that she felt for Scott all those years ago? She had closed that door for so many years. Could she re-open it for someone other than Scott? He had given her a beautiful gift. It brought a smile to her face instantly. It reminded him of her. Did he feel that it was his last chance to show her how he really felt about her, that he actually understood her, that he knew she was searching for something? He told her not to hold onto the branch too tightly, that it may not be the right branch, that it may not be strong enough. Was he referring to her relationship with Scott? Was he suggesting that *he* was the one for her instead?

Her heart sank. What was she talking about? It wasn't possible. The door was definitely closed. In fact, it was locked and bolted. George was with Toni. Once again, she had missed out on the man who could offer her all the things she craved in a relationship. She had such a wonderful time with him at the cruise. He knew who she was as a person. *"The way you dress. You strive to create the right space with your clothes, with your accessories: the right you,"* he had said. She had felt so exposed. He was right! She had been too afraid to be herself. He knew that her small odd additions were almost a cry to be her true self — or some hope that one day she would live the life she wanted ... that she had been holding on to that small part of her that was still real. *"The light in your eyes reveals a lot, about the 'right' you."* He saw right through her. *"Hey,"* he had said. With that one word, she knew that he knew that she had so many repressed emotions. What had she done? George was the one — the "right" one for her! But she refused to pursue a man who was with another woman again. It wasn't her style.

"What's wrong?" Cassandra looked concerned.

"It doesn't matter. George is with someone else. In fact, they are probably engaged. They were meeting at the jewellers. That could only mean one thing. She probably wanted to choose her own ring. She's the type of woman that would want to choose her own ring. Everything she wore looked like it was straight out of the pages of a fashion magazine. I did think she was too high maintenance for him," Julie added vindictively. As nice as the woman was to her when she met her in the city, she couldn't help how she felt. She was completely wrong for George, Julie decided.

"Julie. You need to take action. If George knew how you felt back then, he might've not gotten involved with someone else. He did see you with Scott that night so he probably gave up hope. Besides, they're not married yet. Just be honest with yourself and with George. You don't want to lose him and keep asking yourself, 'What if?' Maybe that's why you were the last one to be with George in your dream. Tanya is no longer a threat, and maybe in your subconscious you don't believe that Toni is either."

Julie looked at Cassandra like she was onto something.

"That's my amateur dream analysis, nothing I studied. I just don't want you to miss out again. I know you are at a happy place right now with your life, but you can't deny your feelings for someone. Just tell him how you feel. I saw how much your face lit up when you realised that you have feelings for him, and don't think we didn't see how hurt you looked at the restaurant that night when you first noticed George with Toni. Why do you think you haven't been able to get rid of that image? It kept appearing in your dreams because it hit a nerve."

Julie looked at her empty cereal bowl. Cassandra was right. She did feel excited about the prospect that she and George could be together. She had still been shell shocked that night at the cruise. Scott had just told her that he had a daughter.

"I can't believe you both knew all this and you didn't say anything. Does everyone know me more than I know myself?"

"You had been hurt for so long thinking that Scott and Tanya betrayed you. You couldn't consider another relationship until you dealt with those feelings. You had to figure it out for yourself."

"I guess you're right." Julie shook her head in disbelief. "I can't believe what I'm saying. How could I even be considering getting involved with another man after I had such high hopes for my relationship with Scott? It doesn't feel right for someone to be able to move on so quickly."

"Of course it feels weird but you need to move on, Julie. You've spent too many years already wondering what went wrong with you and Scott. You deserve to move on and so does he. It's normal to be scared to venture into something new but I don't think it's a rebound thing. Yes, you just lost something and you are grieving. It's not the same as being on the rebound though. You are grieving the idea of you and Scott together as you were in the past. You are also grieving the image that you imagined of you and Scott together in the future."

"Why don't you talk to Stacey? She seems to hang around with George and Toni. I'm sure she would know what's going on," Maria offered.

"I think I will. Thanks for listening again, both of you. One thing I'm definitely certain of is that the tall figure who was walking hand in hand with me definitely is George. The blue eyes that I remember staring at me in my dream are suddenly very clear in my mind."

Julie spent the rest of the day feeling oddly excited. She couldn't believe that her feelings for George were so strong. Julie could feel an intense, but pleasantly familiar burning feeling in her heart again. She couldn't get rid of it. It was always with her.

As she walked into the Design Institute that was beginning to feel so familiar to her, she decided to call Stacey. Sitting at one of the many desks in the library, surrounded by an abundance of design books, Julie took out her mobile and dialled Stacey's number. There was no response so she left a message.

Deciding to take an intermission from the melodramatic conflict her feelings evoked, she walked over to the computer and typed in "Space and Design". She had an hour to do some research before her tutorial. Later, at work, she would help Maria with the display window and the store's presentation. Julie felt proud that her friends were taking her design abilities seriously as Maria looked to her for advice on the store's layout. It made her feel capable and her dream of becoming an interior designer all the more real.

Julie also thought Maria was very savvy with her marketing ability and clearly had a lot of business acumen as her store encouraged customers to take a peek and purchase something most of the year, but they were flocking in droves for Christmas gifts. Her Christmas gift ideas were especially inviting.

"That looks great, Julie. I can't believe how beautiful the whole shop looks. People will never want to leave, but hopefully when they do so they do it with many purchases."

"Your idea for the 'Three wise gifts' set is sure to be a winner. The fact that they come free with any other purchase they make over fifty dollars embraces the Christmas spirit of giving."

"And I get to make a bit of a profit," Maria laughed wickedly. "Don't make me out to be a saint, Julie. As much as I'd like my customers to leave the store with a free gift, I couldn't do it without them purchasing something that costs a lot more than the gift."

"Well, you're not running a charity. At least your products are certified organic and environmentally friendly as well."

"Yes. You're right. I am contributing in a positive way to society. I think that design course of yours is making you see the bright side of life."

"I guess it's the same with creating a beautiful space to live in. You have to focus on the positives that the space has to offer and draw attention to it. It doesn't matter how small or old something is, once you find where its beauty lies, all you need to do is bring it out and let it shine."

Julie realised that she got carried away when she noticed her friend looking at her sceptically.

"So, what's going on with George? Did you talk to Stacey yet?"

"I actually left a message on her phone," Julie responded, struggling to avoid taking a look to see if there were any new messages.

"Maybe she left a message. Have a look at your phone. It would have been difficult to hear it with the Christmas choir that has been singing jovially all day and every day this week. It's enough to drive you crazy. I can't even play my ambient, new age music, and it's not even December yet."

Without responding, Julie looked at her phone and tried to remain calm as she realised that she had a voicemail from Scott. He told her that he had recently talked to Tanya and she mentioned that they should all catch up one day, including James and Jenny, however, it would be difficult at the Christmas period as he, Ashley, and Victoria were off to Surfers Paradise in Queensland for Christmas. Victoria was apparently really excited. He hoped that she was all right and he couldn't wait to see her again. He told her that Tanya would organise a get together soon, and that was it.

As Julie placed her phone in her bag, she made a decision. *I will move on,* she promised herself. It was obvious that Scott had. He sounded very happy and Julie knew that he was at the right place in his life. She needed to move on without him. Cassandra was right.

The rest of the afternoon passed quickly. There were still no messages from Stacey and Julie looked forward to a relaxing night on the sofa with a glass of chilled Pinot Gris, which, in tandem with the air conditioner, would no doubt help deal with the sudden unbearable heat. As she locked up the shop, having sent Maria home early as she looked fatigued and was getting bigger by the day, she heard her mobile ring. It wasn't Stacey but to her surprise, it was Christina.

Oh no, she thought with dismay. *The date! That's what she's calling about, the blind date!* Julie had completely forgotten about the agreement she had with her sister.

"I finally got some time to call you. I was in the middle of something and I couldn't get away. I'll tell you about it another time. It's so exciting. Anyway, I just wanted to make sure you haven't forgotten about the date."

"I haven't forgotten. Well, maybe I did but that's because I really don't want to do this. I only agreed because I couldn't hear a word you were saying and then I completely forgot about it. Anyway, I don't know if I can make it. I've had an epiphany about something, or someone I should say."

Right then, Julie realised that another call was coming through.

"You have to go now! You can't stand him up. It's too late to cancel. He's probably on his way to the bar. I have to face him tomorrow and he'll think I played a cruel joke on him."

"All right, all right! I guess one drink won't hurt," Julie grudgingly agreed. "I've got to get another call. I'll tell you all about it after. Bye." Julie switched to the other call.

"Hi Julie, it's me Stacey. I received your message and I finally got the chance to call you back. I've been working flat out. Anyway, I was surprised to hear from you ..."

"Stacey," Julie interrupted a bit too abruptly. "Did George ever have feelings for me?"

Julie couldn't believe her own abruptness. But as bold as she was in her frankness, fear took over as she awaited Stacey's reply.

Stacey was laughing.

Julie felt naked and exposed. Was it such a ludicrous idea that George would have feelings for her? Was she so off base it was funny?

"Julie, I can't believe it. It's a Christmas miracle, that's what it is. I'm sorry that I'm laughing but I am so thrilled that you finally realised."

"What?" Was she hearing correctly? "Realised what exactly?"

"You finally realised that George Giveski, our handsome and suave ex co-worker, is madly and deeply into you. The poor guy has been for ages, but you were too blind or too obsessed with your work, or impressing Colin, to see it. I can't believe you finally realised it."

"How do you know exactly? Did he tell you, and why didn't he let me know all this time?"

"Did he tell me? He had to. He felt that he would burst if he didn't. He was positive that you felt nothing for him though. He thought you despised him so he gave up on the idea. He also thought that there was another guy in the picture. You seemed to be carrying a torch for someone. He told me that if he could take a hint from a woman that she wasn't interested in him, you were that woman. He'd had enough, though. He wanted to tell you how he felt the night of the cruise. That's why I made sure you sat across from him. He had seen a different side to you at the work lunch. He realised that you didn't despise him. In fact, he felt that you and he had a connection. I thought that it would finally happen that night at the cruise but it didn't. Instead, his heart was torn in two. He saw you with Scott and he got his answer. He always suspected you were in love with someone else and he found out that he was right. I felt really bad for him as I was the one who had encouraged him. Didn't you see how much I tried to get you two together? I mean, I organised a whole harbour cruise for both of you. I like my work colleagues but I could have waited more than a month for a reunion. Anyway, the poor guy was devastated, especially when he witnessed that kiss. It was as if you and Scott were the only people in the world."

Julie had to sit down. She felt herself sliding down from the wall she was leaning on down to the timber floor. She was in the store again. She couldn't even remember unlocking the door. She needed a quiet place to ensure that she heard every word.

"When I ran into you the other day with Toni, I have to admit, I was relieved that it was over with you and Scott. He's probably a great guy, and very hot, but I guess I'm biased in this situation."

Julie remembered Stacey's odd reaction. She did seem pleased that she and Scott were not an item. She had brushed it aside though. Then she remembered Toni.

"When I found out that Scott was no longer a prospect for you, I contacted George. He didn't buy it though. He still can't believe that you would get over him so quickly, especially the way you and Scott were going at it that night."

Julie remembered how George's jaw had dropped when he witnessed Scott with her, but she thought she was being ridiculous. He was with Toni soon after.

"Anyway, he still talks about you. He is proud and he doesn't want to admit that he has feelings for you. I can't believe he even confided in Toni. He wouldn't let her watch *Dancing with the Stars*, one of her favourite shows, because he couldn't stop talking about you. It's not like George to confide his feelings so willingly."

"What! He confided in Toni? That doesn't make sense. Why would he confide to his fiancée, of all people? Do they have one of those weird arrangements?"

Once again all Julie could hear on the other side of the line was Stacey's uncontrollable laughter. "What did you say, Julie? His what? I'm sure you said his fiancée."

"Okay, so maybe I'm wrong about them being engaged, but how can he confide about his feelings for another woman to his girlfriend? Is she that self-assured?"

"Oh Julie, please stop. I'm going to have a cardiac arrest. You really crack me up. Listen to yourself. Who said Toni was romantically involved with George?"

"Okay, so then it must be one of those casual, no strings relationships."

"Wrong again. I can't believe how you form these ideas in your head and then you believe them to be true without any concrete evidence. Why did you assume that Toni was George's girlfriend? Oooh! The thought of it makes me sick. Are you sitting down?"

"Yes." Julie was firmly planted on the ground. In fact she was frozen with anticipation.

"Well, my dearest, poor Julie, Toni is George's sister. She's staying with him for a few months while her apartment in Melbourne is being refurbished. George asked me to show her around since he's busy with setting up his tennis coaching school, and she doesn't have any friends here in Sydney."

"What!" Julie felt like a complete idiot. Then she remembered how he had his arms around her at the Indian restaurant. Why would he hold his sister in that way? "Well if she's his sister, why was he hugging her at the Indian restaurant? I saw them both. They looked like they were on a date."

"What Indian restaurant? Oh, actually I remember now. George was pestering Toni to try Indian food as he couldn't believe she had never tried it. I went shopping with her the next day. It was on a Friday, right? Anyway, apparently the vindaloo that George made her try didn't agree with her, as she was on the brink of getting a cold. George was probably just comforting her. He felt bad that he made her try one of the more spicy options, especially when she was already feeling sick. Honestly, guys proving they can handle spicy food. It's so immature. Why couldn't he start with butter chicken?"

"Oh." Julie didn't know what to say. Now she thought about it George had mentioned that his sister was staying with him. It also explained Toni's warm greeting and her mentioning that George had told her a lot about her. The poor girl was obviously trying to be friendly. In fact, now that Julie thought about it, she was probably trying to score points for George: her brother, not her boyfriend, not her fiancé.

"Oh, and they were meeting at the jewellers that day in the city because their mother's birthday is coming up, and they thought it would be great if they both pitched in and bought her some type of jewellery. Does that explain everything for you? Before you answer that, though, I'm dying to know, are you interested in George? Do you definitely have real feelings for him?"

Julie paused for a while and then she responded confidently. "As a matter of fact Stacey, I do have feelings for him. In fact, I can't stop thinking about him and I'm so worried that I have missed the boat. I was unaware of how I really felt all these years but now I'm sure. I think I'm falling for him. My heart aches as we speak. I want him to know how I feel, that I don't despise him at all. I think he's intelligent, witty, passionate, exciting and extremely sexy. It's taken me this long to realise it."

"Well, why are you telling me all this? Go tell George. Tell him exactly what you said to me. I'm so excited for you both. Don't waste another minute though. I think he had given up hope on you. Now that I think about it, he did hint that he may be moving on. Oh God! I hope he hasn't already. I hope he hasn't met another woman. Call him Julie. I'll give you his number. He had just stepped out when I called earlier. I was responding to a message he had left me. He wanted to talk to me about something. Toni had answered the phone."

Julie frantically wrote down the number as she hadn't stored it in her mobile. She had wasted enough time.

"Okay … bye Stacey. Thanks for your help," she said abruptly, and hung up.

After calling George and only getting his voice mail, she grabbed her bag, locked up the shop and ran out the door.

Within minutes she was tackling the crowds in Pitt Street mall, walking hurriedly but not knowing what exactly she was doing. Where would she find George now? Suddenly a plan came to her mind. Julie would call him again and this time she planned on leaving a message. She would tell him that she wanted to talk to him and then ask him to meet her somewhere. Julie was taking control of the reins again.

Yes! She would tell him exactly how she felt. Taking chances and being spontaneous and bold seemed to be working for her lately. There was no stopping her now. She would start by going to the wine bar and telling her blind date that she was sorry but it would not work. She would apologise for having wasted his time and tell him that her heart belongs to another. Well, maybe she wouldn't tell him all that, but something along those lines anyway.

Her steps became quicker with the urgency of the situation. She was practically running now. Even the street name was beckoning her to him. George Street was packed with commuters, workers, and shoppers. Everyone seemed to be walking at a frantic pace. They all seemed to have a mission, somewhere urgent to get to. Julie blended in with the rest of the crowd, apologising for bumping into people as she walked. No one looked or cared; they were all fixated on getting to their urgent somewhere. Market Street was just as frantic. There was no mercy. Her shoes, which had a slight heel, let her down as they bruised her with every step. The ground underneath them seemed rougher than usual as her feet ached with pain. She felt that she was sinking into it as her legs felt heavier with each step. It seemed that the closer she got to the wine bar, the further it was as fatigue set in. It had been a long day. She felt the perspiration on her face as the humidity was still making its unwelcome presence.

Her watch did not take pity on her either, as it cruelly conveyed that she was twenty minutes late for her date. The last thing she wanted was to reject someone who was already upset with her for being late. He was a friend of Christina's after all, and she would definitely get an earful from her sister if she didn't handle the rejection with sensitivity. *I have to do this quickly and tactfully*, she acknowledged to herself when she suddenly noticed a familiar figure approaching her.

It was him!

She couldn't miss his tall frame anywhere. His walk was very familiar to her. His hair was shorter than he usually wore it. He was walking towards her. He looked focused as though he had to be somewhere. He also looked serious and slightly frazzled. Where was he heading? He was still walking in her direction, on the same path. He hadn't noticed her yet, but in a moment, their paths crossed.

"Julie!" His blue eyes looked at her just as they had in her dream. It was as though they were talking to her. They were so deep and inquisitive. He was about to speak, but paused, taking his time as though he wanted to choose his words carefully. "Where are you off to? Are you late for some appointment?" He was smiling now. It was the same confident smile he usually gave her, except she used to think that smugness lay underneath it. She had been wrong.

Julie didn't speak for a while. She needed to catch her breath and she didn't quite know what to say. She wasn't expecting to run into him.

"George. Hi! Actually I do have an appointment, but I need to get to it to cancel it. It's actually a bli— I mean I just need to tell this guy something, I mean, it's a long story."

Julie flicked a strand of hair from her forehead self-consciously. She knew he was attractive but she never noticed that he was this sexy. Now that she had him in front of her, she didn't quite know what to say. The smile he was giving her didn't help her attempt to construct a sentence. He seemed to be amused by her flustered state.

"So, who's the lucky guy? Are you running late for a date?"

Julie decided to be honest with him. The last thing she wanted him to think was that she was meeting Scott. "No, not really. I mean, I am meeting a guy but it was actually a blind date my sister set up on my behalf. I realise it was a bad idea so I'm going to cancel."

George was still smiling at her. "Poor guy, he'll be really disappointed once he takes a look at how drop dead gorgeous you are."

"Yeah, I know. I mean I don't know that I'm drop dead gorgeous, I mean I don't think I'm that bad … I'm waffling aren't I? What I meant was that I feel bad for having wasted his time. The fact that he's a friend of my sister's makes it complicated."

George seemed to be struggling to contain himself from laughing. It was as if he knew how nervous he was making her.

"Anyway, I'm supposed to meet him at one of the wine bars in this street and I'm really late."

"Don't let me keep you. Good luck. Do you want me to come with you for moral support? What does he look like?"

"Um, he's … I don't know. I actually don't know what he looks like. I can't believe I don't know anything about his appearance or even what his name is. How will I know who he is?"

"Sounds like you really wanted to go on this date," George commented smiling. "You took a lot of time to find out everything you can about him," he continued in the same sarcastic way. "Seriously, I'll come with you. I'll try and stay out of view."

"If you're not too busy, did you have to be somewhere?"

"Actually I have a date with a girl I know. The problem is I forgot my mobile at home and I wanted to call her to find out if she'll be able to make it. Don't worry. I have a few minutes to spare."

"Oh," Julie responded, feeling as though her whole world was suddenly collapsing.

Say something, she told herself. *Tell him how you feel before he gets serious with this girl.*

Julie struggled to hide her disappointment as she walked towards the wine bar, George walking close behind her. She nervously opened the door. When would she tell him? What would she do after she cancelled her date? She decided to take it one task at a time. She stared at the faces in the wine bar but she didn't see anyone. All she could think of was how she would tell George.

"Julie, are you all right? You seem to be a million miles away. You really feel bad about rejecting this guy don't you? Do you think that it's a bad idea that I'm with you?"

"No, I was dying to see you anyway." Julie couldn't believe what she had said. She wasn't thinking clearly. The jazz music playing in the bar pierced her ears. It seemed to be interfering with her thinking.

"What did you say?"

Julie froze. She could feel his curious gaze as she stood still with her back turned towards him. She couldn't bring herself to turn around.

"Julie. What did you say?" She heard him ask the question again. She still couldn't answer.

Suddenly, she felt a smooth hand on her wrist. He gently turned her around. She was standing close to him but she couldn't look at his face. She worried her own would betray too much. She finally dared to look at him. He looked so delectable in his light blue polo shirt. He hadn't fully shaved, and his blue eyes stood out from his tanned face, no doubt the result of having spent many hours on the tennis court. They were staring intensely at her, awaiting her response. He wasn't smiling anymore. "It's okay Julie … it's okay to let go. Just give me a chance …

you can trust me. Just tell me … tell me what you said. I need to hear it."

Julie took a deep breath. "I said that I was dying to see you. I was dying to see you because …" She couldn't control her emotions any longer. Unable to find the words to complete her sentence, she instinctively placed her hand on his face and just looked at him. Without thinking, she leaned close and felt his soft lips on hers as she clumsily kissed him. Insecurity instantly took over. She backed down, feeling embarrassed at her brash and impulsive move.

"I'm sorry. I don't know what I'm doing … I shouldn't have done that," she blurted out, avoiding eye contact.

"You know what I think, Julie?" he said as he stroked her face, gently guiding her to look into his intense, blue eyes.

Julie didn't answer. She was too embarrassed.

Obviously sensing her uneasiness, George continued. "I think you should have done that a long time ago. Then I would have known that you didn't despise me, that you might even like me. You would have spared me a lot of sleepless nights."

Before she had a chance to respond, Julie could feel the same soft, sensual lips again. Only this time they were moving rhythmically with hers and awakening every part of her. He was kissing her softly and she was responding. His hands had made their way around her waist. They caressed her back. She could smell his cologne. It made her want the moment to last forever. Still holding her close to him, he leaned down and looked into her eyes.

"So have you finally realised? Have you finally realised why I did the things I did, why I tried so desperately and relentlessly to get your attention?"

Julie couldn't talk. She didn't want to. She wanted to be in the moment and process what was transpiring.

George looked at her knowingly. He took her hand in his. "Why don't we sit down and have a glass of wine? It will give us a chance to really talk." He began to lead her to one of the tables, the touch of his hand instantaneously making her tremble. She wouldn't need any wine. She felt as though she was tipsy already.

"What about my date? I can't be so callous and insensitive," Julie commented, a calmness taking over her. Suddenly the task of cancelling her date didn't seem so daunting. She felt that anything could be achieved and that all would be okay. It was as though the ferocious, hungry fire that had been ignited inside her heart had settled and now flickered peacefully, allowing her to enjoy its warmth. George put his arm around her.

"He won't care. He might even meet someone else."

"George!" Julie was shocked. How could George be so insensitive about the dating plight of another guy? "I'd better find him," Julie continued, suddenly feeling a bit disheartened at George's insensitivity. Was she wrong about him not being smug?

"He's isn't here anyway," George continued in the same tone. He was now smiling.

"How do you know?" Julie queried, looking at her watch.

"I know these things and I know for a fact that the guy is probably with a beautiful girl right now, one with a very worried and puzzled look on her face."

"How do you know that?"

"I know, because I'm the guy. The blind date you have is with me. So do you still want to cancel?"

"What are you talking about? I don't understand. How can it be you? Is this one of your jokes? Are you still teasing me to get a reaction out of me?"

"I'm your blind date, and you can thank your dear sister."

Julie felt that she was starring in one of her own bizarre dreams. What did Christina have to do with this? How could she possibly know George? Julie had mentioned him occasionally to her, well more than occasionally. Now that she thought about it, she mentioned him quite a lot.

"I actually saw Elisabeth and John this afternoon. I think they really have potential. Elisabeth serves well, and John is really trying to add more top spin."

"How do you know my niece and nephew? What do you mean more top spin? What does … ? Oh!"

Julie sat back in her chair smiling. She looked at George who looked pretty pleased with himself before she looked at her mobile, which had been buzzing for a while.

"George!" she said slowly. "Could my lovely niece and cheeky nephew have had tennis lessons lately?" Julie suddenly remembered her sister and Brian discussing tennis lessons for the kids as they were driving back home from the Hunter Valley.

George smiled at her. "Their last lesson was 3:30pm this afternoon. They've only been playing for a few weeks but they seem to be naturals."

"So you have met my lovely and intuitive sister, Christina?"

"I sure have. She recognised my name. She filled me in on a lot of things. Apparently you have strong feelings for me and you always seem to be talking about me. She is sure that you like me, but you're afraid to get involved because of something that happened with an earlier relationship. Anyway, that was a misunderstanding, and the guy came back into your life and you finally have closure so you can move on. You are definitely over him and in fact you weren't really involved with him lately anyway. Have I understood everything correctly? Sorry to sound insensitive but I'm just summarising. Anyway, I assumed that the guy was Scott, that guy I saw you with at Circular Quay. You are not involved with him anymore? That ship has definitely sailed?"

"Well, I see Christina has covered most of it and she's right. That ship has definitely sailed. In fact, it's already reached the next port. Actually, now looking back, it hadn't really left that port to begin with. She's also right about me having strong feelings for you and having being scared to act on them, and she is also right about the guy I was meeting tonight being handsome," she added, remembering Christina's words. She caught George smiling at her before continuing. "I am puzzled about one thing though."

"Oh? What's that?"

"What about the date that you have with the girl you already know?"

"Oh that! Well, I'm looking at her beautiful face right now. I already know her but I can't wait to find out a lot more about her. She seems very interesting in more ways than one. I was lucky to have kissed her and I am looking forward to exploring things further."

"Okay. So if I'm that girl, then who were you going to call? You said you needed to call her to see if she would still make the date."

"Okay, that part was a lie. I was actually going to tell Stacey who my date was with. I felt bad that I had led her to believe I was seeing someone else. She's our number one fan, you know. She'll be so upset if she finds out that your sister set this whole thing up and that she had nothing to do with it. I also wanted to spare her from planning another work reunion to try and get us together."

"Well, she may have encouraged me to go after you when I spoke to her earlier, so she won't feel that left out. However, it seems that we have another fan who wants to see us together: my sister. I still can't believe you and Christina both tricked me like this!"

"Are you telling me that you're not pleased with how things turned out? I mean, as you put it, you were dying to see me. I'm curious, what did you want to tell me? I already know what you wanted to do to me, if that kiss is any indication."

"You're relentless. Seriously though, I meant what I said. I was dying to see you. I wanted you to know that I don't despise you. In fact, I got to see a lot of the real George and I liked what I saw. Not that you weren't always like that, but my mind was too cluttered to see you for what you really were. I would have made sure you knew it whether Christina or Stacey helped or not. I guess I'm grateful for their support, but I'm living my life with a new motto, and that's to be proactive and make things happen."

"And how has that been working for you so far? Wait! Before you answer that, what do you mean when you say the *real* George?"

Before Julie could respond, her mobile buzzed again. She decided to answer it figuring that whoever it was really wanted to tell her something. It was Christina. She had left a text message:

"So sis, do you still think I don't know you?

Thank me later, much later hopefully, maybe even in the morning.

GAME SET & MATCH."

CHAPTER THIRTY-SIX

Music blared from the designer house in the beautiful tree lined street in Mosman. Tanya was certainly doing well for herself. The street was full with cars from guests invited to Tanya's "Pre-New Year's Soirée" as it was described on the invitation. As Julie opened the gate and began to walk into the landscaped entrance of the house, she felt George's arm around her.

"Looks like everyone's here. I hope she's friendly with her neighbours. There isn't a parking spot left," George said.

"She probably didn't want to leave anyone out."

As she had confided to Julie on the phone, Tanya felt that they had all wasted too many years already not seeing each other. Even Christina, Brian, and the kids were invited.

"So are Maria and Antonio still able to make it?" Julie asked Cassandra, as she walked with Connor behind her and George following. They had decided to take one car and George had agreed to be the designated driver, being the newcomer and all. He scored some bonus points with Cassandra and Connor who planned to have a drink or two. They had spent too much time studying. Their studies were nearly over and it was time to party.

"Maria sounded frantic when I spoke to her earlier on the phone," Cassandra replied. "She didn't know what to wear. Everything she tried made her look pregnant. Those were her words, not mine," she said, looking at both Connor and George who were staring at each other, baffled.

"Okay. I'll be the one to say it. She *is* pregnant," Connor stated matter-of-factly.

"Yes, but she doesn't want to wear something that makes her look pregnant." Julie decided to be the translator.

Both men still looked perplexed. "Only a woman would understand that," George remarked with a sly smile on his face. "It's too complicated for us two simple guys. Actually maybe Connor can shed some light, being a counsellor."

"It's not a woman thing. It's a Maria thing," Cassandra interjected. "As much as she likes being pregnant, she doesn't like *looking* pregnant. Give her a break. She's feeling slightly depressed. She hates maternity clothes. Besides, you know Maria, she'll really lose it if she gets one more person touching her stomach and predicting if it's a boy or a girl."

They were at the front door step. Julie took a deep breath as she rang the doorbell. It was her first official party with George. They had been seeing each other for a month, but she didn't think that the awkwardness that came with being introduced to the world as a couple was what she was nervous about. Her closest friends had already seen them together, and even Christina and Brian had, not to mention John and Elisabeth. If she could endure Elisabeth's incessant, "Is he your boyfriend?" question in front of strangers, in a queue at a popular restaurant, she could endure anything. Her parents would be next. She felt safe with her emotions around her family these days.

The issue was Scott. He and Ashley would also be at the party, as would Victoria. Would Ashley feel threatened by her? And more to the point, how would George feel about seeing Scott? He had told her on numerous occasions that he was okay with her and Scott being friends, and she loved him for it.

"Don't worry, Julie, it will all be okay." George placed his hand on her arm. Julie turned around and looked at his reassuring smile. Ever since she started seeing him, he always managed to remain positive in the face of adversity.

If there was a ninety per cent probability that things could go wrong, George would focus on the ten per cent that things would go right. That was exactly what she needed in her life.

He was right. Everything would be okay. She just had to dig deep and find the courage to deal with it. That's exactly what she had done at her recent job interview. Julie couldn't believe that they wanted to see her for the position of assistant to the head designer. In fact, she had even dismissed the fact that she had expressed her interest for the job, only to receive a phone call during a leisurely day at the beach with George.

"I can't believe they want to see me. I've just started my studies in the field!" she had cried out to George in disbelief. Apparently, as they told her in the interview, her passion for interior design was evident in her letter. They had been even more impressed with her at the interview as her eyes lit up whilst answering the head designer's questions. Besides, she also had office experience which a lot of the other candidates didn't. Her only problem had been how she would break the news to Maria. She didn't want to jump ship when her friend needed her the most. As she expected, Maria was excited for her, but also a little disappointed. Julie had to admit, she would miss working with Maria in Eventually You. It had been an exciting time of her life. She promised Maria that she would help her find a replacement.

"Hi Tanya," Julie greeted her friend with a kiss and stepped into the wide hallway. There were tea light candles scattered casually all over the house. The house had a very unique layout and Julie couldn't wait to take the grand tour.

"You must be George. Julie and I go way back. We were friends from university. I've heard a lot of great things about you already."

312

"Well, I try my best," George replied, his face breaking into a charming smile.

"This is my husband, Nathan. He's been dying to meet you. He designs furniture, so I'm sure you'll have a lot to talk about, Julie. He studied industrial technology and woodwork at university."

"Nice to finally meet you, Julie." A man with short hair and contemporary looking glasses offered his hand. "It's great that you and Tanya are friends again. She's so excited that you're back in her life."

"I feel the same," Julie responded, warmly shaking his hand. "We've sorted everything out now so I hope you don't mind if you see me here more often. We've got a lot to catch up with."

"Feel free to drop in any time. Besides, I hear you're studying to be an interior designer. I hope you like some of the pieces I've designed. Tanya and I will show you around later and we can have a chat."

"That would be great. I've already noticed some wonderful pieces and I'm still in the hallway." Julie smiled at him as she continued making her way into the house, trying to avoid knocking down a tripod floor lamp, while she waited for George who was greeting Nathan. "I was telling Julie that she's welcome anytime and that goes for you too," she heard him say.

Julie's eyes combed the spacious and very white open plan lounge and dining room, while Tanya greeted Cassandra and Connor. Her eyes circled the room until they stopped their reconnaissance, landing on Scott, who stood with a beer in his hand in one corner of the room, talking to a pretty woman with straight, long, dark brown hair. Little Victoria was holding on to the woman's dress. He and Julie locked eyes. Julie felt warmth in her heart when she saw them. Who could forget those kind eyes? As she looked at him, she knew that he would always have a special place in her heart. He was definitely a friend to her. Scott whispered something in the woman's ear and they both walked over to where Julie and George were standing, followed by Victoria. Julie's heart skipped a beat and she took a deep breath.

"Hey Julie, it's great to see you again," Scott greeted her with a kiss on the cheek.

It was all so friendly. Julie didn't feel uncomfortable at all. She couldn't believe how Scott managed to turn what could have been an awkward situation in to one that was so natural and non-confrontational.

"Hi, George. You remember me, don't you? Why don't I introduce myself again, this time with less anger in my voice? My name's Scott. I'm sure Julie has filled you in on our melodramatic past. It's all sorted now so there's no need to worry."

"No problem. I'm cool with everything. I'm glad it's all sorted. Otherwise my beautiful and over-analytical Julie here would not be able to move on with someone else. Finally, she realised that after all these years of working with me that she actually liked me and that we could be more than work colleagues."

Julie couldn't believe how natural and mature they were being about the whole situation. Scott looked at her affectionately as George hugged her. It seemed that he was really happy for her. She felt that he would always have her back.

"Julie, I'd like you to meet Ashley, my wife."

The pretty woman offered her hand. "Hi Julie, don't worry, I'm not going to strike you or anything like that. I prefer to leave the drama at the theatre. I know all about you and Scott and I agree with George. If you didn't work all that out, we wouldn't be at the place we are now. Besides, we all have a past. Did Scott tell you? I still keep in touch with my ex-boyfriend as well. We realised we were better as friends than anything else and unlike a lot of other people who say that when they break up, we really meant it."

It was too easy. Ashley was being so nice to her. *They must have really worked things out,* Julie thought, relieved that there was no ambush awaiting her.

They headed towards the garden. Victoria walked apprehensively, holding her mother's hand. Outside, people congregated on the tiled patio where a chef seemed to be performing tricks with a variety of ingredients on a large outdoor grill. Caterers were walking around serving appetisers and there were plenty of drinks at the bar. The DJ seemed to be enjoying himself as much as the guests. Julie quickly noticed her sister with Brian, John and Elisabeth. She headed to them instinctively.

Her sister hugged her warmly. "Julie, you won't believe it. Guess what? Brian and I are starting our own accounting business together. I'll have to thank Cassandra. The career counselling surveys clearly highlighted what I have known all along. I need autonomy in the work force. Brian also realised that about himself so we thought, why not? We're both business savvy people and we know our stuff. I know that you are both going to tell me that those surveys are merely a guide, but I've been thinking about starting my own business for a while. I just didn't have the courage to go for it. Being my own boss and spending more time with Brian is what really matters to me."

"I think it's a great idea. Besides, it will also give me time to spend with my delectable wife," Brian added, hugging Christina and kissing her on the lips. John and Elisabeth began giggling. "That's how we first got together anyway. Remember our economics team project? We definitely were successful with that and we've been together since then. Maybe money can't buy love but in our case discussing it helped us get together. We make a great team you and I," Brian added, looking at Christina as though they were falling in love all over again.

Julie was so pleased to see Brian and her sister so happy together.

"Oh! There's Cassandra. I'll thank her personally. You and George seem to be doing well. Don't forget to thank me in your wedding speech," she whispered in Julie's ear.

Julie rolled her eyes and then smiled. "Just go and thank Cass. I think I've acknowledged your contribution in our getting together already. I might add though, that I also played a part in it as well."

"Yes. I know. You took matters in your own hands," Christina replied and headed towards Cassandra.

Just then, Julie noticed Victoria hiding behind Scott. Instinctively, she took John and Elisabeth by the hand and led them over to Victoria.

"Hi Victoria, remember me? Can I introduce you to my niece and nephew?"

Victoria looked at Elisabeth and John cautiously.

"Hi Victoria," Elisabeth decided to take matters in her own little hands. "Do you want to play with us?"

With a shy nod, Victoria joined Elisabeth and John. They walked off together into the garden, chatting amiably.

"Thanks for that," a familiar voice said from behind her. She turned to face Scott, who smiled at her appreciatively.

"My pleasure, Scott."

"Bonjour! So how are my two fellow travellers. Is this a reunion?"

Scott and Julie both turned around. It was James. Jenny was nearby and was in deep conversation with Nathan. A tall, cool-looking man with a ponytail and tattooed arms was by her side. When she noticed them, she walked over to them with a smile on her face.

"Hi all, hi Julie, how's my roommate?"

"We're all fine," Scott replied on their behalf. You seem to be fine as well, Jenny. Could our cynical realist be in love?" Scott enquired playfully.

Right then, a stylishly dressed Maria walked out into the patio with Antonio by her side.

"Hi everyone!" She looked in their direction. "Have I missed anything? I couldn't find anything to wear," she confided as she approached Julie. "Be honest with me, Julie. Tell me. Do I look pregnant?" Antonio rolled his eyes.

"Maria. Honestly. I've never seen you look more radiant. You're absolutely glowing." Maria looked at Julie with a slightly stunned and embarrassed look on her face. Julie was sure her friend was touched. She was positive that a tear was threatening to stream down Maria's smooth face.

"See Antonio, that's all you had to say. If you told me that, I would have been ready five outfits ago."

"So is everyone all right for drinks?" Tanya enquired.

"We're fine, Tanya. This is a really happening party. Just what I needed after all the IT fires I had to keep at bay," Scott quipped.

Tanya walked over to where Scott was standing. Julie happened to be standing next to him as she had momentarily stepped away from George who was having a conversation with James about tennis.

"Thanks, Scott. I'm just glad that you could all make it. It's great being with friends. It's what really matters in life, being with people you can trust, right Julie?"

Right then, a familiar tune burst from the speakers. It was "Losing my Religion" by R.E.M. Instinctively, Julie looked at Tanya and then at Scott.

"I think this calls for a toast," Scott said, raising his glass. "To friendship!"

"And to no misunderstandings," Tanya toasted.

"To closure, forgiveness, and honesty," Julie added, raising her glass.

"Cheers!"

***

"Spectacular!" That's the only word that came to Julie's mind. The New Year's Eve fireworks were as spectacular as everyone expected them to be. George and Julie had found a great spot at Blues Point. Living in North Sydney definitely had its perks when New Year's came round. While others had to fight through crowds of commuters, and some very optimistic people believed a parking spot would miraculously appear, Julie and George simply walked from the terrace house to Blues Point, one of the well-known vantage points which offered panoramic views of the harbour. The bridge lit up in one amazing, extravagant firework finale. It was as though Champagne was flowing into the harbour. Julie could see the little boats and yachts all lit up as the people in them charged their glasses to welcome in the New Year. Everyone cheered with approval and appreciation for the pyrotechnical masterpiece that they had witnessed. It was surreal.

Julie felt tears of happiness stream down her face. The spectacular display touched the core of her being. It was as though it sealed the spectacular year that was now ending, just like a passport stamped after arriving home from a wonderful trip. As she pondered her thoughts, George handed her a glass of Champagne. "Happy New Year, Julie," he whispered in her ear.

She looked at his sincere and affectionate smile. "Happy New Year, George."

He kissed her gently and she leaned on his shoulder, as they marvelled at the harbour which was now calm and serene, a complete contrast to a moment ago.

EPILOGUE

Julie yawned as she hugged her sheets, enjoying a few more moments of blissful sleep. Moments later, she awoke to the aroma of freshly brewed coffee. She automatically sat up and leaned against her pillow as she eyed George's bare toned arm. He handed her a cup of coffee and gently kissed her head.

"Good morning sleepy head. Are you sure you still want to go for our morning walk? We did have quite a late night."

"Well that was because you couldn't keep your hands off me," she teased.

"Well, it did get very intense. I do recall you not being able to keep your hands off me too, though," he said as he stroked her hair, smiling at her affectionately.

Julie smiled as she took a sip of her coffee. "I can't believe that a year has passed since I was in Europe. It was so wonderful watching the live coverage of the race and seeing all those amazing sights last night."

"Well, we'll have to create our own memories. Maybe we should consider going overseas as well. Cassandra and Connor seem to be having the time of their lives."

"I know. The photos they emailed are spectacular. I think they're going to Sweden next. I guess they deserve it. They've both been studying so hard. It's a great idea to see the world before they get stuck into their counselling roles."

Right then Julie's phone rang. It was Maria.

"Hi Julie!"

"Hi Maria, how's that beautiful baby boy of yours? I can't wait to see him again. I bought the most gorgeous outfit for him."

"Julie, you and Cassandra have nearly bought me everything there is to buy from the baby boutiques. Please stop! Cassandra just emailed me saying that Italy had the cutest baby clothes. It was hard enough convincing her that she didn't have to be here for the birth. I think she feels so bad that she wasn't here and she's trying to compensate by buying gifts for me and the baby."

"I guess even counsellors have their weaknesses. Seriously though, how are you coping Maria?"

"You know everything they say about looking after a baby?"

"Yes."

"Well, it's true. I thought running my own business was challenging. This entails being tired 24/7. But I must admit, I also didn't expect to enjoy it so much either. He's so adorable. I think I'm learning a lot about myself now that I'm a mother."

"How's the shop going?"

"That's why I'm calling. Thanks so much for suggesting I hire Stacey. Of course, no one could replace you, Julie, especially your creative flair, but Stacey has definitely surprised me. She's practically running the place. Do you know how good she is with the books? That girl really has some great marketing ideas as well. It doesn't stop there either. She has taken control of her own finances and is even doing a business course on the side. Now that I have the baby, she has really saved me."

"Wow! That's wonderful for you and for Stacey. I always thought that if she used her organisational skills to manage her finances, she wouldn't have the financial problems she had for so long. I guess a lot of people surprise themselves when they discover what they are capable of doing."

"Well, you're a good example of that. I hear you have been filling in for your boss and doing some of the design work."

"Yeah, things are going really well. There have been some challenging days of course, especially balancing work and studying. I don't know when I'm going to complete my latest assignment. I love it though. It's what I thought it would be and more."

"Glad to hear that. Anyway, I was wondering, when can you drop by and help me with decorating the nursery? You won't believe that the terrace house is for sale and Antonio and I put in an offer. Our agent thinks we have a great chance. I've always loved this house. I would hate to lose it. I'm so grateful that you and Cassandra let me and Antonio stay here when the baby was born."

"You don't need to thank us. I guess it worked out well for us too. Living with George, close to the beach, is wonderful. Cassandra is loving being free and travelling the world with Connor for now. She said that she's enjoying living in the moment, and her travels should help her decide where she wants to live. I'm sure it will be close by, since she beat me to it and offered to be the baby's godmother."

"Don't worry. You'll have plenty of chances to be part of my son's life. My only problem is that my parents are coming to visit from Melbourne. I'm sure I won't hear the end of it. Apparently, I'm living in sin with Antonio and we should be married, especially now that we have a baby together."

"Don't they know that Antonio proposed to you, and that you are so excited to marry him since he is 'the man of your dreams?' They were your words remember?"

"I didn't tell them yet. I don't want them to think that the reason we're getting married is because I agree with them. I'll surprise them with the news when they least expect it."

"You are unbelievable, Maria. You really make me laugh!"

"I know, I know! I'm stubborn and proud. Anyway, the baby just started crying and Antonio's out buying more nappies. Give my love to George. Bye!"

As Julie hung up the phone she smiled to herself. It was hard to believe how much their lives had changed — how one good thing could lead to another. She took a look at George sitting across from her. She had definitely found a good thing.

"We'd better get dressed if we're going to go for that walk. We can have some breakfast at the coffee shop on our way back."

"Don't worry. I'll be dressed in a jiffy." Julie jumped out of bed, realising it was later than she thought. She knew that she wouldn't take long to get dressed. These days, as much as she loved to look her best, she wasn't so hard on herself. She felt good on the inside and it showed on the outside.

"Don't forget my parents' barbecue is around one o'clock, so we don't want to have too much for breakfast," she reminded George.

"You're right. Your parents never stop offering me food. They won't take no for an answer."

"You're right about that." Julie was looking forward to the barbecue. She couldn't wait to hear all about Christina and Brian's accounting business. It had taken them a few months to get it off the ground.

Twenty minutes later, Julie was dressed in a tracksuit and sneakers. She looked in the mirror and applied some pink lip gloss, some mascara and some moisturiser. After brushing her hair and tying it in a simple ponytail, she smiled at the young woman staring back at her. She looked into her hazel eyes. It was the same woman, but she wasn't hiding behind anything or anyone anymore. She then noticed the new dress she had purchased. Julie planned on wearing it to the barbecue. Or maybe not. It didn't really matter. George was right. Her eyes revealed the truth: the "right" Julie, the one that lived according to her own values, and not what others thought was right for her.

As she searched for her keys, she glanced at the jewel-shaped bottle that Maria had given her with the beautiful scented oil inside, noticing how often Julie admired it. The crystals shone from every angle of the room just as they had on the display table in the shop. Julie loved how every little facet of the bottle contributed in making it look beautiful as a whole.

"I'd better remember to get back to Scott. He left a message about Victoria taking tennis lessons," George informed Julie as he glanced at his mobile.

"He's lucky he knows the boss," Julie said, feeling a warmth in her heart at the mention of Scott.

Julie grabbed her keys and headed out the door.

"Don't walk too fast. We just had coffee," she pleaded with George.

"That's what you said last time, and I'm the one who couldn't keep up with you," George laughed.

How about we start by seeing more of Australia?" she enquired.

"What on earth are you talking about?" George looked genuinely perplexed.

"I mean for our holiday. Remember you said we'll have to create our own travelling memories?"

"Oh! I'm on board now. That sounds good. How does far North Queensland sound? In summer of course."

"What about South Australia? I'm thinking vineyards."

"That sounds good too."

As they stepped outside of the apartment building, a drop of rain landed on her nose. A few more drops fell as they started to walk.

"We'd better head back to the apartment. This is becoming more than a light drizzle."

"It's just a bit of rain," Julie responded. She began to twirl around as though she was dancing. "It feels great, it's liberating!"

"Well, it's official," George was looking at her with a smile on his face.

"What's that?"

"You're officially crazy."

"Come on, George. It's exhilarating. I feel so alive, so carefree." She continued in the same tone. Julie felt calmness inside her. She felt content, raw and real, just like all the products in Maria's shop. She felt organic: certified organic.

Just as she was about to plead with George to continue their walk, more heavy drops fell. Suddenly, walking in the rain didn't feel so exhilarating. She began to walk fast and began heading back towards the apartment.

"What happened to feeling free and liberated?"

"Forget that. I just washed my hair last night. Let's go back, get our umbrellas, and head for the coffee shop," she shouted, running towards the apartment building. *A bit of vanity never hurt anyone*, she told herself. *Besides it's nonsensical to walk in the rain, especially in July!* She smiled to herself, comforted by the fact that she could always rely on her rebellious, or, at times, not-so-rebellious self.

"That, Julie, is an excellent idea."

ACKNOWLEDGEMENTS

I'd like to send a heartfelt thank you to my husband who supported me from the onset in my quest to write *Eventually Julie*. His IT expertise and continuous assistance in such matters is deeply appreciated. Thanks also for being my sounding board for many ideas while writing this novel.

Thanks also to my children for their support, and for taking an interest in the writing process itself.

Thanks to my editor for her feedback and suggestions.

A special thanks to the team at Bespoke Book Covers for answering all my queries, and for their expertise and exceptional service.

I greatly appreciate all my family and friends who have supported and inspired me throughout this journey. Julie's plight, and her need to be true to herself is a story that I felt needed to be told. It *eventually* came to fruition, and for that I am extremely grateful.

Finally, thanks to all of the wonderful readers who have read my books. I hope they have touched your life in a positive way. Please feel free to note your thoughts by writing a review.

The Greek Tapestry (Julie & Friends, Book 2)

Maria and her older sister, Nicki, were childhood friends with Dimity, the girl who lived across the street. Growing up in Sydney, they even came first in an art project with a tapestry they made by hand, which depicted island life in Greece. They believed nothing would separate them - but would sadly find that nothing was a tall order. When Nicki and Maria's parents uproot them to move to Greece, leaving Dimity behind, they discover that even the strongest friendships can disintegrate.

Now, almost twenty years later, each of them has their own life. Dimity lives in a designer house with her sexy husband, an industrial designer named Malcolm, and their two daughters. She loves Malcolm, but is tired of playing the accommodating wife and daughter-in-law. In need of change and inspiration, she sets off to Greece.

Maria has both the career and the family, but still feels the need to prove herself to her mother. After her mother hides invitations to her cousin's wedding in Greece from her, Maria is spurred into action. She is sick of her mother's interference and heads to Greece in search of answers.

Nicki also has a successful career, but she and her husband, Marco, are unable to have what they really want - a child. Needing a change in life, she follows her sister to Greece, and stays in a peaceful, historic village outside the town of Ioannina.

As Maria, Nicki, and Dimity each try to untangle their complex lives, will they find their way home and weave their own beautiful reality?

Fasten your seatbelts and get ready to join the fun in magical Greece!

"Anthea's new novel reads like you're watching a very well made chick-flick movie! Someone make a movie out of this, please."

The Rambling Boho

ANTHEA SYROKOU is an author who grew up and resides in Sydney, Australia. Her novel, Eventually Julie, is an intelligent and delightful read that can inspire anyone who is stuck in a rut. At the very least, it will add a sprinkle of warmth and laughter to their day.

Anthea's love for writing was planted at a young age when she studied Greek mythology. Her love for literature continued well into her teenage years when she enjoyed reading novels by many of the great English writers.

As a young adult, she immersed herself in reading women's contemporary fiction and writing about topics, that many could relate to, in a witty, light-hearted way, which became a passion — one that she takes very seriously.

Anthea has a BA degree, majoring in psychology and industrial relations, and a diploma in counselling. She also studied Greek literature at university and has worked in direct marketing, and insurance and investments.

As well as writing fiction, Anthea also writes articles and posts on everyday issues; often adding her dash of humour.

When she isn't writing or reading, Anthea enjoys spending time with her family, travelling, yoga, and escaping to the vineyards. A quiet house with some jazz playing in the background, surrounded by a few lit scented candles is her idea of relaxation. Anthea lives with her husband and their two sons.

For more information please visit **antheasyrokou.com**

Made in the USA
Monee, IL
11 October 2021

79839927R00192